About the Author

Mary-Anne O'Connor has a combined arts education degree with specialities in environment, music and literature. She works in marketing and co-wrote/edited *A Brush with Light* and *Secrets of the Brush* with Kevin Best.

Mary-Anne lives in a house overlooking her beloved bushland in northern Sydney with her husband Anthony, their two sons Jimmy and Jack, and their very spoilt dog Saxon. This is her first major novel.

GALLIPOLI STREET

MARY-ANNE O'CONNOR

HARLEQUIN® MIRA®

First Published 2015
Third Australian Paperback Edition 2016
ISBN 978 148920699 2

National Library of Australia Cataloguing-in-Publication entry

Creator: O'Connor, Mary-Anne, author.
Title: Gallipoli street / Mary-Anne O'Connor.
ISBN: 9781489206992 (paperback)
9780857996169 (ebook)
Subjects: Families—Australia—Fiction.
World War, 1914–1918—Participation, Australian—Fiction.
World War, 1939–1945—Participation, Australian—Fiction.
Dewey Number: A823.4

Published by
Harlequin Mira
An imprint of Harlequin Enterprises (Australia) Pty Ltd.
Level 4, 132 Arthur Street
NORTH SYDNEY NSW 2060
AUSTRALIA

Printed and bound in Australia by Griffin Press

FSC
www.fsc.org
MIX
Paper from responsible sources
FSC® C009448

For Nana and Da

We lived, felt dawn, saw sunset glow,
Loved, and were loved, and now we lie

Colonel John McCrae, 1915

Part One

One

Beecroft, Sydney, Australia,
November 1913

The rumble echoed through the faint drone of cicadas and Jack lifted his head, listening.

A flash of grey caught his attention through the branches and his country-honed senses fell into instant alert.

'What's wrong?' asked Rose.

Jack held up his hand to silence her and parted the trees, emerging from their lovers' hollow. Squinting in the late-spring heat, his eyes made out the green snake of creek line twisting through the valley, the telltale artery of a landscape that had lazed too long in sunshine. Parched and dry, it seemed ready to self-ignite from lack of rain.

The smoke had disappeared…but no, there it was.

The rumble echoed again and he registered that it was actually the sound of a horse and wagon at full pelt. The cart could be glimpsed between bushes as it careened along Cowpasture Lane, and he could now make out that the grey 'smoke' was in fact dust billowing in its wake.

A woman's scream carried across the expanse and he jumped to his feet, annoyed at himself for taking off his boots moments before. Jack glanced back at the beautiful, flushed face looking up at him enquiringly and cursed the wretched timing of it all, hoping she would heed his instruction.

'Stay here!'

With that, he leapt onto Tilley, snatched up the reins and hurled her down the slope.

Tilley wasn't nearly as fine looking as Ebony, Iggy's mare, but Jack had only had her a few weeks and already she was outstripping a few of the others out on Riley's track. He felt reasonably sure he could catch the bolting horse and wagon before they hit the mush that had replaced the shallows in recent months. Thinking about what would happen if the wheels met with that thick clog of mud, he gripped the leather saddle hard with his thighs and urged Tilley on faster.

He tore across the paddock, taking the fence at a gallop before cutting down towards the lane, weighing up the unappealing option of cutting through Stan's Gully without boots to save time. His mind was made up as he caught a glimpse of the runaway. Yes, it was a woman on her own, standing up in the wagon, dragging on the reins.

'Bloody fool's gunna break her neck,' he muttered. He turned Tilley towards the gully, taking the rocky slopes and gritting his teeth against the sharp tear on his shins as the sword grass lashed him. Sweat ran into his eyes, piercing them into momentary blindness, as he swerved against the large sandstone boulders: rough grazes added themselves to the lines of cuts. Jack vaguely registered the trickle of blood, and supposed his legs were by now a mess, but then Tilley found the sudden rise that bordered the road and he forget all else, finally gaining a clear view of the situation.

The sight was not what he expected.

With her honey-blonde hair loosened from its usual tight braiding and her cotton dress tucked into a belt about her waist, Veronica Maggie O'Shay was standing up in her father's cart, one leg firm against the front-board. Her arms were taut and she was obviously in full control of Bessie, who was galloping along in front. The girl let out a loud catcall, which Jack recognised as the 'scream' he'd heard earlier, then took a bend in the lane with precision, laughing in exhilaration.

It was the laugh that did it. Jack's high-pitched whistle made Veronica start and she turned and stared at him in surprise. Her confident pose became a confused moment of imbalance as she contorted in alarm, the cart careening dangerously before she managed to regain control, slowing Bessie down to a canter then finally to a walk.

She jumped down from the wagon and rounded on Jack as he dismounted, her hair twisting and bouncing about her, reminding Jack of a pet cockatoo he'd once had, who used to gallop across the floor, crest fanning in fury, whenever he saw the biscuit tin being put away.

'What the hell do you think you're doing, Jack Murphy?' she demanded. 'You could have killed me!'

'Me? You seemed to be doing a pretty bloody good job of that yourself!'

'Don't you swear at me!' She waved a warning finger at him, her breath coming in short gasps, from exertion or fury. 'Sneaking up like that...I nearly ended up in the ditch!'

'Sneaking up? With the racket you were making?' Jack glared back at her, feeling a wave of anger overtake him. So much for rescuing a damsel in distress. Bloody Veronica and her secret rebellions. He'd thought she would have well grown out of such things by now. 'I'm sure your mother would be interested to know that her daughter was running about the place with her legs bare to the wind, making a scene!'

Jack indicated at the still half-tucked-in dress, distracted by the limbs that were being hastily covered from his sight.

'She wouldn't…she…' Veronica swatted angrily at the unruly blonde curls blowing across her face and Jack knew he had her there. Mrs O'Shay would not be amused by this escapade. Veronica seemed to run out of logic and reverted to one of her brother Tom's favourite retaliations instead. 'You're – you're nothing but an ugly man's dog, you know that?'

'Sure she'd love to hear her supposedly refined daughter talking like that too,' Jack said, beginning to be amused by Veronica's outrage, and the way she'd copied Tom's slang, clearly the worst insult she knew. He could tell the comments about her mother were unnerving her; she was biting her lip and he noticed he was staring again. He became uncomfortably aware that they were very much alone, both in varying states of undress.

'I'd better escort you home,' he said, quickly pulling up his braces, which were hanging down limply, and running his fingers along the edges of his shirt front for the buttons.

Veronica blushed and glanced down. 'What happened to your legs? You're bleeding.' She bent and peered at the scratches and cuts on his shins. 'What on earth possessed you to take off your boots?'

She reached out to touch his leg and he grabbed her arm, hauling her upwards.

'Don't. It's all right.' Jack stopped abruptly as she stood in front of him and his eyes came to rest on the pulsing in the damp hollow at the base of her throat. A sticky strand of blonde curl still clung there and for a moment Jack felt a strong pull towards her, a lapse of conscious thought. An insane desire to brush that curl away and trace her skin with his fingers.

Then he met her eyes. O'Shay eyes. The same colour as her brothers, Mick and Tom.

His two oldest, closest friends.

Their little sister.

'Anyway, you'd better do something about that hair,' he said, almost shoving her away and turning to needlessly tighten Tilley's girth.

Veronica seemed to steady herself before climbing back onto the wagon. Sitting on the bench seat she braided her hair furiously as Jack determined to look away. This is Vera, for God's sake, he told himself sternly, purposefully using her brothers' pet name for her. Get a hold of yourself.

Forcing a neutral expression, he mounted Tilley and deliberately adopted an authoritative, paternal tone. 'Just take more care in the future, Vera. You would've been in serious trouble if I hadn't come along. What if you'd ended up in the creek?' He received a haughty sidelong glance in response, and felt his frustration rise again, forgetting the new, mature approach. 'When are you going to bloody grow up a bit and stop acting all wild?'

Vera turned quickly on the bench seat. 'When am I going to grow up? What about you? You can't even walk around with your...your shirt tucked in and your boots on! And for your information I was in perfect control of Bess the whole time, and I've lived on this lane long enough not to be so stupid as to drive a cart into the creek.'

Jack thought he detected a slight tremble as she picked up the reins, and he sighed. 'Better give me the cart. You're too upset to drive.'

'You just get yourself back to whatever crevice it was you crawled out of! I am quite capable of getting myself home,' she said, flicking the reins and adding over her shoulder: 'And stop calling me Vera!'

She set off up the track at a pace, leaving him enveloped in plumes of dust. Jack moved to the side, shielding his face, watching the angry little cloud all the way to the corner until she disappeared from view.

What the hell was wrong with her? And, even more disconcerting, what the hell was wrong with him?

She was like family. Growing up on neighbouring farms, the Murphys and the O'Shays had been inseparable as kids – barefoot and unencumbered, they had grown as wild as the bush itself within a thousand adventures of childhood. He supposed they'd never looked ahead, to when adulthood would arrive and drive them into responsibility and restriction, reining them in and strapping them down. He suspected Veronica was resentful. She'd had the worst of it at that suffocating school her mother had sent her to and now, when it was finally over, she had come home to find that the rest of them had long moved on into adult lives. The adventures were of a different nature, the friendships altered.

Even his sister Pattie, Veronica's closest friend, had been home schooled by a governess and was never made to leave. Another wild one was Pattie, though in a different way from Veronica.

Pattie was a tomboy, straight out.

Veronica was…well she was Vera. Vera would be the one standing in the mud, squishing it beneath her toes or sitting in the tree humming songs to herself, always the last one to want to come inside. Such was the girl. He wondered at the adult version of this nature child. He'd thought she would come home after four years away a polished little clone of her refined English mother, yet here she was tearing along the track, bare legged and as wild as ever. Jack's mind filled with the image – like an ancient goddess on a chariot, he mused to himself.

He shook his head, rejecting it. It was just the shock of seeing her suddenly grown up. They hadn't had the chance yet to try to be friends as adults. Working in the city meant he'd only seen her sporadically during the past four years, and then only on the occasional weekend when she was home. Even now that she was back for good, those precious two days were likely to be taken up with cricket and courting Rose.

Good Lord, Rose!

Jack immediately snapped out of his reverie and mounted Tilley, who made short work of the sprint back to the stand of trees in the high paddock where the other world lay waiting. Spying Rose's horse Arrow grazing nearby Jack let out his breath, relieved that she hadn't left in a huff. He ducked his head through the whispering casuarinas that secluded their secret spot.

'You sure took your time,' she said. 'What was it? A runaway horse?'

'Hmm? Oh yeah, just some local kid.' Jack lay down next to her, marvelling at the fact he could have forgotten about her for so long as he cupped her soft cheek. 'You feel hot,' he observed, tracing the damp line along her brow.

'Still getting used to the Sydney weather.' She smiled, pushing her dark red hair back in a thick curtain and baring one creamy shoulder from her blouse. Jack stared, his mouth going dry. He'd never been with a woman like Rose before. The girls he'd courted were mostly strictly raised Catholics whose mothers were never far away – he'd been lucky to steal a kiss or the occasional brush against them at a dance. He'd visited Kings Cross, of course. All the men in his circle did, mostly to play cards and dine at some of the more risqué clubs, however a few times the night had ended in darkened rooms between perfumed sheets. But that was different. It had been perfunctory, fast, professional. Detached.

Rose was a delicious cocktail of Catholic girl and seductress. She was a lady, yet she responded with free abandon to her passion without seeming to harbour any guilt or restraint. These past two months with her he had learnt how to please a woman: where they liked to be touched, how they liked to be touched. How much fun a lady could have without completely surrendering her virtue.

He leant forward and lifted her hair, kissing her softly behind her ear, noticing that his breath raised little bumps along her arms. She closed her eyes as he found her mouth, playing against it until she sighed, her eyes heavy and asking for more.

'Did you miss me?' he asked.

She reached behind and showed him a pile of unlaced corsets, raising her eyebrows in answer.

'I'll take that as a yes.' He laughed, rolling her onto the blanket and kissing her deeply again, this time running his fingers across the thin fabric to feel the bare skin beneath. He stretched her arms up above her head and traced circles against her breasts, watching her gasp as her skin met his touch.

'You're a bad, bad boy Jack Murphy,' she whispered, tracing one nail across his chin. Jack kissed her again, the sweet scent of the splintered leaves baking above them, all thoughts of runaway carts swept from his mind.

Veronica didn't go straight home; in fact she decided heading to the creek and cooling off was a much better idea. After tying up Bess she took off her shoes, welcoming the familiar feel of the large smooth rocks under her feet as she picked her way downstream to her favourite spot. This was a small pool to the side of the creek, hidden behind an enormous log and ringed by sand.

It was here, to this secret oasis, that she came to escape the confines of her life, a life once as natural and easy as these surrounds. How she had longed for it as she endured the stuffiness of the classrooms at her hated finishing school; now, in her newly prescriptive role as young lady of the house, this place was her only solace from routine. Here, soothed by the clear water and the light dappling the leaves in multiple shades of green, she could distance herself from expectation and restraint and savour the freedom that had once been hers. Back when being with Jack was an everyday event. Back when being with Jack was simple.

Veronica undressed, absently watching the rainbow lorikeets squabbling among the grevillea, their jewel colours brilliant alongside the strangely curling, long red flowers. Laying her clothes on the sand, she placed her shoes on top and walked gingerly into the water, its coolness soothing her overheated skin as she lay alongside the log, her head resting on a smooth branch. She breathed in deeply, welcoming the familiar honey of the gum blossoms hanging overhead and tracing the scribbly gums' little pathways with her eyes, forcing her mind to relax.

'Hello, Eddie,' she said. The butcherbird had jumped up beside her, tapping his beak expectantly on the log. She smiled and he hopped a little closer. 'No, I haven't got any bread for you today. Go and catch something, you lazy thing.'

He waited for a while, then eventually accepted there would be no free lunch and began to dig about in the leaves for grubs.

Veronica's mind wandered back over the events of the past hour, scowling as she remembered the condescending way Jack had looked at her, his dismissive words. The moment he had pushed her away as though he suddenly realised she was just a child.

The way he ordered her about as if he were her brother. Who was he to tell her she couldn't race a wagon and enjoy herself? So what if she'd let out a few calls and her skirt had ridden up a little?

Veronica blushed. Actually she had tucked it up and Jack Murphy had just seen more of her body than anyone else since her mother dressed her as a child. Sighing, she leant back in the water, staring at the sky. There would be hell to pay if she was found out, so what had possessed her to do it? She didn't really know, she just knew she needed to do things like that sometimes, to remind herself how it all used to feel. Before she'd had to grow up.

Sinking into the cool water she ran her hand down her arm, reliving the moment he'd touched her, remembering the feel of his fingers, as if they'd burnt her. She'd been so close to him she could breathe in his scent; every part of her alert. His open shirt and his low-slung trousers had revealed a flat brown stomach with a trail of fine dark hair. She blushed to think what lay at the end of it.

No, Jack Murphy was definitely not like a brother to her. He never had been really.

What was he doing, riding around half dressed like that? she wondered distractedly. Maybe he'd been for a swim. That would explain it...although he didn't look as if he'd been swimming. Maybe he'd been about to, and that was where he was headed when he saw me. Or – maybe he had been taking his clothes off for other reasons. Maybe Rose even took them off. Veronica sat up straighter, not liking that idea at all. No, he wouldn't do such a thing...would he?

The O'Shay and Murphy children had been brought up going to the same small local church with the same teachings every Sunday, and they all knew that sins of the flesh only led to damnation. Jack would surely resist, even if this particular temptress were Rose, with her generous cleavage and flirtatious ways. Veronica sighed, looking down at her own breasts, wondering if she would ever tempt him in the ways that Rose did. As if I'd want to! she told herself primly. But as she emerged from the water and put on her clothes she knew somehow that was exactly what she wanted, and she had no idea how to pray for that.

Two

Highview, Beecroft

It looked as though it was going to be a long, lazy Saturday afternoon, and Catherine O'Shay was just settling onto the rocking chair on the porch, her favourite Austen and a nice cup of tea on the table beside her, when she spied the buggy coming over the rise.

She rose with a sigh and smoothed her hair. 'Veronica, the Dwyers are coming. Tell Eileen, will you?' She paused, waiting, then repeated, 'Veronica?'

Her daughter started from where she'd been sitting on the front step of the family homestead, Highview, lost in a daydream as was usual. She was even more prone to them of late. 'Pardon? Oh, yes, Mother.'

Catherine watched her rush off and sighed, wishing her children would stop growing up. All this mooning about was obviously due to one thing, or one young man to be more precise, and as she considered the competition Catherine didn't envy her daughter's plight. Watching the carriage approach she reflected there would be little respite for any of them from Miss Rose

Dwyer that summer, especially if the hot weather continued, and the socialising that came with it.

Her English sense of propriety had never quite become accustomed to the 'surprise pop-in visit' that was so popular in this part of rural Sydney, though at least after so many years she knew to expect it. She didn't mind if it was the Murphys visiting: they were practically family. No, it was more these new neighbours, the Dwyers, who had her on edge.

Her husband Kevin joined her on the verandah with a wide grin and a kiss on the cheek. 'Here comes a bit of fun, eh, Cate?' he whispered in her ear. 'Should I fetch you a sherry?'

'Behave,' Catherine warned him, but patted his cheek just the same. 'Where are the boys?'

'Checking out the race results down at Riley's. You didn't ask who won the game.'

'Judging by the superior expression on your face I can see that we did.'

'Victory to Beecroft once more, my dear girl! And there was some other excitement this morning –'

'Hush. Here they are.'

The Dwyers alighted amidst a flourish of courtesies. Mildred and Rose were ushered into the front room while Kevin stole Dr Dwyer away to smoke cigars, discuss the cricket and leave the ladies to their 'nattering'.

'What a lovely dress, Rose. You look very pretty today,' Catherine said, settling her skirts on the velvet settee. She acknowledged that Rose was masterful when it came to promoting her natural advantages, appearing cool and crisp in the dark green dress, its rich hue finding the gold in her skin and the cut emphasising her much admired curves.

Rose curled one red tendril about her finger and smiled. 'Thank you, Mrs O'Shay.'

'And how are you faring in this heat, Mildred?' Catherine addressed Rose's Irish mother, nodding in anticipated sympathy.

'Oh, 'tis dreadful hot, Catherine. I don't know how we're to bear it this whole summer long.' Mildred fanned at the round expanse of her face, flushed in mottled pinks, her greying fair hair already clinging about her neck. She looked nothing at all like her attractive daughter, who had inherited her red hair from her father, along with his cooler complexion and brown eyes. The Dwyers' son, Iggy, also looked like his father and younger sister, and Catherine often thought poor Mildred looked like a weed in the flowerbed. Even so, despite being a bit of a fusspot, Mildred radiated genuine kindness, and Catherine had liked her instinctively. Her opinion of young Rose, however, was far less favourable.

Veronica arrived with the tea. Although the O'Shays had two maids, Catherine believed in having her daughter assist in the finer points of entertaining, including supervising in the kitchen and bringing the tea. An unintended result of this excellent training was an appearance of servility she suspected Rose thoroughly enjoyed exploiting to advantage. The child was an artful player in the games women employed, Catherine observed. She had encountered many a Rose in her debutante days in London and knew when her dreamy daughter was walking straight into Rose's traps. Sure enough, as Veronica poured the tea, Rose slyly dipped her cup, and its contents splashed on the spotless white tablecloth.

'Veronica, please, do be careful! Dear me, Rose, are you all right? You're not burnt?' Catherine dabbed at the stained cloth with her napkin, inwardly seething.

Mildred clutched her handkerchief to her mouth, her watery blue eyes round. 'Blessed saints, are y'scalded?' She turned her daughter's palms about in alarm and examined her wrists.

'Oh,' Rose breathed, 'I'm sure it was my fault for holding my cup the wrong way. And no doubt Veronica will get better at pouring tea as she becomes more accustomed to entertaining company.' She smiled sweetly at Veronica, who could only gape back at her. Catherine knew her daughter was aware she was being toyed with but was helpless against it. She'd little practice in societal scheming.

Mildred flapped with her handkerchief, blowing on the clearly non-existent burns. 'Oh…oh there now, 'tis fine. A storm in a teacup,' she said, calming down and nodding herself into reassurance, smiling at her little joke. She turned to look at Veronica and patted her hand, obviously confusing her frustration with guilt. 'Don't ye fret there, child. My now, that cake looks delicious. Is it one of your own fruitcakes then, Catherine?'

'Actually it is. Would you care for some?' Catherine gave Veronica an imperceptible nod and she handed each lady a slice, taking extra care when placing it in front of Rose. Catherine observed that her daughter looked as if she was half tempted to squish it into Rose's perfectly smug face and sent her the slightest of frowns.

'And what have you been up to today, Rose? You appear to have the sun in your cheeks,' Catherine manoeuvred deftly, sipping her tea.

'Oh, I just took a little walk along the lane earlier,' Rose said. 'Although I did hear something from Iggy that made me think twice about the safety of stepping out these days.' She leant forward, her tone hushed. 'They're saying at the cricket there was a runaway cart along the road this morning, completely out of control. And apparently Jack Murphy was able to stop it and prevent a terrible accident.' Veronica dropped a piece of her cake just as it reached her mouth and it landed neatly in her cup. Fortunately no one seemed to notice – except Catherine, who decided to completely ignore it. Truly, her daughter seemed to have learnt nothing about poise at that school.

'Goodness, do you know who it was in the cart?' Catherine asked, her focus firmly on Rose.

'A young woman on her own; not much more than a child, he said. Honestly, if I may say, some of these girls are given entirely too much freedom. I am so grateful Mother brought me up to behave in a ladylike fashion.' Rose shook her perfectly coiffed curls from side to side. 'It's just terrible to think of how this younger generation flout the rules of propriety. Apparently she had no bonnet, hair flying about and skirt high enough…Well, I needn't go into further detail, I'm sure,' she finished, looking scandalised.

'A child, ye say? And how is she getting a hold of a horse and cart?' Mildred gasped.

'An older child, apparently,' said Rose airily. 'It's a wonder she wasn't old enough to know better, I suppose.'

Catherine nodded slowly, wondering at the machinations at play beneath Rose's words.

Just then the men entered, carrying glasses of whisky and laughing loudly.

'Looks like the boys are back from the tracks,' said Kevin, gesturing towards the window and the sound of Tom and Mick's voices carried towards them, and someone else. 'Looks like young Dan is here too,' he observed happily. 'What say we make a party of it this afternoon, eh? I'll send Tom to round up the masses. Who's in for tennis?'

So much for a lazy afternoon with Austen. Catherine sighed inwardly as she watched her husband and Dr Dwyer head out onto the verandah to welcome the boys. Kevin, the youngest of seven children, believed wholeheartedly in the adage 'the more the merrier' and felt that parties should be held spontaneously whenever possible. The minor detail of feeding said masses was left to Catherine, Veronica and the maids, Eileen and Molly.

Catherine had soon organised lemonade and racquets for their guests, then bundled Veronica off to the kitchen to help create a miracle. Somehow, between the four of them, they rolled out extra loaves of bread, carved the pumpkin and potatoes, strung the beans and dressed a turkey and a rabbit. Catherine herself made the sponge cake for dessert, to be filled with farm-fresh cream and blackberry jam that evening, as well as an enormous crumble made with apples picked from the Murphys' orchards.

Life on a dairy farm in Beecroft might be a far cry from her own genteel upbringing in the English countryside, Catherine mused as she worked, but at least she was never idle.

By the time the others were done with tennis, Veronica was adding the finishing touches to the table, leaving her with only a few minutes to run upstairs and change.

The other ladies had freshened up earlier, none of them actually partaking in tennis in 'this perishable heat', as Mildred described it, and each enjoying a rare afternoon off from her own housekeeping duties as they applauded the men. Veronica was sure Rose had enjoyed that immensely, especially as Jack had arrived a few hours earlier and she'd probably been able to flirt and flatter to her heart's content. She seethed to imagine it, resenting her strict mother's rules tying her to the duties of the house when she longed to be outside with the others. Pattie had arrived with her brother Jack, and Veronica was somewhat cheered by the consolation that she was sure to be entertained by her friend's accounts of the afternoon.

With that thought in mind, and the exciting prospect of seeing Jack bubbling away in her stomach, she ran up the staircase and into her room, opening the wardrobe and pondering the options within. Not that there was much choice: white, cream or lavender. The other girls were wearing modern styles of darker fabric and with lower necklines, but her dresses were all very conservative and plain. Even though she'd finished school these two weeks past, her mother was apparently inclined to keep her in girlish dresses forever. She chose the lavender, wishing she were allowed to wear her hair loose and pinned up at the sides as Rose and Pattie did. Instead she had to content herself with twisting her braids to one side.

Veronica paused and stared at the mirror, and gave in to the plaguing thoughts that had been racing through her head all afternoon. Did Rose know it was she, Veronica, who had been in that cart? Had she and Jack been seen? The laws of her social world had been thoroughly drilled into her at school and by her mother, and she was quite sure it was frowned upon for young ladies to spend time alone touching half-dressed men on a public road or even a quiet lane. Actually, especially not a quiet lane.

As a finishing touch she grabbed a pin and set a single deep lavender rose from their front garden in the hair behind her ear. Meeting her reflection she acknowledged that she at least looked innocent and pure. You *are* innocent and pure, she reminded herself, but her wrist warmed in memory and she felt as guilty as if she'd thrown herself into Jack's arms and kissed him. Turning for the door she banished that tantalising thought.

The sun swept away the last of its gold, surrendering to the night in lengthening rays between the tree branches. Even the birds seemed relieved to Mick as he watched them from his favourite position, perched on the sandstone ledge that ran along the verandah. The white cockatoos arrived in their dozens, calling to each other as they came, gathering their families together. They settled in a series of flurries, dotting the heights of the old Sydney red gums down by the milking sheds. The noise of their activity was almost outdone by the rising song of the kookaburras, who were also settling their clan for the night.

Mick watched it all, letting the sounds of home drift over then sink within. How he loved it, even though he was no farmer. The O'Shay boys were ever the scientists. He'd fought Tom for the medical tomes in their library from a young age, devouring information wherever he could find it. It had taken some convincing before their father acknowledged that Nigel Gregor, their housekeeper Eileen's husband, was a far more suitable farm manager than either of his sons would ever be, and they were finally permitted to pursue their academic aspirations. Of course it hadn't hurt that their mother was keen to see them follow in her family's footsteps, she being the daughter of a noted science professor at Cambridge University in England. She was an extraordinary woman, his mother, Mick acknowledged. A gentlewoman made of steel; although he was glad he was her son and not her daughter.

'Looking a bit thirsty,' Tom remarked, walking up with Dan and handing him a glass of beer.

Mick turned and grinned. 'Man cannot live on grass alone.'

'Lucky we're not cows then.' Tom took a deep drink then whistled in mock appreciation as Jack walked up the wide steps in evening dress. 'I take it back! We seem to have a fine-looking young bullock right here.'

Jack laughed, patting his slicked down, black hair that had been forced into submission from its usual forward lick. 'Well something sure smells like bull out here,' he replied, accepting a glass from Molly as she passed by with a tray.

'What did you use on that hair? Paint?' Tom pretended to investigate and Jack waved him away, trying not to spill his beer.

'So how did you enjoy today, Dan? Settling in all right?' Mick enquired, pushing his brother behind him.

'Yes, thanks,' Dan said.

'A whole year exiled back in Braidwood after, what? A decade boarding at Joey's? You must have forgotten what girls look like by now!' Tom nudged at him. Dan blushed and gave a small shrug. 'What do you make of our Beecroft fillies, eh?'

Mick was sure Dan was wishing himself back at 'Joey's', or St Joseph's College, right about then, or even on his parents' isolated farm. He was on Highview to learn about the latest dairy-farming practices on behalf of his family, but spending a summer with his older brother's schoolmates might prove to be a little more than the country boy could handle.

'They seem…very nice,' Dan managed, the crimson still staining his face.

Tom nodded knowingly. 'Well one of them is our sister, remember, so you'd better do the right thing by her brothers. Just the essential bribery: money, jewels. No camels though. The horses get offended.'

'Surely Veronica must be worth more than a camel,' Mick suggested.

'She runs a bit like one,' Tom said, screwing up his nose. 'A bit of a gangly old clomper, really, but don't let that turn you off, young Dan. Other members of her family are remarkably gifted and talented, especially the second eldest son.'

'Although fortunately she looks more like the eldest,' Mick added, pointing at his fair hair for emphasis.

'Yes, I've always thought you were the more feminine brother,' Tom said, and they all laughed.

'She's pretty,' Dan blurted out, seeming a bit shocked by his own admission. 'I mean, she…well she is.'

Jack moved away from where he had been listening, propped against the wall, and Mick noted he didn't seem as amused as the rest of them. Putting his glass down, he looked directly at Dan. 'She's too young.'

As he watched Jack's retreating back Mick wondered why he had felt the need to act the big brother.

'Well, I don't know about that.' Tom shook his head as they walked towards the parlour. 'She must be at least forty in camel years.'

The last of the twilight sent a soft crimson glow through the open French doors and between pale blue silk curtains held to each side with corded silver tassels. All the candles had been lit and the crystal chandelier turned on, each little flame and bulb making diamonds dance on the glassware. It was still warm, but the open doors sent the slightest of breezes across to the windows, carrying the scent of baking bread, turkey, rabbit and cake.

Catherine breathed it all in, humming along to the gramophone as she checked each detail. The soft strands of violin touched the night outside, inviting the languid evening indoors, as she smoothed the fine lace on the table once last time. She loved the soft white cloth, a gift from her mother as part of her trousseau. It reminded her of the elegant folds of her childhood home, such as the blankets of snow across their English lawns or the gentle meander of the river as it played with the trailing feathered branches of the willows. Cream roses spilt from the enormous cut-glass centrepiece, a wedding gift from her aunt, and the silver cutlery from her cousin's family gleamed from the polish Eileen had applied that afternoon. Her dressed dining table always reminded Catherine of the way her family had so graciously accepted her marriage to a mere farmer, and an Irish-Australian of all things. It was a shrine to their forgiveness.

Catherine O'Shay had no regrets. She was no pining English lady, wilting and faded. She was a modern success, proof that an aristocrat could marry for love and bring her gentility with her. Probably an impossibility back in Cambridge, but here, in this hopeful, strange land, such things could happen.

Not that this meant for one moment that she had forgone the rules that made such a life possible. Catherine knew that contentment could only be attained if one behaved as a lady should. Thinking upon her daughter, she wondered if she would ever truly make Veronica understand the difference between being wild and being free. Wildness placed one in danger, an unpredictable state of being that could only end with others taming you by force.

But true freedom, well that was a happiness no one else could touch.

Patting her dark chignon into place and smoothing the white silk of her dress, Catherine's eyes came to rest on her wedding photo and she smiled. She was free indeed.

Three

The large table was full when Veronica arrived, and she wondered if she imagined a flicker of admiration from Jack as she entered the room. She certainly didn't imagine it from their guest Dan Hagan, who stumbled as he stood up and hurried to pull back her chair, bowing slightly.

'Look out he doesn't catch any flies there, Vera Mags,' her brother Tom whispered in her ear as Dan returned to his seat to gape at her from across the table, his movements awkward but his brown eyes earnest. She slid her gaze along to see if Jack had noticed and it collided with his, which made her stomach so unsteady she felt she could have been the one swallowing flies.

'Well now, let's have a toast then,' her father announced. 'Here's to the heroic efforts of our boys in the First Eleven today. Well played, especially our Tom who got his first fifty of the season, and young Dan who is promising to be our best fast bowler in many years, ably supported by Mick in slips. Well done.'

'Hear, hear,' chorused the men.

'And to the ladies for putting on a fine spread as usual,' Kevin went on, smiling at his wife, 'and for gracing our table with their beauty, even our little Vera here, pretty as that rose, my dear.'

Veronica blushed, touched the flower in her hair and noted a flash of annoyance pass across Rose's face. 'And finally to young Jack, who I hear tell was quite the hero this morning, saving some girl from disaster. Nice to know our womenfolk have a quick-thinking man like you about to keep them safe. To good company!'

The crystal glasses chimed as dinner was served, conversation centring on the heroic rescue, although Veronica was grateful to note that Jack deftly avoided elaboration, stymieing all efforts to find out who had been the young lady in question. Her heart pounding with the fear of discovery, she tried to stay focused on her food and remain inconspicuous. The latter wasn't really that hard. For much of the meal it was Rose who drew all of the attention with her animated conversation, until she apparently decided to send some of it Veronica's way.

'Do you know who the girl may have been, Veronica?' she asked. 'Jack said he'd never met her before.'

'I-I'm...not sure,' stammered Veronica, feeling trapped as all eyes turned towards her along the table.

'You are probably around that age, are you not? Fifteen or so?'

'Seventeen,' Jack corrected her.

Veronica noticed Rose didn't seem to like that.

'Perhaps you're not being completely honest, Jack. You seem very knowledgeable about the girls in this area,' she said.

Veronica thought Jack laughed a little uneasily, but then he kissed Rose's hand and said: 'Well, everyone knows the girls in Beecroft are the prettiest around. Look at the one I'm sitting next to.'

Rose simpered and Veronica felt like yanking her stupid ringlets, but then the redhead redirected the focus onto her once more and annoyance slipped back to nervousness. 'Surely you have some idea who it could be, Veronica? After all, how many girls are there in this little town?'

There was nothing to fault the logic of her questions, but Veronica knew without doubt now that Rose had full knowledge it had been she on the road that morning and was steering the conversation towards humiliating exposure. Worse still, her brother Tom was kicking her under the table and grinning at her knowingly. Lord knew what he was about to say, surely finding this opportunity to tease her irresistible. Veronica shifted her desperate gaze to her father who winked in return and cleared his throat.

'It seems to me that we have a case of a young lady who needed some fresh air and got a bit carried away, but whoever it was I think we should allow her the dignity of anonymity. I'm sure she's learnt her lesson, and we've all longed for a little taste of freedom in our day, have we not? No harm done, thanks to young Jack here…speaking of fresh air, who would like to join me on the verandah for a breather?'

Veronica breathed a sigh of relief herself but it was short lived as Catherine stood, directing raised eyebrows her daughter's way, and beckoning her to the kitchen to supervise dessert. Pattie Murphy followed her in a swish of dark pink silk.

'A word if you will, Veronica.'

Jack's sister Pattie waited impatiently as Veronica stood in the next room being dressed down by her mother in hushed tones. The phrases 'not a child any more' and 'reputation to consider' came floating under the door.

Pattie sighed, absent-mindedly stirring the cream. She had arrived that afternoon hoping to spend some time with her friends. Unfortunately, she hadn't dressed for tennis, which she usually thoroughly enjoyed, and she was forced to miss out on the joys of flinging herself around the court and trading banter with the boys. Instead, with Veronica busy in the kitchen, she'd been forced to spend an interminable afternoon with Rose. After only two months in the neighbourhood, that gigantic know-it-all already seemed to fancy herself an expert on everyone and everything in it. It was almost as if Rose chose every word as part of some fiendish plan to antagonise her.

And now here she was at it again, only this time it was Veronica at the mercy of her scheming ways. A proper little viper that one, Pattie decided, and definitely not someone she wanted as a sister-in-law.

Catherine emerged, a subdued Veronica in tow, and Pattie pasted a suitably serious expression on her face, replacing it with a grin as soon as Catherine exited through to the adjoining room.

'Don't. I don't want to talk about it.'

'Why not? It was only Jack. And it wasn't as if you were flying along in your drawers, although Rose would have us all believing this mystery woman-child was practically nude.'

'How did she know it was me? I mean, who saw, for goodness' sake?' Veronica hissed, looking over her shoulder to make sure her mother was busy organising dessert aperitifs with Eileen in the other room.

'She was probably lurking in the bushes, trying to accidentally stumble across Jack so she could twirl her stupid parasol his way.' Pattie stuck out her tongue in disgust.

Veronica thumped the spoon as she assembled the desserts, adding extra cream and jam to each bowl of cake and crumble. 'Well, she's ruined my summer. Mother will watch me like a hawk. She said I have learnt "nothing about behaving like a lady and everything about becoming a hooligan".'

Pattie laughed. 'Oh piffle! So what if you had a bit of ankle showing and hair flying about? It's not like I haven't horrified a few old biddies with my adventures. Trust me, she'll get over it.'

'Your mother isn't like my mother.'

'It's not your mother who caused the problem. That Rose really riles me up! You know, she really deserves her just desserts.' Pattie stuck her finger in the jam, tasting it. 'Hold your horses!' she declared suddenly, clutching at Veronica's arm and pointing at the wall. 'Let's squish that huntsman up. Put it in her jam.'

Veronica watched agog as Pattie climbed up onto the stool with a bowl and spoon to catch the spider. 'Stop it! You'll get caught!' Veronica gasped, giggly and nervous at the same time, but Pattie was something of an expert at spider catching. Despite the impediment of her 'blasted skirts', soon the unfortunate creature was being buried in the last of the sticky jam at the bottom of the bowl.

'What's taking you so long?' Catherine demanded, entering the kitchen with Eileen and eyeing the desserts impatiently.

'Just finishing adding the jam.' Pattie smiled innocently, heaping a large blob onto the final plate as Catherine marched out, telling them to hurry along.

'This one is for *Rose*, Eileen,' Pattie instructed her carefully. 'She said there was no possibility that your jam would taste as nice as their housekeeper's.'

Veronica watched round eyed as Eileen jutted out her chin indignantly.

'We'll see about that, miss.'

'You'll be fine, dear boy,' Dr Dwyer assured Tom, who was busy lamenting his loss of sleep during his final exams. 'If you've made it this far you'll be sure to pass next year as well. Then you can join your brother and take an internship down at St Vincent's. They didn't haul me all the way from Melbourne without giving me a bit of clout! I'll take care of it for you.'

The desserts were being finished and Veronica tried not to stare as Rose lifted her fork towards the bit she'd obviously been saving: the jam.

'You're enjoying it there, aren't you, Mick?' Dr Dwyer asked.

Mick looked to choose his words carefully. It wouldn't do to offend the chief surgeon of the hospital. 'Of course! Although in the long term I had been considering the possibility of working locally. I've always imagined myself a rural doctor. Being able to spread myself about a bit.'

The jam perched in dark globs as it headed towards Rose's mouth.

'Less serious city problems such as plagues and more rural problems such as spider bites?' Pattie suggested, just as Rose landed the contents firmly into her mouth and began to chew.

Pattie's father George chuckled. 'We're hardly dealing with plagues these days, my dear.'

'I saw a spider-bite patient just this week,' Tom piped in. 'Head like a horse he had poor chap. Not unlike our Mick here.'

Veronica watched horrified and fascinated as Rose reloaded her fork.

'Beastly creatures. I can't imagine what the good Lord was thinking when he made them,' Rose observed, turning to smile at Jack. 'I'm afraid I'm quite terrified of spiders in general. They seem to be everywhere around here.'

'Oh you'll find you'll develop a taste for them,' Pattie assured her as Rose ate another mouthful. 'Are you quite all right there Vera?' she added innocently, her eyes dancing wickedly at a choking Veronica.

Veronica nodded, red-faced, sipping her water.

'Perhaps we should adjourn to the parlour?' Catherine suggested, moving the party to the next room and casting an exasperated look at her daughter.

'That was a little hairy,' Pattie whispered in Veronica's ear as she walked by.

It was some moments before Veronica could compose herself to follow.

The men filled their whisky glasses and the conversation turned to hospital politics; the ladies listened, sipping their sherry.

Catherine relaxed, able to do so at last now that dinner was finished and her guests were satisfied. This was by far the best time of evening for the hostess, she observed, settling comfortably into her armchair in the soft light of the parlour and focusing on Mick's story.

'So he had only moments to decide either way and went with his instincts. Luckily for the patient he was right and it was appendicitis.'

'Extraordinary,' said Dr Dwyer.

'The poor girl would have died if he'd listened to that damn charlatan,' Mick finished.

'Mick, please,' Catherine admonished.

'Oh he can call a spade a spade there, my dear. Dr Smythe is an old quack – isn't that right, George?' Kevin deferred to his old friend, George Murphy, who knew the man well.

'I have found in life it is best not to disagree with one's host,' George replied, 'however it is even more advantageous to refer to the lady of the house in all matters of polite society. They are the ones who feed us after all.' He nodded and tipped his glass at Catherine and she noted, not for the first time over the years, that he really was a very nice gentleman. Alice was a fortunate woman. A charming husband, a successful handsome son in Jack, and Pattie...well Catherine had to admit, the girl was unfailingly likeable even if she was a bit wild. Not that she was in a position to judge, after her own daughter's antics that morning. Noticing

Iggy Dwyer standing quietly by the window she realised he had hardly said a word all evening.

'And how about you, Iggy?' she said, after acknowledging George with a smile. 'Have you never thought to study medicine like your father?'

Iggy looked to be considering his response. 'I'm afraid my studies were somewhat interrupted during my formative years, Mrs O'Shay.'

Mildred leant on her husband's hand. 'He was terribly ill with scarlet fever, I'm afraid. Spent a good five years bedridden, poor lamb. Only got well again this past year.'

'Oh I am sorry. I didn't mean to pry,' Catherine said.

'Not at all, not at all,' Mildred assured her. 'We don't like to mention it, but so far the Sydney weather seems to agree with him, bless him. Never seen him so well and strong.' She smiled at her son, still patting at her husband's hand. 'What God takes away with one hand, he gives with the other.'

'Can't say I wasn't disappointed,' Dr Dwyer said stiffly.

'Now, now,' Mildred said. Catherine felt the tension from Iggy as he shifted his weight away from the curtain he'd been leaning against. She knew he had endured some kind of ill health – Mildred often alluded to his 'disposition' then seemed to catch herself – but she'd no idea it had been for so long and of such a serious nature. She looked at the doctor, figuring it wasn't something he liked people to know about his son.

'It's no use denying it was a great disappointment to me that he couldn't continue his studies for many years. He has a fine mind but he missed too much school in the end – and wasted his opportunities to boot.' Dr Dwyer took a gulp of his brandy.

Mildred added quickly, 'Of course he's excelled at his piano. The master at the Conservatorium said as much, did he not, dear? Says he's got real potential.'

'Humph.' Dr Dwyer drained his glass. 'Yes, piano playing. That's quite a career choice for a man.'

Catherine shifted in her chair, wishing she'd never broached the subject, as Iggy placed his glass on the mantel.

'The boys were talking about the trouble in Europe today,' he said lightly. 'Perhaps you'll get lucky and end up with a son in uniform. That's something any father can be proud of, is it not?'

Silence stretched across the room.

'Let's hope it doesn't come to that,' Kevin said reassuringly, noting Mildred's stricken face.

'Surely not,' she said. ''Tis a long way off from us.'

'If the Brits need us then Australia will rally,' Jack said firmly. 'Half our relatives are over there.'

'What about your family here?' Pattie countered.

Everyone seemed to consider that for a moment.

'They say if you join the Light Horse you get to take your own mount over with you,' Dan said shyly. 'Imagine that. Riding across Europe. I've never even been out of Australia.'

'I doubt it is much of a holiday,' Mick remarked. 'Still, if it comes to pass I'll be doing my bit, no doubt about that. They'll be needing doctors.'

'And I couldn't let you sail off alone and charm all the nurses in your shiny new uniform. I'd better come along and pitch in a stethoscope too.' Tom grinned across at his brother.

Catherine eyed her sons with concern. She supposed if war came she would be grateful that both had chosen to study medicine and would therefore tend the wounded rather than fight on the front lines, but no one was safe, of course. Already the ladies at church were atwitter with patriotism, but she knew only too well that casualties always exceeded glorious, unsupported expectation. Her brother had sailed off to the Boer War filled with confidence and survived all kinds of horrific battles, only to die in a field hospital while being treated for dysentery. Remembering her mother's face when she'd received the news of his death, Catherine felt the sudden urge to hold the hands of the clock above the fireplace. To cheat the fools who made war. She bent her head as the memory of her brother's cheerful wave goodbye returned to her with full force. Then she felt someone move to stand behind her shoulder and a hand covered hers. Looking down at the long brown fingers, she saw her own tear land upon them.

'Now, now, I'm sure it will all come to naught,' Kevin said, smiling gently down at his wife, patting her hand. 'Let's move into the parlour and see what Iggy's been learning on the piano and have a little singalong. Where's Pattie? Come along, young lady; give us a tune or two.'

Mischievous Pattie had certainly given her parents a few extra grey hairs over the years, but all was forgiven when she sang. Her beautiful voice washed over them as she began with 'When Irish Eyes Are Smiling', which made Mildred cry openly. Pattie's parents rocked back and forth, arms linked, misty-eyed. With the applause barely over, Rose whispered in Iggy's ear and he played the opening chords to 'You Made Me Love You'. Pattie didn't seem to have much choice but to sing as Rose curtsied in front of Jack. They danced in the lazy familiar way of lovers and, even though others soon joined them in the centre of the living room, they seemed isolated in their own world. Catherine observed the expression on her daughter's face, feeling her pain as she tasted the cruel sting of heartache for the first time in her young life.

Veronica watched them and knew somehow that the race had been run and that Rose had won, although what exactly she'd done to win didn't bear considering. Nor did she want to stay to watch Rose enjoy her victory. She was heading for the door when Dan appeared in front of her, his expression hopeful as he bowed for the second time that night and held out his hand. He was closer to her in age than Jack and nice enough looking, she supposed, with his brown hair and eyes and broad shoulders. She knew she should have been flattered by his attentions, but all she could feel was disappointment that he wasn't Jack. Finding herself unable to refuse, she allowed him to waltz her around the floor and, in spite of herself, the music began to lift her spirits.

Soon they were all dancing, her brothers singing with exaggerated adoration to Pattie, which made them all laugh.

You made me love you
I didn't want to do it I didn't want to do it…

Tom sent Veronica a grin before donning his mother's riding bonnet and placing one of her scarves around Mick's face; they hammed it up again in loud falsettos.

She felt Dan's eyes upon her and turned to him, shrugging. 'I do apologise. They're a bit mad, I'm afraid.'

'I think I need a bit of that in my life.' Dan smiled back. He really did have a nice face, she noted, trying not to look past him to where Jack stood, his arm still on Rose's waist.

The parlour resounded with applause as the brothers finished their duet on bended knee, before begging their father in squeaky girlish voices for their favourite Irish jig. Kevin promptly produced his fiddle. The music was like an elixir running up the dancers' veins as the room spun, the floorboards easing beneath the rug, flexing with the rhythm of the dance. Singing along with the familiar songs, Veronica found herself lost in the music, her feet moving effortlessly in time.

'Hand her over unless you've got a spare camel!' Tom laughed, grabbing Veronica off Dan and twirling her about.

'Slow down, you great ape.' She giggled as he pranced her back and forth, whooping as he went. He gave her an extra enthusiastic spin and somehow she landed in Jack's arms. Every part of her fell into alert and for a moment both of them stood still. The last time he'd touched her felt like years before, although impossibly it had only been that morning, and the same strange feeling of burning ran along the place where his hands lay.

She glanced up at him, unsure what to say just as Tom went sailing past, imitating an ape.

Suddenly they both began to laugh and Jack took one hand off her waist, leading her with ease about the floor as they let go of the troubles of the day and enjoyed each other again, old friends. They were young for a moment, with all the freedom she missed so much, the freedom that had driven her to stand on a cart galloping towards the sun.

The music ended and a voice broke through the hum of conversation. 'Jack? There you are. Come on, darling, sing this one for us all.'

Rose had called him to the front and Jack dropped his arms from Veronica and went, leaving her feeling suddenly empty.

Like his sister, Jack was a gifted singer. His voice rang through the night, clear yet intimate, wrapping itself around the listener.

I wandered today to the hill, Maggie,
To watch the scene below;
The creek and the creaking old mill,
Maggie,
As we used to long ago.

Rose held his hand and he looked down at her as he sang, the meaning of the gesture clogging in Veronica's brain, then forcing its unwanted way in. The words followed her as she quietly left the room.

But she missed the lift of Jack's gaze to the departing lavender dress.

But to me you're as fair as you were, Maggie
When you and I were young.

Four

Beecroft

I need to get that stupid girl out of the way.

Although she had played the situation artfully to regain the advantage, Rose was still seething over the sight of Veronica and Jack on the road earlier that day. She had followed him across the ridge, unable to contain her curiosity, hiding herself behind the rocks in Stan's Gully. Even from a distance she could read the heat between them. Despite her confidence that she had successfully driven the girl from his mind in the hours afterwards, she knew she had competition.

And the last thing Rose needed right now was competition, not if she was going to get what she needed from Jack Murphy.

'Stop scowling, Rose. The wind will change and you'll stay that way!'

Her brother Iggy was in a better mood, as he usually was after he'd played the piano for hours. Not so the cricket and tennis parties for him: he much preferred spending time with his music, the one constant positive throughout his invalid years. Although fit and hale now, he'd little interest in attaining sporting skills, with the exception of horse racing. He watched Ebony's sleek form with pride as they took off in the buggy for home, his parents having left a little earlier, Mildred still a little teary from the 'sweet music' (although Rose suspected it was a mite more due to the sherry).

'You got your way. I went to the damnable cricket and got the story out of Jack, then spread it around.' Iggy cast a look at Rose. 'You should be happy! He was by your side the whole night.'

'You didn't manage to get the most important piece of information! It wasn't much use without naming her.'

'Oh well, it made him look like a hero, and you were on his arm all night so you got some reflected glory out of the situation,' he reminded her and she smiled a little. 'Come on now; tell me what's going on. Why was I helping you name and shame this girl? She's no competition to you; she's only a kid.' In fact Iggy secretly considered Veronica very much a woman, and a beautiful one at that. He hadn't minded trying to help squash any potential romance between her and Jack Murphy. Besides, he was really trying to protect her. He loved his sister, she was the only one who had kept him sane when he was ill, but he also knew that jealousy was a poison in her veins and he didn't wish her enmity on anyone.

Especially not Veronica O'Shay.

'Well, it's finished with now. I was hoping her mother would be a bit more scandalised and lock her away but it obviously wasn't enough. I need something more.' She furrowed her brow thoughtfully.

'Just get him to propose. She can't be a threat to Mrs Jack Murphy,' he suggested.

'Of course that's the goal, but it's not that easy...Wait. That's it!'

'What's it?' Iggy was wary. Rose seemed obsessed with this man, and that wasn't like her. Usually she just toyed with an assortment of admirers, dangling them before her like pieces of jewellery before throwing them back in the box. But since their family had moved to Beecroft she'd seemingly shut the lid and set her eye on the prize diamond that was Jack Murphy.

She was terribly spoilt, he acknowledged, beyond the suspicion of their innocent mother, who wouldn't have believed Rose capable of such scheming. Besides, Mildred had spent their childhoods far too focused on fussing over her sickly son to pay much attention to the secretive side of her daughter. Iggy sighed, remembering the years of cosseting.

She was their father's favourite of course. Why wouldn't she be when she gave him exactly what he wanted in a child? Healthy, confident, uncomplicated. The opposite of his son. Rose never gave her father one minute of concern. With dimply smiles and manipulations, Rose had managed to completely bamboozle Dr Dwyer, who never saw the hard selfish streak that coursed through her.

But Iggy knew. He was probably the only person in the world she was ever herself with.

Perhaps she was serious about wanting to marry Jack. In fact, observing her calculating expression he was starting to wonder just what she was capable of doing in order to secure him.

'Let's just say that Mrs Murphy could be the answer to everything,' she said thoughtfully, and fell silent the rest of the way home.

Shaking his head, Iggy thought, not for the first time, that his piano was far better company than people; after all, he knew what tunes it could play.

Even though he was exhausted from the day, Jack twisted and turned in the sheets, the dampness of his body meeting the thick, still air as sleep continued to elude him. Sweat bit at the deep scratches on his shins, and it occurred to him that Rose hadn't even commented on them that morning. In fact, she hadn't seemed interested in the story at all until there had been company and she relayed what he'd told Iggy. Then again, he allowed, there'd been other things on her mind. He closed his eyes, picturing her lush body beckoning him, arching her back, her long blonde hair...His eyes flew open. *Red* hair.

It was no use trying to sleep after that. Getting up, he went out onto the back porch, where he rolled a cigarette and stared up at the stars, clear and bright with the lack of the moon. He knew Rose expected him to marry her, and he would have to do so, and soon. He had taken liberties, after all, far more than he should have with a lady, and she was becoming increasingly more difficult to resist. Besides, he'd been head over heels since he first laid eyes on her.

He'd been at mass that Sunday morning, home from town for the weekend and sitting with his family, when he noticed something unusual was going on. Tom and Mick were a few pews ahead and acting very strangely – dropping hymnals and bending down, craning their necks to the side. Glancing around, he saw the source of their distraction. Across the aisle sat a family who were new to their parish; and seated primly between her parents, in a glow of white cotton, was an angel. A sunbeam through the stained-glass window cast a pattern across her face and she'd lowered her lashes, then redirected her vision his way. When his eyes met the dark brown pools of her irises, he'd swallowed hard. He couldn't recall a time when he'd paid less attention to the mass as he surreptitiously drank in every detail of her, from the faint outline of her corset to the honeyed skin of her neck curving into her collar. By the time mass had ended he'd made up his mind to speak to her, although what to say to such a girl he'd no idea.

To his delight, Catholic etiquette saved him the trouble. The Murphys and the O'Shays had walked as a group over to the Dwyers to welcome them to the parish, and his mother made the introductions.

'I see ye have a cake stall running there,' Mildred commented after the niceties had been observed.

'Yes, to raise money for the orphanage,' Alice said.

The angel had smiled up at him and Jack had felt himself gape, all words evaporating under her gaze.

'Do they sell butterfly cakes? I do so love them.'

Jack had managed a nod and somehow thought to offer her his arm.

The O'Shay boys had watched in envy as he'd led her to the tables, and Jack vaguely registered Tom's muttered amazement.

'Cheeky bastard.'

The courtship had blossomed from there, at a speed that sometimes took even Jack by surprise, and he knew that she would be the perfect choice to warm his bed and grace his table. There really was nothing else to consider, was there? The blonde hair flashed through his mind again, and he frowned. Veronica had stirred something within him. The girl who'd been like a little sister had grown into a woman. He thought of her bare legs today, the perspiration on her skin as she stood so close, the feel of her beneath his hands as he'd danced with her tonight. Suddenly he wanted her. It rushed through him and he couldn't deny it. But if he was going to be a married man he had to accept that there would always be desirable women in his path. He wasn't an animal that couldn't control his lusts, was he?

Jack threw his cigarette into the night, forcing the images of Veronica away.

He decided he'd better look into buying a ring that week while he was in town.

Decision made, he headed back to bed. Closing his eyes, he imagined Rose, her corsets in a pile, her body awaiting his touch. But when he woke at dawn it was images of purple roses that left him in a sweat.

Monday dawned with glaring brilliance, the heat already radiating off the tin roof of the shed. Alice Murphy bent down to investigate underneath the coop towards the back and laughed as the largest rooster, King Henry, strutted out, puffed up as usual with self-importance. Henry had been so named by Pattie, and Alice thought it was the perfect name for the pompous-looking rooster, who appeared to consider himself royalty among chickens. As she thought of her daughter she shook her head, but then couldn't help smiling at her impish ways. Alice might sometimes succeed in dressing her as a lady, but Pattie was a free spirit at heart. Whoever took her on was going to have to have an open mind about decorum – not that Alice really worried about her very much. Pattie could look after herself.

She cast a look down at her basket, satisfied that the two dozen or so eggs would be well received at the orphanage, and headed back towards the house. The long white verandah ran around its entire circumference, and Alice admired it as she approached, noting the jasmine was growing thickly post its flowering and would need a good prune before Christmas. It wasn't quite as grand as Highview's, but the Murphys' farmhouse was renowned as the prettiest in the area, situated as it was in a spot near a dam shaded by several jacaranda trees. The purple flowers had dropped a carpet on the lawn, disguising the dry, patchy grass and rows of apple trees lined the nearby paddock. It was a sight she never tired of, the beauty of her home.

Alice turned her mind to the upcoming Christmas season. For many years now, she and George had taken their family over to join the O'Shays' relatives at their residence in Wahroonga. Situated little more than five miles away, this lofty area on the North Shore was renowned for its large, beautiful homes and their extensive gardens, but the grandest of all was Greenshades. With its manicured lawns, fruit-filled orchard, tennis courts and swimming pool, Greenshades was a delight, and Christmas there was the highlight of the year. Marjorie, Kevin's sister, had married a wealthy importer and, much like her brother, was a generous host who loved a good party. The result was a Christmas event that rivalled all others in the area, with tennis and champagne, swimming and riding and the traditional pavilion dinner party.

What drew Alice's especial attention every year, however, was that the family and its connections also provided a Christmas event for the orphans cared for by the Mercy Sisters nearby. Alice had been heavily involved with the orphanage since she first moved out that way as a young bride, and was grateful for the opportunity to put her comfortable financial position to good use.

Unfortunately it couldn't buy her a choice of daughter-in-law. She sat down on the porch step, taking a moment to drink in the reflections on the water as the occasional jacaranda bloom twisted its way down into the dam. No, it wasn't Pattie that concerned Alice right now: it was her son.

Rose certainly looked the part on his arm – elegant, assured, fashionable – however it was the undercurrents beneath the polish that concerned Alice. Her only son knew his own mind, a characteristic for which she was usually grateful. Determination and decisiveness had served him well in his studies and now his business career. He'd all but taken over the family packaging company, leaving George to enjoy an early semi-retirement. Yet now it seemed his strength could become his weakness, because once he decided on something he couldn't be swayed, casting aside advice and warnings and focusing only on his goal.

And this girl was undoubtedly in his sights, however blinded by the vision he might be. Alice knew any criticism of the match on her part would fall on deaf ears.

Alice sighed, drawing herself up and swinging the door open into the cool interior to deposit the eggs on the kitchen table. 'I'm just off to town for a bit, Maude. I shouldn't be too long.' She gathered up her hat and nodded at the maid.

'Before you go spendin' more on presents for them little ones, you might want t' take a look at the growing mountain under that tree,' Maude said dryly, pointing at the parlour.

Alice smiled as she headed off to the sulky, mentally ticking off all the things she still needed to buy as she took the reins. Tilley seemed to enjoy the exercise of pulling the lightweight cart and Alice soon found herself relaxing into the drive. It was only a mile and a half to town and the sky was cloudless in an endless blue, the thirsty, golden fields shimmering slightly in the breeze. A few wallabies flicked their ears at her with interest and the cows grazed in their slow way, one occasionally lifting its head in idle curiosity at the sound of the sulky.

By the time she arrived at the general store Alice felt quite peaceful, all thoughts of Jack and Rose pushed from her mind and replaced instead with purchasing considerations. She had decided on pink ribbon to trim the new bonnets she was making for the orphanage girls, and some bright red and blue paint for George to finish off the train set he was making for the boys. The other little gifts would be gratefully received, but she was sure the train set would be the hit of the day. George had enjoyed building it, with some help from Pattie, who loved to tinker with tools and design all manner of contraptions down in the shed with her father. Alice smiled as she hitched the horse up outside the store. That girl really should have been born a boy.

Hannah Street was mostly empty save a few sleeping dogs, some older men discussing the contents of the paper outside the general store and the postmaster who waved at her from the stately post office entranceway. Walking gratefully out of the hot sun and into the shade of the store, she headed first towards the selection of ribbons.

'Good morning, Mrs Murphy.'

Alice turned to see Rose Dwyer standing near the window, looking striking as usual in a white blouse and navy hobble skirt. So much for pushing the girl out of her mind, she sighed inwardly. 'Good morning, Rose, how nice to see you,' she said, forcing a smile. 'Doing some Christmas shopping?'

'Yes, I want to buy Mother some new winter gloves,' Rose replied, turning to the shopkeeper. 'Hilde, could you show me what you have in store?'

'Got some nice summer ones just 'ere.' Hilde nodded at the counter hopefully, then grimaced as Rose shook her head. 'Think there were a few winter pairs left over 'fore I put 'em away. I'll have t' look at what we have out back,' she added, not looking very keen to do so.

'That would be lovely, thank you,' Rose replied.

'Don't know what ya mum's gonna want 'em for in this heat, 'less she's stopped melting since I saw her last,' Hilde muttered under her breath, heading out to the back storeroom slowly, her large frame ponderous in her enormous apron.

Rose turned back to Alice. 'Are you making a new bonnet?' she asked, nodding at the ribbons Alice was holding.

'Yes, just choosing some trim for the Mercy girls.' Alice always preferred to call them that rather than 'orphans', which sounded so cold and sad.

'Actually I'm glad I saw you today,' Rose said. 'I wanted to ask…well, I wondered if I might have your permission to help with the orphans. I'm sure you are very busy and I would so love to be of use. I mean, I assume there will be a celebration of sorts at the orphanage for Christmas?'

'Actually, they attend celebrations elsewhere,' said Alice, feeling slightly embarrassed. She was hardly in a position to invite Rose to Greenshades, where their Christmas would take place.

'Oh, I see,' Rose replied. 'Well perhaps I could visit the orphanage with you and help in some way. I'm desperate to be involved, missing the children from my old parish as I do.' Her eyes filled with tears as she added, 'Especially at this time of year, poor lambs.'

'I didn't know you were involved with this kind of work, my dear,' Alice said, surprised. Rose didn't seem the type.

'Oh well, one doesn't like to boast about doing God's bidding,' Rose said demurely. 'I would love to be a comfort and help in some small way again. I do so love children. Look at me, I'm sorry. Being all sentimental and foolish.'

'Just don't weep on me new ribbon there,' Hilde sniffed, having returned with a selection of the previous season's gloves. She eyed Rose with obvious suspicion, plonking the box on the counter. Alice studied Rose too, wondering at her motives.

'Come with me on Sunday,' offered Alice, deciding to call her bluff. 'Pattie and I visit every week with the O'Shays and I'm sure there will be plenty for you to do. No doubt the girls will enjoy the company.'

Rose's lips gave an almost imperceptible twitch before settling into a benign curve and she held out both her hands prettily to Alice's, thanking her warmly. Turning to leave she was halted by a loud 'Ahem' from Hilde.

'Oh Hilde, I do apologise. I think I've changed my mind about the gloves – I'll knit them myself instead.' She looked back at

Alice and smiled again. 'After all, handmade things mean so much more.' Hilde's mouth drew into one long, grim line as she closed up the box and took the gloves out to the back again, mumbling something about a certain 'useless baggage' who 'wouldn't know her backside from a knitting needle'. Alice had to stifle a giggle at that.

But all the way home in the buggy she puzzled over this new, unexpected side of the Dwyer girl.

On one hand, she found herself sharing Hilde's scepticism. There was something a bit too good to be true about Rose's pious behaviour, yet on the other hand Alice supposed the younger woman might truly just desire to be a good Christian. She thought about the reading from the previous Sunday's mass, translating the Latin in her mind: *Nolite iudicare ut non iudicemini: Judge not lest ye be judged.*

'Did ya find whatcha were lookin' for?' Maude asked as she walked into the kitchen on her return home.

'Perhaps,' Alice replied, lost in thought and missing the confused expression on Maude's face. She sat down to cut the bonnet trimming, reflecting that one comment by Rose was certainly true: handmade things did mean so much more, especially to the hands making them.

Five

Waitara

Pattie thought the trip would never end. An hour in a chaise with Rose Dwyer and her own mother was torturous, not least because Pattie, who usually liked to handle the horse herself, had to let Alice take the reins today. She cursed herself again as she fidgeted with her bandaged hand, annoyed that she hadn't been more careful working on the train set with her father. As a result, she had a rather sore gash to contend with, which was nothing compared to the torture of sitting opposite Rose in a confined space for half an hour. Her only entertainment during the trip had been trying to decide which was worse, her mother's gullibility or Rose's lies. Surely her mother could see through the pathetic fabrications about the 'poor souls' at St Bernard's, Rose's old parish orphanage in Melbourne.

Rose was appointing herself the heroine of every tale, describing how she had saved little Stan from drowning in the river, sewn Sally a dress with material bought with her own allowance (so the 'poor darling' had something pretty to wear on her First Holy Communion Day), and how Father Colin O'Donnell had openly cried at the pulpit the final time they attended mass, devastated to see her leave.

'He told me later he was most embarrassed, but he just couldn't seem to help himself,' she said with a dainty shrug.

'It's a marvel he can get through mass each week then if he's so emotional,' Pattie remarked. 'The Bible is hardly a comedy.'

'Pattie!' said her mother.

'And however does he cope with funerals?' Pattie went on, undeterred.

Rose darted a half-amused look her way then feigned an expression of sadness. 'I suppose a priest's life is a lonely one. Losing a friend can't be easy, even for them.'

Pattie couldn't help herself. 'I wasn't aware they were permitted lady friends.'

'Pattie that is quite enough– ' her mother began.

'Oh, Mrs O'Shay, don't be concerned. Pattie is just teasing me,' Rose said. 'She and I are becoming bosom friends.' Alice missed the mocking glance Rose threw at Pattie's flat chest as she took a deep breath, expanding her own, impressive bust.

Pattie seethed. How could Jack be so shallow as to parade about with this insufferable cow? She needed to say something to him before it got more serious, and judging by her mother's look of tentative approval today, it was going to have to be soon. The realisation made her slightly nervous. Jack had never been one to listen to advice, especially from his little sister.

She was saved from further thought as the orphanage finally came into view, a collection of dark brick buildings surrounded by bushland on the tallest hill in Waitara. The O'Shays had already arrived and, as she began to unload the eggs and apples they'd brought with them from the farm, she waved at Veronica. The latter waved back, pausing briefly in the game of hide and seek she was playing with the children in the garden.

Catherine was already in the kitchen organising a midday feast, a weekly treat of roast beef and potatoes followed by apple pies and cream, while the Sisters of Mercy enjoyed some quiet prayer. Pattie figured their mothers were in their element here. Sunday mass was well and good, but Catherine and Alice were practical women who believed in practising what was preached, and the two of them were a force to be reckoned with in that kitchen.

Catherine smiled to see Pattie come in with the supplies, then looked down at her bandaged right hand in consternation. 'Oh Pattie, whatever have you done to yourself now?'

'Runaway track, I'm afraid, Mrs O'Shay,' Pattie explained laconically.

'Indeed?' Catherine raised an eyebrow. 'Well I suppose that's a little better than blaming a runaway horse,' she said, taking the crate of apples and casting Veronica a look as she arrived in the doorway. Pattie could have sworn she saw Catherine hide a smile as she turned away.

While the children were eating lunch, Catherine took the girls aside and asked if they would go up to the work site nearby. The foreman was a family friend and had kept some leftover wood for the orphanage whose dark walls would become freezing in winter.

'I'm not sure I can lift anything today,' Pattie apologised, holding up her bandaged right hand.

'I'll go,' Rose volunteered, and Pattie stared at Veronica's dismayed expression, unable to help her.

'I'm not sure…it may be a little too heavy for you, my dear, and I wouldn't want you to damage your pretty frock.' Catherine eyed Rose's soft yellow dress dubiously.

'Oh, this old thing can stand getting dirty. I'm sure I can handle it, especially if it means warming these poor dears in winter,' Rose said sweetly, picking up her hat. Pattie pulled a face at Veronica, who couldn't seem to bring herself to smile back.

'Shall we take the cart?'

Veronica stared straight ahead, gripping the seat as Rose failed to avoid yet another rut on the steep road. It was horribly hot. So hot the tree shadows up ahead were making water mirages on the track. They hadn't spoken a word the entire way and Veronica was mentally inventing and discarding conversational topics when, to her surprise, Rose spoke.

'You seem nervous, Veronica. Would you feel better standing up, perhaps?'

'I…I'm not sure I understand– '

'I saw you,' Rose said in a matter-of-fact way. 'It's no use trying to deny it. I watched the way you flaunted yourself in front of Jack on the road, and the way you tried to flirt with him at the dinner party too. He has no use for a child, Vera, so stop embarrassing yourself.'

'Veronica.'

'I beg your pardon?'

'My name is Veronica,' Veronica ground out, feeling her anger build, 'and I have no…interest in Jack Murphy, if that's what you're implying.'

'The little girl has a temper. Well, well, well.' Rose raised an eyebrow. 'He's going to ask my father for my hand soon, so it's just as well you have no "interest", as you say, although I think you're lying.' She glanced at Veronica casually before adding, 'Not that it matters. Jack is in love with me, as I'm sure you can plainly see. I'm just trying to save you from making a fool of yourself again.'

'I'm sure I have no idea what you're talking about.' Veronica stared across towards the thickly forested hills, focusing on breathing normally to keep her voice light.

Rose sighed, shaking her head. 'Just keep well away from Jack, Veronica. He's going to marry me and sticking pathetic little flowers in your hair won't change that. Do we understand each other?'

'Oh, I understand you perfectly,' Veronica responded, unable to resist adding, 'although I'm surprised you feel so threatened by a child like me.'

'Not threatened, I'm just a realist. Even the bull will sniff at the calf.'

Veronica felt her heart thump hard in her chest and clamped her mouth shut, determined not to react. They drove along in a frosty silence until the workers finally came into sight. Seeing them approach, the foreman, John Parks, waved to them. Veronica waved back.

'Here's a turn-up for the books! Hello there, Miss Rose.' He tipped his hat at Rose who flourished the reins to the seat and held out her hand to be helped down. Some of the workers nearby stopped and stared at her. 'Mind y'step. Well, well, look at our young Veronica.' He smiled at her kindly. 'How's your dad going? Hey.' He'd noticed the men watching them. 'Don't just stand there gawking like frogs!' he yelled. 'Get this wood on the cart for the ladies!'

Rose studied her nails and enjoyed their admiring glances while Veronica donned her gloves and helped place the smaller blocks on the cart.

After a good twenty minutes the tray was full and John raised his hand in salute.

'Tell your dad I'll pop in and see him next week,' he said, pausing to bark at the young men who were still hovering. 'Go on, get back to work! And put your eyes back in y'heads, ya bunch of prawns!'

They waved goodbye and drove away. Veronica was flushed and dirty from her work in the hot sun and glanced alongside at

Rose, who remained immaculate and cool. She had to hand it to her. Despite the fact she hadn't lifted a single piece of wood, somehow Rose had still received the lion's share of the praise from the men. It's a pity she doesn't apply her enthusiasm for speeding along bad roads and flirting with men to other pursuits, Veronica reflected, noting that the load was being flung to one side. She twisted in the seat and bent over to secure the ropes as best she could, pushing the hair back from her face.

'Would you mind driving a little bit less like a lunatic?' she exclaimed as the cart swerved yet again, forcing her to grip on tightly.

'Would you mind not acting like a martyr all the time?' Rose replied, rolling her eyes.

Veronica glared at her, half inclined to push her off the bench.

'Is there any water left?' she asked, eyeing the canteen tied around Rose's waist.

'Didn't you bring any?'

'The canteen was supposed to be for both of us.'

'Was it? That's a shame. All gone.' Rose shrugged, flicking the reins. The cart veered as the horses further lengthened their gait.

Veronica doubted that, but decided she would rather go thirsty than beg Rose for anything.

Ten minutes later, her thirst now overwhelming, she was starting to relent on that decision. She was just about to ask Rose if she wouldn't mind checking the canteen again when the horses slowed down, shaking their manes.

'Get on there,' Rose said, whipping them. Suddenly both horses began to shy and buck, whinnying in fright. Concerned that they might bolt, Veronica jumped down to hold the reins and try to calm them. Then she saw the reason for their distress.

On the side of the track, only a metre or so from her, was a large black snake, his neck held high, poised to strike. Veronica gasped, stepping back, but she was too late. The snake struck, hitting her leg several times, the sharp fangs piercing through her dress. Veronica was so shocked she barely made it back on to the cart before Rose hurled her up and tore them away.

The horses went at a gallop, eventually calming down to a walk before Rose managed to stop them altogether. Even then, their ears and tails were still twitching nervously. By this time Veronica was slumped over in her seat and groaning in agony, her stomach churning. 'It…it was a black snake,' she managed.

'I know,' Rose said, quickly fastening the reins and kneeling down. She tore Veronica's skirts back, examining the wounds closely and pouring water from the canteen to clear the small dots of blood.

'Thought you said there was no water left,' Veronica panted.

Rose ignored her, unlacing her boots.

'Three on the leg, one on the ankle. This one only just went through,' she muttered, reaching for her bag and tipping out the contents. She grabbed a tiny pair of nail scissors and grasped the hem of Veronica's petticoat.

'W-what are you doing?' Veronica gasped, struggling to focus through the haze of pain.

'Making a bandage,' Rose replied. 'Stop moving.' The air was rent with the tearing of cloth as she cut and then ripped strips off Veronica's petticoat. With surprising speed and efficiency she sucked at the bite marks, spitting out what venom she could, then wound the bandages tightly around the wounded limb. Veronica found herself staring at the beads of perspiration on Rose's forehead, reflecting she'd never seen her so much as dab at her face, let alone break out in a full sweat.

When she'd fastened the makeshift bandage, Rose leapt back up onto the seat and flicked the reins. As the horses took off, Veronica slid helplessly sideways.

'Hold bloody still.' Rose grabbed at her, pinning her down with her arm. Veronica had never heard Rose swear before either. She started to wonder if she was hallucinating.

The cart careered dangerously as Rose held onto Veronica with one hand and tried to control the horses with the other. Veronica felt the darkness beckon, her head pounding as a strong nausea assailed her.

As her head lolled from side to side, and the waves of blackness washed over her, Veronica felt Rose shaking her and heard her calling, as if from a distance, 'Oh no, you don't. Wake up! Come on, stay awake.'

The orphanage came into view just as Veronica lost consciousness. Her last thought was that she must be hallucinating as she heard Rose begin to cry.

Six

Highview, December 1913

She felt the warmth on her face as she was pulled from her dream. Jack was there, standing on a boat, but she couldn't get to him and he was floating away, far away over giant, angry seas. She wanted to run to him but there was a snake in front of her, poised to strike, but she had to go. She had to bring him back home. The snake struck and her eyes flew open.

The curtains rippled along in little waves in the breeze and she stared at them, confused, blinking against the glare, her head aching. She was in her bedroom at home. It had all been a dream. No, not all. Her leg ached. Slowly it came back to her: the baking sun, the striking snake and Rose, ripping at her petticoat, winding the bandages.

'She's awake,' she heard Eileen call excitedly. 'Thank the Lord. Thank the Lord,' she wept, as Catherine and Kevin came in to the room, ashen faced.

'My baby,' her mother crooned, holding Veronica close. It was a mark of how sick she must have been for Catherine to call her that, an endearment she hadn't heard in years. Her father looked like he hadn't slept, the tears running down his face unchecked.

'Can't tell you how worried we've been, little pet,' he choked, kissing her forehead.

Dr Dwyer followed. He checked her pulse and examined her wounds as the parish priest, Father Francis, stood nearby.

'How do you feel?' the doctor asked finally, watching her closely.

'Thirsty,' she croaked, looking at Father Francis whose presence indicated to her just how close to death she'd come. Dr Dwyer seemed pleased with that answer and Eileen immediately poured her a glass of water from the nightstand. She drank gratefully.

'You're a lucky young lady, Veronica. It was a close call I have to say, but you're out of the woods now. It seems that daughter of mine has been paying more attention to my work than I realised.' Dr Dwyer patted her arm and walked out with her mother, talking in low tones about how she would need plenty of rest and only toast and black tea for the next few days. Eileen fussed about with her pillows as a beaming Molly came in with a tray, placing fresh flowers on her dresser. No sooner had the maids left, leaving her with a cup of tea and some dry toast, than Pattie burst in, taking off her gloves and hurling herself onto the bed, grasping her friend's hands and holding them for a moment, her eyes glistening with emotion.

'Hear you lost in a bust-up with a serpent.'

'You should have seen…the snake.' Veronica smiled.

'I did. She's parading about town boasting as we speak.' Pattie wiggled her eyebrows.

'Don't.' Veronica giggled a little then shook her head. 'She… she saved my life.'

'Hmmm. Yes, I'm still trying to figure that one out. She is the daughter of a doctor after all, so I suppose she felt some kind of duty towards you…or else…'

'Or else what?'

'She's looking after herself as usual.'

'No. No…Pattie, she was scared for me. She was crying. I think maybe…there's a bit more to Rose than we thought. I mean… maybe she is, you know…not all bad.'

'Humph,' Pattie snorted. 'You'd save your dog under the same circumstances so I don't see why we should be so shocked she showed some basic human values. Though actually I am surprised she's human. Anyway, enough about snakes. Let's focus on getting you well enough to come to Greenshades. Only two weeks to go, you know. I was thinking about wearing a bathing costume this year. What do you think? Too daring?' She bit her lip, striking a pose and lifting her skirts, making Veronica laugh again.

Eileen bustled back in and shooed Pattie out of the room so the invalid could rest.

Veronica was sleepy, but she stretched out her leg to examine her wounds before lying back against the pillows again. Her aching head spun as she processed the facts. Rose had cared; she had treated her and feared for her to the point of tears. Veronica knew she should be grateful but found herself strangely resentful instead. Not only had Rose taken away the man she loved: she'd now taken away Veronica's right to hate her – how could she continue to despise someone who had saved her life?

She stared at the flowers Molly had brought in: purple roses, a large bouquet and obviously not from their garden. Someone must have sent them in from the city.

And holding onto that intriguing thought she fell into a blessedly dreamless sleep.

Jack tore open the telegram, registering its contents in a rush before sitting down heavily in his chair and gazing out unseeing at the harbour. The relief ran through his veins like a drug. It had been the worst Sunday of his life, going through the motions of comforting friends and family as they all feared the worst. Dr Dwyer's report had been brief and sombre as he'd passed by the Murphys', where they had all gathered to wait: her breathing was shallow and she was still unconscious. Rose had been suitably humble under the praise that had been directed at her all day, particularly from Alice, who had marvelled at her composure and how it may have saved Veronica's life. Rose's parents had seemed quite stunned that their daughter knew what to do in an emergency, but Iggy had simply given her a wink and a kiss on the cheek when he found out, obviously proud of his little sister.

Jack was proud of her too, he told himself, it was just...He couldn't quite put his finger on it. He only knew that the engagement ring had stayed in his pocket as they kissed goodbye at the gate that night and as he rode back to the city the next morning he felt somehow guilty. As if he were leaving a part of himself behind on the road with every passing mile, and it wasn't Rose.

Too many sleepless nights later he'd had enough. He was in the last stages of a deal with a Queensland packaging company that had taken months to close, but he was about to get on the train and head back home nevertheless, when the telegram arrived.

He stared at it again, reassuring himself that the words were still there, before folding it and placing it in his pocket next to the little box that sealed his future. Time felt like it began to pass at normal speed again. Now he could move forward and get on with his life.

But as he journeyed home that Saturday the circle of gold and diamonds lay heavily against his chest, just as the decision weighed upon his mind.

Veronica breathed in the sweet summer breeze as she lay on the garden seat, an unopened book in her lap. She was still a little light headed, but the lure of fresh air after a week cooped up in her room was too much to resist that afternoon, and her stomach was churning not so much with the nausea of the past week but with anticipation. She heard the boys arrive and Tom bounded across the lawn to her, pretending to be a monkey. He was busy picking imaginary insects from her hair when Mick walked over with Jack.

'Hello dearest,' Mick kissed her cheek, 'feeling better?' Both brothers had stayed at home from the city that week, unable to bear leaving, and today was the first day they had parted from her side.

'Much.' She smiled, finally forcing herself to look at Jack. 'Who won?' she heard herself asking as if from a distance. It was unbelievably good to see him, away from the nightmares, in the flesh.

'Us, no thanks to me. I got a duck,' he grinned, leaning over and kissing her hand, suddenly serious. 'Gave me quite a scare there, Vera,' he said simply, but he didn't let go. The sound of a car and then women's voices carried across the lawn as Pattie, Alice, Mildred and Rose arrived.

'There you are!' Rose waved, floating towards them, a vision in a flowered lilac dress that flowed with her every movement. Veronica withdrew her hand.

'And how is our little invalid? Don't you boys go over-exerting my patient,' she reprimanded playfully, tapping her little parasol on Tom's head before offering her arm to Jack.

'She's much better, aren't you, Vera Mags?' Tom grinned at his sister before gazing at Rose as if entranced. She looked very beautiful, Veronica had to admit, feeling suddenly insignificant. All three boys were staring at the sight of Rose lit up from the sunshine behind her, and for a moment no one said a word until Tom broke the silence.

'Off on your rounds? Crikey, these new female doctors dress to kill. Don't know if the elderly fellows will be able to take it.' And he clutched at his heart for effect as they all broke into laughter.

'Now, now,' Rose smiled at him, 'just behave yourself and come on up to the house. Your mother has made the tea. Don't get up, Veronica. I'll get Eileen to bring yours down.'

'Actually I think they're bringing it down for all of us as we speak.' Mick pointed, as Eileen and Molly appeared on the verandah with trays of tea, sugar, cream, scones and jam, led by Pattie holding a large blanket.

'Come up and get some cushions will you, boys?' she called across the lawn and the men set off to do her bidding.

Finding herself alone with Rose for a moment, Veronica found the words she been trying to form for days.

'I want to thank you, Rose. I…I am so grateful to you, the way you helped me and stayed so calm and focused. You saved my life.' She held out her hand in appreciation.

'Don't bother with thanking me, Veronica. I'm sure we both know how you can repay me.' She ignored the outstretched hand, pulling at her gloves instead.

'Repay you?' Veronica stared at Rose, perplexed.

'Stay out of my way, and by that, I mean away from Jack. Don't dance with him, don't flirt with him and most importantly, do not attend Greenshades. I have secured an invitation via Jack's mother and it will be the perfect opportunity for him to propose, so I certainly don't want you around distracting him with your sweet-little-sister act.' She waved and giggled as the others came closer, before rounding back to face Veronica, her mask slipping.

'But I…I thought…' Veronica stammered.

'What?'

'I supposed that after you saved my life we would be, I don't know, friends. I thought things would be different.'

'Women are never truly friends, Veronica. Men are fickle creatures and women are always each other's competitors. Honestly, you really are naive, aren't you? I forget how young you are sometimes.' She opened her purse and took out a lacy white handkerchief, patting Veronica's brow with it as the others arrived.

'Poor lamb. Boys, I think she may be suffering from the heat out here. Perhaps she should move back inside.' She lifted large worried eyes to Mick and Tom, whose medical studies quickly came to the fore, and they felt Veronica's brow and checked her pulse as Pattie eyed Rose suspiciously.

'You are a little on the boil,' Tom confirmed.

'Really, I feel quite fine,' Veronica began to object, hating to miss out on spending time with Jack.

'Come along, let's get you inside.' Mick lifted her up and carried her back to the house, Pattie in tow. Tucking the sheets about her Pattie hummed a little tune before freshening up the flowers until Mick left.

'Who sent you these, Vera? They're lovely. Must be from the city.' She looked at her sideways. 'Don't tell me Jack actually sent flowers? He must have been worried. And purple roses, no less.'

Veronica tried to smile, but didn't quite make it, and Pattie sat on her bed, waiting.

'What is it, darling?'

Veronica's eyes swam. 'With you calling me darling and Mick calling me dearest I must be a sorry sight.' Pattie stroked her hair and for the first time since the snake attack Veronica cried. She cried for the fear of nearly dying, for the look on her mother's face, for her father's tears and for the gentle care of her brothers. But most of all she cried because the man she loved would marry a woman who didn't believe in their world. He would marry someone who used people, who played at life like a puppeteer pulling the strings. Who thought women could not be friends. She would take him away from them, bit by bit, and they would never again share in his life and walk along together. Jack would never be hers; that was hard enough. But her bitterest tears flowed because the Jack she knew would eventually cease to exist, perishing in the coldness of Rose's heart. All of this flowed out of her in the form of broken sobs as Pattie waited.

Finally she managed to speak. 'We're losing him, Pattie.'

Pattie nodded slowly, looking at the purple roses again then back at Veronica.

'You mean...*you're* losing him, don't you?'

Veronica pulled at the thread on her coverlet as Pattie stared. 'Does he...I mean have you...?'

'No, no it's nothing like that. I just...' Veronica ran out of words as she wiped at her tears. 'It's just me,' she admitted.

'I wonder.' Pattie looked thoughtfully at the flowers. 'You sure are one for secrets, although I think Rose may be cottoning on to something.'

'She...she says I need to repay her by keeping away from him. That she's waiting for him to propose and she doesn't want me at Greenshades. She said I'm not to c-come...'

'Not to come to your own auntie's Christmas party? Since when does she rule the roost?' Pattie scoffed.

'Since she saved my life.'

'Well I saved your life plenty of times when we were kids. Remember the crazy mule in the east paddock?'

Veronica smiled. 'Pickles?'

'Yes, that's the one. Chased you cross-eyed into the shed until I convinced it the cricket ball was an apple? Never seen an animal so determined to break its teeth.'

Veronica's smile turned into a watery giggle.

Pattie stood up and wagged her finger. 'Seems to me you need to obey Pattie and I say do what you want!'

Veronica laughed a little more as the tears subsided into small shudders and Pattie closed the curtains, kissing her cheek before leaving.

'She said women can never truly be friends because they are always com-competitors,' Veronica whispered.

'Humph! Charming. Well…just goes to show then, doesn't it?'

'Show what?' she sniffed.

'Rose can be very, very wrong.'

Pattie winked and closed the door and, staring at the vase of flowers until her eyes fell closed at last, Veronica felt a little hope.

Seven

Greenshades, Wahroonga, 24 December 1913

'Hurry up, Vera!' Pattie shouted, laughing as she ran down the stairs, her long limbs covered by a large towel. Veronica stood in her bedroom at Greenshades, peering nervously out the window. Her aunt Marjorie had placed her in her usual room overlooking the pool and she looked out below across the sparkling, kidney-shaped water and green lawns and down the frangipani-lined driveway, seeing who was about. Or, more importantly, whether Jack had arrived. She bit her lip and stared down at the new swim-suit Pattie had bought her as an early Christmas present. She was surprised her mother had let her wear it but Pattie had done an excellent job of convincing her that the new fashion was a far safer option that the contraptions women usually bathed in. Veronica's wellbeing was obviously still high on Catherine's priority list. She found herself wishing she had been forbidden, feeling very unsure about the outline of her shape showing through the thick black fabric. And bare legs! No one had seen her legs in public for a very long time.

Except Jack when you drove the cart.

She told the voice in her mind to hush. She'd made a pact with herself to try not to focus on him while she was there and to just enjoy herself with her family and friends. After all, Pattie was right: what right did Rose have to tell her she couldn't come to Greenshades? It was her family Christmas after all. And besides, if she'd stayed at home fabricating a relapse as an excuse her brothers would undoubtedly want to stay with her, which would mean they all missed out. No she was right to come, she assured herself. And who cares what Jack thinks of the swimming costume?

Brilliantly done, Veronica. Almost a full thirty seconds of not thinking about him.

She shook her head clear, deciding she couldn't really hide in her room all day. Wrapping herself in a towel she timidly slipped out the door and headed down towards the pool, picking her way quietly along the bushes.

'Hello, Vera Mags! Going for a dip?' Tom jumped out and scooped her up onto his shoulders, running down to the pool as she screamed and wriggled, finally landing with an enormous splash in the middle to shrieks of laughter from Pattie.

'At least he saved your towel.' Pattie pointed to her own saturated sheet with exasperation before inclining her head towards a snoozing Mick, who had found a nice shady spot beneath the camellias. She snuck over with exaggerated stealth as Vera giggled. A flurry of splashing followed as Mick was rudely awakened and took immediate revenge, imitating a mad pirate as he thrashed about after them around the pool.

'Stop it!' Pattie laughed as he cornered her.

'Ye'll have to pay the fee,' Mick growled, loping over and making some effective 'arrrr' noises.

'I haven't brought my purse so worse luck for you, y'mangy dog!' she declared, showing her empty palms.

'Hmm. Then I'll be feeding ye to the sharks,' he roared, closing in as she made a last-minute dash for safety.

Veronica's cousins Mary and Agnes interrupted them in an excited clatter as they arrived on horseback, their faces flushed.

'You won't believe it. Come on!' Agnes urged as the two of them dismounted and grabbed arms, pulling everyone along with them towards the front drive. 'Clarkson promised us a visit to the beach on New Year's Eve, although I don't know if we'll all fit.'

'Fit what?' asked Mick, rubbing his wet blond hair with one hand and being dragged along by Mary with the other.

'In that!' Agnes beamed as they rounded the corner, and her older brother Clarkson tipped his hat at them all from behind the wheel of a brand-new automobile.

'Is that…a Sunbeam?' Tom asked reverently as Mary and Agnes clapped and the boys went forward to shake their cousin's hand. Clarkson laughed in a rich, deep rumble, sounding so like his father Clarkson Senior that Veronica had to smile. She adored these larger-than-life relatives, who were as generous as they were flamboyant.

'Certainly is, young Tom. Good to see you!' They shook hands and Clarkson clapped the boys on the shoulder. 'How are you, Mick? Long time between drinks.'

'Where the devil did you get it from?' Tom asked in amazement, running his hand along the gleaming white bonnet and staring at the gold finishes in awe.

'Just came back from picking her up in Melbourne: gorgeous, isn't she? Speaking of which, who's going to introduce me to that bathing beauty back there? Wait on a minute…Vera? Come here and give me a kiss.'

Vera giggled as he wrapped her in a bear hug and swung her about.

'This is a beaut day, eh? What shall we do first? Drive down to Bobbin Head? Take you into town and show off the family genes?' He kissed Vera on the cheek, then finally noticed Pattie standing behind his sister, being uncharacteristically shy. Clarkson took his racing goggles off and smiled a slow dazzling grin at her, incredibly dashing, with his dimples and moustache, even to his sisters and cousins.

'And could this possibly be Patricia?' He stood before her, taking in her shapely legs and tangled hair, stretching to his full six foot and two inches, then bowed low, never taking his eyes from hers. 'Seems I shouldn't have stayed away last Christmas after all. The London lasses pale compared to such Aussie beauty as this.' They all watched in amazement as Pattie opened her mouth to respond and closed it again.

'Blimey, he's turned her into a mullet,' Tom observed, causing them all to laugh.

'Would you care to take the front seat?' Clarkson invited, opening the door for her. Pattie obliged dreamily as the rest of them piled in. The new Sunbeam raced up and down the drive in a plume of dust, to the thrill of its occupants; it was an exciting if short ride. With promises of heading up to the race that afternoon, Clarkson set them down at the house before driving back to town to pick up a friend.

Vera watched the beautiful car wind away as the others went off to change for lunch, taking a moment just to drink it all in, the beauty of Greenshades' front gardens enveloping her. Walking beneath the row of frangipani trees, she inhaled deeply, loving the summery fragrance and touching their velvety blooms, her face towards the sun. Veronica hadn't been able to sneak off to her spot by the creek since she'd been ill and it felt good to be barefoot, outdoors.

She scrunched the grass between her toes and smiled at the feeling one last time before turning towards the house and running up the stairs, feeling the carefree joy of summer at Greenshades embrace her.

She had completely forgotten about Jack and Rose in the fun of the day until that moment, when she landed on the enormous cream verandah and found herself face to face with them both. Jack's stare caused Veronica to instantly regret leaving her towel by the pool as she stood before them, clad only in her new black swimsuit, her hair wild and loose from the impromptu ride.

And you thought having bare legs in a cart was bad.

She told her mind to hush for the umpteenth time that day.

Rose glared at her from beneath her white umbrella, her impeccable peach dress and white gloves seeming to recoil with her as she stepped back and snapped it shut. 'Veronica. What a surprise. I thought you had decided you were too unwell to attend,' she gritted out.

'Hello, yes, well, I am quite fine now and...I couldn't really miss my family Christmas.' Veronica tried for calm defiance, but found herself bumbling. 'So, you…you've arrived. Guess I'll just be off to uh…change.' She tried to exit gracefully but stubbed her bare toes on the step instead, tripping into Jack's arms with force. There was nothing to stop the momentum as her body collided with his and she saw Rose's expression contort to fury at the same moment as Jack's hand landed on her breast.

'Sorry!' Veronica mumbled, disentangling herself, her face flaming. 'The step,' she added, looking back at it in dazed confusion, as if it had suddenly appeared there as a way of explanation. Rose glared and Jack gaped and Veronica decided to limp off with what little dignity was left, reflecting that greeting Rose by thrusting her chest into Jack's hand wasn't the finest way to let her know she'd decided to attend Christmas at Greenshades after all.

Rose was no fool. She knew that Veronica in a swimsuit was stiff competition, even for her. Especially when her would-be fiancé stood there grappling with the other girl's bosom.

'Veronica is such a pretty girl, isn't she?' she said casually.

'Hmm? Oh yes, I suppose she is,' Jack replied.

They were walking about the front lawns, which were refreshingly green and lush compared to the dry farming paddocks at home. The tiered waterfall sparkled in the midday sun and Rose stopped their stroll to watch it.

'It's a pity she doesn't like me, although I thought, after the incident, she might have seen that there is something more to me than this.' She picked up her pearl necklace and dropped it back against her neck, drawing his eye in the right direction, along with his feelings. 'I believe I'm just not the sort of girl who ever makes female friends easily. They always seem to think I'm too… too…' Her eyes began to well as she continued. 'I'm sorry. I don't know why I'm telling you this. I try not to let it hurt me, but she so obviously dislikes me, and the way she looks at you…I think she and Pattie wish I'd never come along, and that you and Veronica…' she dabbed at her wet cheeks with her handkerchief.

'Of course they don't wish that. Veronica isn't like that, Rose. I think she just…doesn't know how to talk to someone as sophisticated as you. Oh come now,' he crooned as she continued to cry. He pulled her behind an enormous gardenia bush and held her close as she sniffled into his shoulder. 'Just give them time.'

'I just don't know what else to do. I've tried to help out at the orphanage and visit with Mother and…and join in the fun around the piano. What else is there? I mean I even…you know…looked after her that day. Some might say I saved her life. I supposed at least then she might warm towards me a little.'

Jack seemed thoughtful about that. 'Hasn't she thanked you?'

'No,' Rose lied, pulling back and shaking her head. 'It's all right. I don't expect any thanks. I'm just glad she's all right.'

Jack held her hands protectively. 'Don't you worry. I'll have a word with them, and soon they'll get to know you better and grow to love you the way I do.'

'What did you say?' Rose stared at him, urging him on.

'Surely you know how I feel, Rose,' he began. 'I think the time has come– '

'Lunch!' called Pattie, ringing the giant cowbell on the verandah and spying Jack and Rose across the lawn. 'Hurry up there, Jack. It'll get cold.' Even from a distance both could feel the hostility Pattie sent Rose before heading back indoors.

'See what I mean?' Rose shrugged. 'Anyway, it doesn't matter. What were you saying?' She lifted her face to him and gave him her sweetest, most encouraging smile.

'Wait up, Jack, we're putting bets on for this afternoon. Are you still in?' Tom called, running across towards them.

Jack looked at Rose, exasperated.

'Don't worry, darling, we'll continue this when you're not so in demand shall we?' She kissed him softly on the cheek, stroking his chin before heading for the house, feeling the relief wash over her. Soon there would be nothing to worry about.

'Can I have a word?'

'Better make it quick. I'm starving,' Jack replied as Pattie chased after him towards the stables. She knew he would want to give Tilley a quick check before this afternoon's race and she grabbed these few minutes while she could.

'She's looking strong,' Pattie observed as they arrived and Jack gave the mare a once-over as she dipped her nose and nuzzled against him in welcome.

Jack nodded. 'Pass me that brush, will you?'

She handed it to him and stood, trying to find some rare tact. 'Jack,' Pattie began, 'I wondered if I could talk to you about Rose.'

'Funny, I wanted to talk to you about her too.' Jack glanced over and continued brushing.

'I don't know if you are aware of it or not but...she isn't exactly...a nice girl.'

He paused and stared angrily at his sister. 'What the hell is that supposed to mean?'

Pattie frowned, kicking her toe at the stall.

'Spit it out, Pats.'

'The woman is a two-faced, lying pain in the neck!' she blurted. So much for tact.

Jack glared at her.

'And she is horrible to Veronica behind your back. Did you know she tried to forbid her from coming here?'

Jack looked momentarily confused. 'I'm sure she was only worried about her health...'

'She only worries about *herself*. She sees Veronica as a threat.'

Jack said nothing but Pattie sensed there was some level of admission there. So Veronica was competition. She pressed on. 'She only pretends to like you, Jack. She's just trying to trap herself a husband.'

'Now you're being ridiculous.' Jack banged down the brush hard, causing her to jump.

'It's true.'

'Are you quite finished?'

'No,' Pattie said firmly. 'She isn't...good enough for my brother and she never will be.'

Jack shook his head in disbelief. 'You know, I really thought if I could talk to you about Rose you'd come to see what an amazing woman she is, but I can see now how wrong I was.'

'She's amazing all right…amazingly conniving.'

'Watch it.' Jack's tone was low and Pattie stopped, recognising that she had pushed him too far. They faced each other, neither backing down.

'I just don't want you to be unhappy, especially when there is someone else who– '

'Don't tell me who to marry, Pats.'

'But– '

'Rose will be my wife, and, whether you like it or not, your sister. God help her. And if you don't accept her then God help me, because you won't be mine anymore.'

She watched him head back towards the house and realised Veronica's tears had been well founded. They were losing Jack and the time to stop it from happening had long passed.

Lunch was a seemingly festive affair that day as the four families joined for the first time, though in fact not everyone at the table was in a celebratory mood.

Veronica avoided all eye contact, especially with Jack, taking her seat and attempting to slip into the background as much as possible. She had changed into a dark blue blouse and skirt, pulling her hair back tight and smooth, and felt safely back in conservative territory, although somewhat drab and dull compared to the warm epicentre that was Rose.

The latter seemed to have recovered her composure and was now holding court over the men nearby, charming them with her flirtatious comments and tantalising glimpses of cleavage beneath the soft peach gown. Meanwhile Alice was busily singing her praises at the other end of the table, retelling the story of the snake bite and Rose's brave rescue. 'And to think she managed to stop the venom spreading by making her own bandages! It really was quite ingenuous. You must be so proud, Dr Dwyer.'

Dr Dwyer looked across and tipped his glass. 'Yes, quite. At least one of my children seems to have taken notice of my work over the years.'

An uncomfortable moment followed and Veronica felt for Iggy as he stared hard at the table.

'I hear Ebony has an excellent chance at the races this afternoon,' she said, forgetting to feel self-conscious around Jack and changing the subject.

Iggy lifted his eyes, looking surprised.

'I've got two bob on him either way,' Tom said. 'Which reminds me, I think I might go down and give Tilley a pre-race brandy. Just to calm her nerves.'

'Keep your devilish paws away from my mare,' Jack said pointedly as the others began to laugh. Soon the conversation flowed easily again and Veronica turned to her mother, who sat beside her.

'When do the children arrive?'

'Tomorrow morning. I think Cook has outdone herself this year,' Catherine said.

Vera could see that Catherine and Alice had thoroughly enjoyed their morning in the kitchen with Marjorie and 'Cook', catching up on all the news and laughing over old times. (Mildred was lying down in her room with the curtains drawn, shielding her aching head from "t' hellish sun'.) With over thirty children, a dozen nuns and forty or so other guests due for the lawn party on the morrow, there was still much to be done. 'We will be requiring your help this afternoon, ladies,' Catherine addressed them.

'But Clarkson has offered to drive us to the race,' Mary protested.

'The men work hard all year and can go on a drive if they please, but the young ladies are needed, I'm afraid,' Catherine said in her gentle yet firm way.

'Has he already arrived then?' Clarkson Senior asked from the end of the table.

'He's just gone to pick up a friend from town, but he should be back soon,' said Agnes.

'Oh Daddy, it's marvellous!' Mary exclaimed.

The conversation turned to automobiles, the men excited by the prospect of seeing a brand new Sunbeam. Although cars were becoming more commonplace about town, many of the men still preferred to ride by horseback. Yet even this horse-mad company felt the excitement of having the fastest model of car in the world in their own backyard.

By the time Clarkson arrived they were all out on the front verandah waiting for him and he didn't disappoint, putting on a dazzling show as he arrived with a flourish and a grin.

'May I introduce the Sunbeam, winner of the French Grand Prix 1913 and freshly imported to sunny Greenshades to grace Mother's lawn?' Marjorie laughed as he continued. 'Oh, and may I also introduce the importer of this fine automobile and a new friend of mine from good old mother England, Gregory Chambers?'

A large muscular man stepped out of the car, taking off his hat and revealing a head of white-blond hair, dramatic against his olive skin and white suit. He was impeccably dressed and made a perfect foil for Clarkson's dark good looks. Veronica suspected they'd made quite an impression in town.

Introductions were made as Kevin set up his camera and took a photo of them all surrounding the car and afterwards everyone clamoured to take turns sitting behind the wheel. Veronica hung back and noticed Rose did the same, which was unlike her. Then she noticed her expression. Rose was frozen to the spot, looking at Gregory Chambers as if he were a ghost. And Gregory Chambers was staring straight back at Rose, although he didn't seem surprised to see her at all.

Rose stood at the end of her bed, gripping the rail and staring out at the date palms as they bobbed about in the breeze. Funny, she thought. There'd been date palms outside the bedroom window of Gregory's house in Melbourne too. She remembered watching the green and gold fronds dance at the precise moment that her life changed forever.

And now here they were again, waving their long, thin fingers. Changing her fate.

'How did you find me?'

Gregory moved up to stand behind her. 'I missed you too, Rose, or should I say I missed this.' He grabbed her, turning her about and kissing her hard on the mouth. She resisted and he twisted his hands into her hair and pulled her close against his big frame.

'Stop it.' She pushed at him. 'I thought…I hoped I'd never see you again.'

'You say the words but your body says something else.' He spoke against her mouth, kissing her again hungrily.

She felt herself weaken, then remembered and pulled away, distancing herself back against the door. 'I don't know how you found me but it doesn't matter because I won't go back to you, Gregory. It's over. I told you before and nothing you say can change it now.'

'Marry me, Rose.' He closed in on her, holding her face between his hands. 'Let's just stop this nonsense and get married once and for all.'

She allowed him to kiss her, just once, and it felt familiar, echoing moments of stolen passion she'd tried to forget. He held her with a restrained forcefulness that made her shiver, her body on high alert to his touch.

'You were a bad girl, running away like that,' he whispered, kissing his way down her neck as she leant in towards him. 'I don't know how long it will take until you make it up to me.'

Then she remembered and opened her eyes, moving along the wall as he followed close, their breathing heavy with desire. 'I can't.' She shook her head, desperately trying to gain back some control of her reeling senses. She couldn't let it happen again. He would take her, then control her, and she would lose herself in the process. Gregory was an overwhelming force and she knew if she went back to him she would bend to his will and surrender more than her body.

He studied her for a moment, pinning her with his pale blue eyes, then smiled in a sudden flash of white teeth against brown skin. 'You can and you will,' he instructed.

'You...you ask for too much.'

'Yes, but this time I'm willing to pay, Rose. This time you can be the wife *and* the whore.'

'Don't call me that!' she flashed at him.

'You know you want me to,' he whispered and she felt a damning rush of desire. It was so wrong but it felt so good to give in and let him take charge. Maybe she could let him do this. Maybe he could just rescue her and take her away.

'I'll give you everything your greedy little heart desires. The estate in London, the house in Melbourne, the family name. Marry me, Rose. Be my woman.'

He reached into his pocket and presented her with a large yellow diamond set in a platinum ring.

Rose gasped. It was exquisite. 'You're serious...'

'Very.'

'I can't, Gregory…you…you take me over…' Images of him looming over her the last time they were together flashed through her mind. The day she'd feared him. He was both powerful and dangerous and it excited her and terrified her at the same time.

'So give in,' he instructed, his breath against her ear as he reached for the door behind. 'I can never give you up now, Rose.'

The latch clicked behind him and her legs gave out as she collapsed on the bed. Now there were two ways out and time was closing on the deal. She had to make her move.

Eight

By the time the men returned and washed up for dinner that night the women had prepared the feast for the pavilion party the next day, as well as an informal dinner.

The night's fare was buffet style, mostly consisting of cold meats, pickles, breads and an assortment of fresh fruits from the orchards. Tradition dictated that the family Christmas was held now, before the greater number of guests arrived on the morrow. Marjorie also insisted on an informal concert every year, and delighted in the news that Iggy was an accomplished pianist. He was in fine form, having won the race on Ebony in a close finish against Jack on Tilley, and was itching to play.

Clarkson Senior got the ball rolling after dinner by handing out various costumes and masks, this year choosing Tom and Mick to perform the first number of choice. Seeing as they were already dressed as gypsies thanks to their host, they sang a version of 'The Gypsy Rover', interspersed with impromptu 'readings' throughout. These included the prediction that they had an 'inkling' Pattie's legs would grow so long she would turn into a gigantic squid and that Alice would divorce and marry a certain rooster and become queen of England. This was followed by an almighty performance by Clarkson Senior, Dr Dwyer, George Murphy and Kevin who sang 'Danny Boy' in strong, rich voices. Kevin interspersed the singing with sweet variations on his violin before the whole group eventually joined in.

Veronica watched Jack sitting next to Rose, who had donned a princess crown, his arm around her as he sang along in his beautiful voice. Rose's fingers fidgeted somewhat nervously with the string of pearls at her throat and Veronica wondered at it. Perhaps she was expecting a Christmas proposal. Veronica felt sick at the thought of that cold heart beneath the pearls beating against Jack's warm loving one for the rest of his days.

Suddenly she needed air and slipped onto the porch, wandering out to walk the frangipani colonnade, breathing the summer night in and trying to exhale the ache within.

'Hello, Veronica.' She looked up, her heart in her mouth, only to be confronted by the sight of Dan, still in riding clothes on the drive. 'What are you doing alone out here? Too much for you?' He nodded at the house, grinning at the rowdy rendition of 'Good King Wenceslas' occurring within.

'Dan! We didn't expect you till tomorrow,' Veronica exclaimed. 'Have you eaten? Goodness, you must be ravenous. Let me fetch you some dinner,' she said, starting towards the house, but Dan seized his opportunity, turning her about.

'It can wait. Actually I'm glad to find you alone. There was something I wanted to ask you. That is, something that has been bothering me. Not bothering me, just you know, on my mind so to speak…Blimey, I'm not much good at this am I?' He laughed self-consciously.

'I'm not sure I understand,' Veronica hedged.

'Not much good at…talking to girls. Pretty girls especially, which is stupid because you're not like that.'

'I'm not pretty?'

'What? No. You are! Very! I just don't know how to talk to you, even though I know you're, you know, normal. You're very...normal.'

'Were you expecting something to be wrong?' She began to laugh a little and he relaxed, laughing too.

'Point is, look I know you are young and all but I...I think– '

'You're right, she is young, and definitely too young to be standing out here with you alone.' Jack's expression was stern as he walked towards them. 'I'm sure you're hungry, Dan. Why don't you go inside and wash up? Vera, a word if you don't mind.'

Dan had little choice but to obey Jack, whom he knew was practically Veronica's brother. She felt for him as he stammered an apology and left, making his way into the house.

'What the blazes do you think you are up to now?' Jack rounded on her angrily.

'Nothing, he just saw me and spoke to me...Nothing!' she ended, feeling angry herself. 'Anyway it's none of your business what I do.'

'Of course it's my business. You're like family and I won't have you behaving like that. It'll ruin your reputation, Vera, and you can't ever win that back once it's lost. Don't you get that?'

'And I suppose Rose hasn't done any damage to her reputation, draping herself all over you like...like *seaweed*.'

Jack looked taken aback.

'That's completely different. Anyway, I'm not always going to turn up at the right minute to save you. Start thinking about how things look!'

'Oh, I've got to start thinking how things look, do I? What about you? Walking about half dressed and putting your...your hands all... everywhere...' she stammered, regretting each word as she said it.

The frangipani trees above them swayed gently in the moonlight, the shadows across their faces seeming uncertain where to land.

He gazed at her for a moment, and she remembered the feel of him that afternoon, his hands upon her. Jack lifted a strand of her hair that had escaped its confines, tugging on it slightly, and she did not breathe as he pulled her towards him until their mouths were close. Veronica leant in slightly, unable to resist what she had imagined for so long.

She brushed her lips against his, so light a touch, yet she felt every part of her resided there, in that one place.

Jack closed his eyes and she thought for a moment he felt the same.

'Damn it!' He swore, turning away.

'Jack.' The word slipped out, a pleading, desperate sound she couldn't take back.

It halted him and he stood still, his back to her. 'What are you trying to do to me, Vera?'

'Nothing. I…Nothing.'

'You know I'm with Rose. How can you treat her like this?'

His hostility struck her hard, as if he'd reached out and slapped her, and she flinched as if it really were a physical blow. 'What do you mean?'

'Seriously, Vera, what do you want me to do? Say that I won't marry her now because you threw yourself at me?'

'Threw myself?'

'Hell, she saved your life. What does she have to do to prove herself to you all?' He ran his hand over his face. 'She deserves better than this…and God knows I expected more from you.'

Vera stood frozen to the spot as the nightmare played out before her. He was going to marry Rose. She had offered herself and he'd rejected her.

'Why do you assume I'm just trying to hurt her?'

'Oh I don't know, Vera, maybe because you just kissed me, when you know I'm going to marry her!' He moved closer, tilting his head. 'You've been trying to break us up all along, haven't you? Did Pattie put you up to it?'

Veronica felt her anger flare. 'This has nothing to do with Pattie!'

'Oh really? So you expect me to believe you just happened to drive past me on a cart with your skirt around your waist and you just happened to fall into my arms in a bathing suit and you just happened to accidentally kiss me just now…'

'Actually…yes.'

'All accidents, eh? No other motives? No actual feelings?' She couldn't find any words as he studied her face and for a moment she thought he might soften. 'Vera, how can you do this? She saved your life.'

It was Veronica's turn to explode then. 'Stop saying that! Saved my life! If I hear that one more time…you bloody fool, Jack, she didn't do it to save me!'

'The fact that you're alive seems to indicate otherwise. And you haven't even so much as thanked her...'

'I did thank her!'

Jack frowned in confusion. 'That's not what she said...anyway, the point is she did save your life. It's a straight-out fact. How can you be so ungrateful?'

'Because she doesn't care two hoots about me or anyone else, she only cares about herself and trapping herself a husband and she…she used me to get to you, can't you see that? You're just blinded by her. All of you men are, even my own brothers!'

'Stop it, Vera.'

But she was furious with him now, and lashed out with all the pent-up feelings of the past few months. 'Stop calling me that! You don't get to call me that any more! It's Veronica to you, and if you're stupid enough to go and marry that…that *wench* then go ahead. You deserve what you get. And by the way, the only feeling I have for you is pity.'

She turned to walk as he grabbed her arm.

'Oh really? No other feelings?' He swung her around and they stood face to face, neither noticing as the parlour curtain parted nearby. 'Then how come every time I turn around you're trying to…to tempt me?' Their breathing was hard as he inched closer. 'Don't lie to me, Vera, I know you too well. And we both know what's going on here.'

'Oh we do, do we?' She flung his arm off, finding her senses again and poking his chest hard. 'You know what you are? You're… you're Henry. You're the puffed-up rooster in the henhouse who thinks he's king of the chickens, but let me tell you something, Jack Murphy, there are plenty more fish in the sea, and I wouldn't want you if you were the last one swimming!'

'So what's that supposed to mean? That I'm a chicken or a fish?'

'Both!' she flung at him, stalking away again as he followed her.

'You know what I think? I think you're the chicken. I think you're only mad because you're too chicken to admit the truth.'

'Oh really? And what might that be?'

'That you're in love with me.'

She felt sick in the stomach, pausing only slightly in her march. 'Don't be so ridiculous.'

'You're in love with me and you can't stand the thought that I'm marrying someone else. It's the only explanation. If it isn't just a ruse to get rid of her then it must be real. You love me.'

She stopped then and turned towards him, her hands on her hips. 'You…you puffed up self-important– '

'Admit it.'

'I am n-not in love with you,' she declared, her hands trembling as she hid them in her dress. 'I've done nothing wrong at all. You, in fact, have taken it on yourself to save me when I needed no help, several times now. I have not asked to be watched, or chaperoned, or…or…touched…or – I'm just trying to protect you from…making a mistake. But like I said, if you want to go ahead and marry that…that woman– '

'Oh I'm going ahead all right. I'm just trying to figure out how you can be so cold towards a kind-hearted girl like Rose. I reckon you're just not the person I thought you were, Vera. I'm marrying her and you know why? Because she's the only woman I know these days, aside from my mother, who I can trust!'

Vera gave a short laugh, shaking her head. 'You know, I was wrong. You're not Henry the rooster, you're Pickles the mule. Stubborn, stupid and too cross-eyed to see what's right in front of you.'

'Oh yes, very mature. Got any other farm animals you'd like to compare me to?'

'How about the back end of a horse!' she yelled over her shoulder, slamming the kitchen door after her and taking some deep breaths as she leant against it.

'You all right, Miss Veronica?' asked Cook, startled.

'Uh, yes, just coming in to see if things are…all ready for tomorrow,' said Veronica as calmly as she could, smoothing her skirts.

'Yes, miss, we're quite prepared. Did you want something else done?' she replied, gesturing towards the tables laden with food.

'No, no. Everything looks fine, thank you. Nice trifles,' she added, trying to sound pleasant, then gave up, noting Cook's now amused expression.

She headed back out into the parlour where the merriment was in full swing.

'Here she is! Come on, Vera, share the floor with y'dad,' invited a jubilant Kevin, who grabbed her hand to join in a jig led by Clarkson, who was playing a merry tune on the harmonica.

She was swung about, but kept looking for Jack over her father's shoulder until she finally spied him walking back in, his expression ominous. He scanned the room, landing his gaze upon Rose, who was in deep conversation with Gregory and, with a sinking heart, Veronica saw defeat. Immediately her anger slipped away to be replaced with an empty, engulfing despair. Jack looked furious and determined and that meant only one thing: he had made up his mind to marry Rose and she, Veronica, had helped make it up for him.

Suddenly she found herself unable to stand it and raced to the solace of her bedroom to cry out her grief to her pillow alone, falling asleep to tidings of comfort and joy.

Jack had watched the kitchen door slam and resisted every urge to throw it back open, grab the maddening creature and throw her in the water trough. Of all the stubborn, interfering, irresponsible women he'd ever met, she took the cake. He had a good mind to tell her brothers to keep a tighter rein on her! What was she thinking, standing in the dark talking to Dan? Then turning around and throwing herself at him, Jack, who was practically her brother?

Being holed up in that convent school had obviously turned her into a proper little strumpet.

Jack strode about the lawn, cursing her with every breath before eventually lighting a cigarette, trying to calm down. And that bathing suit! What was her mother doing allowing her to wear that? He'd been able to make out every curve on Veronica's body, not to mention the fact that he'd actually been forced to grab some of them in front of Rose.

Another bloody thing Veronica had done to him to try to ruin this courtship!

Jack flicked the cigarette in frustration. Truth was he couldn't get those damn curves out of his mind. Or her wild hair, or her damnable lips and the saucy words that poured out of them. Jack thought about Rose and the confident appeal that poured out of her. Why didn't that frustrate him and make him angry the way Veronica's raw, earthy sexuality did? He enjoyed Rose. She was beautiful, sensual, mesmerising. But the stark fact right now was that he wanted Veronica. Jack shook his head, trying to erase that last thought. A man just wants what he can't have, he reminded himself. Maybe it was just time to push this engagement forward so he could bed Rose properly and be done with all this tension and frustration. Surely he couldn't want for more than her every night. It was probably just all the waiting that was causing him to act like an alley cat.

And a bit of a horse's ass. Veronica was right. Why had he pushed her like that, asking if she loved him? Jack wasn't even sure he believed in love. Surely that was just romantic guff women carried on about.

No, there was no other choice, he reminded himself. He had to marry Rose. After all the liberties she'd given him it was the only honourable course of action. The right thing to do. Besides, comparing Veronica and Rose, he had to say the latter would be a far easier companion. He couldn't imagine fighting with a woman like Veronica every day of his life!

That decided he went back to the house, determined to push Veronica away and marry Rose as soon as possible. He couldn't go on like this.

Rose watched the palm fronds silvered with moonlight, shimmering in silky strands outside her window. It was only a few hours earlier that she'd looked out from the window below, onto the same night, under the same moon, watching a different scene altogether. A scene that sealed her fate once and for all. Destiny had tipped the scales; the contents had been amended and re-weighed.

And a new winner had been declared.

Nine

Jack arose at dawn, the little box that had been living in his pocket now resting in his hand. He would ask her father formally of course, but he wanted Rose to be the first to know, and after Pattie and Veronica's ridiculous attempts to undermine her, he decided it was time to put an end to any more interference and be done with it. He would ask Rose to be his wife and blast everyone else if they didn't like it.

Jack stepped quietly down the hall towards her room and paused at her door, confused, to listen to muffled sounds within. He pushed it open and found Rose sprawled naked across the bed, Gregory Chambers buried inside her. They both groaned with pleasure as he rocked back and forth, lost in their passion. Rose opened her eyes and saw Jack standing there. Their gazes locked as they registered the moment of betrayal together, then Jack found himself backing down the hall, out into the sunrise, and onto Tilley. Away.

He raced her as far as she could go without tiring, finding a neighbour's dam. There he flung himself off, tearing at his clothes and plunging into the water, trying to expunge the image from his mind – to no avail. Over and over again it played, his dark skin against her white flesh, taking what Jack had denied himself, the look of passion on her face. The weight of the ring in his hand. He vaguely remembered throwing it into the garden somewhere.

Jack marked the moment of realisation on her face – shock, guilt – and wondered if she felt regret, or if this had been her plan all along. He thought the two had seemed familiar with one another last night. Was that what they had been talking about? Perhaps he had been used to make this Gregory Chambers jealous and force him into action. His mind ran wild. He had to know. Jumping back onto Tilley he made his way to Greenshades to get some answers.

He wondered if they were still there or if they had slunk off together in the early hours. He picked up the pace. Just let them try and hide.

Veronica opened her present from her mother and father and was shocked to find that it was a dark green silk gown.

'We had it made based on your lavender.' Her mother smiled at her.

'I had to convince her to let you grow up,' her father whispered, kissing the top of her head. It may have been based on the lavender, but gone were the high buttons and conservative design. This dress had an actual shape. She found herself almost excited, which was really something, considering her mood. But it didn't last. Folding the paper carefully she placed it back down next to her other gifts, which included a beautiful emerald brooch from Mick, obviously chosen, she now realised, to match her dress, and very high boots from Tom with a comical '*Beware of Snakes*' sign on each.

Rose was strangely bright eyed, she noticed, but didn't need to guess why as she waited for Jack to walk in and make the announcement. The mood was subdued compared to the previous night and Veronica suspected a few sore heads were being nursed, particularly by Kevin, who was staring suspiciously at the tomato juice Catherine was forcing him to drink. Clarkson, meanwhile, was busy at Pattie's knee drawing caricatures of them all and her friend was giggling at everything he did.

'Blimey, first he turns her into a mullet, now she's a kookaburra,' muttered Tom as he walked past.

To Veronica's surprise Gregory Chambers clinked his spoon against his juice glass and the room fell silent.

'I would like to propose a toast, if I may, to our generous hosts, Marjorie and Clarkson Senior: thank you for this splendid weekend. You certainly know how to make a stranger feel welcome. To the hosts,' he prompted, as everyone raised their glasses, 'and to present company. And if I may, I would like to make an announcement– '

'An announcement or a confession?' Jack stood at the door and the roomful of people looked from one to the other, like spectators at a game of tennis. Veronica stared in shock.

'Jack, please, Gregory is making a toast,' Alice reproached her son. 'Go ahead, dear.'

Gregory met him straight in the eye and continued in a loud clear voice. 'Perhaps a confession, yes. I have not been entirely honest with you. I am not a stranger to one particular person here. Rose Dwyer and I have known each other for quite some time and my visit here was quite planned on my behalf, I must admit. I apologise for that, Clarkson, but my reasons were honourable, I assure you.'

'Honourable, you say?' Jack walked into the room, standing across from Rose, his blue eyes narrow. 'Is that what you call it?'

A look passed across Gregory's face. He continued. 'Rose and I became acquainted while I was working on setting up the

Australian arm of the import business in Melbourne. She was volunteering at the orphanage nearby where I also volunteered as a driver on weekends, taking the children on outings and so forth. Rose often came on those outings and, well, we formed a friendship. I had planned to come and meet the family sooner, but as you know, I had other Sunbeams to chase.' He smiled, nodding towards Clarkson whose expression remained neutral. 'But here I am now and, well, after a conversation with her father earlier, I am pleased to announce our engagement. Ladies and gentlemen, may I present my fiancée, Rose.'

He held out his hand to Rose who walked gracefully over and took it. A nervous-looking Mildred and Dr Dwyer stood as well, as one by one the stunned onlookers came to their senses and congratulated the couple and her parents. But the atmosphere was charged and Veronica's eyes stayed on Jack, her heart pounding. The conversation petered into silence again as Jack and Gregory faced one another down, until Rose stepped forward and forced Jack to meet her gaze.

'I am so very grateful for your kindness these past few months, Jack. You made everything…bearable for me.'

Jack stared at her in disbelief, and Veronica watched him trying to reconcile what was true only yesterday with what was true now. Suddenly, he turned and left, Pattie running after him.

'Jack! Jack, where are you going?'

But Veronica knew it didn't matter. Wherever he went he wouldn't escape this.

Alice watched them walking arm in arm about the gardens, a spectacularly beautiful couple both dressed in white, his blonde hair dazzling in the sun, hers as red as its setting glory. Never mind that everyone else is involved with the children or looking for Jack, she thought bitterly. Obviously they are too preoccupied with themselves to care about anything else. Let alone her parents. Alice felt no malice towards the latter for her son's public humiliation. They were being forced to accept it like everyone else, with the added scandal of a secret courtship to deal with. No wonder poor Mildred could be heard weeping in her room.

The children ran about, the girls all wearing their new bonnets, delighting in the horse rides Iggy and Dan were supervising, the lemonade Veronica was distributing and the swimming pool, where Clarkson and Pattie were playing games and watching out for their safety. Mary and Agnes were taking turns giving tennis lessons and the rest of the children had gathered in the annex with Clarkson Senior, Dr Dwyer, George and Kevin, still in raptures over the wonderful train set.

The pavilion dinner was set to start at six, followed by a Christmas performance by the children, then it was off to bed for the little ones in the huge shed. The grown-ups would then attend the ball this evening until the wee hours, with morning mass set for nine, after which a large breakfast would be served before everyone set off back home.

They used to have the Christmas tree after the dinner but every year it had become earlier and earlier, and today everyone felt they needed a boost, so the presents were given out pretty much on arrival. It had lifted all their spirits to see the young faces alight with joy, although Alice noted Rose hadn't bothered to watch.

So much for her love of the children, she thought angrily. She may have met this Chambers through an orphanage but Alice doubted she had done much charitable work while they were together, judging by the way she was pressed up against the man.

She scanned the drive again, waiting for her devastated son to return, her mind alive with worries. Mick and Tom had left a few hours earlier to check for him at the Greengate Hotel, suspecting he was there drowning his sorrows, but as the hours stretched into the afternoon and more and more guests arrived she became increasingly concerned. How could she have been so blind? She should have listened to her own instincts; she knew what Rose was. Yet she had invited her here, given her free range into their friends' kind hospitality, sung her praises for all to hear, only to be rewarded with this. The betrayal of her only dear son.

And it was a betrayal. No young lady of honour would ever lead a man on in such a way, allowing him to court her openly, parade her about town for months, monopolise all her dances and be serenaded again and again in public, without expecting a proposal. Even the night before Jack had draped his arm about her on the couch in an intimate fashion, right in front of this Gregory person. Everyone had been expecting an engagement announcement this weekend between Rose and Jack and up until this morning she had suspected Rose was angling for her acceptance purely to gain a foothold in their family. Why else pretend to be so charitable and pious? And something else troubled her. Jack had known about the engagement this morning, yet he hadn't known last night, judging by his behaviour. When had he found out, and worse, *how*?

Alice sighed, moving into the house to see what she could do to assist the others with final touches to the dinner. The question wasn't so much whether Jack would return, but what his temper would lead him to do when he did.

Gregory Chambers watched his fiancée with amusement. Only Rose could turn a spurned lover's world to her advantage, working the room with a grace and charm that melted every man into a puddle. Not so the women, he observed with a small smile, noting the hostility that greeted her every nod their way, but Rose was never concerned with what women thought of her. As she once said to him, it was the men that ruled the world: women were mere competitors for the associated power. A smart girl, his Rose. And beautiful. Despite the fact that she knew every woman there would know she had practically dumped that fool Murphy at the altar, she'd chosen a brilliant gold low-cut gown for the evening, prompting a ripple of scandal as she walked into the pavilion, almost causing the trumpet player to swallow his mouthpiece. She dared people to gossip about her. Let them say their worst, I've got my man, said the gown as she draped herself next to him like a cat.

It was all part of her game. She might appear cocky and in control to the rest of the world but Gregory knew she really wanted a man to take her and possess her. Make her his plaything behind closed doors. Punish her for being the one who made all the men hot. Jack Murphy was a lightweight. He could never have handled a woman like Rose.

She was a woman of insatiable appetites.

He knew she would be tempted by the carrot he had so deliciously dangled before her, or should he say carat. Yes, they were two of a kind. Negotiators of the highest skill, although she had only made one request of him: an immediate wedding and an extended honeymoon in London, which she professed she had always wanted to see. He had no trouble agreeing, needing to attend to his business interests regardless, and six weeks in a luxury cabin with Rose followed by a year of living in London was a tantalising proposition. Besides, she would need to meet his English family and assume her role at his mother's side. He wondered what she would make of Lady Chambers.

Gregory watched the enormous diamond ring glide down the satin of her dress, sparking indignation from the women nearby and lust from the men and, all in all, counted himself a lucky, lucky man.

Veronica felt it had been the longest day of her life, despite the sweetness of the children, who had earlier finished a touching performance of the Christmas story and were now lying bundled in their beds. Her stomach churned the entire time as she waited for Jack to return. What could she possibly say to comfort him now? 'I told you so?' Even in her worst imaginings she couldn't have foreseen Rose playing this card. She'd known she was devious but this was just plain cruel.

'Dan, rounding in on the left,' whispered Tom as he passed by and Veronica quickly scuttled into the crowd to avoid him. He was after her for another dance but she'd had enough of trying to concentrate on deflecting his clumsy compliments, as nice as he was. All she wanted was to see Jack and know that he was all right.

She found Mick at about the same time as Dan found her and she looked to her brother for rescue.

'My dear sister, I don't think I've had the pleasure all evening.' Mick grinned and offered his arm. 'Excuse me, Dan, family first.'

Dan stood watching in disappointment as Mick waltzed her about the floor, laughing.

'Dearest, if you don't want men falling in love with you, stop growing up and wearing dresses like that.' He shook his head and she smiled, slapping his arm.

'Stop it, you're embarrassing me.'

But he looked at her quizzically, adding, 'I'm quite serious. You gave me a little shock, you know. You seem to have changed overnight. ''S awful. Now I have to swat my mates away from you. Look at that pup Dan. That's it: he's banned from all future parties. And I think Iggy needs to put his eyes back in his head too...Made you look.' Veronica found herself smiling again, as she turned her head back around, but not before she noticed Iggy was indeed staring at her, as were a few others. She had barely looked in the mirror, consumed as she was with Jack, but she had to admit the Christmas dress from her parents did suit her. Her mother had excellent taste and the folds were modest enough not to raise eyebrows, yet flattering to her shape. Mick's brooch was secured at the centre of the neckline, the deep emerald stone adding a rich, exotic statement to the simple design of the dress.

'Thank you for the brooch. I do love it. And I'm so sorry about this morning, I should have thanked you properly.'

'Well I did buy it just after you were sick so it cost me most of my savings, sentimental fool that I am,' he lamented, pulling a face, 'and now here you are, using it as bait to trap my helpless friends and leave us all for good with some undeserving mug.'

'I'll never leave you,' she promised, craning her neck to the doorway for what seemed like the hundredth time that night.

'Still looking for Jack?' Mick looked at her knowingly. 'I already told you: my mate Bob said he'd left the Greengate and taken off for home. He'd hardly want to come back here now. Don't worry about him Vera. He won't do anything stupid.'

'Hmmm,' she replied, still looking to the door, her eyes suddenly widening.

'Bloody hell,' he muttered, following her gaze. 'Famous last words.'

Veronica watched transfixed as Jack walked through the crowd, striding towards Rose and Gregory with a slight swagger to his gait. He still wore the same clothes he'd had on that morning and his expression was wild.

'A word with you outside,' he slurred, his fists clenched.

'I don't think that will be necessary, Murphy. If you have something to say you can do it here, in front of this fine company,' Gregory replied, sipping his champagne. Rose looked at them calmly, but Veronica noted the whiteness of her knuckles as they clenched the skirt of her dress.

'I don't think Rose would like that, would you, *darling*?' Jack's eyes were locked on her.

Gregory placed his glass down and stepped forward. 'I appreciate you have a friendship with my fiancée, but mind your familiarity,' he said in a low voice, his large body now menacingly close to Jack's athletic but by far slighter frame.

'Oh we are familiar with one another.' Jack laughed harshly, squaring up. 'Very familiar.'

Gregory clenched one meaty fist and Veronica eyed it anxiously. Spurred into action, she broke away from Mick to walk over and stand between them.

'Jack,' she cried brightly, 'there you are. I do believe you promised me a dance.'

Everyone waited, including the band, as Jack wavered: he focused on Veronica's face. Then, after a look back at Rose, he seemed to make up his mind. 'Shall we?' he obliged, pulling her rather crookedly into his embrace.

Veronica looked at Jack, unshaven, reeking of alcohol, dishevelled. And hurt. Lifting her chin she began to dance. Tom made hasty motions to the band to play something and they quickly did so. Slowly others filled the dance floor as Veronica and Jack whirled around, missing steps but never taking their eyes from each other's. Neither said a word and, as the song ended, they continued to dance the next. And the next. They danced until the couples gradually fell away. They occasionally nodded and smiled at passers-by but they kept on dancing.

And when the final song ended and the band packed up, he bowed and kissed her hand, staring at her for a moment before whispering, 'Thank you, my Vera.'

Her eyes filled with tears as he stumbled away, shoulders heavy, and she stood alone for a while, the pavilion empty, save for the maids clearing away. Finally her mother came and gently took her arm, leading her up to bed and helping her into her nightie as she had when she was a child.

The moon sailed across the sky through silver-lined clouds that turned gold as it passed. Veronica watched its voyage until her eyes finally closed against the night, one that would change the course of her life.

Because she knew before she opened them again in the morning that her Jack would be long gone.

Ten

Bobbin Head, Turramurra, August 1914

'Last one in is a rotten egg!' called Pattie, running into the shallow waters of the bay, Clarkson chasing her. Gum-lined hills rested in a eucalypt haze and the sound of their laughter echoed through the valley. It was sunny but still a cool winter's day and Veronica smiled as Pattie shrieked from the splashing of cold water.

'Mad.' Dan shook his head, watching them and grinning.

'As a hatter's tea party, I'm afraid,' Veronica said agreeably. 'Speaking of which?' She offered him a cup from the Thermos and they sat in companionable silence, watching the others and enjoying the view. It's peaceful here, Veronica reflected, if one discounted the raucous yelling and screams. It felt good to smell the earth and the damp and touch the sand. She had felt boxed in these long winter months, going through the motions of dreary household duties with a heaviness that woke her in the morning and drugged her to sleep at night. And it was more than that. It was an emptiness in her heart that made her feel as if nothing could ever be right in the world again.

Dan looked at her over his tea. 'Must feel good to get outdoors for a while.' She smiled at him, thinking not for the first time how alike he was to her. If not for him things would have been worse, she admitted. Over the past months she had found a kindred spirit in this country lad. He too felt most at home in the bush, barefooted and close to the earth. Both enjoyed socialising, but preferred not to be the centre of attention, and she knew that he shared her restlessness, a feeling that life was on hold until the real adventure began. And so they had waited together, sometimes just sitting in companionable silence, like now, other times chatting as he milked the cows, shot the crows or fixed fences. And other times, when they could steal away, they had hiked down the creek to talk about possibilities and secret ambitions. He filled a void now that Pattie spent all her spare time with Clarkson and she knew she had made a true friend. But lately she feared something reckless was building in him, a new edge to the wilder side of Dan, and something more she wasn't ready to face.

'Feed me, you fool!' cried Pattie from the water.

'What's this? I expected you to have baked for days preparing my luncheon!' Clarkson replied, his long arms spread in mock outrage.

'Open the larder sir or pay the forfeit!' She laughed, running from the water and wrapping herself in a towel.

'And what, pray tell, is this forfeit of which you speak?' he demanded, shaking his hair dry as he followed.

'I'll set Buggles on you!' She pointed at her furry winter hat, so named by Clarkson.

'No! I surrender! In fact I may have just the thing…'

Clarkson moved to the 'larder' as Pattie called the large trunk he had strapped to the back of the Sunbeam and began to produce an array of foodstuffs, including a baked ham, several bottles of lemonade, a loaf of bread and an enormous cauliflower.

'A token of my esteem,' he said, kneeling and placing the last in front of Buggles.

The laughter continued throughout lunch and Veronica found that she was truly enjoying herself, relishing the simple fare, the beautiful surrounds and the excellent company. She had been looking forward to this picnic for weeks and it was well worth the wait.

'If only every day could be like this,' she sighed, packing the dishes as they finished.

'Come on, it's not over yet. Let's go for a ramble.' Dan helped her to her feet and they set off for the carriage track nearby, leaving Pattie and Clarkson to laze on blankets in the sun.

It was steep going at first but it soon levelled out as they reached the edges of the rainforest, and Dan hoisted her onto a large sandstone ledge to sit and soak in the view. The blue-green river lapped against the narrow sandy shores, occasionally disturbed in expanding circles by jumping tailor fish.

Dan broke the silence. 'Do you think the water is the same colour in Germany?'

Veronica pondered the question for a moment. 'Well, they are quite deep, I suppose, and they wouldn't have the sandstone, so I'd say no. Definitely darker.'

He nodded, considering that. 'I imagine I may have the chance to find out soon. If it comes to it.'

Veronica felt her insides tighten. 'No, I'm sure it won't. It can't.'

'But if it does...' Dan picked up a few rocks, rubbing them against the ledge thoughtfully. She stared at the water, searching for words that would stop what he would say next. What the young men would all say if it came to pass.

'Veronica, I'll be joining up.'

It sat there between them, a giant rock, bigger than the one beneath them and just as immovable and dense. And there was nothing to say because of course he would go.

'It's not just for duty, is it?' she asked. 'You want to go.'

'I don't want war, Veronica – '

'Yes you do.' She said it simply, detaching herself.

He seemed to struggle then, frowning. 'No, I don't want war, but I do want to go. It's true. All the fellows will be going and it's the other side of the *world*, Veronica! Just think! The fighting will probably be over by the time we get there anyway. I just…I don't want to sit here twiddling my thumbs and leave my mates to it.'

'But you're underage– ' she began.

'They'll take me.'

'Your parents– '

'Are too far away to stop me.'

He turned then, reaching for her hand. She let it lie there, still not looking at his face.

'If I do go…I want, I mean…will you…?'

She shook her head as even more unwanted words came towards her.

'Please…?'

The sound of horse's hooves pounded down the track and they stood as one as Mick and Tom cantered towards them.

'It's happening…just heard…' Tom panted.

'England has declared.' Mick looked at his sister. 'It's war… we're at war.'

Veronica remained where she was as Dan ran over to the brothers and they made their way down to tell the others.

She stared at the rock, at the heart that Dan had carved as they'd sat, her initials inside. Suddenly her world had turned. Declarations had been made and she felt useless against the force of their pull.

Pattie squashed Buggles further onto her head as the Sunbeam bumped its way up the track.

'Just let the rodent jump off and be free,' Clarkson suggested, yelling over the noise of the engine.

'He's a rabbit.' She scowled.

'Rat!'

She cast him a haughty look then continued to stare straight ahead.

Clarkson sighed, pulling over to the side of the road and cutting the engine. The stillness of the rainforest immediately engulfed them, cool and whisper-quiet save the tinkling sound of water. They had stopped near a running creek and he traced its journey through the thick bed of undergrowth, a sea of dark green ferns beneath white-pillared gums.

'Out with it,' he said, waiting.

'Why the Royal Flying Corps? Why not just be a regular soldier? Oh no, you can't just be a...a foot soldier! You have to be the daredevil! Give yourself the best opportunity to be *killed*.' She glared at him from beneath the fur. 'It's not a bloody game, you know.'

'Why would you think it's any worse than– '

'Because you're going over there to hang upside down in front of German machine guns.'

'We don't just hang upside down like fruit bats!'

'It's ridiculous! What possible use could you be up there, other than providing a sitting duck?'

'Just think what we could do, Pats. We could find out more from the air than we'd ever know in a month of Sundays on the ground! And we could drop bombs from the sky...imagine what that could mean.'

'Yes, but you'd have to survive for five minutes first.' She sniffed, looking unconvinced. A lyrebird walked across the track and they both watched it as it made its careful way along, its delicate tail nodding behind. 'Even he knows he's not supposed to fly...and he's a bloody bird!' The lyrebird looked at her, startled, then ran off into the forest.

'Why London?' she asked, after a pause. 'Why can't you be based here?'

'We only have two planes in the country and about a thousand blokes wanting to fly them! I'm just lucky I'm half English so I can even join the RFC.'

'Yes, lucky...' she scoffed, folding her arms and sinking back in the seat. 'Lucky you can go and die for another country.'

'It'll be over before I even get there,' he soothed.

'Humph.'

He watched her determined chin jut out and her eyes flash beneath that damnable hat and knew in that instant what he had to say.

'I can't promise that, can I? I can't promise I won't die either. But I can promise you this,' he said, tilting her chin towards him with his fingers. 'I will love you all the days I do live.' Her eyes searched his and her face crumpled as he continued. 'Marry me, Patricia?'

She nodded as he kissed her and he held her as tight as he could, knowing soon the memory of her would be all he had left to hold onto.

Eleven

Beecroft, October 1914

Kevin O'Shay watched his sons walk up the drive of Highview together, their Medical Corp uniforms looking stiff and overly new, although he didn't like to imagine how they would appear after months of wear, stained with the blood of their countrymen. He thought of the many times he had stood here, watching them come home, children carrying fishing poles, schoolboys home for summer, lads in their cricket whites. And now young men, army doctors, home for the last time before heading off to war.

He dragged on his cigarette, noticing the lines on his own hands and wishing desperately they could be put to use. His country didn't want him; he was forty-seven years old. He and his friends were cast aside, considered too old against the fresh young bodies of their sons. Australia wanted youths, eager to show their mettle; passionate and energetic; and with their patriotic convictions as yet uncomplicated by the weight of experience. He couldn't be of medical help like his sons, but Kevin wished he could take their places on the boat and keep them at home, safe from the stray bullets and shells.

Catherine had taken to her bed again that afternoon, still too overcome to stand the thought of them leaving tomorrow, her worst nightmare having come to fruition. Some of the other young men had already gone, including Dan. Iggy was due to leave on the morrow, having volunteered for the Light Horse Brigade, which Mick and Tom were to support. Jack was due home any day and they all waited to see what uniform he would be wearing when he arrived. Pattie said he was trying for the Light Horse as well.

Veronica came out to stand next to him and Kevin looked down at his beautiful daughter with affection, grateful she at least would be staying at home with them. She had grown even lovelier over the past months, her face and figure blossoming into full womanhood in her eighteenth year, her understated style echoing her mother's quiet grace. Today she wore blue, which suited her well, and she gazed at her beloved brothers sadly, gripping onto the flowers she had picked for her mother's bedside.

'Vera Mags! For me?' Tom grinned, kissing her cheek before grasping his father's hand firmly, clapping him on the back and marching indoors.

'Hello, dearest.' Mick hugged her and put his arm around his father's shoulders and they all followed Tom, who was busy investigating the mail.

'Where's the love letters from my sweethearts? I thought the girls all went dopey over a man in uniform.' Catherine had emerged and managed a smile at her son, who was bounding about like an overgrown puppy.

'Mumsy!' He grabbed her in a big hug and kissed her cheek with a loud smack.

Too innocent for the ravages of war. Kevin sighed inwardly.

'Calm down, silly boy; hello, darling.' She held onto Mick, her eyes teary. 'The Murphys are coming for dinner. I was going to invite the Dwyers but I think Jack may be back any day so I didn't want to chance it. Pattie is bringing Clarkson with her so that will make a nice party of things.' She was doing her best to sound cheerful, and they all pretended along with her, chatting about Pattie and Clarkson and the upcoming wedding.

Kevin watched his wife's face, saw the pain etched around her eyes, and felt a sudden urge to grab her, his daughter and his sons and head to the hills, over the mountains and far away where no one could touch them. He had friends out west, and money. They could all escape this lunacy and come back when it was well over, safe and sound. Then Mick met his gaze and nodded at his father, just the once. Kevin felt the twist inside and knew escape was impossible. His boys were now grown and bound by honour.

He had to let his sons be men.

Veronica looked out her bedroom window, down the drive and out to Cowpasture Lane, waiting for the man on horseback who never came. The lights were on over at the Dwyers' home and she felt for Iggy, saying farewell to his family tonight. It had been just him and his parents since Rose left for England. She wondered how he was coping with the inconsolable Mildred. At least his father might show him a little more respect now that he'd fulfilled his own prediction and joined up for war. She was glad she'd gone out for a ride with him that morning and regretted she hadn't spent more time with him since Christmas. It had just felt disloyal to Jack to be too close to Rose's brother. And now he was leaving and it was all too late.

Veronica let her mind drift to Rose, imagining her in her mansion in London with all the aristocrats. How different things might have been if Rose Dwyer had married Gregory Chambers in Melbourne and never moved to Sydney. Or if Jack would come home again instead of staying in town week after week, seeing his family only when they came to him on the occasional weekend. With the impending war, food packaging was in higher demand than ever and he claimed he was too busy to leave the city, but she knew that was just a convenient excuse. They would be doing well enough without him when he went off to war.

The irony – that the man she loved was free to love her, but chose to stay away – wasn't lost on Veronica. She'd always felt that if not for Rose she and Jack would be together, but now the fact that Rose was out of the way was the very reason they weren't. He was too hurt to love; and, even if he weren't, she was too close to the memories for him to start a fresh life with her.

Besides, it was all too late now in more ways than one.

Still, she took her time getting ready as she always did when the suggestion that 'Jack might come' was bandied about. She had learnt not to get her hopes up after almost a year of disappointment, but her stomach fluttered slightly every time. She didn't know if she would ever get past that.

The table glittered with candles in the dining room in anticipation of a large roast dinner, but Jack's place was conspicuously empty as usual. Veronica, let down by his absence despite her best efforts, walked in slightly late and greeted them all. She sat down next to Mick, who said he was pleased she wore his brooch, pinned upon the white collar above her navy dress.

She was about to comment when the door opened and suddenly he was here. Her Jack, handsomer than ever in his new Light Horse uniform, complete with the New South Wales wallaby trim on his hat, his dark hair combed back and his smile in place. He was thinner, she noticed, and the smile didn't quite reach his eyes, but he was there! They all stood up, his parents and Pattie weepy to see him home and in uniform and the others just glad to see him at all. He took his place next to Pattie, sitting directly opposite Veronica, who couldn't be happier with the view. She had stood with the others but had only managed a shy smile; and now words failed her completely as he caught her eye. She could look all she liked, though without realising it, she had her heart in her face as he returned her gaze.

Jack stared at Veronica, wondering how the hell he could have stayed away so long as the force of her hit his senses. She had grown even more beautiful this past year and the way she now let her hair down made her seem ethereal. But it was her expression that gave him pause: her eyes were filled with an open love. So different from the women he had been courting in town to fill the void, with their empty chatter and flirtatious games. What a waste of time when he could have been here, with the woman who visited him in his dreams. The woman who was a part of his home, his family. Him.

The woman he realised only now he desperately loved – something he didn't even know he believed in – the night before he would sail away to war.

He realised the others had been asking him questions and he forced his gaze away, answering them all as they ate the delicious meal, enjoying the company of his closest friends and family whom he had so missed, and who had so missed him. With Tom, Mick and Jack sailing away together in the morning, and Clarkson in a few short weeks, there was a deep sense of closeness in the room that night. The uniforms around the table served as silent, stark reminders that this was a memory to treasure in the coming months as oceans separated them, possibly forever.

'Feels like the bloody Last Supper,' said Tom at one point, as Kevin distributed the wine. Jack laughed along with the rest and he noticed Catherine even forgot to chastise him for managing blasphemy and profanity in the same sentence. They all needed that comment, a moment's reprieve, and Jack felt a surge of gratitude that his two best friends would be with him at least.

Gazing at Veronica yet again, he resolved to do everything he could to bring her brothers back home to her.

It was over too soon, the candles low, the wine drunk and the plates emptied.

They stood on the verandah together, looking out at the road, no one wanting to say goodbye.

'I'd best be off,' Jack said, his throat tight as he shook hands and kissed cheeks, leaving the most difficult until last. Those heart-filled eyes poured into his and he touched her chin softly, whispering he would write, before holding her tightly for the briefest of moments.

'I'll write too,' she promised softly and he turned and walked down the stairs, mounted Tilley and rode down the drive, pushing her to a canter lest he change his mind.

It was as if he'd never existed, Veronica mused, as she brushed her hair in the mirror later. Like a beautiful dream. She turned off the lamp and lay back on her bed again, gazing at the moonlight in her room and watching the shadows dance, not wanting to close her eyes on this night and start the difficult future that lay before them at dawn.

The tree branches were tapping against the window and she watched the patterns on the curtain. *Tap, tap, tap.* That wasn't a branch. Her pulse leapt.

'Vera.'

She got out of bed and opened the window, standing back in shock as Jack climbed in.

'I know how this looks and I'm sorry. I just got halfway home and I realised…I realised I'm going to war, Vera. And I couldn't leave without telling you…that is…' He broke off and moved closer, lightly tracing her cheek with his fingers.

'Oh God, I've been such a fool.'

She stared at him, barely allowing herself to breathe, incredulous that Jack was standing there, in her bedroom, in the middle of the night.

'It doesn't matter...'

'Yes, it does.' He held her hands, shaking his head. 'You were driving me crazy and I wanted to blame you for it. I was every farm animal you called me and probably a few more.'

'Is that why you're here? To apologise?' She stared as he laced her fingers, entranced.

'Yes. And to tell you that...that I'll write.' Veronica shivered as he trailed little kisses up her arms. 'You already told me that,' she said absently, staring as his lips moved closer.

'Did I? Well then I forgot to tell you to write to me.'

'I already said I would.' She gasped as he pulled her into his arms.

'Well, then, maybe you can tell me what I forgot to do.'

'I think…you forgot…' He leant forward, ending her words with the lightest of kisses.

'This?' he asked against her mouth as she nodded, leaning in for more. This time there was no restraint. A white-hot rush of desire spread through her as he poured out his passion in a devastating, desperate kiss then moved his mouth across her throat.

'Vera,' he breathed against her, kissing her once more. Then from somewhere it came, unwilling against every instinct. She remembered.

'No...I…I can't.'

Jack looked momentarily confused.

'Yes, you can. I'm free now. I'm here. And I promise I'll come back. I promise.'

She lost herself again as he found her mouth and kissed her with such feeling that at that moment she almost could have forgotten the past few months and thrown herself into it.

Almost.

'No,' she said again, this time pulling back. 'Jack, please.'

'But I'm free to– '

'But I'm not.'

His arms still held her waist as he searched her face, waiting.

'I'm...not free.' It was his turn to pull back as he dropped his arms, his expression clouding.

'Jack, I never thought...You stayed away! I just assumed you couldn't bear the thought of being around me anymore. That I reminded you too much of what went on and after a while I think...I think I just gave up. And Dan was there...'

'Dan?' He said the word as if testing its sound for the first time.

'Dan Hagan. He has been...courting me these past few months and I...I didn't have the heart to say no...He was going to war and he asked me...the day he left...' Meeting his eyes, she let the words fall. 'Jack, we are secretly engaged.'

'Secretly?' he said slowly.

'Yes...I said I'd rather nobody know. I didn't want a...a fuss about it all.' I didn't want it to be true, she thought guiltily.

She reflected later it would have been better if he had ranted and railed at her, flung himself to the floor or punched the wall, anything but that look; that devastated look. Like she'd broken him in half. And then he was gone. She'd even wondered if she had dreamt it but then there it was, the same look the next day as she waved goodbye from the crowd. Even across the Quay she could feel the emptiness he carried and it made her ache to run up the gangway and take it all back. Tell him she never loved Dan – she couldn't love Dan. That she only said yes because he was off to war and he'd begged her. That she had thought she was facing life alone anyway, and a kind man at her side was a better companion than loneliness.

That she would give anything to be free to love him.

'If England needs a hand, well, here it is!
If England wants a hand, well, here it is!'

Catherine looked over at Veronica as the boat made its slow yet resolute way, taking their boys, leaving them with their dread. The cacophony of gaiety and song fell like a warning drone upon their ears, the streamers thrusting the air like swords, the confetti raining like tears.

'England needs a hand, well, here it is!'

Then Catherine turned back and, forcing a brave smile, waved her handkerchief and blew Tom and Mick a kiss. Veronica realised it was all any of them could do. Pretend. The only weapon of those left behind and the greatest gift they could offer those departing. These young men they so loved. These precious, precious lives.

Pretend. *Everything will be all right. We are not worried. We know you'll come home safe to us again and we'll laugh at your adventures and the folly of it all.*

And so Veronica waved her handkerchief and blew her kisses at Mick and Tom too, and, as they sailed away, she added one more message to her list of pretendings and sent it to the man who stood alongside them. *And we'll marry other people and grow old as friends and forget that silly night long ago, the night before you left for war.*

And we'll live happily apart, ever after.

Part Two

Twelve

Cairo, Egypt, February 1915

Iggy eyed the old piano greedily, running his hand across the dusty keys as Simmo pulled up a chair behind him.

'Come on, give us a song!' he urged, laughing. In the interminable months of his illness, Iggy had dreamt of this moment, when he could speak to his beloved keys again. His fingers found their way and began their familiar dance as the others roared with delight and began to prance about to the sprightly tune.

Simmo was a very tall, very large country boy from just outside Orange, and a fellow patient in the Cairo rehabilitation hospital, where both had recovered after the voyage; Iggy from seasickness and Simmo from appendicitis. He had kept Iggy continually amused with his distrust of all things foreign, insisting on smuggling in good 'Aussie tucker' whenever possible. Iggy was in constant bemusement as to how the intrepid Simmo managed to find white bread, blackberry jam and the occasional bit of pudding in Egypt, later finding out his sister was a maid for one of the 'toffs' in command.

In return Iggy had entertained him with stories from home, describing to the incredulous Simmo a world of glamorous women, tennis courts and swimming pools, racing cars, sleek horses, music and balls.

Somewhere along the line they had become firm friends, and Iggy knew that this party was all his doing. Apparently, when Simmo had seen the old piano in the corner of the brothel the day before, he had decided his mate could use a pleasant surprise on his first day out after weeks of 'bein' crook'. He and a few of the others had made a deal with Delilah, the madam, promising a swag of men with pocketbooks full of money if she would allow them to have a private party, including use of the piano and 'some decent plonk, not Gippo rotgut'. Delilah kept her part of the deal and the men were amazed to find real whisky in their glasses, served by scantily clad exotic beauties who were soon scooped up into burly arms and spun about the dance floor.

Iggy had to hand it to Simmo: if you wanted something, he was your man.

Jack was laughing as Tom and Mick dragged him along through the streets of Cairo, all of them feeling the effects of the cheap booze they had been swilling, which Tom figured was possibly camel urine.

The past few weeks of training in the desert had been a distraction of sorts for Jack, but an exhausting one. In some ways he felt the strangeness of the camp reflected his general state of mind. Mena House sat at its centre, a graceful hunting lodge that had been converted into a hospital, and the Australian camp surrounded it in a city of tents. Against the backdrop of this circus-like scene rose the ancient pyramids and the Great Sphinx, and Jack felt eerily that they watched the soldiers' games of war like benevolent gods.

It was good to have a break from training and spend time with Tom and Mick.

His riding boots were covered in dust as they urged him to keep up, promising him great fortune if he bought a lucky charm from a certain shop they had discovered a week earlier.

Jack guffawed in amusement as they wandered into the wrong shops time and again, taking pleasure in the escape the alcohol provided from his constant, troubled thoughts. Especially the last image he had of Veronica as they left. Just one small face in a crowd, yet he couldn't get it out of his mind. He hadn't even been able to bring himself to wave goodbye as the list of things that separated them grew from Dan Hagan, to oceans, to war.

Tom and Mick had been standing with him and, somewhere further along, Iggy. It seemed it was his destiny to be best mates with the brothers of women who had broken his heart. Not that he had spoken to Iggy that day. It was a few days later, when he'd visited Tom on duty in the infirmary to find a writhing, clammy Iggy restless on his bunk, when the confronting moment finally arrived. And not that it was much of a confrontation at that, just a small bolt of shock at that face, so similar to the one that caused him such hurt, then an awkward moment broken by Tom.

'Anyone fancy an afternoon drink? I think I'll just go visit the cocktail lounge,' he'd said in a lofty voice, holding a penny on his eye like a monocle and humming a waltz as he made pretend cocktails with bedpans in the corner. The other patients laughed and called out requests, giving Iggy and Jack an excuse to laugh a little themselves, and the tension eased.

Jack stood by his bed, twisting his hat. What to say to the brother of the woman who had betrayed him, a man who he'd considered a friend only a year ago? A man about to walk into battle alongside him. They needed to put the past behind them and all the foolishness of women and romance because, with Iggy in his regiment, there was no room for anything but absolute trust. Jack realised that was it. Trust. Suddenly there was only one thing he needed to ask.

'Did you know?'

Iggy stared up at him, his eyes large and sunken. 'Absolutely no idea.'

Jack nodded. 'Fair enough then.'

'Well come on, kiss and make up. I have vomit to tend to by the bucketload here. The King of Thomas Island absolutely cannot hold his liquor down by George!' Tom pranced over, waggling his finger at a patient he had crowned with a bedpan.

And that was all there was to it in the end. With Tom and Mick kept busy with seasick patients in the first few weeks, Jack had spent many hours playing chess and cards with Iggy, discussing music, horses and politics mostly, finding he had much in common with the amusing, articulate invalid. He missed their chats now they were in Cairo and training each day and looked forward to Iggy's release from the rehabilitation hospital, which Mick had heard through the medical grapevine would be some time in the next week. It would be good to have his mate in his unit.

During the entire voyage Iggy never made mention of Rose, which Jack appreciated, but at the same time he wouldn't have cared if he had. It seemed so long ago and so unimportant.

Veronica was another story. How he cursed the fact that he was privy to her secret.

One particular night on the crossing, after a few drinks, Mick had said something that made his heart ache for a while. They were sitting in the infirmary and Mick had been talking about a picnic they had enjoyed courtesy of Clarkson and his 'Sunbeam of Wonders', when Veronica's name came up.

'She was so funny. She actually believed Clarkson when he told her there was a puppy in the larder. In fairness, he had already produced a chest of ice with champagne and a collapsible table. And a chicken.'

'Well, you've got to have chicken with champagne,' argued Tom.

'Yes, but it helps if you kill it first.' They all laughed loudly at that. 'Anyway, she heard this whining and opened the boot and out jumps Tom! Bounded around after her the rest of the afternoon until Dan had to build her a little fortress out of sand and stand guard.' Mick stopped as the laughter faded and there was an awkward silence. Finally it seemed Tom couldn't stand it.

'You don't have to hide it from us, mate. We saw on the last night as plain as day how you feel about Vera and you never know what might happen when we get home. Chin up!'

'Think I missed that boat, lads,' Jack replied, wishing they knew the truth.

'Nonsense,' Tom declared, 'I reckon you've got just as much chance as that young fella…all's fair in love and whisky…*hic*…I mean war. Who's been spiking my drink?'

'Rather not talk about it.' Jack drained his cup, giving Iggy a thankful glance as he changed the subject.

'So did you kill the chicken?'

'No. Pattie and Clarkson married her to King Henry,' Mick revealed, laughing. 'A wedding practice run of sorts they said. Apparently there was a lot of chicken feed throwing instead of confetti.'

Jack knew he just had to put up with the fact that Veronica's brothers would talk about her and make him ache even more, because there wasn't any question of Jack ever trying to stay away from them. They seemed to consider a mate's morale their personal responsibility, especially Tom, who bounded through life on the boat as if he were on holiday. He forced Jack out of his melancholy time and again, dragging him about to meet every other Tom and Dick and Harry on the ship whenever he was off duty. A one-man party was Tom, and so well liked the three of them couldn't go five paces in Cairo without somebody hailing them over to clap him on the back and swap a few jokes, Australians and Egyptians alike. Combine that with the camel urine and Jack could almost say he was enjoying himself.

Tom and Mick had located the shop at last, larger than the rest and with better quality goods, and the shopkeeper Ammon greeted Tom like an old friend. Mick was busy haggling over a silk scarf he wanted to buy for a pretty nurse back at the camp hospital when Tom eyed Jack staring at some jewel-encrusted rings in a locked glass cabinet.

'Contemplating a new look for yourself? Can't say you won't get thumped if you wear one of those, but don't worry, I'll patch you up,' he assured him. Jack cuffed him about the ears before asking the eager shop owner for a closer look at a beautiful deep sapphire and gold ring. Ammon unlocked the cabinet and handed it to Jack, who turned it into the sunlight. It shone a pure dark blue, which Jack figured was close to the colour of Veronica's eyes. It was probably the alcohol fuzzing his common sense but for some reason he had to buy it, even though he knew he could never really give it to her, especially as she was about to become someone else's wife. But he didn't care. It reminded him of her and he wanted it.

Glancing over his shoulder to make sure the others weren't looking, he impulsively purchased the ring, stumbling a bit to use a good portion of the roll of notes he stashed into his sock each day, along with his other precious belongings.

Ammon noticed his bulging boot and handed him a beautiful flat tin, pausing as he held it.

'Bringing luck. Khepri will protect.' He pointed at the winged beetle holding a sun at the centre and nodded at him. Jack nodded back, focusing with a little difficulty on the ancient symbol before placing his things inside and securing it in his top breast pocket.

Mick bought some silk scarves and Tom a pharaoh head lucky charm (which looked suspiciously to Jack like an ashtray) before the three of them tumbled back out onto the street, declaring it was time for another drink. They twisted down some alleyways towards the seedier part of town, known as the Wazza, joining the trail of some fellow Australian soldiers.

'Hang on, what's going on over there?' Tom led them towards the sound of music and laughter and they turned a corner to the sight of a brothel that had prostitutes baring parts of their bodies out through the windows. The stench of stale perfume mixed with tobacco smoke assaulted them as several soldiers lazed against the doorway.

'G'day, Mick! How ar'ya Tom?' greeted one of them, holding up his bandaged hand in recognition of the brothers.

'Neddy-no-ride! How's the paw?' Tom greeted him.

'Gettin' 'sential function back.' He grinned, showing the cigarette perched between two fingertips poking out of the bandages. 'Fella in there's been bashing away on the pinny all arvo, and them Gippo birds are making a killin'! Saw some blokes lining up six deep for a go.'

Mick, Tom and Jack looked through the door with interest.

'Better not go for it, Ned. Half the blokes I'm treating at the moment have VD,' Mick warned him, peering over his head for a better view of one particular 'bird' just the same.

'Bit late for that,' he grinned. 'They know a thing or two, lemme tell ya. And get a load of this gay 'n' frisky!' He held up the whisky glass and Tom took a swig, smacking his lips in surprise.

'Blimey, I can still see,' he said, making his way in to the party.

'Wouldn't mind having a closer look, just in the interest of medical responsibility, you understand,' Mick declared, walking through as well. Jack followed, his eyes wide at the sight of bare-breasted women dancing with half-dressed soldiers. The room was filled with smoke and the noise was deafening as the men sang along to the piano.

'Tom! Mick! Jack! Over here!' called out a familiar voice and they recognised Dan Hagan approaching, drink in hand and shirt off. Tom and Mick shook hands and greeted Dan joyfully, excited to see a face from home. Jack turned away to grab a drink first from a passing tray, trying to hold his resentment and jealousy down with the whisky. When he turned back Mick and Tom were already trying to chat up some of the girls.

'How are you, Jack?' Dan yelled over the din, clinking his glass.

'Dan. Good to see you,' Jack responded, noticing he'd grown taller and broader and disliking the fact. It was easier to see his competition as a boy.

'Hear you fellas in the Light Horse are coming over to Turkey with us,' he yelled.

'Yeah, can't take the horses with us, which seems a bit pointless after all the training,' Jack yelled back, pleased to be discussing war and not home. 'Seems we're all destined for the infantry after all.'

'Still it's got some perks.' Dan nodded at Jack's riding boots. 'Women go wild for the uniform. Might have to get myself a transfer over.'

'Well we Beecroft lads should be able to bowl over a few maidens if we stick together,' Jack ventured, wondering if Dan had lost interest in Veronica.

Dan laughed, shaking his head. 'I've still got my eye on one back home to be honest,' he said, 'although you tried to scare me off her one night, as I recall.'

Jack smiled through gritted teeth, remembering that night and the argument he'd had with Veronica. And that first kiss. He wondered how he ever could have been so stupid as to push her away, let alone let Dan get another chance.

'You know the girl,' Dan continued. 'Gorgeous blonde – couple of brothers with a few mental problems though.' He nodded at Tom, who was wearing a veil and doing his own version of a belly dance, his drink perched on his head.

Jack continued to nod amiably, resisting the urge to punch Dan's happy face through the wall.

'How about you? I'm sorry about what happened with Rose, mate. Hope that it's all right to mention it…'

Jack looked at Dan who was offering him genuine condolence while still obviously a little nervous of him, and he felt slightly ashamed. 'Of course. Ancient history now,' he assured him.

'In that case, I have a surprise for you,' he declared, relieved, and nodded over to the piano in the corner.

Jack craned his neck, welcoming the sight of Iggy playing his heart out and whistled over to the brothers, pointing. Tom, Mick, Jack and Dan all made their way over to the piano, clasping hands with Iggy and laughing.

'I thought I recognised that out of tune tinkling!' Jack grinned.

'Outa tune nuthin! Who's this clown?' Simmo roared, overhearing.

'Easy there, big fella. Feeding time's coming,' Tom reassured him.

'Uh Simmo, these are my mates from Sydney; the fellas I've been telling you about.' Iggy stood up. 'Mick, Tom and Jack. And you met Dan earlier.'

Simmo's thunderous expression transformed into an enormous smile; and, as Jack felt his arm get pumped by a massive paw, he reminded himself to have a word with Tom about potential head-thumping incidents for future reference.

By now the crowd were becoming restless for more music and Iggy played a few opening chords, raising his eyebrows at Jack. The latter didn't need much prompting and soon the room resounded with a rousing rendition of 'Waltzing Matilda'.

'Give us one for our lovelies!' called a shirtless lad at the song's end, holding a photo in the air then kissing it. The cheers of approval were deafening as Iggy began an old favourite.

The room quietened to a man, the laughter dying and the dancers stilled as the words reached them, drinks remaining in hand.

The sun burnt in deep orange surrender across the ancient city of Cairo, resting on the walls behind Jack as his clear voice filled the room.

Oh, all the comrades e'er I had,
They're sorry for my going away,
And all the sweethearts e'er I had,
They'd wish me one more day to stay,

But since it falls unto my lot,
That I should rise and you should not,
I gently rise and softly call,
That I should go and you should not,
Good night and joy be with you all.

If I had money enough to spend,
And leisure time to sit awhile,
There is a fair maid in this town,
That sorely has my heart beguiled.
Her rosy cheeks and ruby lips,
I own she has my heart in thrall,

Then fill to me the parting glass,
Good night and joy be with you all

Good night and joy be with you all.

The words travelled out to the dusty, foreign streets, out towards a future the Australians were trying to drink away. But for each, they knew the time was coming, and as sure as this day was ending, the days of war were about to dawn.

Thirteen

Beecroft, May 1915

'*We publish today a brilliant description of the landing of the Australians and New Zealanders on Gallipoli Peninsula by that experienced war correspondent, Mr Ashmead-Bartlett. It is a thrilling story, a story that will make us all feel proud of our soldiers.*' Alice read the newspaper aloud to the Ladies' Auxiliary as they knitted that afternoon. It was raining outside and Veronica found herself staring at the patterns on the windows as the words came alive.

'*They have shown that, though transplanted to these southern skies, the breed is still the same as that of the men of Mons and Waterloo, and a hundred other great battles.*'

'Hear, hear,' said Constance Dickson, the woman in charge of the local Red Cross.

Veronica wondered why the author felt that being under southern skies would somehow have rendered them less than worthy of being killed in the name of the British Empire. She decided Mr Ashmead-Bartlett was a pompous fool.

'*They were in a desperate position when they landed on the narrow beach in the dawn, but they did not hesitate. They carried the Turkish trenches on the beach and on the cliffs, and, without the support of artillery, held on all day of Sunday, 25 April. Their dash and courage saved the situation, and no troops that ever marched have done better.*' Some of the ladies gave a spontaneous flutter of applause.

'Would the 1st be there, do you think?' Catherine asked Alice.

'I'm not sure,' Alice replied, looking up from the paper, 'although they are bound to have to go to this Gallipoli place. Listen to this: *The latest news is that a great battle is proceeding, to prevent a division of Turkish reinforcements from joining the main forces. It is probable that it is the Australians and New Zealanders that are engaged in this operation.*' She put the paper down and rubbed at her eyes.

Veronica noticed Alice looked older these days and felt a rush of compassion. Jack's welfare was in her heart every day that passed too. And Dan's, she added to her thoughts quickly. And Iggy's and her brothers. She stood and walked over to the refreshments table, a wave of frustration overwhelming her as she poured a glass of water.

'Iggy said naught about this Gallopololi, although he can't as you know. Very strict they are about such things,' Mildred said, holding the silver cross she wore at her throat anxiously.

'Gallipoli,' Constance corrected her. 'It's on the Turkish coast.' Constance knew everything there was to know about the war. Well, everything the newspapers tell her, Veronica thought, feeling bitter. She had a healthy scepticism of the accuracy of the news they received, littered as it was with 'heroic rhetoric' as her mother described it. Only in private of course.

'I do hope Miles takes his swim trunks,' said Priscilla Enright, the mother of an overweight, lazy lad who was now part of the infantry. 'It sounds terribly hot over there.'

'I think feeling the heat is the least of their problems,' Catherine said, clicking her knitting needles a little loudly. Veronica knew her mother found Priscilla and her ignorance of the realities of war a trial.

'Oh, I'm sure they'll have time for a little bathing,' Priscilla continued. 'Miles needs the seawater to help him with his skin. Gets dreadful rashes in the heat. I told him to make sure he told the sergeant that he'll need to bathe at least twice a week.'

'I don't think skin rashes are a high priority during battles,' Catherine said tightly. 'I think avoiding machine guns is more the issue.'

Veronica felt like patting her mother on the back for that comment. It was almost like having Pattie there, although the latter might have boxed Priscilla's silly ears by now.

'Well!' said Priscilla, pushing her spectacles up onto the bridge of her nose. 'I don't think they'll be close to much of that.'

'Yes, I'm sure the Turks are on the run by now,' Constance soothed her, casting Catherine a warning look and changing the subject. 'And how is Pattie faring, Alice?'

'She's been terribly ill throughout I'm afraid,' Alice replied. 'And miserable as can be.'

'She's not the type to like being forced to sit idle and wait.' Constance said this with a tone of approval. Pattie was an active member of the Red Cross, Constance's favourite volunteer in fact, although Pattie didn't hold too much stock in that. Only pregnancy had been able to slow her down from the whirlwind lifestyle she usually led. She was finding the confinement of her latter stages unbearable. Veronica decided to pop in to see her later that afternoon, rain or no rain.

'And what's all your news then, Veronica?' Constance looked over at her and she started, realising she was still standing by the table and not knitting like the rest. She went back to her chair and answered.

'Just waiting like everyone else, I suppose. I just wish I could do...something,' she finished lamely, trying not to reveal too much of her frustration.

'Well, you're not only waiting. You're here, helping our boys be more comfortable. That's something isn't it?' Alice suggested. Veronica shrugged, unconvinced, looking at the socks she was knitting.

'Perhaps when yer older y' could join t' Red Cross over in Egypt,' Mildred suggested.

'I don't think that is a very good idea,' Catherine interjected quickly.

'Nonsense,' said Constance. 'They can certainly use more volunteers, especially with this push in Turkey. I've heard the medical corps are in dire need of the support of young ladies who aren't afraid to work hard and show good character like this one here.' She nodded at Veronica approvingly.

'Oh now, I'm no too sure there, Constance. Could be terrible dangerous for a young girl such as she is.' Mildred shook her head. 'I was thinking more organising supplies and the like. Not hospital work.'

'We old biddies can do that well enough. Veronica here has nursing written all over her. Both her brothers are doctors after all.' Constance snapped her fingers. 'I've got a wonderful contact for you. My cousin Wilma George is the sister in charge at the holding station in Cairo. I could write her if you like.'

Veronica sat forward, hope rising. 'That would be wonderful…'

Catherine shook her head. 'No,' she said firmly. 'She's too young: it's out of the question.'

Veronica stared at her, opening her mouth to object.

'Surely she is well out of danger in Egypt,' Priscilla interjected. 'Why, it's a whole other country. They don't put nurses near the war.'

'Actually that's exactly where they do put them,' Alice said. 'But you're quite right. She would be well away from the actual fighting.'

'My brother survived battles in the Boer and was killed by a bomb attack when he was in a field hospital,' Catherine said, her voice shaking slightly. 'Hospitals are not necessarily safe.'

The room fell silent as the other ladies digested this piece of information. Veronica had known about her uncle's death through her father but she had never heard her mother speak of it until now.

Mildred reached over and patted Catherine's hand. 'I wouldn't want my daughter anywhere near it, truth be told,' she said, nodding at Catherine, then blushing slightly, Veronica suspected for mentioning Rose in front of Jack's mother.

'I'm terribly sorry to hear of your loss. Truly. But surely that was a freak accident,' Constance said, seeming to be unable to restrain herself. 'If all mothers refused to let their daughters be nurses, who would care for our wounded?'

'Other mothers can make their own choices. My daughter is staying here.' Something in Catherine's tone forbade any further comment but looking across at her Veronica determined that this was far from over. In that moment she knew she would find a way to do it. Somehow she would get on one of those boats and go to her boys. Her knitting days were over.

Veronica woke from her dream in a sweat, taking a moment to bring herself back to the present. Jack had been in a maze and there were giant rats chasing him out but then, when he found his way to the open spaces, enormous mosquitoes swooped and attacked, tearing at him as he ran. She screamed but no one could hear her – she was locked in a cage far away.

She stood and dressed in the clothes she'd laid out, putting the last of her things in a valise as quietly as she could. She'd packed what she knew she would need and nothing more. Stuffing the much-read mail from her brothers, Dan and Jack in the pocket, she closed it and placed the note on her dresser.

'They won't take you without a letter,' said a voice from the doorway.

Veronica turned, facing Catherine, her heart thudding.

'I've written my own,' Veronica said, her chin raised as she clutched her bag.

'I know you think I can't stop you, but I can. Dr Dwyer knows half the board. They'll never approve you.'

Veronica knew this was true. The Voluntary Auxiliary Defence or 'VAD' had an enlistment age of twenty-three and older. But there was a way.

'You could make it happen.'

Catherine folded her arms. 'And why would I do that?'

'Because I'll run away anyway, even if you don't.'

'And where will you go?'

'Queensland, Victoria...anywhere I can reapply. Whatever it takes, Mother...I have to go...' Veronica's hands shook and she felt the tears well in her eyes.

'Why? Is it so terrible to stay here safe with us?' Catherine threw out her arms, encompassing the walls.

'Yes!' Veronica cried. 'I...I have to go to them. Maybe I could be near Tom and Mick – or if not, then *any* hospital – I can't stay waiting here any longer, not when our boys might need me. Not when I could be of use. Don't you see?' She wiped at her face. 'It could be Iggy lying there or...or Dan – '

'Or Jack?' Catherine said, her gaze pinning her daughter to the truth.

Veronica hesitated then broke down. 'Or Jack.'

Catherine stepped into the room and gathered her close.

Veronica subsided, to sob in her mother's arms. 'Oh, Mum, please let me go to him...please...I know he needs me.'

'I can't lose you...' Catherine began to cry too, pushing back Veronica's hair and holding her face in her hands. 'I can't.'

'I'll come home, I will,' she promised and Catherine rocked her against her heart.

They held each other as the rose of dawn stained the sky. It had cost the admission of her greatest truth but Veronica knew her mother had heard her at last.

Three weeks later Veronica stood at the gangway of the departing ship and embraced her parents one last time.

'Goodbye, my dearest pet.' Her father shook his head, tears streaming, and she could barely stand to let him go from her embrace.

'My baby,' choked Catherine and Veronica clutched at her, wishing she could take her mother's strength and wisdom with her.

Pattie was there too, her eyes bright as she held Veronica close, whispering in her ear before she ascended the ramp.

'Keep an eye out for a certain dashing Australian airman for me, won't you? And tell him his child seems to share his taste for adventure.' She laughed through her tears as the baby kicked between them.

Veronica picked up her bag, her initial steps resolute as she climbed towards the unknown but she paused halfway up the gangplank, staring at the enormous ship and feeling very much her paltry nineteen years. Veronica looked back at her mother, fighting the temptation to run back to the protection that at times had smothered her, but had always kept her safe.

Then Catherine smiled at her, pride and love in her gaze, and Veronica knew if her mother believed she could do this, then she believed it too.

Fourteen

Gallipoli, Turkey, June 1915

She was walking towards him, barefooted in the summer fields, trailing her hand across the long grass. Her dress was white and he could make out the shape of her as the sunlight filtered through the sheer material; and the look on her face showed him everything he had ever wanted her to feel.

'Jack,' she mouthed towards him.

'Yes, darling?'

'Wake up, ya bloody galah!' Simmo's boot kicked into his ribs and he blinked awake. 'You and Bullseye are orderlies and I want me scran…and ya better hop to it before I shove my rifle up yer ass fer calling me darling!'

Iggy and a few of the others laughed heartily at this and Jack turned over, groaning. Being orderlies meant they were responsible for getting the 'scran', or breakfast, a much-hated job. It meant running the length of the trenches down to the cookhouse and back, never an easy task.

'You're on fatigue today too, so hurry back,' Iggy said, sending him a sympathetic grin. Jack rubbed his head, wishing he could go back to his dream.

'Come on, Dan.' He poked him with his foot. If he couldn't dream about Veronica then why should he? Not that they got much sleep in this hell-hole. If the Turks weren't sending over grenades or picking up on their every move with snipers, the rats, lice and flies were there to do their best to make sure they were as tortured as possible.

Dan, or 'Bullseye', as he'd been dubbed, met the news about being an orderly with about the same level of enthusiasm but soon they were off, ducking as showers of earth rained down from the Turkish snipers having some fun.

'Oh they are gunna get theirs when we get back,' Dan said between clenched teeth as they flattened themselves against the wall, a bullet sending a tin sailing into the trench. He'd earned the name 'Bullseye' over the past few months by applying his honed crow-shooting to sniper work, and bets were often placed on him and Iggy for marksmanship. The latter had also shown remarkable skill with the gun, much to his own surprise. Jack figured they were mates you were happy to have in a place like this, especially when shooting ability was one of the Anzacs' few strengths. They were at a constant disadvantage, located as they were right under the Turks' noses, and the defenders seemed to have an endless supply of grenades. The Australians had to make their own bombs out of jam tins.

They reached the cookhouse, already sweating in the morning heat, and Jack noted that the flies were thick on top of the billy tin.

'Sure miss a decent cup of tea,' Jack sighed, flicking the buggers off, though they immediately landed straight back.

'And some fresh baked scones with some real butter,' Dan sighed, looking upwards and pretending to pray before inspecting the contents of the scran. 'Nup. Just bully beef and rock-chewers again.'

'Think I might have to start putting these in the jam tins and see if I can soften them up,' Jack said, holding up a 'rock-chewer' army biscuit and shaking his head. 'My kingdom for something fresh!'

'Simmo said he would grab me a fish when he went down swimming later. I'll ask him to get one for you too if you like.'

'How does Simmo catch the fish?'

'They get blown up from the bombs.' Dan grinned.

'Fish bomb stew.' Jack shook his head. 'Only in Turkey.'

They made their way back, cursing the occasional flying debris from the snipers.

'Bloody hell,' said Jack as a sudden series of explosions shook the earth. Dirt rained down upon them and the scran went flying as both men flattened themselves against the trench wall, several sandbags falling from the top.

'Look out!' Jack grabbed a sandbag and hugged it to his chest, launching his body across the trench on top of the live grenade. The explosion shattered through him, lifting him off the ground like a bucking mule before landing him hard back on the earth. Jack lay there, waiting for the blackness, but it didn't come. Instead someone was flipping him onto his back and Dan grabbed at him frantically in a cloud of dirt.

'You…you alive?'

Jack barely nodded, the middle section of his body a fiery pit of pain, and allowed Dan to half drag him to the side.

'Turks,' he panted, pointing to their right. Jack heard it too.

'Allah! Allah!' The Turkish voices came closer and Jack tried to heave his gun onto his shoulder. It seemed to weigh ten times what it had moments before.

'Ahhhhh!' roared Simmo, barrelling past them, bayonet first. He was closely followed by Iggy and the others.

Gunfire pitted the air, and Dan raced after them, Jack clawing his way behind. He rounded several corners, stumbling and clutching, his head swimming in a daze, then suddenly he was in it. Dan was already lying behind a crate, taking deadly aim in quick succession as the Turks came in over the top. Simmo fought like a wild animal, stabbing the enemy at close contact with his bayonet, and several others were in heated crossfire with some barricaded Turks around the bend. Iggy had picked off several of the enemy from behind a pile of sandbags and Jack collapsed next to him. He felt heavy and awkward but his heart pumped at him to keep going.

It was fast. He tried to make sense of it as bodies fell in the deafening noise and debris.

Then suddenly it all stopped. The shots petered out and it was still. It took a moment for Jack to realise, of course, as his heart-beat thudded in his chest and his senses tried desperately to search for any movement, but the raid had indeed passed. Simmo and the others began to walk back, kicking at the corpses to make sure they were dead. Jack tried to focus on their sightless eyes then closed his own, sickened.

'Anyone left?' Iggy called.

A single shot rang out and a Turkish soldier fell next to Simmo from the edge of the trench above. They all crouched immediately.

'Thanks, Bullseye,' said Simmo, staring at the man then back towards Dan, nodding.

Dan nodded back and Jack thought he looked like he wanted to be sick. Come to think on it, he felt the same way.

'What the hell happened to you?' said Iggy, turning to Jack who was by now wheezing quite heavily.

'Decided to take a nap on a bomb,' said Dan, shaking his head, still incredulous, as Iggy undid Jack's shirt and cut away the frayed edges with his knife.

'Well, you've got to get some sleep around here somehow,' said Iggy as he worked. Over the past few weeks he had displayed some impressive medical skills, showing he had learnt a lot more during his invalid years than his father ever gave him credit for.

Jack knew his chest must be a pretty sight, judging from the grim look on Iggy's face, but he couldn't seem to lift his head to investigate.

'Hey, where's me scran?' Simmo bellowed at Dan, remembering.

'Hold it down up there,' said a voice from behind them as reinforcements arrived.

'Sir,' they all acknowledged. Sergeant Blockley was gruff but respected by the men, who admired any officer who put himself alongside when enemy activity struck.

'Any more up further?' he asked Simmo, scanning the dead bodies in the trench.

'Don't think so, sir. One juz up there but we got him in time.' He nodded at the rim.

'Right, move back you lot. You two, get these bodies out.' He pointed at two newly arrived men and the others retreated, glad to be relieved of that duty.

'What's the verdict, Dwyer?' he asked Iggy, his eyes narrowing slightly at Jack's chest.

Iggy checked each of Jack's pupils, holding the lids apart as Dan hovered nearby. 'Concussion, sir. And several broken ribs at the least.' Jack tried to comment but found his chest hurt like hell.

'Grenade?' asked the sergeant.

'Threw himself on one actually, sir,' Dan informed him. 'Holding a sandbag. Saved both our lives,' he added, still looking shocked at Jack's brave action.

The sergeant didn't comment but looked at Jack with a flicker of surprise. Jack tried to look back but his sight was blurred.

'Permission to get him down to get checked out,' Iggy said.

'Actually I want a word with you, Dwyer. Crawley, Hogan,' he said to the two men who had begun disposing of the bodies. 'Leave that. Get this man down to the doc first.'

'Permission to assist?' Dan asked and the sergeant nodded as the former began to gently help his mate off the ground. Jack was hoisted and carried off to a stretcher, wondering what Sarge wanted with Iggy just as the sharp pain of the lifting hit him and the blackness did take hold.

There were no dreams of Veronica in that dark void, only flies and exploding fish and sightless eyes that screamed 'Allah!' as they stared into his soul.

Fifteen

August 1915

The perspiration beaded on his forehead but Iggy didn't notice. His entire focus was on holding his aim and squeezing slowly: the perfect balance. The shot split the air.

'Yes!' crowed Simmo, who was watching through another scope. Jack checked the sights through the periscope rifle and confirmed that Iggy had indeed managed to hit the mirror the Turks had been using in the opposite trench.

'That's five bob for me!" Simmo grinned.

'Not so fast,' Jack reminded him, handing the rifle to Dan. 'Aim for the one throwing the grenades.'

'I'll try and get the one that owes you a sandbag.'

The men all watched as Dan searched the ground above them, coming to rest on another glint in the sunlight on the far right. He pointed it out to Simmo, who nodded in confirmation.

Dan held steady, taking aim.

'One Turk mirror, far right,' he said.

'Come on, Bullseye,' muttered a few of them.

'Miss, ya bastard,' whispered Simmo.

The shot rang.

'Haha!' Simmo yelled, slapping Iggy on the back with glee.

Dan apologised to his supporters, looking regretfully back at the glittering target. 'Sorry, mates.'

'Double or nothing!' they dared, challenging Simmo and the other men who'd backed Iggy's side in the bet. Some general ribbing broke out and Iggy laughed as Simmo gave one objectionable fellow a dressing down.

'You're just gutless!' said the soldier hotly.

'And you're about as useful as tits on a bull but we still don't shoot ya! Now git outta here before I clock ya one!'

Just then a messenger ran towards them, breaking the argument.

'Sarge wants to see yas,' he panted, pointing to Jack and Iggy. Jack looked to Iggy, who shrugged and they set off together, still grinning as the argument continued behind them.

'Typical bloody New South Welshman! Ripping a man off.'

'Yeah well I'd rather be from the south than a Queenslander with a face like a half-sucked mango!'

Iggy wondered at the summons. He was still getting used to his new rank as corporal, a promotion he had heard about the day Jack was injured. Sarge had told him the news as the dead Turks still lay around them and he knew that moment would stick in his memory for the rest of his days.

It made sense that Sarge would want to talk to him if any movement was afoot. But why Jack? Hopefully they were promoting him too.

'Wonder what they want with me,' Jack said, reading his mind.

'Maybe they want to wrap you up in sandbags and throw you at the Turks. Our new secret weapon,' Iggy suggested.

Jack grinned. 'Anything to end the bloody thing.'

They had arrived at the bunker and stood outside waiting, the sun beating down as they enjoyed a rare view of the cove. It was really quite beautiful, Iggy had to admit. The water was very blue, shading to pale green where it met the yellowed sand of the beach, and the sky's expanse felt enormous after the confines of the trench. It was cloudless and clean. Iggy soaked it all in, ignoring the war that littered the landscape and trying to imagine it as it would have been before. He couldn't, though. The hospital ships lay waiting for them beneath that sky. The beach was half-covered in equipment and horses and supplies and the men who were trapped there ran into that glittering ocean, trying to avoid snipers as they drowned the lice that infested them all.

They were waved in to the sergeant's bunker and saluted him as he sat behind a desk, poring over maps.

'Sit, sit,' he instructed, pointing at two chairs. They obliged, waiting.

'How are you faring now, Murphy?' He looked at him over his glasses. It was more of an order than a question.

'Well, sir. Quite recovered.' Jack replied.

Iggy knew Jack's ribs still bothered him but also that he'd never admit it.

'Good,' the sergeant said briskly, straightening his papers. 'Can't have our two new corporals unfit for duty. Especially now.' Jack leant forward and Iggy felt a smile tug at his mouth. Good on him.

'Had a little word to HQ,' the sergeant continued, allowing them a brief smile, the first either had ever seen him produce. 'Bloody brave action you took the other week, Murphy. Congratulations Corporal.'

'Thank you, sir,' Jack said, taking the official letter the sergeant was handing over and looking a bit stunned.

'Right, onto some urgent matters at hand. It seems there's to be a major offensive and it looks like we're going over the top.' He paused, looking at their shocked faces. 'Stalemate's over, gentlemen.'

Jack chewed on the bully beef, his hunger overriding his disgust for the wretched stuff as his body took refuge in the hard walls. Iggy flopped beside him, cursing his boots as he shook out his socks and examined the sores on his feet. Jack threw the food away in disgust, rubbing clammy hands along his legs and lighting a cigarette instead. He stared at the dirt as the glow of shelling flared and waned. Corporal Murphy of the 1st Australian Light Horse. It sounded so noble, but here he was wretched and infested, filthy as any foot soldier in any war, any sense of superiority a nonsense. But there was responsibility. Yes, there's plenty of that, he thought, looking down towards the others, his eyes landing on Dan.

It seemed impossible he could ever have wanted to punch this boy's face. He was a damn nice bloke, Jack had to admit. A kind, loyal and decent fella. How pathetic to hate a man because he has something you don't have, he chastised himself. Isn't that how we ended up fighting a war?

It had ceased to matter to Jack that Dan was engaged to Veronica because here, the only thing that mattered was that Dan was his mate. With so much death around them, that was all that *could* matter. Worrying about life after this was a waste of time. Tomorrow morning they could all be dead anyway.

Jack ran through the sergeant's brief again. Their regiment had been given orders to take Dead Man's Ridge. Simultaneously the 10th and the 3rd Division would attack the Nek and Quinn's. Jack understood the logic all right. It would serve two purposes. One, it would gain the position at Baby 700, the valuable high ground they had been desperate to take for months, and two, it would take the focus away from the English and New Zealanders attempting to take Chanuk Bair, the overall goal.

Yes, there was nothing wrong with the plan on paper, Jack mused, flicking the cigarette butt into the dark. It was the idea of running across open ground under machine-gun fire that didn't seem quite right, especially as they'd be running towards a place called Dead Man's Ridge.

They were quiet to a man that night with the knowledge of it. Jack wondered how Mick and Tom were faring back in Egypt, tending to the wounded and fearing they would find familiar faces on their tables. He wondered if they would see him soon and privately prayed at this point they would. 'Wounded' held a lot more appeal than 'dead'.

The orange tips of their cigarettes traced their movements as each man pondered his fate.

Jack knew it had to come to this: a decisive strike. A proper battle. It couldn't go on as it had been: men trapped like fish in a net, beaten down by the hellish conditions and the constant shelling. He also knew he was becoming a harder man, more detached from killing each day. But tonight was different. There was no detachment. For the first time they knew they would kill in advance. Tomorrow they would all end life. Or die. It was one thing to fight from the trenches, reflexively. Quite another to know ahead of time that you would stare into the face of the enemy and stab a blade into his heart. Or have him stab one into yours.

'Did you hear what Simmo here did this morning?' Dan broke the silence.

Jack sat up, needing to hear it, knowing if it involved Simmo it might make him laugh.

'Got in trouble for not saluting some snooty pom on the way up from the beach,' Dan continued, 'so he said, "Certainly sir, and what should I address you as? Captain Headless?"'

Simmo saluted them all and Jack laughed a little but the silence descended once more.

Tonight the joking around wasn't enough, not with death lurking over that rise. All thought could end tomorrow with the slice of a single bullet and Jack felt his mind empty in advance, resembling the stretch of ground above him; a desolate landscape devoid of life, stilled in anticipation of carnage.

Jack decided to provide his mind with some focus and slowly performed his nightly ritual, pulling out the Egyptian tin he had in his breast jacket pocket and examining the contents. He paid each his special attention: the letters he knew by heart, the jacaranda flower he'd picked off the ground on the last morning at home, now dried and flat, his mother's rosary beads, a small velvet pouch that held an exquisite sapphire and gold ring and, most treasured of all, a photo taken that last night at home. Just the two families at dinner, and innocent enough if he were shot and Dan was the one who sorted the tin's contents. No one would ever have to know that it was Veronica's face he stared at every night. His eyes roamed over the others and he missed them all, but always his gaze came back to land on her. It was her smile he traced. Her figure he tried to visualise through the grainy image and layers of clothing she'd worn. Her voice he tried to remember. Just Veronica, and the unlimited imaginings of his parched mind.

He usually held onto this for a good minute before carefully putting each item back into the tin and placing it in his pocket again, close to his heart, but tonight he couldn't seem to let it go, almost as though if he did he would never see her again.

Glancing over at Dan he saw he held on to a photo he kept in his wallet, a photo he also looked at every night, little realising Jack was a few feet away staring at the same girl. The more time Jack spent with Dan the more he regretted this secret between them, but it was something he knew he could never confess.

Along the trench he watched the men clean their rifles and say their farewells, the pit a sea of frightened men in private ritual, until each fell into an unwilling sleep.

Jack and Iggy waited together, awake, side by side, the minutes closing in towards the dawn, vaguely registering Simmo's snores among the nightly sounds of war.

'Still holding that photo.' Iggy nodded at his hand.

Jack had forgotten about it.

'May I?' Iggy took it and stared for a moment. 'Had a bit of a thing for her myself you know.'

'Vera?' Jack said, surprised. 'You never said.'

'Bit too much competition to be putting my horse in that race.' He shrugged.

'Yeah well, I don't suppose any of our chances of finishing are that high right now.' Jack sighed, leaning back to look up at the stars. 'Do me a favour, Ig?' he said after a while.

'I'm not writing a note to Sarge telling him you have a sore throat and can't go to war school, if that's what you're asking,' Iggy replied, lying down and handing the photo back.

Jack tried to smile. 'No, mate. Was kind of hoping you could see to it my folks get the tin. I put a little note in there for them.' He saw Iggy nod slowly before adding his last request. 'And Ig, if you ever get the chance...tell Vera...just tell her I'm sorry I acted like the back end of a horse.' He laughed a little, but his eyes had filled with tears and he cleared his throat.

'Hey I'm not bloody showing up at home without you. Pattie would skin me alive!' Iggy tried to joke back.

'Just do that for me, will you, Ig?'

Iggy's smile faded and he nodded at the sky. 'Sure thing, mate. If that's what you want.' And they watched the sky light up then fade for a while before he spoke again. 'While we're on the subject, do me a favour too, won't you? Take care of Ebony. I'd hate her to end up a tourist ride around the pyramids. And sing "The Parting Glass" for me. Always best to go out with a bit of class.'

'I can't very well sing it without my piano player, so it looks like I'm not coming back without you either. Have we got a deal?'

Iggy grinned. 'Deal.'

And so they fell asleep at last, knowing they would awake to death, but with the knowledge that they'd done what they could to say their farewells.

She walked through the grass and came to stand in front of him at last, the white dress brushing against him. She stroked his face, love in every touch, and he inhaled the scent of her, a lingering earthiness that clung to her hair. She'd been swimming in the creek again.

The bombs startled him out of his dream and he found he was covered in sweat, his skin on fire in the cool morning as the sergeant crept along the lines, waking the men and preparing them to advance. In an instant they were wide awake, clinging to their guns, some praying, others white faced, too scared to think, and a few determined, fiercely poised to get it over with.

'Take over, lads.' He nodded to Iggy and Jack. Jack nodded back, trying not to notice the flash of sympathy that crossed Sarge's grim countenance.

'Face the wall,' Iggy called, moving along, then doing so himself.

'Straight and fast, boys,' Jack called loudly, putting as much confidence into his voice as he could manage. Dan's brown eyes were wide as he looked over at him and Jack gave him what he hoped was a nod of assurance. 'We'll be right, mate.'

Dan nodded back, white faced.

Life paused for an unbearable few seconds.

Then the whistle pierced the air, slicing it like a knife. Boots hit the rungs of the ladders and suddenly they were running. Jack registered a pale-pink sky and an expanse of ground, then felt the blind panic of exposed prey. Men collapsed as the bullets found them, warm bodies spilling in sickening collision, then still. Jack's terror propelled him forward as he swerved and ran with Iggy and Dan by his side. Launching themselves into the first trench they shot their guns, stabbing blindly, ending the lives of those who would take their own.

The bombs pounded in close succession as they waited, strained against the sides, and prepared for advance towards the second trench. Heaving air, the whistle forced their legs once more.

They shot wildly as they ran, suddenly face to face with the Turks. Jack tried not to register expression, eyes, fear. He lunged, feeling the flesh give way beneath his bayonet, the blade exiting in a bright red smear. Launching over the carved, bloodied mess they slammed their bodies against the earth, hearts in frantic drum within their cages. Jack felt vaguely grateful the cries were silent against the roar of guns.

The third and final push came as they crossed deeper into Turkish lines, like fleas on the back of a lion. The lion roared, slashing at them, and there were heavy casualties alongside as men fell all around them. They found the next crevice on its back, desperately throwing themselves into the job of killing for a third time until the enemy ran out and they clung to the walls, stained with blood, every inch of their bodies wired.

The bombs were thick in a deafening rain and Jack felt a sudden weight on his leg.

'Jack.'

He couldn't hear the word, he could only see Dan's mouth move as he collapsed in a pile of flesh and limbs, as if he were suddenly made of parts that had no relation to each other. He held onto Jack as he slipped away, his last expression frozen in a plea to live. Jack watched those brown eyes lose their sight, saw the young face without its owner. A gaping hole was ripped in the place where Dan's heart had beaten only moments before.

'No!' Jack squeezed his own eyelids shut. No God. Please no.

'Oh God. Oh sweet Jesus,' Iggy cried out and Jack opened his eyes, seeing Iggy's stricken expression as he stared at Dan, shaking his head back and forth in denial.

'Don't look…we can't look.'

Iggy turned away and they stared in the opposite direction to wait for what hell would come next, survival instinct the only thing guiding their frantic minds.

If he'd a rational mind at the time Jack might have noticed his fingernails were clinging to the dirt deep to the cuticle as he hung against the trench and waited that morning. The sun was full by the time they realised all officers were either dead or injured and they were out of grenades. Jack and Iggy, although only corporals, were now in charge of their section and knew without ammunition they were all lost.

And all the while, Dan lay at their feet, an unbearable reality and a constant reminder of their probable fate.

The call came down the trenches from Major Glasgow for volunteers to go back for more supplies. Their objective of reaching the trenches at Dead Man's Ridge had been achieved, but the other battles at the Nek and Quinn's had been lost. They were stranded.

'I'll go,' Simmo volunteered.

'No,' Iggy said immediately, but Simmo squared his enormous shoulders.

'I'll do it, mate.' He turned to Jack, who gave him a grim nod.

Simmo took one gigantic breath then leapt out of the trench. Iggy held the scope but Jack noted his trembling hands and took it off him.

In the end Jack wished he hadn't looked.

Simmo was cut down just a few feet before making it and Jack watched helplessly in the mirror as he writhed in pain then lay still. Iggy didn't ask as he lowered the scope and Jack didn't tell him.

Several others volunteered, a few making it across but none making it back. After two agonising hours peppered by the pitiful sounds of the wounded, the major sent a new message informing them they had to retreat. Jack and Iggy stared up towards the open ground, ground they had given so much to gain, only to give it back. Both knew the Turks were now free to shoot at their retreating backs, but there was no other choice.

Jack took one last look at Dan, wishing to God he could bury him, before holding his hand up and giving the signal with Iggy.

They went as one, the survivors carrying the wounded, hopelessly exposed to heavy machine-gun attack. Jack saw the rip through Iggy's upper arm and his legs folding.

'No you bloody don't.' Jack grabbed at him and he hauled him along, every muscle straining those endless final yards until at last they fell together into the trench. Iggy looked at the blood spreading down his sleeve, then at Jack's retreating back.

'Where the hell do you think you're going?' he shouted.

Jack had seen Simmo a few feet out and decided it was one body he'd bloody well bury, grabbing his belt and dragging him in as well. His last thought was that someone had kicked him in the chest as he flew backwards into the wall, landing across Iggy.

By the time help arrived the trench was red with the lifeblood of what remained of the two hundred men who'd made up the 1st Australian Light Horse that morning. Only fifty remained unscathed.

Sixteen

Cairo

Veronica wet the towel and wiped the young lieutenant's forehead, soothing him as best she could. So many had arrived in the past few hours that she had barely time for such things, but this man had waited so patiently, in such terrible pain, and now the majority were settled into beds she felt she could spare him a few moments. He was young, perhaps not much older than she, and as slight as a girl, but there was a strength in him that she recognised in so many of these young officers and she suspected he commanded his men's respect.

The wounded began to pour through the doors again and Veronica put down the towel, patting her charge on the arm and moving across to inspect the new arrivals. She thought about tomorrow then tried to put it out of her mind again. After two weeks in Cairo she still hadn't let her brothers know she was there, although she thought they would likely have received word by now that she had joined the VAD, and that they probably weren't very happy about it. The last thing she'd wanted was to cause them even more worry by working alongside them green as a leaf, but fortunately an understanding doctor on board the ship had allowed her to spend time in the infirmary. Then, when she'd arrived, Sister Wilma George, Constance Dickson's cousin, had taken her under her wing for two weeks here at the holding station.

Tomorrow was the day she had been waiting for these many months, having secured a place at the hospital where her brothers worked, the converted 'Luna Park'. She hoped they would be proud of her and not try to shield her from her work, which had become a passion. Every day she saw men suffer indignities and torment, but with it came the opportunity to do something about it, even if it was only to be there for the wounded. If she had to put a word to it, this hellish place allowed her something she couldn't find at home: purpose.

Mick cursed as he read the letter again. What were his parents thinking allowing Vera to come over here to this? He hated to think that he couldn't protect her from witnessing the horrific costs this war was inflicting on body after body. It was hard enough for him and Tom, who worked long hours operating on them, often only to send them off to live their lives maimed, crippled, blinded or scarred – or back to the front, God help them. How could Vera possibly be expected to cope with it? A young, untrained, emotional girl? Especially with everything going on over in Turkey.

He looked across the ward towards Tom, who was examining some poor blighter's leg, yet still managing to lift the spirits of the man in the bed beyond the curtain by telling him some rather ribald jokes. He's amazing, my brother, Mick reflected. Never let the idea of despair overtake him, cracking jokes and making friends even here, in the worst nightmare imaginable. It made all the difference to their patients who often managed to laugh despite everything they had been through, thanks to Dr Tom.

'Hear we're getting some new recruits today,' Jerry Rankin, a Canadian doctor, said, stopping to stretch for a minute before starting his next procedure. Jerry was from Vancouver, where he'd worked mainly with a group of other doctors in the development of X-rays and their impact on operative procedures. He was therefore somewhat of an expert in limb surgery, so Egypt had come as a shock. He'd had to accustom himself to just sewing bits back on as well as possible. Still, he tried to bring some of the latest ideas into their makeshift hospital. Mick and Tom had been most interested in the rudimentary X-ray area he had set up out the back.

'Ambulance driver says there's a knockout blonde arriving,' Jerry told Mick, 'so keep back and give us ordinary fellas half a chance for once, will you?'

Mick sighed. 'Just keep away from anyone named Veronica.'

'Don't tell me you have a sweetheart hidden away?'

'No, a sister likely to arrive any day and definitely out of bounds to anyone who likes breathing,' Mick warned. No sooner had the words left his mouth than the new staff walked in, the last one causing him to drop the letter.

'Vera!'

She turned, letting out an ecstatic 'Mick!' before running across the hospital floor, much to the Matron's disapproval, and flinging herself into his arms. Mick hugged her tight, then pulled away to see her dear face.

'You're a bloody sight for sore eyes! I only got the letter today!' He shook his head, incredulous.

'No chance to object then.' She smiled up at him. 'Where's Tom?'

Mick looked over to where Tom stood, taking off his gloves and staring at Vera in shock. She rushed over to him, laughing, as his face broke into a huge grin and he let out a great whoop.

Matron scolded as Tom and Mick took turns swinging her about and talking excitedly. 'You're disturbing the wounded!' she raged, shaking one fat finger.

'Yeah well they're disturbing my Egyptian holiday,' Tom quipped, causing the conscious soldiers to laugh.

Mick led the trio outside and over to grab a quick cup of tea in the mess, introducing an awestruck Jerry and telling him to give them a yell if new casualties arrived. Veronica's eyes were wide as they walked past roller coasters and rides.

'We've put some of the customers in the Haunted House,' Mick told her, explaining how the lack of room had led to beds at the ferris wheel and even the ice-skating rink, with the operating theatre in the former ticket office.

'Goodness, imagine waking up to that!' Veronica exclaimed.

'Seems kind of appropriate to me,' Tom mused, draping his arm around her as they walked. 'Roller coasters, haunted houses, everything feeling like a bit of a circus…'

Veronica laughed, hugging him close.

'What the bloody hell are you doing here?' He shook his head.

'Seriously, what did you have to do to convince Mother?' Mick added.

'What do you mean? She's obviously still tied up in the kitchen as we speak,' said Tom. The trio laughed again and as they walked into the mess Mick figured whatever reservations he had about her being here, it was damn good to see her.

He just didn't know how he was going to be able to break things to her in person.

About ten minutes later she'd figured out something was up. Yes, they were happy to see her and yes, Tom was making jokes as usual and Mick was talking earnestly about the hospital, but something else was going on.

'Any news about the boys?' she said, trying to sound casual.

Tom and Mick went very quiet and neither seemed to want to meet her eye.

'You've heard something haven't you?' She tried not to let panic overwhelm her. 'I saw a few from the 1st down at the holding station. They said there was a big push a few days ago.' Mick twirled his fork on the table and Veronica placed her hand over his.

'Please…' she said, looking from Mick to Tom.

Mick cleared his throat. 'There was a push from the 1st a few days back, yes, and some of the wounded are only just arriving now. They've had a lot of issues with evacuation and overcrowding on the hospital ships.'

She watched his face closely as he played with his cigarette case and felt her heart beat in her throat.

'What aren't you telling me?' She swung her gaze to Tom. 'Oh God…oh God no…'

The dread flushed through her and she felt the air close in like a suffocating blanket. Jack.

'It's Dan,' Mick began gently, reaching for her hand. Veronica felt the sorrow shoot through her stomach and clenched his fingers, fighting her tears. And to her shame something else too. Relief that it wasn't Jack. Then Dan's face flooded her mind and she began to shake. Dan. Her friend.

'He's gone, Vera,' Tom said softly.

'No…'

'One of their mates, Simmo, arrived yesterday and told us Dan died right next to Jack. It was instant, which is one mercy I suppose,' he told her.

'Jack's a bit of a hero by all accounts,' Mick added.

'Dragged Simmo and Iggy into the trenches and saved their lives. Simmo said he was unconscious so he doesn't know any more than that about Jack…or Iggy,' Tom said, deciding not to tell her that Simmo saw Jack afterwards on a stretcher, 'pale as a ghost and all clammy'. He and Tom suspected typhoid fever.

'He only knew that much because someone else told him. I'm so sorry, dearest.'

Veronica stared at them, willing them to tell her it wasn't true. Dan was dead. Barely twenty years old and as good a man as anyone would ever be likely to meet. She thought of his parents in Braidwood, losing their youngest child. She thought of the carved initials on the rock and the secret she'd carried each day. A man who loved her was gone.

But Jack's alive. Veronica closed her eyes and felt guilt consume her that she could think about that after hearing her fiancé was dead and lying in a Turkish battlefield.

She opened her eyes to her brother's concerned gazes as they waited for her to speak but she had nothing to say. How could she possibly voice what she was truly feeling? That Dan had been her secret fiancé but she actually didn't love him? That part of her was relieved they hadn't said it was Jack? How could she show such a callous heart to her two loving brothers? Finally she said the only truth she was willing to share.

'I can't imagine him not alive.' Dan Hagan had been life itself, a bundle of energy and youth, impossibly now as lifeless as the stone walls around them.

All too soon the messenger came to tell them more wounded were on their way, and they returned to their work, but Veronica carried with her two new weights upon her heart. Her guilt for not mourning Dan as he deserved, and the enormity of what bit at all their heels, because it was no longer just a fear. Death was now an intimate acquaintance. Now it held one of their own.

Seventeen

Gallipoli

The guns lit up the sky as the boat pulled away from the shoreline. It moved steadily towards the hospital ship, whose lights looked almost festive in the night sky. But the large cross on the ship's tower glowed ominously, spilling a red pathway across the water, like a haemorrhaging animal. From his stretcher on the floor of the boat, Jack watched the dark cliffs of Gallipoli sporadically light up, thousands of men struggling against the walls like confused ants under a piece of glass.

Jack still didn't know how he was alive. His chest hurt like hell but there was no blood, yet somehow he couldn't seem to lift his arms to investigate the damage. They were so heavy. He supposed he had concussion or shock or something. It felt so hot that he kept wondering if it was day, especially when the sky was illuminated. It was confusing. Perhaps it was day after all and he'd been drifting in and out of sleep. He was sure Simmo had been stretchered past him, alive and saying something Jack couldn't hear over the shelling, and Iggy had also been taken aboard at some point. Was that only today? Had they really survived or was it just dreams telling him what he wanted to be true?

Jack stared up at the top of the ridge and thought about Dan, lying there in the trench with the Turks, a corpse they would throw away, uncaring. And yet, only this morning, there he'd been, looking over at him. Trusting him.

It didn't seem possible that he was gone; that there was no longer a heart left to beat within him.

That he didn't speak or think or move or laugh.

The memories crowded in of legs, arms, faces strewn across in a bloody pile as they ran the last few yards to make it back. Bodies housing men no longer. Mates. He thought of the mothers and sweethearts, fathers, babies, grandparents and children, all waving goodbye with such faith in the mad adventure that came to this. He felt their sorrow wave over him and, along with it, the desperate urge to pull every one of the dead into an Anzac trench to bring them home. He wished they could bury them all in Australian soil, where their loved ones could erect a fitting headstone and lay flowers every Sunday.

As the boat reached the ship and they hoisted him up he took one last look at Gallipoli and knew that part of him would remain there too, lying with the dead, until the soil found their collective dust and the breeze whispered their spirits across the cove.

Jack knew he had changed in that place – that the breeze would carry with it the man he used to be; who they all were on the other side of time before living included killing. Every man who had landed there would leave the ghost of his former self behind.

Jack overheard them talking through his delirium as he moved in and out of consciousness, his body on fire. The doctor had said on his way through earlier he would need to cut the poor chap's arm off but there was some doubt expressed in the nurses' whisperings: they believed the arm could be saved if they could get him to Egypt in time. Trouble was, they couldn't find the doctor to approve the inclusion of the man in the emergency transfer as the last bodies were being loaded to the departing vessel. Jack managed to focus on the man and, after squinting hard to make sure, suddenly began to cry out.

'Iggy! Oh sweet Lord! Don't do it! He's a musician…a piano player! Don't do it, for God's sake!' The nurses rushed forward, trying to calm him down as he started to crawl off the bed towards his mate. 'Don't do it! You can't!' He wept, falling to the floor of the hospital ship, hysterical. '*Iggy! No! You can't! Get your bloody hands off him! Get away!*'

The doctor arrived and helped the struggling nurses restrain him, finally grasping what Jack was saying. Walking over to Iggy's bed, he gave him a quick examination before sighing and shaking his head. 'I just don't think he'll make the journey. He's too weak.'

'He won't want to live like that. He won't…' Jack sobbed, struggling to stay conscious, his head rolling from side to side as the nurses held him down. But it was no use and, as the dark engulfed him, his last thought was of Iggy's talented hand lying on the sheet.

Veronica had been trying to shake the feeling all day but it had only grown stronger. The main influx of casualties had tapered off as the hospital spread to capacity, every possible space housing a bed, but still Jack and Iggy didn't come. She knew there was a good chance they had been sent to one of the other hospitals, but it didn't seem to make sense that they wouldn't send them here with the majority of wounded from their regiment. Unless they were still at the holding station.

Mick and Tom had worked tirelessly since dawn and now, at nine o'clock in the evening, were finally washing up and taking off their blood-soaked coverings.

'I need you to drive me to the holding station,' Veronica told them straight out, putting on her hat as she did so.

'What the blazes for?' Mick watched her don gloves with almost enough energy left to feel annoyed.

'It just doesn't make sense they're not here,' she said simply. 'We need to hurry.'

Tom sighed, knowing it was useless to argue, but Mick gave it a go, pointing out the nonsense of driving there in the dark, at this time of night, when the seriously wounded had already been transferred and they were needed on call here. Putting on his coat Tom walked to the door, Veronica following briskly.

'What am I supposed to say to your patients if they wake up?' Mick admonished him in exasperation.

'Tell them the most stubborn woman in the world owes them a kiss good night,' came the answer.

They barely spoke as Tom steered the ambulance through the night, arriving at the station without incident. Veronica leapt from the car and ran straight up to a tall man smoking a cigarette outside, recognising him as the ambulance driver who had been delivering patients all day.

'Captain know you've pilfered his bus?' He nodded at them in greeting.

'Just checking on a late arrival. Was there a patient called Dwyer transferring today?'

'Not today. He and the other chap are too weak. Don't know how they made the trip to be honest…Hey, where ya goin'?'

Veronica ran into the building, straining her eyes down the rows of mostly empty beds and recognising one dark and one red head in the corner. She and Tom wove their way through; her heart was in her mouth as she came face to face with them both. Grasping Jack's hands at last and feeling his brow, she searched wildly for the nurses in charge.

'He's burning up,' she told Tom, pulling back the sheets.

'So's Iggy. Nurse!' he called out. A solitary nurse came out of her office in surprise.

'What do you think you're doing? Move away from those patients!'

Tom silenced her by pointing at the patch on his coat and gave them a quick examination before responding. 'When did they arrive?'

'This morning. I'm sorry, doctor, I didn't realise…they were too weak to risk transfer. Dr Sommers was going to send for a second opinion in the morning regarding surgery for Corporal Dwyer. Corporal Murphy's fever has been high all day. He's soaking through the towels quicker than I can change them.'

Tom examined Iggy's shoulder and arm and turned to the ambulance driver, who had been watching with interest.

'Help me get the stretchers.'

'Righto, Doc,' he responded, and they rushed outside.

'Is it all right if I help myself to towels, Sister George?' Veronica asked her former superior.

She looked at Veronica's face for the first time. 'Goodness, is that you, O'Shay?'

'Yes. Do you mind?' She went to the store cupboard, not waiting for a reply, and fetched some towels and a bowl of fresh water. Now that she'd found Jack she had no intention of leaving his side.

She stroked his face, love in every touch, and he inhaled the scent of her, knowing it was her by the lingering earthy scent clinging to her hair. She'd been swimming in the creek again.

Opening his eyes he felt the breath catch in his throat at the sight of her, softened in a golden light. How did she get here? Was she dead too?

He closed his eyes again. It didn't matter. If she was here then heaven was fine by him.

The first thing Jack thought when he awoke was that he'd lost his mind. Was that a ferris wheel overhead? He wished he could go back to the other place, where Veronica was. Then he remembered.

'Iggy…' His voice felt distant and his throat ached with thirst, but he tried again, louder this time: 'Iggy.'

Then she came after all, although she didn't have the scent of the creek about her. More like soap and fresh linen. But she was bathed in light and so beautiful.

'What happened to…you?' he asked the vision.

'What do you mean?' She was crying, but she was smiling too.

'How did you die?'

'I'm not dead, my love,' and she held his hand. 'See?' It didn't pass through him. It was warm and real flesh. And he could feel it.

'Vera?' he choked in disbelief. He drew her closer and touched her hair and her face. 'We're…alive?'

'Very much.' She was crying in earnest now, clinging to his hands and kissing them.

'And…Iggy?'

'He's alive and with two fully functioning flippers, thanks to you,' Tom told him from behind Veronica. He stared in disbelief at the sight of Tom, Mick and Iggy, the latter lying in the next bed, complete with bandaged but attached arm.

'Am I home?'

'About as close as you're going to get in Egypt, mate,' said a grinning Mick, coming in closer to check his pulse and forehead as Veronica poured him some water. He stared at her uniform.

'How on earth did you talk your mother into that?'

'Same way she talked me into driving down to the holding station to search for you.' Tom shrugged helplessly. 'Pure stubbornness.'

Jack shook his head, then looked back at Iggy's arm. 'What happened?'

'Oh this little scratch? Fell off a ferris wheel,' Iggy responded. Jack looked taken aback then burst out laughing. They all joined in until the tears rolled.

'What is it with that bloody thing?' He gestured at the ride, setting them off again.

Jerry walked past just then, and Mick called him over, introducing him.

'This is Dr Jerry Rankin, the man who saved Iggy's arm. Just so happened we had a bit of an expert handy, 'scuse the pun.' They all laughed again, so happy they couldn't seem to stop it bubbling forth.

'And…how…what about me?' Jack managed.

'Typhoid,' Tom informed him. 'Somehow you've managed to come to the other side of the world and go to war but instead of getting shot you nearly die from a fever.'

Jack rubbed at his chest. 'But…but I was shot, wasn't I?'

'Not quite.' To his surprise Iggy pulled out a battered tin from his pocket, which Jack recognised as his.

'Reckon we should make these compulsory issue,' he said, passing it over. Jack traced the deep valley in the centre in amazement. The image of the winged beetle that held the sun was obliterated, and he registered that it had indeed protected him. It had saved his life, stopping the bullet from piercing his heart.

Veronica stroked his arm as he held the tin, acknowledging his close shave with death. The others shuffled and cleared their throats and ostentatiously left them alone. 'Vera, I don't know if they have told you…'

'About Dan? Yes, I know.' Her face clouded and she looked away.

Jack looked at her downcast face and felt ashamed. What kind of man covets his mate's fiancée when he probably isn't even buried yet?

'I'm so sorry. He was...a good friend.' Jack eyes clouded with tears. 'And a damn fine soldier. Bullseye, they called him. Crack shot.' He wiped at his eyes. 'I wish...I could have got him back to you safe. I'm...I'm sorry.' He meant it. He would give anything for Dan not to have died. Even Veronica. 'I know he would have wanted me to tell you that he thought of you...always.'

Veronica nodded and they sat for a while, as Jack traced the dent in the tin thoughtfully. Eventually he let himself reach for her hand, squeezing it with what little strength he could muster before his eyelids closed once more, and wishing the barriers didn't exist that made him have to let it go.

Eighteen

London, England, October 1915

Rose was late for lunch at the Savoy as she pushed through the crowds surrounding the entrance and dashed inside, giving the doorman a brief impression of a daringly short skirt that edged towards her knee as he opened the heavy glass doors. Clarkson rose in greeting, his expression wary as he noted her expensive black coat and matching suit. She gave him her hand and an amused smile before ordering a drink.

'What's the matter, Clarkson, haven't you ever seen a woman in black before?'

'Not out of mourning,' he replied.

'The whole city's in mourning. It's considered bad taste to wear bright colours these days, haven't you heard?' She sipped at her wine and gave him a once over. 'You look positively thin. Don't they feed you boys?'

'We get by.' He signalled to the waiter for another scotch. 'Why am I here, Rose?'

'My, my. You're being a bit frosty today. Can't a girl just want to catch up with a friend from home?'

'I would hardly say we are friends, considering the way you treated my brother-in-law.'

Rose paused. 'Yes, congratulations on your wedding. I was sorry I couldn't be there.'

'I don't recall asking you.' He lit a cigarette and waited.

'Perhaps the invitation got lost in the mail,' she smiled, 'regardless, I'm sure you'll never have a dull moment with Pattie. I certainly didn't,' she added dryly, signalling to the waiter for another drink. 'Were there many there?'

'Just close friends and family,' said Clarkson. Truth was it had been a very small affair with Tom, Mick and Jack already gone, but he'd enjoyed nearly a full week with his bride at Bondi Beach before shipping out. The memories of it kept the loneliness at bay, especially at night.

'I hear you are getting some flying time. That was very fast. You must be making friends in high places,' she said with a little laugh at her own joke, but something in her tone made his eyes narrow.

'Who do you need me to introduce you to, Rose?' He drew on his cigarette, watching her casually.

She attempted an innocent look before apparently deciding it was easier to be direct.

'Major Hitchcock.'

'Why Hitchcock? Hold on, let me guess. You want to be invited to tea.' Major Hitchcock was at his base and Clarkson was under his direct command, a fact of which he was sure Rose was well aware. The Hitchcocks had a beautiful estate just outside of Bath and Rose certainly wouldn't be the first woman to hanker after the social coup of such an invitation. The question was, why did Rose want it badly enough to risk exposure from the only man in London who knew what kind of person she really was?

'Not exactly. I want an interview for a job with his wife.'

Clarkson was thrown. 'What on earth for?'

'I want to become a member of FANY. Surely you've heard of them by now.'

He had, of course. The First Aid Nursing Yeomanry were fast building a reputation as a vital medical unit in France, where they had set up a hospital in Calais. Unlike their sisters in the VAD and nursing, who were under the strict supervision of the army, members of the Yeomanry were independent – and renowned for their daring. They were currently taking matters into their own hands in France, having found untended masses of wounded soldiers in desperate need of care. Clarkson stared at Rose, trying to comprehend her undoubtedly ulterior motive.

'I suppose you know Iggy's joined the Light Horse,' she began. Clarkson nodded, waiting. 'It's useless all of this sitting about when the boys are over there facing goodness knows what, and London has grown so tiresome with all of these ridiculous restrictions. I feel so bored by it all. Elspeth Hitchcock is interviewing women as we speak and, well, being Australian and without the right contacts as yet, I need a recommendation.'

'Go on,' said Clarkson.

'I learnt a thing or two growing up watching my father and we both know I'm useful in a crisis.'

'A snake bite hardly compares to someone's leg being blown off, Rose.' He paused, swirling his drink for a moment. 'Why do you really want to go?'

'I told you– '

'How's Gregory?'

Rose crossed her legs and smiled nonchalantly. 'Busy. So, can you get me an interview?'

'Seems to me he might have something to say about his wife going abroad and being in the line of fire…And if I know Gregory he won't be too keen on the idea of you being around all of those men for months on end. Look what happened last time you were out of his sight.'

She let that one go, draining her glass then tapping it thoughtfully. 'Are you going to help me or not?'

Clarkson tilted his head to one side and considered her request, watching her beautiful face, trying to guess at the thoughts racing through her mind.

'I suppose it's no skin off my nose if you want to go and join the Yeomanry. God knows they're short out there from what I've heard.' He stood and finished his drink, throwing a few notes on the table. 'Just do me one favour, Rose: don't tell anyone I've helped you. I have a wife who might not be quite so understanding.'

She found herself able to take her first deep breath once he'd left, her face clouding over as she considered her next move. One step closer to her goal; she felt her chest constrict with anticipation of the next one she would need to make, the one that would release her from the hell of her own creation.

Her composure belied her dread as she crossed the room, tossing her coat over one shoulder and causing several heads to turn in admiration, but Rose had long since got past caring. Whatever hope she'd held for happiness lay on the floor of Cabin One aboard *The Princess Dream* and nothing could ever bring it back.

'Tell my wife I need to see her in my office as soon as she arrives, Collins.'

'Very good, sir,' Collins replied, taking his coat. Gregory pushed open the polished oak door and strode over to his desk, throwing his gloves down and pouring himself a drink. He gazed sightlessly out the mullioned windows, his mind racing as he replayed the meeting he'd just had over in his mind. Hiring a private investigator was a mere formality. He'd never expected her to actually dare to court danger and see another man, yet that very afternoon the report had been clear. She had been seen having lunch with no other than Clarkson, in broad daylight at the Savoy of all places. The very place he'd lunched only yesterday with some very important business associates. His hand gripped the desk at the thought of them seeing her there, alone at lunch with another man.

The front door opened and he waited for her to enter the room. She did so after a few minutes, smoothing her hair with one still-gloved hand.

'You wanted to see me?' she asked.

He struck her hard across the face, causing her to reel backwards, slamming her left side against the desk before she collapsed to the floor.

'I won't be made a fool of, Rose,' he told her, his voice low. 'If I ever hear of you meeting with another man again you'll be sent home alone and Elizabeth will stay here with me, away from the influence of her slut of a mother. Do you understand?'

'She…she's only a baby, Gregory…please. She needs to be somewhere safe. These Zeppelin raids– '

'Elizabeth will remain in London with me. As will you, my wife, as long as you behave as a wife should.'

Rose pulled herself to her feet slowly, grunting in pain. 'Gregory, I promise you, I was only meeting Clarkson to ask about home. I would never betray you.'

'What about Jack Murphy, Rose? How can I ever trust a woman who was already pregnant when I married her?'

'She's yours! Gregory, for pity's sake, look at her!' Rose pleaded with him, pointing to the photo on the mantelpiece of a white-haired child wearing christening robes.

'Yet you would have married Murphy and fobbed her off as his. My child. It didn't even occur to me until later that you must have been lifting your skirts for him right from the start. How else did you plan to get away with it? You never would have told him the truth. Just like you never would have told me...bloody *bitch*.' He hit her again, this time grabbing her throat after he slapped her face and squeezing her chin so she faced him. Tears fell down her cheeks.

'I know she's mine. Unfortunately my child didn't get to choose her mother, but I choose whether or not you are fit to be in her life, so you'd better start warming my bed again and doing as you're told. That includes keeping your legs together around other men and staying at home, or so help me Rose I'll make you pay before I send you away.' He shoved her backwards before walking out.

Rose made her trembling way to the nursery and picked Elizabeth up gently from her nap, cradling her close as she sat in the rocking chair beneath the window.

It was the first time he had mentioned Jack since that terrible night in the cabin on their honeymoon when he'd noticed her rounding belly in the morning light and confronted her about her pregnancy. She'd still felt hopeful enough to confess she was carrying his child until he'd smashed her head hard against the wall, accusing her of tricking him into marrying her as she carried another man's bastard. He'd kicked her until she was unconscious on the floor, the blood pouring from her head into a dark pool, causing the maid to scream when she'd arrived later with the linen. Gregory was in the bar by then, dismissing the incident as his wife being 'clumsy' when called to the infirmary to speak with the ship's doctor. He never once came to visit her for the rest of the voyage as the older man fought to save both her and the baby, finally coming to inform Gregory that both would probably survive just days before they docked. Despite the doctor's protestations, the captain treated the whole affair as 'an unfortunate accident', and Rose saw him a few months later driving an expensive new car about town.

She rocked Elizabeth, her tears drying as she smiled down at the serene face of her beautiful little daughter. Funny how she never cried, this child whose womb had been housed within a body wracked by worry then pain. She had arrived on a Sunday morning, a tiny child but perfectly formed, easily passed off as 'an early baby', due in part, Rose was sure, to her own ill-health during the pregnancy.

Gregory had walked in and taken a long look at the infant before instructing Rose to name his daughter after his mother, Elizabeth. Then he left without so much as a glance in her direction. His so honoured mother, the widow Lady Chambers, was equally cold, arriving one day in her black robes to observe 'the child' and inform Rose which schools she would be attending. She stayed all of ten minutes before leaving in a matching black coach, like a malevolent spider crawling back to her lair. It was the only time Rose had met her and she hoped fervently it would be the last.

Rose had expected him to come back to her bed after the birth but as yet he had avoided her altogether, seeing her only briefly in the mornings at breakfast, or occasionally at dinner, when her presence was required at his table. So it had been until today.

She knew he would expect it of her now.

Rose shuddered to imagine how his violence would distort their already borderline dangerous bedroom passion. What was once a game of lust-fuelled domination would surely tip into darkness. She prayed Clarkson could arrange the meeting as soon as possible. Everything depended upon it.

Nineteen

It was a bitterly cold day but Clarkson sat outside the hangar anyway, waiting for his flight time. He sipped on his tea for a while, holding it in his gloved hands to warm them before pulling the letter from Pattie out of his pocket and re-reading it yet again.

> *Your daughter has a remarkable talent for throwing things. If she weren't only four months old I would swear she does it on purpose! Only yesterday I was changing her and she grabbed the talc and threw it at my head. I was nearly knocked out, let me tell you. Aside from her violent ways our May is adorable in every way and she does have extremely good taste, as you can see from the photo.*

Clarkson held up the picture of little May wearing Buggles and grinned, wishing he could see the exact colour of her eyes beneath the fur. He guessed they were the same blue as Pattie's. Re-reading the rest of the letter with amusement, Clarkson paused, savouring the last few lines. Tracing over the ink, he ached to kiss Pattie goodbye for real as he counted her little Xs across the bottom. Eleven. He grinned again. God he missed her.

A man waved at him from the front steps of HQ and Clarkson recognised him as Major Hitchcock's secretary. He ran over and the man ushered him in.

'The major said he'll see you now.' Clarkson had forgotten all about Rose and her request and quickly composed himself for the interview, wondering why he was bothering.

Even in London, that woman was nothing but trouble.

She stared at the back of the door, dreading the sound of his footsteps but knowing they would come. Just one more night, she reminded herself. One more night until she could hold Elizabeth again. One more night and she would never have to feel his fists upon her, his hands, his heavy form as it crushed her beneath him and ripped away whatever was left of her sensuality. What had been a beautiful part of Rose's life had become a painful, violent assault of body and mind and soul. Gone was any desire to be touched because touch now meant hate and blood and tearing. Touch had destroyed her life.

Standing up she walked over to the mirror and stared at the sorry soul who lived there. Pale, hollow and thin; a ravaged face, a battered body. Her once rounded curves had faded to the bone, her creamy complexion was now mottled in purple and green bruises. She looked about the room for something to cover herself in but found only silks and satins, lace and delicate cottons. Like a slave in a whorehouse to be dressed up for the show, she mused vaguely, shrouding herself in a blanket instead and huddling against the window.

She stared out at the world, registering that it moved on without her in bemusing normality; a world where sunshine met the skin and a woman could hold her child's hand, eat ice cream and laugh. A world she would fight to rejoin tomorrow, regardless of the enormous risk, because Rose knew that despite everything Gregory had done to her over the past weeks, locking her in her room, banning her from her own child, the violent abuse, the raping of her fragile body, he had not broken her. She was stronger than all of it because she had a secret weapon he could not destroy: her determination to be with Elizabeth. She knew that to her dying day she would fight and scheme, manipulate and claw her way back to her child and away from him, even if it truly meant that dying day came far sooner than it should.

The footsteps sounded and she braced herself as the door swung open and his shadow crossed her. She didn't speak as he ripped into her flesh, his hands cold, his body an enormous force ripping at her breasts, her thighs, inflicting as much pain as he could in between her legs as he thrust inside her in a sudden assault. Weeks earlier she would have begged, cried, reasoned, attempted to oblige him, but all of her efforts had only furthered his anger. She knew it was best to lie still and silent until it was over, squeezing her eyes shut against the blinding agony he inflicted, telling herself it would eventually end. Swallowing her cries of pain.

He finished with a grunt and rolled off her, spent. Rose vaguely registered the sound of Elizabeth's baby talk down the hall and focused on it, blocking out his heavy breathing.

'Put something on that hides those bones tonight. I have guests for dinner,' he ordered as he sat up and began to dress. She shrugged her way into her robe, hands shaking, and nodded. 'Answer me when I talk to you, slut,' he spat. 'You look like a threepenny whore. Put some makeup on and hide your shame.' He stared at the swollen eye and cut lip he had given her two days earlier. 'On second thoughts, forget it. I don't think anyone could eat looking at that.' He shoved her back and she felt her head collide with the bedhead before he strode out of the room, bolting the door.

Rose sat unsteadily, rubbing the back of her head and wondering if she would pass out. It didn't matter as long as she was able to stand and walk out of here in the morning. There was a soft knock at the door and she told Mary to enter, struggling to stand.

'Good evening, m'lady. Oh, sweet saints, don't get up. There now.' Mary bustled in, rushing to her side as she noticed the blood on the sheets. 'What's happened now? Oh me poor love…' Mary looked to the back of Rose's head but found more blood running down her mistress's leg. She tended to her gently, changing the bedclothes and helping her into a warm bath, laying out towels, all the while talking in hushed tones of the plans they had laid.

'I'll come at dawn. The master won't be up after I've slipped a little something in his nightcap, and Collins is off to see his brother tonight. I've packed all the things and they're stored down at the port, so not to worry there. There's more than enough money from the sale of your fur so I've set it up that you'll have cash in the valise and the tickets are all paid. Ah no, pet, let me,' she interrupted herself, helping Rose from the bath as delicately as she tended the baby, wincing at the state of Rose's body and cursing the master under her breath.

Rose held onto every word, knowing the plan already of course but comforted by Mary's calm tone that made the end of the nightmare seem more possible. Mary reminded her of her mother Mildred, with her soft comforts in Irish and gentle fussing. A kindness she'd never really appreciated. How she longed for her now.

'I'll bring yer dinner up and please try to eat, m'lady. Ye need yer strength.'

Rose thanked her and lay against the fresh linen, physically depleted but determination renewed. No matter what else happened, this would be the last time she lay in the aftermath of his assault. Whether her escape was successful or not one thing was true: if there was a next time she probably wouldn't survive.

Twenty

Cairo, November 1915

The rooms were filled with contrasting shadows and brilliant light, the glare of bandages and bed linen burning in apricot hue as the last of the sunset sank below the edge of the windowsills. Jack picked his way through, offering greetings and shaking hands with those whose faces were familiar, nodding to other poor blighters whose gruesome injuries were reflected in their haunted eyes. He was glad to be leaving this nightmare, although discharge from rehabilitation unfortunately meant rejoining the war and his battalion, or what was left of it, at the Mena camp. Jack definitely wasn't complaining though. At least he would still be in Egypt for a little longer and he would gladly take any more days that he could to be near Veronica.

His recent promotion to lieutenant had enabled him to swing a few advantages his way for his date with her tonight and he had the evening planned like a general before battle: dinner at a private little restaurant on the river, champagne courtesy of the resourceful Simmo followed by a walk in the gardens. There he would show her the contents of the tin that saved his life, ending with the little velvet pouch.

Jack paused at the gate and lit a cigarette, surprised at how nervous he was. Surely she would say yes. She was still in love with him, wasn't she? These past weeks it had been difficult to tell, busy as she was with nursing the steady stream of wounded, and army hospitals were hardly romantic places. But there was something else amiss as well. Something in the way she avoided his eyes and the sadness around her mouth when she smiled. Perhaps she had been in love with Dan after all. This thought plagued him until she finally arrived half an hour later, draping a scarf over her hair and out of breath.

'Sorry, I had a patient who wanted to get a letter home to his mother and I'd promised him all week to help him write it, then Matron had me change dressings at the last minute and anyway... I'm sorry I didn't have time to dress up a bit more. I know you want to celebrate tonight before you go.'

She sounded nervous but Jack was too struck by her appearance to care. The aqua green of her dress made her seem otherworldly, fresh and clean in a dirty, sweaty dustbowl. He wanted to undress her on silk sheets and revel in the life exuding from every perfect pore of her skin. It was intoxicating after so much death and destruction to be around something so beautiful. So whole. She was staring at him expectantly and he shook himself back to the plan.

'Shall we?' he asked, offering his arm. She tucked her hand in and, as they walked to dinner, he congratulated himself that he was the luckiest man in Cairo.

About an hour later he was wishing he were back at that point and starting over. 'Don't you like the lamb?'

Veronica had been toying with her food for a while and Jack was running out of conversation starters. For God's sake, it never used to be this hard to talk to her.

'Oh yes, it's fine.'

'You said that before when I asked you if you like the view.'

'Did I?' she said surprised, staring out across the Nile. 'It's lovely. Really.'

Jack watched the boats glide along with their yellow lights and sighed. 'All right, Vera, spill it.'

'Spill what?'

'What's going on in that little blonde head of yours?'

'Nothing,' she said again, staring down.

'Blast it!' Jack tossed his napkin on the table and pointed across at her. 'You're not going to do this. Not this time.'

'Do what?'

'Sabotage us!'

'Me sabotage?' Veronica glared at him. 'You're the one who… who– '

'Who what? Made a fool of himself over the wrong girl? Rejected you? Left you waiting?'

Veronica stared back, unable to disagree.

'But I grew up, Vera, and came to my senses…'

'You were too late,' she blurted out.

'You didn't wait for me.'

'You gave me no indication I should!'

'And you said yes to Dan– '

Veronica stood up, pushing back her chair. 'Don't mention his name.'

'Why? Because you can't bear to hear it or you can't bear to hear it from me?'

She walked towards the door, pushing chairs out of the way in her hurry, and he followed her out onto the street, tossing money to the waiter as they left.

They walked in silence as Jack searched for the right words, noting the strain in Veronica's face and the tears she brushed aside.

'We can't just pretend he never existed.'

'I don't want to talk about it,' she said, walking swiftly.

'Well we're going to, damn it,' Jack replied, stopping. 'Because right now it's like he is standing right here, between us.'

'I can't,' Veronica said, her steps slowing and she bent forward, hugging herself.

'Because you were so in love with him?' The words cut him.

'No. It's just…it's wrong…it's all wrong.'

'What's wrong?'

'Us!' she cried, the tears falling as she turned towards him. 'We are wrong. How can we be together now after…after Dan died and I was…'

Jack held his breath. 'Heartbroken?'

'*Relieved*. I was relieved because…because it wasn't you.'

Jack felt his heart constrict and reached out his arms, pulling her close against it. 'I know, darling, I know.' He rocked her close, loving her with a fierce intensity. 'But don't you see? You weren't glad he died: you were happy that I lived. Don't you think I felt guilty too? Asking myself if part of me was glad he was out of the way? But I'm not. How could I be? He was a good man and a good mate.' His voice broke, memories of Dan flooding him – his laugh, his trusting nature, his lifeless body. 'A good mate.'

They stood together, letting the pain flow, until a group of soldiers wandered near, singing loudly.

Jack took her hand and steered her away to the nearby gardens, sitting her down next to him on a bench beneath a massive fig tree.

'I want to show you something,' he said, reaching into his pocket and taking out the tin. 'Every night in the trenches Dan took out his photo and I took out mine.' She held the photo and stared. 'We both loved you, Vera. Do you really think he would have wanted you to be unhappy for the rest of your life?'

Veronica shook her head slowly.

'I kept this too. A jacaranda flower to remind me of home, the letters you all sent which I re-read a hundred times...and this.' Jack upended the little pouch and the ring landed in his palm. 'Even though I never thought I could give it to you, it was still yours in my heart. Vera, you deserve to be loved. You deserve to be a bride and a mother and a grandmother and a great-grandmother.' Jack slipped the ring on her finger and it glittered in the moonlight. 'Veronica O'Shay, will you marry me?'

Veronica stared at the beautiful stone then back at Jack's face, the face of the man who she had always loved, and suddenly she knew it wasn't wrong to do so at all. In fact it was so very, very right.

'Yes,' she breathed onto his lips as he kissed her at last, because for all that had been lost, they both knew now that whatever was left had to be taken in this moment. Such was love in war.

Twenty-one

December 1915

The bride wore a dress she'd had made for the occasion by Tom's friend Ammon, the shopkeeper who had sold Jack the little tin that had saved his life. Ammon was not only a seller of fortunate trinkets and precious rings, he was also a fine tailor, insisting on sewing the dress himself from the softest ivory silk. Veronica had shown him a picture from a magazine and he'd made a beautiful job if it, the soft tone a perfect match against her skin. In her hair she wore a single blue lotus flower instead of a veil – Ammon's wife Nefi told them the bloom was the symbol for beauty and healing. Jack figured that summed her up perfectly.

She had become a favourite among staff and patients alike, her kind ways making the men feel nurtured, something all of them were starved of after months of being away. Many envied Jack as he stood at the makeshift altar in the gardens. His eyes filled with love as she walked towards him – he doubted any woman had ever looked more breathtaking than his Vera, with her soft gold hair, and her blue eyes shining at him. Tom and Mick had managed to borrow Delilah the madam's piano and had it sitting beneath the giant fig nearby; an almost fully recovered Iggy played his own interpretation of Mendelssohn's Wedding March, a lilting, romantic version that was his best man's gift to them both.

They spoke their vows before the priest and took communion, bowing their heads as he blessed them both before rising to hear the groomsmen, Tom and Mick, read the Irish Wedding Blessing.

May God be with you and bless you.
May you see your children's children.
May you be poor in misfortunes and rich in blessings.
May you know nothing but happiness from this day forward.

Finally, they exchanged rings before heading down the tunnel of guests to cheers and whistles as Iggy played, and Ammon and his family threw green wheat into the air to bless them with fertility.

The reception was also held in the gardens, with Veronica and Jack sitting on large cushions and drinking rose sherbet at Ammon's insistence. They feasted on salads, meats and sweets, everyone enjoying the break from monotonous army food, with Simmo in particular relishing the opportunity to stuff himself full. It seemed he'd developed an appetite for foreign food at last, although Jack noticed he still sniffed everything with suspicion first as he limped along the tables. Simmo had also been able to swing some decent plonk via Delilah and the party was already becoming quite merry. The champagne flowed as the afternoon wore on and Tom and Mick tapped their glasses for silence so they could read the telegrams, their favourite from Pattie.

To Mr and Mrs Jack Murphy, may your marriage be like a runaway horse and cart, always held in check by a woman at the reins. With love Pattie, Clarkson and May

Iggy then played the opening chords to 'Waltzing Matilda' and the brothers stood to sing their own special rendition.

Once a jolly horseman
Rather fine at singalongs
Jumped to the fray to fight for country
And he sang as he stuffed a lucky box against his breast
You'll come a-waltzing my Vera with me
Waltzing with Vera
Waltzing with Vera
You'll come a-waltzing my Vera with me
I'm that lucky blighter saved by a ciggie tin
You'll come a-waltzing my Vera with me!

Everyone laughed and cheered, Jack finally asking for some quiet before they cut the cake. 'I stand here today a man without words – '

'Hear hear!' Simmo raised his glass.

'Well. Without many words.' Jack grinned. 'Suffice to say that today I have married my childhood friend, my true love and my wife till the day I die. I cannot do justice to what this means to me with speech, so I would like to give you this song along with my promise that I will love you, my Vera Maggie O'Shay – or should I say Murphy – always.'

Few of the guests could hold back tears as Jack sang 'Maggie', his voice lifting through the trees, each touched by the gentleness of romance in a brief pause during these harsh, violent days.

Later, as Veronica sat in front of the hotel mirror, she reflected that although she'd missed having many of her family and friends there, especially her parents and Pattie, it was a dream wedding from start to finish. It had been hard to accept that her father wouldn't be there to give her away nor her mother to help her prepare, let alone give up Pattie as her matron of honour, but Veronica knew that she was one of the fortunate ones in this war, so she couldn't truly complain. Her man was alive, whole and near her, even if only for a short time. Most of the women at home could wait years before they saw their sweethearts again, if indeed they ever made it back.

The wedding celebrations had moved on into the Wazza district and Veronica shook her head at the thought. Simmo, Iggy and her brothers had looked set to 'tie one on' and she was sure they'd be some of the last ones trying to squeeze onto the midnight tram, the only way to get back before curfew. She had seen the overladen carriages struggle along before, Australian soldiers trying not to fall off the rooftops as they cheered and sang their way home.

Not so for Jack tonight. They had checked in at the Semiramis Hotel, an elegant grand building that sat against the Nile in Cairo, their three-day honeymoon there a gift from Jack's parents. Veronica felt a thrill when she saw it: the sheer opulence of the building caused her to stand and gawk like the tourist she actually was. It was truly a palace, rising in classical beauty against the famous river on one side and manicured parkland on the other.

The interiors held an intricacy of furnishings unlike she'd ever seen. Thick patterned rugs ran down marble hallways, elaborate chandeliers hung high above, and there was an aura of sumptuous decadence in the floor-to-ceiling mosaics. Lush velvet and sheer gossamer curtains framed enormous windows that looked out across the Nile to the ancient pyramids and their vast secrets. Veronica had felt she was walking into a hedonistic world of eastern mystery, heavy in its seduction. Delicious, forbidden, exciting.

And now nerve-racking. She stared wide-eyed at the enormous bed, a shrine of gold silk and fine Egyptian cotton, grateful that Jack had given her a moment to change.

She brushed her hair loose and put on white cotton under-things trimmed with pale pink satin ribbon. They'd been a wedding gift from Pattie, who'd ordered them over from London from a catalogue. She wrote in the following telegram that she hoped it sped up the arrival of a cousin for May. Veronica blanched at the thought. Not because she didn't want children – she did, as many as she could bear. It was the thought of being sent home if she fell pregnant that concerned her, and being separated from her brothers and Jack again.

She saw him in the mirror and turned, smiling shyly, feeling self-conscious with her exposed arms and ankles. She couldn't believe this moment had finally arrived, that they were allowed to do what they were about to do.

Jack soaked in the image of her, knowing he would revisit it many times in the coming months, and they shared a moment of pure happiness, alone at last. And free to do whatever they wanted now that they were man and wife.

He moved towards her slowly, holding out his hand to lead her to the bed. He was a little nervous himself. Jack had never made love to a virgin and he didn't want to hurt her or frighten her. They lay down and he propped himself up on one elbow, handing her a glass of champagne, and they both drank rather quickly, calming their nerves. Then he took the glasses and placed them on the nightstand, turning back to trace his vision downwards, pulling the strings, as she held her breath, looking fascinated, excited and scared all at the same time. He drew the cotton away to reveal her breasts, which were full and soft to his touch as he ran his fingers across them. Veronica gasped, then tentatively reached out one hand and drew his face in to taste his lips.

Jack groaned and pulled her into his arms, delighting in the passion that she returned as they kissed, hungry and urgent. She pulled at his shirt and he flung it off over his head, ripping it at the shoulder; she laughed, then they were kissing again. He kissed her breasts, her stomach and her hips, pulling down her drawers to kiss even lower, causing her to gasp again. She kissed at whatever part of him she could reach; his hands, his neck, his shoulder, before he raised himself up and entered her, unable to wait. She flinched and he paused.

'All right, my love?' he asked, and she nodded, moving slightly against him. It was all the encouragement he needed.

He cried out a few minutes later and fell against her, rolling onto his back and dragging her across his chest. 'I'm sorry...about that.' He panted. 'Just let me...get my breath back...and I'll do a better job of it.'

She just kissed him again and smiled, lying content in his arms. He looked at her curiously, realising she didn't understand what had just happened. Letting his hand wander downwards he decided he would spend the next few days showing her just what 'a better job of it' meant.

Several hours later Veronica heard her own voice cry out as she reached a place where the red and black behind her eyes exploded and her thighs tightened about him. The Egyptian cotton wrapped about their sweat-soaked bodies, her hair clinging against his arm as he joined her. They collapsed as one, exhausted, and slept, only to awake in the dawn hours and begin again.

It was two full days until Veronica donned her dressing gown and finally drew the long, sheer white curtains, emerging from their room onto the porch. She stared out at the rising sun as it lit the Nile and touched the faces of the pyramids, sending shadows beneath them. Deep in those dusky brown patches Jack's division were now gathered, in the last throes of slumber. An army in respite.

The pause from war was sweet, even sweeter for her.

Jack would have to report there tomorrow and she was expected back in Cairo, but he had leave in a week and they would be able to spend the weekend together. She knew she was lucky, but she hated to leave him for an hour, let alone a week. Sighing, she acknowledged that soon a week would feel like an hour in comparison to the months he would surely be away.

He came to stand behind her, wrapping her in his arms and brushing her hair gently across her shoulder to kiss her neck. She arched it towards him, leaning back into his warm body, hugging his arms. They stood together, soaking in the magnificent scene, both of them reflecting that soon enough the shadows would be his world again and she would be unable to share in it.

The room service arrived with a hot breakfast of bacon, sausages, eggs and coffee, but they ate it cold in the end. They could eat and sleep when they were apart. For now, both needs just seemed to get in the way of the far greater one they had discovered in each other's arms.

The great monuments above them scored the sky, an ancient attempt to defy the passing of time and find immortality upon and below the earth. But the mortals beneath knew that no matter how hard they clung, the earth would move forward, taking them with it into the unknown.

Part Three

Twenty-two

Boulogne, France, June 1916

Rose focused as best she could on the road ahead, but without headlights and a windscreen, it was a difficult business and extremely dangerous. The wounded men in the back of the ambulance were tended by Beatrice and Emma, two other members of the Yeomanry, who were more than happy to leave the driving to Rose. They hurtled through the warm summer night and the distant rumble of artillery grew fainter with each mile.

During the day the sun had lit the fields a luminous green seemingly from within, their colours rich beneath the blue sky as the poppies waved and bobbed delicately in the breeze. Rose felt the sunlight there was somehow softer, comparing this gentle landscape with the vast, sun-baked expanses at home. Even the smallest of cottages were beautiful, with their white walls and red-brown roofs.

Then again everything about France was beautiful to Rose, aside from the brutal reality of casualties. Firstly, it had given her ideal refuge from Gregory, as he would find it very difficult to locate her there, in the full flush of the war, especially under the false names they had adopted of Agnes and little Eliza. And secondly, it had given Elizabeth a hiding place where she was loved and cared for. In all, to Rose, war-torn France meant freedom.

Of course she found it hard living in Boulogne while Elizabeth stayed in Calais, but she had to keep her daughter a secret from FANY who wouldn't have allowed her to join if they'd known she had a child. She had Sundays off, thanks to her arrangement with Stella, her supervisor. Rose had told her that she needed to tend to elderly relatives that day. This was partly true – she did have an older relative she visited on Sundays, however she hardly needed 'tending'. On the contrary, she was as capable a person as anyone was likely to meet. Her aunt Joelene was the reason Rose had chosen France in the first place. She had made it all possible, and the day they had arrived on her doorstep had been the beginning of Rose's salvation.

She had fallen into her aunt's arms, weak, exhausted and, for the first time in her life, without access to money, clutching her belongings and her small child. Yet, as her aunt told her that day, holding her chin and accentuating each word, she'd 'chosen to fight for a life worth living, and that makes you stronger than you ever knew you could be'.

And she did feel strong, in a different way from anything the old Rose would understand. The old Rose would see strength in getting her own way, or being admired and envied for her beauty. The new Rose had learned a whole different meaning of the word.

Elizabeth seemed to have inherited this strength too, displaying it in her own charming, baby way. A regular little miss she was, Rose reflected, smiling to herself.

Elizabeth adored Joelene and was blossoming living in the pretty coastal town of Calais and playing with her little French friends. She was already saying her first French words and sat with

Joelene on the balcony overlooking the port like a grown up, sipping at her milk and calling 'Bonjour!' to passers-by. Their aunt, in turn, was relishing the opportunity of showering Elizabeth with attention, telling Rose again and again how much she reminded her of her own daughter, Marguerite, who had been killed at the age of sixteen in a train accident. Personally Rose thought Elizabeth looked almost exactly like herself, with the exception of her white-blonde hair, and was very unlike her cousin who had been dark haired with an olive complexion. The only real similarity lay in the large brown eyes that were consistent throughout the Dwyer family, and perhaps it was there that Joelene found traces of her long-lost daughter. Or perhaps it was the determined nature of Elizabeth's character, a quality the Dwyer women seemed destined to possess.

This same character had driven Joelene across the ocean when she was young: she'd somehow managed to talk her parents into allowing her a European artistic expedition. In truth, she was really just trying to find a way to escape a monotonous world where the men all studied medicine and the women all 'married well'. She knew she would never go back home. Arriving in France from Australia in 1884, Dr John Dwyer's eldest sister had immediately fallen in love with the windswept northern coast, not to mention a certain French baker called Henri. Although widowed not long after losing her daughter, Joelene had stayed, her son Louis with her. Louis was now serving on the front, marching off within half an hour of the recruitment officers arriving, along with most of the other men in the area, and Joelene missed him terribly. Rose's unannounced arrival had turned Joelene's life around and Rose knew she had made the right choice in running to this aunt, who was really a stranger. Being somewhat of the family 'black sheep' Joelene had never been mentioned very much, and most fortunately Gregory didn't know of her existence.

Somehow, even on the other side of the world, Rose's family had managed to save her.

The other rescue came in the form of her work: she had found her niche in tending to the wounded. Working in the Yeomanry suited her almost as much as France did, with her practicality and determination rising to the fore. Here, her naturally bossy nature was a vital skill, her daring an asset and her stubbornness invaluable to saving lives. She sped along the rutted roads with a clear focus, alert to every ditch, and the amount of wounded she was able to convoy out was astonishing to the volunteers. In fact, it had already earned her the nickname 'Redsped' at the hospital.

She found herself not only enjoying her role as an ambulance driver and medical assistant, but also being involved as an instigator. One of the main problems that had repeatedly frustrated her was that so many of the men came out of the trenches covered in lice and rat bites, like wild animals. How were they supposed to win the war when they kept damaging their own men through neglect? It had motivated her and some of the other girls to bring mobile baths out with them, giving the men the great luxury of cleanliness at the rate of forty at a time. It was a small impact on a massive problem, but it gave Rose some satisfaction all the same.

'There's tens of thousands more like me, ma'am. Why bother?' had asked one curious man in the bath.

'They're nothing like you. You're clean,' she'd responded.

'Not for long. Little blighters will feed on me again within the week.'

'Yes well, let's try making you a little less delicious, eh?'

Beatrice and Emma were a surprise to her, taking her bruised and battered self under their wing and protecting her secret, which they'd accidentally discovered when they ran into her at the markets in Calais one Sunday. It was hard to explain the miniature version of herself in her arms as anyone other than her own child.

Now she was glad they knew. It had been the beginning of yet another unexpected blessing: friendship. She'd never had any time for women before, truly believing as she'd once said that 'men ruled the world' and 'women were mere competitors for the associated power', but that seemed a lifetime ago. Watching what men could do, the damage they could wield with that power, and feeling the brunt of it first hand, had altered her irrevocably. Besides, without Mary, her maid back in London, she would probably be dead by now. She prayed she was safe living anonymously in Ireland.

Ironically, through experiencing the worst of humanity for the first time, she had learnt to appreciate the best of it. Whereas once she would have been too self-absorbed to notice the need for compassion, now, after experiencing its benevolence, she had turned her strength to its cause.

Now she was a part of the medical army, striving to reduce the crushing impact of violence, the weight of which Rose knew only too well. It was her determined nature that had saved her in the end, and she had found something stoked and fired inside as the burning desire to save others consumed her. Once spoilt and selfish, she was now a woman bent on a singular goal for herself and others: survival.

Rose thought of the maimed men she ferried to the trains and tended at the hospital, young men, often no more than boys, left without legs or arms, faces blown apart. Perfect forms in grotesque redesign. She often shook her head in disgust at the stupidity of trench warfare, wondering what her father would say if he were here.

Her mind drifted to home, her mother's letter echoing through her mind as she drove along.

Gregory has been here searching for you and Elizabeth. I wish you would tell me what is going on. Why have you left him? What did he do? He asked for my family's addresses in Ireland but we didn't give him any. He seems very angry. Please let us know where you are and what you are doing, Rose. We are worried sick and just want you to come home. I am praying to St Therese every day for my little girl and granddaughter and have enclosed her holy medals – one for you and one for Elizabeth. Wear them for me, won't you?

Rose played with the medal on the chain around her neck, then clenched the wheel tight, determining yet again that anonymity in France was the only choice she had. Rose knew Gregory wouldn't give up until he found her, in all likelihood murdered her, and took Elizabeth to London to be raised by nannies and institutions (or, worse, his mother).

Ultimately she was well hidden here, constantly surrounded by the girls and hordes of medical staff and soldiers.

France had swallowed them up into its gaping wound and Rose felt surprisingly at home.

He stood casually watching her as she unloaded the wounded, handsome as a film star in his Royal Flying Corps uniform, causing the girls to raise their eyebrows and nudge each other, and smile knowingly at Rose. He may have appeared nonchalant but secretly he was stunned at her transformation. He'd expected to find her in a café dressed in the latest Parisian fashion, flirting with some poor mug and confirming his suspicion that her desire to join the Yeomanry was merely an excuse to get out of London and find a lover to sap off. Instead here she was, holding a young man's bandaged arm carefully, mud splattered across her apron, sweat about her cap as she helped stretcher him onto the carriage.

'Hello, Rose.' He grinned at her, feeling rather pleased for some reason, as if he'd caught the rat with the cheese.

'Agnes,' she hissed at him, looking about to see if anyone else had heard. 'Agnes Pascal. What the bloody hell are you doing here?' She slammed the ambulance doors, taking off her gloves.

'My apologies. I was looking for another lady altogether, well dressed, a bit of a snooty pain in the neck. I have some mail for her.' He was still grinning, taking in her caked boots and stockings.

'I'll pass it on.' She grabbed the mail. 'Why didn't you just forward them like the others?'

He shrugged, leaning against the doors. 'S'pose I was curious.'

'It hardly seems necessary to cross the Channel.'

'Well there's a fine thank-you. And here I was thinking I must be the only person in London you can trust.'

Rose looked uncomfortable, confirming his suspicion that the latter was true.

'You didn't look the best last time I saw you.' Clarkson paused, lighting a cigarette. It was an understatement to say the least. When he had last seen her she'd been standing outside a waiting room at the docks, looking very thin and very frightened. He'd almost stopped himself from handing the referral papers over, thinking perhaps he should take her somewhere safe instead, but her eyes had held a wild desperation and he'd known she was set on doing things her way. He was involved enough, he'd decided, placing them in her hands, but not before noticing the purple bruises on her skinny wrists and the marks on her face that powder had failed to conceal.

'I take it Gregory didn't share your enthusiasm for adventure in France.'

She looked around to see who had heard then back at him warily.

'No one knows where you are, Rose.'

'Agnes,' she corrected again.

'Agnes,' he conceded. Clarkson noted her face had regained its beautiful shape. 'You're looking…very well now.'

Rose seemed to want to ignore that and started to flip through the mail, scanning the handwriting. She looked disappointed. 'Have you heard anything about the boys…about Iggy?'

'Yes: I'll be heading down their way soon actually. I've been re-stationed to St Omer for now though, so I'm nearby for a while. Just waiting for a few things to finish off here then I'll be gone.' She flicked her eyes and he noticed her take in his new captain's uniform.

'I heard Iggy was in the Middle East but he hasn't replied to my letters,' she admitted.

'That would be because he's been transferred to the 12th. Promoted, actually, along with Jack. There must be a shortage of officers down there too.' He tapped his stripes and shrugged. Rose considered that for a moment then began to pack up the rest of the supplies.

'Need any help?'

She shook her head as she walked over to a storage building and placed a crate inside the doorway, locking the door behind it. 'That's it.'

They stood awkwardly and Clarkson figured he'd better finish things off and leave, surprising himself when very different words left his mouth. 'I don't know about you but I think it's time to wet the whistle. Care to join me?'

Later, as they sat under the canopy of a quiet café, he questioned what had made him ask her. It wasn't as if they were old friends with stories to reminisce upon, or family members with news to share. In fact he should have shunned her, considering she'd dumped his brother-in-law in such a publicly humiliating fashion. At best they were acquaintances who'd happened to share a few days in common before the war and had mutual people in their lives. He supposed he was just homesick and, although he was unwilling to frequent the brothels like his single mates, he missed the company of women just the same.

And Rose was all woman, he had to admit. Even in her drab uniform she was a knockout and when she shook her newly cropped hair after removing her cap he found it hard to focus on what she was saying. The curls swam about her face but she tucked one side behind her ear, a habit he noticed she frequently employed as she began to relax with the wine, trusting him a little more. She was playing it safe, making idle chitchat, and he was letting her go on, waiting. Finally coming to a pause, she let out a deep sigh as he watched her closely.

'It's not what you think.'

'What do I think?' he returned, lighting a cigar, the orange glow flashing in the dusk as the streetlights flickered in their glass and metal lamps against the stone.

'I didn't come here looking for a new man.'

'I don't think that.'

She frowned at her glass, sipping thoughtfully. 'What *do* you think?'

'I think you came here to escape your marriage,' he said casually, 'but you got more than you bargained for. You found you actually want to work.'

'And that amuses you?'

'Yes, it does rather. Don't think I've ever seen you with a hair out of place let alone splattered in blood and guts.'

To his surprise she burst out laughing and he found himself delighting in the sound.

'C'est la guerre,' she said when the laughter had subsided, shrugging in the French way. 'It's the war.'

'And are you still at war, Rose?' he asked, serious now.

'Rose no longer exists,' she reminded him. He saluted her, ordering more wine and some maroilles cheese as the café began to fill, the murmurs of conversation surrounding them. The waiter brought out both, along with some crusty bread still warm from the oven.

'I'm fighting two wars. One we're sharing right now,' she gestured at their uniforms, 'and one I'm afraid I chose. Rather stupidly, but there you are.'

'Why don't you just divorce him?'

She shook her head, twining her hair about her ear again as she ate. 'Oh, I don't think he'd like that very much,' she said, taking a deep gulp of wine, the glass clinking on the table. 'Bit of a problem with his temper, I'm afraid.'

'Yes, I'd noticed.' He felt the anger rise in him at the thought of his former friend's enormous fists colliding with her fragile bones. 'Why didn't you just go home to Australia? He'd hardly dare hurt you among your own folk.'

'Because there's more than one way to hurt me,' she admitted, 'or haven't you heard? No, I suppose not. Pattie would hardly be interested in telling you news of me.'

Clarkson was confused. 'What am I missing here?'

'It's what he's missing, or to be more precise what he feels he owns. A rather precious commodity I took with me.' She opened her purse and took out a photo, handing it to him.

He stared at the beautiful child, shocked. 'But where was she at the docks when you left? And where is she now?'

'She was with the maid inside the waiting room.' He waited until she added, 'She's with my aunt during the week now.' She took the photo back, smiling at the little face smeared with chocolate. 'She took this photo last week on her second birthday. I really should have cleaned her up a bit, but she looked so sweet. First time she'd tasted chocolate cake…'

'Second birthday?'

'Yes, she was two on the fourth of June.'

'You were married just after Christmas, as I recall.'

Clarkson's expression had changed from shock to suspicion and she faltered, looking down at the table, seemingly unable to meet his eyes as the truth revealed itself in waves through his mind.

'That's why you were after Jack…and why you chose Gregory when he turned up at Greenshades. You were already…' He shook his head, watching her twirl her glass anxiously, suddenly angry. 'What, so you were just going to marry Jack and fob the baby off as an early arrival? How could you use him like that? For God's sake…and here I was feeling sorry for you. That's why Gregory's so angry, isn't it? *Isn't it?* How can you live with yourself?' He spat the last, causing her head to snap up.

'I did what I had to do.'

'Used people.'

'*Survived.*'

'*Lied.*'

She picked up her bag, standing a little unsteadily in the now silent café as the other diners paused and stared.

'Running away from me too, eh? You keep running, Rose, but spare a thought for the child you're dragging through the mud with you.'

She spun back, picking up her glass and throwing the contents in his face, hurling her words at the same time.

'You bastard!'

He stood, enraged, wiping the wine away, towering above her, but she didn't cower.

'Go ahead. Hit me,' she dared him wildly, 'make the blood pour down my face. Down my legs. Smash me around the room. Lock me away. Starve me. But don't ever accuse me of not thinking about my child. Not that…' she choked, breaking down.

Something twisted inside him and the anger faded as quickly as it had come, and then he was holding her, trying to comfort her as the words poured out between sobs.

'I had to…to find a home…I couldn't bring my child up in sh-shame. And J-Jack was so kind. I would have been a g-good wife to him. I never would have told him. I didn't want to hurt him. I didn't…and then I saw him outside arguing with bloody Veronica at Greenshades and I…knew then he loved her and I… couldn't so…I chose. I went to Gregory's bed…I couldn't do it to him…I couldn't…'

He stroked her back as the racking shudders through her body gradually subsided and then sat her down, still holding her hand.

'Haven't told anyone that,' she confessed, wiping away her tears with her handkerchief, a small embarrassed smile surfacing as the people around them began to turn away.

'Well I'll bet that feels like a bit of a load off, then.'

She nodded and he patted then let go of her hand. He ordered another bottle of wine and poured, offering her a cigarette.

'I don't really smoke,' she sniffed.

'After what you've been through, I'd say that's the least of your worries,' he replied, lighting it for her.

They sat in silence, each processing their thoughts, as the café continued its nightly rituals, lovers and friends in murmurs about them.

'Did they marry then?' She broke the silence.

He stubbed out his cigarette. 'Yes, last year, in Cairo. She was working as a VAD.'

'Really?' Rose nodded thoughtfully. 'Bit more than meets the eye there with Veronica. I'm afraid I made rather a habit of underestimating her.'

'Jealous?'

She twisted her curl back. 'No...Well, yes. I kind of hated her for a while, seeing her as stealing my potential husband. It's pretty scary being pregnant and unmarried, let me tell you. Brought out the worst in me, I'm afraid, and I was already something of...'

'A spoilt cow?'

'Thank you, yes. Anyway, she's with him now and I seem to have got what I deserved.'

'Did you love him?' he asked, wondering why it suddenly mattered.

'Which one? Gregory? No, it wasn't like that.' She leant back in her chair, tucking one leg underneath, stroking her ankle thoughtfully. 'It was more just a thrill with him. The forbidden affair with the big powerful man and all of that rot. I didn't mean to let it get out of hand and then we were together and...he kind of frightened me into it. I didn't even tell him we were moving to Sydney, just that it was over. Gregory was very controlling...he would have talked me out of going and I needed to get away from him.'

'And now history repeats itself.'

'So it seems.'

'So why did you choose Gregory? Why didn't you just marry Jack?'

'I told you, I would have chosen Jack if I hadn't seen him with Veronica...and with Gregory turning up like that...marrying my child's actual father just seemed the logical choice at the time, although I don't think I've many friends in that town anymore.' She shrugged. 'Not that I had many in the first place. Never been much good at that at the best of times, although here it's... different.'

'Maybe you're different,' said Clarkson.

'Not different. Just damaged goods.' She waved her hand dramatically at her uniform. 'The airs and graces have fallen by the wayside.'

'Good riddance, I say,' Clarkson raised his glass. 'To the wayside!'

She laughed a little and they drank. 'So now you know everything. Perhaps I have changed. I don't think I've ever told anyone all my secrets.'

'Well now, not quite. You only answered half of my question. Did you love Jack?'

She turned the bottom of her glass as he waited. 'No, I couldn't say I did. He is a good man and a great kisser.' She threw Clarkson a wicked look and he felt his pulse quicken. 'I'm not sitting around daydreaming about him, if that's what you're asking. I just wish for Elizabeth's sake I could be happily married. I feel that I've failed her a bit.'

'Oh I wouldn't say that.'

'You just did, really,' she reminded him.

'Typical bloody woman. Holding things against you.'

'It only just happened!'

'Have a little more wine,' he suggested, filling her glass.

'Typical bloody man. Trying to get a woman drunk.'

'Can't blame a fellow for trying,' he grinned and Rose's mouth twitched in response.

Only he wasn't smiling about it later as he lay awake thinking about how soft she'd felt against him when he held her, stirring feelings he knew he couldn't afford to be feeling after a year and a half away from his wife and a baby he hadn't even met.

Rose was like French wine, he mused. A delicious red with a dangerous kick.

Twenty-three

Highview

Veronica stared out her bedroom window. After almost two weeks back she was still trying to accustom herself to the green and gold landscape outside. Spending a year surrounded by desert or endless, deep ocean, made the fields and bushland along Cowpasture Lane seem surreal to her now, with their constant abundance of wildlife. She watched as the king parrots picked their gentle way along the branches of the wattle tree, the vivid red chest of the male almost glowing amongst the leaves. She counted the family this year: three females, one young male and this fellow, the magnificent patriarch.

How she wished she and Jack could be building their family here, in their home, together.

'Vera! Vera!' Pattie ran into Veronica's room, waving a letter happily. 'I've got the latest from Mr C!'

'Thank goodness for that.' Veronica smiled, stretching out her back. 'I don't know how many more times I can hear you re-reading the other chapters.'

'I never believed it when people said expectant mothers are crotchety old things but you're starting to prove their point,' she sniffed, pretending to be offended. 'Now listen up! All comfy?' she asked as she jumped onto the bed and fluffed up their pillows, lying next to her to begin reading. Veronica loved Clarkson's 'Chapter' letters almost as much as Pattie did, laughing at the funny stories and humorous drawings that filled every page. He had taken to sending one every now and then between his usual letters, claiming they would one day be his famous 'memoirs', which he would name *The Heroic Misadventures of Mr C*. It was just what Veronica needed this afternoon to distract her from her thoughts.

'*Chapter Eight: A Fly in the Appointment.*' Both girls giggled before Pattie continued.

I had the unfortunate duty of having to report to Major several days ago and searched my mind as to its reason. Had he found my secret stash of chickens in the plane? Did he know about my nightly riding sessions on Daisy the milking cow next door? Or, worst of all, had he discovered the master tunnel diggings to Australia under my floorboards?

They laughed at the drawings he had provided for these three scenarios. One was of a man flying a plane with chickens in the back seat, an extra chicken on the top wing, waving with her little goggles in place. The next of a man riding a plump cow across a paddock, saddle and stirrups flapping and a rather crazed look on the cow's face. The third showed a half-dug tunnel through the sphere of the earth, an arrow pointing to Mr C's quarters in London on one side, another arrow pointing to his home in Australia at the bottom of the globe. Mr C was sitting in the centre of the earth, cooking what appeared to be a sausage on a fire at its core.

The dreaded day arrived and I scrubbed myself up, making sure there were no chicken feathers to be seen, and I made my way to his office. It seemed my fears were unfounded. He knew nothing of my secret activities at all! He wished to speak to me regarding a totally different matter: French trousers. It seems the greedy man has outgrown all of his pants due to the amount of milk and eggs he's been served since his arrival at the base. (Daisy and the chickens have a lot of explaining to do!) As a consequence, he has ordered me to fly over to France and stay there awhile until I have found French trousers large enough to accommodate him. I opened my mouth to object to this outrageous waste of my precious digging time when a daring fly flew in and did the tango with my tonsils.

Pattie and Veronica fell about as they looked at the comical drawing of Mr C clutching at his throat as a fly actually seemed to dance with his tonsils, a very fat man standing behind him, frowning.

So, my dear wife, I will now be stationed in France in search of large pantaloons. Tell my little chick her father is a courageous, gallant hero to take on such a quest and give her a thousand kisses from me. Then give yourself about ten thousand more.

Try using a mirror. I do.

Yours in constant, heroic misadventure,

Your loving husband,

Mr C

PS Please send me a little spade. The others are becoming suspicious about all the missing forks.

Veronica made Pattie read it twice and they sat, wiping at tears as they pored over the clever little drawings.

'He's really very good, you know. He should send something in to the newspapers,' Veronica said, pointing at the man on the cow. 'Look at that cow's expression,' she giggled.

'I wish he was working for a newspaper and not flying about Europe,' Pattie sighed, lying back and staring at the ceiling. 'Do you think he is really off to France? Maybe Mr C is trying to break it to me gently.'

'Wait for the next letter. He'll let you know if he is,' Veronica assured her, yawning. 'Lord, is it normal to be this tired all the time? I can't seem to stop sleeping.'

'Make the most of it,' Pattie said, patting Veronica's rounded stomach. 'It'll keep you up soon enough.'

'Oh,' Veronica gasped. She held Pattie's hand still at a spot under her ribs where the baby liked to push its little feet, and Pattie smiled as she felt it kick about.

'He's awake at any rate,' Veronica said.

Pattie grinned. 'You said "he"...'

'I told you I don't know at all; I just have a feeling...'

'I know you know, you witchy thing!'

'Hmm,' said Veronica. Truth was she did feel that she knew. From the moment she suspected it was true, and had started hiding it lest they send her home, she'd believed her baby was a boy.

They lay for a while and the baby settled back down, content beneath Pattie's hand.

'I wish I could have hidden it for longer,' Veronica sighed.

'Jack is far from Cairo now anyway. You may as well be home with us,' Pattie reminded her and Veronica knew she was right.

'I just wish I could snap my fingers and have him suddenly here, just for an hour or so.'

Pattie sat up and crossed her legs, holding the letter in both hands. 'Sometimes I sleep with all of Clarkson's letters under my pillow, hoping I will dream of him and spend some time with him that way. Silly, I know.' She shrugged.

'Does it help? Do you dream about him?'

'That's the silliest part. I can never remember my dreams.'

Veronica rubbed her stomach absently. 'I remember mine clear as daylight,' she admitted.

'I wish I could,' Pattie said turning to look at her. 'Any dreams about Clarkson? Is he going to turn up in our garden at the end of his tunnel any time soon?'

Veronica laughed. 'Well if he does I'll be waddling back down it to go and fetch Jack, fat stomach and all – and just you try to stop me.'

Pattie jumped off the bed and saluted her. 'Yes, ma'am! I'd best be off. May will be waking up and hungry for her goo.'

'What's goo?' Veronica laughed.

'All things food. I'm sure she means "good": at least I hope that's what she means. I'm not the world's best cook, after all.' She shook her head. 'I'm sure that child is already teasing me. I don't know where she gets it from!' Pattie left with a wink and Veronica lay back, leaning over on an impulse to her nightstand to pick up the pile of Jack's letters and stuff them under her pillow. She rested her head and almost instantly fell asleep.

But she didn't dream of Jack. There were giant mosquitoes again, only this time it was Clarkson who was in trouble as he rode on top of one, trying to hold it with reins as crazed chickens flew alongside. The mosquito pointed its long nose towards the earth and they hurtled down. A large bed of red flowers loomed and she knew he thought they would save his fall as he jumped off, not seeing the thorns beneath them.

Veronica called out but once again she was in her cage.

Twenty-four

Boulogne

'Redsped, ya breakin' me heart.' Private Hill held his hand over his chest, imploring her with the other. 'Sit a spell, go on. I'm as bored as blazes and yer a sight for a sore eye. Truly,' he said, pointing dramatically at his bandaged eye.

'Behave, Ben,' she warned him, rushing past to pick up the supplies she was taking out to the front. Mostly champagne, strangely enough.

'Did I tell ya? Bruce and me are gunna be stretcher-bearers. See? Can't get rid of us!'

'In that case, enjoy the boredom while you can!'

'Come back! Yer a cruel woman!' he called after her, dissolving into coughs. She listened to the latter more than his words and prayed he wasn't going to relapse and succumb to pneumonia on top of everything else. The loss of one eye had been enough of a blow to an eighteen-year-old, especially someone like Ben. He was the lively, enthusiastic type and hated hospital almost as much as the trenches, constantly telling her he didn't want to be 'no dugout', a person who hides from the action.

He was one of many she had come to feel were her boys, almost like one large person with thousands of names, a brave giant whose multiple faces were all secretly afraid.

Masked in joviality, they were all united in one cause: each other.

Ben had already been sent home once with dysentery, or 'Gallipoli gallop'. He had been medically discharged and (she would have thought) let off the hook, but now here he was, re-enlisted, maimed and putting his hand up again. When she'd asked why he'd come back he'd simply said: 'Can't just leave me mates to face it.'

It was the only thing that kept them all going, this bond forged at the gate of death: a promise to stand alongside each other no matter what. Gradually, steadily, in the face of their humour and general selflessness, she was finding herself less and less consumed by her own fear and worry and increasingly protective of this giant that was the Australian soldier. The 'diggers', as they had begun calling themselves, after so much trench warfare. As they fought their enemy, she fought her own, pushing every day to halt the cold hand of death that clutched at the giant's clothes, ripping pieces of him away and leaving holes behind that could never be filled. She visited those holes in her sleep and saw them by day, the white crosses starkly fresh, spreading across French soil as the blood of Australia's sons wept into foreign earth.

Her job was mainly to ferry wounded from Australian lines but she saw many other boys too. French, English, Welsh, Irish, Scottish, Canadian, New Zealanders and even Germans writhed in agony in the back of her ambulance. She wondered when it would all end. Sometimes her dream of living a peaceful life hidden away in France with Joelene and Elizabeth seemed like a hopeless fantasy.

And then there was Clarkson.

His visits had become a regular event over the past weeks and, despite her best efforts, she found him drifting into her thoughts with increasing regularity. When he materialised in person her heart rate leapt and her stomach seemed to fall against her spine. Beatrice and Emma said they found it vastly amusing to watch the composed, in-charge Redsped gain five extra fingers and lose most of her concentration whenever a certain dashing airman appeared grinning nearby. Clarkson passed the time waiting for her to finish by visiting with the injured men, playing cards with Private Hill, his mate Bruce and the others, or helping Rose unload the stretchers and equipment. Usually they strolled along between the old stone walls towards the cafés after she was done, which was often quite late, enjoying the extended summer twilight as the waves curled against the sand. They dined on seafood and shared bottles of wine, enjoying the delicious local cheeses and pastries.

Last Sunday she'd even allowed him to come with her to visit Joelene and Elizabeth in Calais. It was strangely moving watching him with Elizabeth, his large form dwarfing her tiny one. She had taken to him immediately, chatting away in her mix of English, French and baby, putting her chubby little hand in his palm and asking for 'choclat'. Joelene and Rose had laughed as she'd led him about the place, introducing him to her dolls, the furniture, even the stove which she'd informed him was 'no, no, hot', pulling him away and shaking her soft white curls. Clarkson had been meekly obliging the entire time, completely entranced by this little fairy of a child, perhaps feeling closer to his own daughter for being in her presence.

They'd walked along the port, buying vegetables and freshly caught fish at the markets as 'Eliza' ran about, charming everyone they met in her little blue dress and white petticoats. Of course she had got wet, splashing about in the water, scolding the waves and crying 'Ne fais pas ça!' before running back into her mother's arms.

Her little legs had grown tired in the heavy wet skirt so she'd ridden on Clarkson's shoulders the whole way home, much to her delight. Rose had watched her daughter's smiling face as she'd waved from her human tower, and had felt the happiness creep into her own heart before reality pushed against it. She wished there was no war, no Gregory, no Pattie and no May. Just this world, this child and this man. She knew it was wrong to want someone else's husband, reminding herself how hard it had been to step aside and let Veronica have Jack in the end, but this was different. She hadn't loved Jack.

She'd stopped still, staring at his back as he held her daughter's shoes in one hand, her little foot in the other, and felt the truth move through her, like a wind blowing her open. When he'd turned back to smile at her, his kind brown eyes questioning, it had exploded as fact. She had thought she was done with foolish choices in her life but apparently not. It was hardly the best move to fall in love with an old enemy's husband while hiding from one's own in war-ravaged France.

Packing the ambulance, Rose saw Beatrice and Emma approach, each checking through supplies in canvas bags.

'Got your hairbrush in there, Em?' Beatrice enquired. Emma pulled one out, making Rose laugh in surprise.

'A girl has to look her best at all times.' Emma waggled it at her. 'You never know when the right gentleman might present himself.'

'It's for the wounded.' Beatrice jumped into the ambulance. 'She's got it in her head that they'll enjoy a good brush. Personally I think she's confusing them with dogs.'

'Bound to get a few tails wagging, I'm sure,' said Rose.

'As long as it isn't tongues!' Beatrice laughed.

Emma giggled, stuffing the brush back in. 'Where to, Redsped?'

'Clearing station. Did you see the champagne?' Rose pointed to the crates near the storage shed.

'Maybe they just want to calm a few nerves out there,' Beatrice suggested.

'Maybe they are worried about running out of morphine,' Rose countered and the three women exchanged glances.

They drove out the gates and Rose soaked in the brief respite of countryside. Hay bales lay in rolls like thick ribbons and behind them the green hills spoke of life and abundance. Incongruous with their destination.

'You were home late,' Beatrice observed as they bounced along.

'Was I?' Rose looked straight ahead, ignoring her teasing tone.

'I'd be home late too if I had a date with Captain Charming,' Emma said, leaning forward to join in. 'Come on, Rose, spill the beans. Have you kissed him yet?'

'No,' said Rose firmly.

'Liar,' Beatrice countered.

'Isn't the hay pretty? Reminds me of home a bit,' Rose said.

Beatrice sighed, giving up. 'Where are you from, anyway?'

'Originally Melbourne then we moved to Sydney. Beecroft actually. It's a rural area just outside the city.'

'Never been to Australia. Actually never been outside England until now,' Emma admitted.

'Me either,' said Beatrice. 'You're a long way from home, though. Do you miss it much?'

Rose thought about the letter she'd been trying to write to Mildred these past few weeks. 'I miss my mother,' she said, surprised at how strongly she felt it. 'She's never even seen Elizabeth.'

Beatrice looked at the photo Rose had pinned on the dashboard of the little chocolate-smeared face.

'What don't you take her home after the war? Seems a shame for her not to know her grandparents.'

Rose shook her head. 'I don't think I can ever go home.'

'Surely your husband wouldn't try to hurt you in front of your family,' Emma said.

'You don't know my husband.'

Emma considered that. 'Well, maybe Clarkson would protect you. I can't imagine anyone messing with him.'

'I don't know about that but I do know his wife would kill me anyway, so not such a great idea.'

'Thought you said nothing has happened between you two?'

'It hasn't...but I jilted her brother.'

Beatrice looked over at Rose and sighed. 'Oh what a tangled web, Redsped.'

Soon enough they arrived at the clearing station, where the sound of bombing was constant, far more so than previous weeks. There was a steady stream of trucks, cars, men and a cumbersome beast that seemed to be driving itself.

'What on earth is that?' Emma shouted above the noise.

'I believe they're called tanks,' Beatrice called back.

'Terrifying.' Rose watched them in horror, imagining the wounds one would see from such machines.

They alighted from the ambulance, walking over to check what wounded needed ferrying out of the mayhem.

'Anyone would think there was a war on,' Beatrice said.

'Or a battle about to be,' Rose agreed. Everyone in town had been talking about it and the bombardment and massing of armies only confirmed it. The time had come for the big push and Rose knew her days of dining after work and having Sundays off would soon be over as she gazed at the thousands of troops heading down the road. If the rumours were true the men would go over the top in a few short days.

As they drove back with some of the injured Rose felt a deep sense of foreboding, envisaging the rows and rows of soldiers they passed being mowed down, falling in bloodied massacre. After all, if she could see the attack coming surely the Germans could.

That night, when she was packing up, a hand steadied her balance as she lifted a stretcher into the truck. She felt her face flush as she met Clarkson's smile.

'Hungry?'

She nodded and they set off together, the evening breeze welcome after the heat of the day.

He turned from their usual path towards the town and she stopped.

'Where are you going?'

'You know, funny things happen to you when you go to war,' he said, grabbing her hand and leading her down a side street. 'You end up in strange places, see terrible things…and you forget…' he panted as they climbed some stairs '…one of the most important things in life.' He stopped at a bright new Model T Ford, opening the door with a flourish and grinning. 'To have fun.'

She climbed in, delighting in the soft new seat and shining chrome, laughing as he turned to the back and pulled out two enormous hats. 'Shall we?'

They sped off, up towards the cliffs, tantalising glimpses of ocean beckoning as the wind whipped at the hats; he handed her his scarf to keep hers tied down. Climbing steeply, they reached the summit and the view opened into glorious expanse around them, the light burning orange against the lace of clouds overhead.

She got out and stretched, breathing deeply of the fresh salt air and revelling in the freedom of senses left bruised by the violent assault they bore each day. The gulls rode the wind and she watched them, envying the simplicity of their existence. When had it become so complicated? Rose wandered forward, mesmerised by the movement of the ocean, dancing in a thousand shades as gold met silver and the twilight approached. Taking off her hat, she lifted her hair, feeling wonderfully small against the vastness of sky and water.

'Dinner is served,' Clarkson announced and she turned to find a full picnic laid out, complete with gramophone. Noticing the boyish expression on his face she felt something akin to pain within and she swallowed her tears, moved by his thoughtfulness. They ate without talking, lost in their own thoughts as the sun bid its spectacular farewell. She wondered what was on his mind.

'Penny for your thoughts.' He beat her to it.

She sighed, pushing her hair back. 'I saw the men today, thousands of them all up near the front, and one of those horrible tanks. I even saw a certain plane flying over a few times as some madman tried to assess the enemy. I'm just feeling worried tonight and then of course here we are,' she gestured outwards, 'and it all seems so…pointless…this war.'

'I'm sure they know what they are doing,' he assured her, though his tone suggested otherwise, 'and I'm glad you enjoyed my flying. Which reminds me, I'll be picking you up at five o'clock tomorrow morning so don't sleep in.'

'What are you talking about? I can't go anywhere tomorrow.'

'Stella is aware you have an important assessment mission to assist me with. Just make sure you don't eat too much breakfast.'

'What do you mean "assessment mission"?' she asked, eyeing him with suspicion. 'Are we driving to the front?'

'Something like that.'

He smiled at her, holding out his hand to help her up, and all thought left her mind as he stopped still in front of her and they stood close, close enough that she could smell the leather of his jacket and the soap on his chin. She froze as his hand slid up to her shoulder and he felt her skin through her blouse. The lightest of touches, but it beat at her heart.

'You should have brought your coat,' he murmured, pulling her gaze into his eyes.

She nodded, feeling herself drawn closer as the burnished light fell across his features, his mouth only inches from hers. Then the image of Gregory came unbidden into her mind and she broke the spell, pulling away and packing up the picnic. It was one thing to want another woman's husband; it was quite another to risk his life. If she let her passion loose and they became lovers his life would be at risk if Gregory ever found her.

He stood for a moment behind her and she knew he was battling with himself. Then he walked over to the gramophone and before long the music reached her ears. She looked up as he held out his arms to dance, his handsome face in soft invitation. She gave in to it and moved with him as the words fell to the wind and the ball of the sun met the water. It descended in blazing farewell, marking time that would never return; unique forever and felt keenly by two would-be lovers forbidden to love.

I would say such wonderful things to you
There would be such wonderful things to do
If you were the only girl in the world and I were the only boy

Clarkson felt her cheek against his, so soft. Everything about her was soft: her skin, her hair, her face. She was so beautiful and so incredibly strong. And sensual. He'd never met a woman this intoxicating. It was as if everything she did made him want her, whether she was packing supplies or taking off her hat or holding a glass. Everything she said brought him closer into her. Every word was another tie that held him. He didn't just want her flesh: he wanted her soul. He wanted to lose himself in her, everything else be damned. The song ended and she moved away, taking the scent of her, the touch of her, from his arms.

They drove back and he walked her home the long way through town, not wanting to leave her. Looking up, he wished they could take a bed inside one of the brightly coloured buildings where the little balconies opened out from darkened rooms, hinting at hidden passions and secret lovers. The city's stone led them along and he felt himself clinging to its prison, knowing that their time was running out and soon he would leave her here in this fortress town. Theirs would be just another love story locked away in the ancient walls, unspoken and unfulfilled.

It was the best outcome, he told himself. He could face Pattie with a clear conscience, knowing he'd kept his marriage vows and remained faithful. It was the right thing to do. The only choice for an honourable man to make. But as she turned slightly to say goodbye, the streetlight touched her hair in a glow about her face and she twisted one curl around her ear in that now achingly familiar way, and he realised it was too late. He'd already betrayed Pattie in his heart.

Twenty-five

Montreuil-sur-Mer, General Headquarters, France

Gregory Chambers stepped out of the car and strode across towards the Officers' Mess, his mind on the upcoming offensive. It was about bloody time they got this whole damn thing over and done with, as far as he was concerned. Giving in to his mother's insistence that he take on his commission had been unavoidable in the end. Forced as he was to stay in Europe in his search for Rose and Elizabeth, he knew he would have to comply with family pressure and do his duty eventually. He'd just hoped that the war would only last a year or so and he would be able to avoid it altogether.

It was an inconvenience he could do without if he was ever going to get on with the two things in his life that actually mattered: his business and his runaway wife and child. The former would surely continue to grow under the careful eyes of his lawyers and associates; locating the latter, however, was proving a frustrating enterprise. He knew they were somewhere in France, or at least that the trail had ended here. Rose had been seen arriving in Calais, a thin woman with red hair carrying a small, white-haired child, but that was where the clues to their whereabouts had stopped. It seemed no amount of money could uncover their location in the chaos that was France right now.

Gregory slapped his gloves on the counter and ordered a glass of wine, nodding at some of the other officers alongside.

'Sir,' saluted Lionel Pankhurst, his second lieutenant, standing to attention. A bumbling fool, in Gregory's opinion. Too many years at pompous boarding schools and not enough life experience to fill a stamp amongst the lot of them, he thought contemptuously as he scanned the room.

'Looks likely we'll see some action soon, eh what?' Captain Charles Rollings tipped his glass towards Gregory. He looked to be well into his afternoon drinking session with his usual partner in crime, Captain Lewis Jenkins. 'Looking forward to getting stuck in?'

Gregory gazed at him over the rim of his glass, thinking how useless this overweight windbag would be in battle. 'Quite.'

'The Australians are arriving: lots of veterans from Gallipoli,' Rollings continued. 'And a load of fresh troops as well. You may have some friends among them.'

'I doubt it,' Gregory returned dryly.

'I didn't know you were a colonial,' Jenkins said, looking up and down at Gregory's English uniform, his eyebrows raised high. 'Bit of convict blood, is it? A few secrets in the closet?'

Rollings swayed, patting Gregory's arm. 'I don't think Lady Chambers has many secrets in her closets,' he chuckled. 'I was referring to Chambers' associations by marriage. The new Lady Chambers is Australian, is she not?'

Gregory felt the glass stem between his fingers, stopping himself just in time before he snapped it. Damn Rollings and his gossipy wife.

'Imagine that! A kangaroo bouncing around in the family. Any young joeys about yet?' Jenkins sneered.

The glass stem did snap in Gregory's hand and he grabbed Jenkins by the throat, holding the sharp edge close. 'Don't ever mention my family again, do you understand?'

Jenkins eyes were wide and he managed a nod before Gregory let him go, leaving the murmurings and musings behind him as he walked out. Let them talk, let them drink, let them stumble their way into battle and get shot for all he cared. But beware the man who mentioned the bitch he'd married, lest he feel first hand some of the vengeance that clawed at him every day.

Bring on the war, Gregory dared the rain as it began to fall hard upon him. The sooner the killing is done the sooner he could track her down and send her traitorous soul straight to hell.

Twenty-six

St Omer, France

She felt the ground leave them with every inch of her body as she clenched the seat tightly, watching in awe as the airstrip fell away beneath them and they whirred over the treetops. She held her breath as they cleared the forest, then the farmhouse then, all of a sudden, the earth dropped. They sailed out over a golden patchwork quilt where little dollhouses rested on soft folds and tiny beings moved about in the early morning light, going about their daily ritual of survival. Clarkson banked and Rose let out a cry of delight, laughing at the sheer madness that they were actually flying. She knew that's what he did of course, sometimes secretly feeling he exaggerated the role these flying machines played in the war, but now she could believe it. Such a viewpoint would take hours to plot on land, yet these marvellous contraptions gave one the eagle's advantage, and she *felt* like an eagle as they veered left and she looked out at the coast. The dawn touched the jagged cliffs, igniting the waves as they hurled themselves against the rocks then fanned in spectacular farewell.

Rose had thought France beautiful on land, but from the air it was even more so. The emerald greens of the trees, the crisp whites and yellows of the houses, the red of the rooftops and the gold of the sand all vied for attention and she felt intensely alive as exhilaration washed through her. Clarkson turned and pointed out the train line and the approach of Calais and she waved at Elizabeth and Joelene, knowing they were probably asleep in their beds. Her baby's soft little face filled her mind for a moment; she blew her a kiss. In the distance she could make out England and felt grateful for the expanse of water that separated her from the dangers lurking there.

Clarkson banked again, turning inland, and she watched the patchwork quilt reappear. The hay rolls she saw yesterday were scattered on the blanket in tiny dots as silvered trails of the river meandered in their creases.

Then it came. At first a distant rumble, then louder, as dark clouds of explosives rose skywards, marking the battle line long before anything was visible on the ground. The soft beauty of France had a death line locked and wrestling across her breast. Two angry beasts roared and screamed, rending the air and clutching at her with sharp claws. Rose saw the line reach in two directions as far as she could see: the beasts stretched out their mighty arms in anticipation of the real battle to come, when this wrestle became a fight and they unleashed full vengeance upon each other.

Clarkson kept heading steadily towards the line and she grew afraid as the German army came into sight. She saw them swarming and hovering at the back behind the firing line, a mirror of their enemy, and felt strangely as if she were watching Iggy play with the toy soldiers he'd had when they were children. These little tiny specks that each had a soul felt like pawns in a giant game of chess, necessary but expendable, a distraction intended to protect the back row. For the first time she saw the war for what it truly was, a deadly game played by men who were once boys, with toy soldiers and chess sets, and who now had the real thing at their disposal.

Clarkson flew for a few minutes as close as he dared with Rose on board, taking photos of the German developments from a camera perched on the wing, then turned for home. He was satisfied that he'd confirmed what they had unfortunately all expected back at base: an enemy on full alert. Just then he noticed something out of the corner of his eye and cursed. Rose, watching him, turned as well, and blanched to see a German plane headed their way. It was unusual for this hour and Clarkson guessed he was on a scouting mission much like his own and that the pilot was probably just as surprised as he was. He made for the clouds and cut through above, knowing that the German could no longer see him and would turn back rather than stay behind enemy lines. Sure enough, ten minutes later, they cleared the clouds and sailed out into blue sky, once again over calm fields.

By the time they landed the sun was well up and they were greeted by a few of the other personnel, including Captain Standing, a tall man who was a fellow pilot and friend of Clarkson's. All of the men stared at Rose as she shook her hair out of her cap and goggles and smiled her dazzling smile.

Captain Standing gave a low whistle and stepped forward, taking her hand and kissing it, introducing himself as, 'Standing. Captain Standing. But you can call me Roger.'

Rose greeted them all as they walked across the field and Clarkson stayed close in protective hover.

'How is the Hun this morning?'

'Curious.' Clarkson went on to tell them of the massing troops and their unexpected encounter.

'Probably Löwenhardt looking for a few more dances on his card,' said Standing.

'Must have changed his mind when he saw it was you. Didn't want to become the extra in your baker's dozen.' The others agreed and the conversation steered towards ace fliers and the upcoming battle.

'I hear they're boasting the Baron is up to twenty now.'

'Only eighteen at my count.'

'Well he's dancing with the devil painting himself red, but I doubt we'll get to see him. Artillery is set to blast them to smithereens before the boys go over the top. The war will be over in a month once we clean up the last of them. They can't do much without archies.' Standing ducked as they entered the tent near the strip.

'I didn't even get to shoot down one,' grumbled a young man as they sat to eat.

Standing clamped his large paw on the young man's shoulder. 'Don't worry, Rookie, I'm sure you'll be an ace before we're done.'

'I really want that car,' he sighed.

'Rookie here has a grandfather who says he'll buy him an auto if he shoots down a Jerry,' Standing explained to Rose.

'I just need to get my hours up, Captain.' Rookie looked at Clarkson hopefully and he felt a surge of affection for his young charge.

'Maybe Standing will take you for a whirl this afternoon,' he suggested. 'Get some more fly time in.'

Rose watched this interaction, sickened by Rookie's naiveté. All of this talk of aces and kills was shedding a new light on Clarkson's world. As much as she wanted to like them, their nonchalance stung. She felt a driving desire to take them all down to the hospital and introduce them to the maimed bodies that manned the 'archies', or machine guns. Let them see what artillery did to a faceless infantry, German or not.

Clarkson seemed to have noticed her silence and suggested they get going, waiting until they'd made their farewells before asking her what was wrong.

'How can you even ask me that?' Suddenly she was angry, really angry, and as they reached the car she turned and let the full vent of it fall upon him.

'It's just a game to you flyboys, isn't it? Who can shoot the most ducks in the pond and get the highest score! They don't care about the cost...they don't see it. How can they be so...so cavalier? You men, you're all the same. Just overgrown children playing at war, and it's still the women who tend to the scrapes, only now its severed arms and missing eyes and dead boys. *Dead.* It isn't a game. What's wrong with you all?'

'I think you misunderstand them– ' Clarkson interrupted.

'Oh I understand all right. And what about you? Aiming for a baker's dozen? So you've already killed twelve men? When were you going to tell me that?'

Clarkson held open the door. 'Just get in the car, Rose.'

She threw herself in, her heart beating wildly as they took off, neither saying a word until another plane flew overhead in a whirring roar and she saw young Rookie waving excitedly in the seat behind Standing.

'How can you do it?' She felt the tears prick at her eyes. He stopped the car and they watched the plane recede into the blue.

'How can I not?' He lit a cigarette and she waited. 'You think we play at war? We're just trying to survive it, for God's sake.' He stared out at the field. 'Yes I've killed a dozen German fliers. Am I proud of it? No. But do I regret it? No, I don't.'

'But you are taking a life. Every time. They're not just...just chess pieces...' she argued.

'That's what it is. Kill or be killed. Don't you understand that if we don't shoot them down they'll take photos and tell their artillery exactly where to point their bloody cannons? We need to stop them getting back. Rose, killing one of them could save hundreds or thousands of our men. It could win the bloody war.'

She watched his face sadly. 'And it's all about winning, isn't it?'

'Yes, it is. They threw down the gauntlet, not us, and we could either wait to be taken down or fight. So we fight. I'm sorry you clean up the blood but you chose it. You begged for it. And don't tell me you had no choice. There's a perfectly sedate life waiting for you in Calais with Joelene. You wanted to be a part of it and so did I.' He drew on his cigarette. 'We may not like what it does but we do like what it means.'

'And what is that?'

'We get to go home and live in a free country.' He shrugged, still avoiding her gaze.

'Weren't we already doing that?'

He sighed, stubbing out his cigarette. 'Yes, but for how long? If Britain fell, how long could we last? The Germans want empires, not countries.'

'So we trade our pawns for a different king.' She watched as he faced her at last.

'We do whatever it takes to protect the queens.'

'And play at death?'

'So they make a game from a game. How else do you expect them to face it?'

She felt his hand cover hers, never taking her eyes from his as he curled her hair behind her ear with the other and smiled, the defensive frown leaving his face to be replaced with a tenderness that made her ache.

'Don't be too hard on them, my love.'

She felt her breath catch in her throat. 'Is that what you're doing? Playing a game to avoid facing death?'

'No,' he stroked her chin, 'I think I'm finding what I want to live for.' He drew her towards him and she wanted to fall, like the surrender of soldiers who stood resolute for so long, then realised they wanted to give in and just go home. She wanted to stop resisting.

Rose watched as his mouth lowered, unable to pull back against the force between them as he touched her lips lightly with his. The last of her resolve melted into desire, her every sense alive to the softest of touches asking for permission.

The sound of an oncoming car forced them out of their trance and Clarkson recognised the man's uniform and pulled back, saluting as the major drove slowly by, taking in the scene but not saluting back.

'Are you in trouble?'

'Probably, but he'll get over it. He has bigger things to worry about than me,' Clarkson said, turning back.

'Wait. I need you to understand something...Gregory– '

'Is just another person who'll be trying to kill me? I think, given the odds, he'll have a hard time jumping the queue.' He went to kiss her again.

'No.' Rose pushed at his chest. 'Not here. Let's go back to Boulogne and find somewhere...private.'

He had no argument with that, and turned onto the country road towards the town. Rose leant in against him as he wrapped his arm about her, kissing the top of her head. She watched the sun glide between the gathering clouds, heavy with impending rain. Her mind was consumed with delicious sensation, then slowly went to greet a tide of thoughts.

She thought about Gregory and what he would do if he found them. She thought about Pattie and May and how he would ultimately choose them over her. She thought about Elizabeth and how she would eventually need to leave France with her daughter and throw Gregory off their trail. She thought about the ace fliers and how he could so easily die at any time.

She thought about the tanks, the men, the blood and the impending push.

She thought about it all as she watched the drifting sun. How different the world seemed up there in the clouds, where human problems were small matters of insignificance against the mighty scope and beauty of earth.

Then the delicious sensation consumed her once more. Warm, comforting, safe. And something more. The memories of violence she'd met at her husband's hand melted away beneath the reverent longing she discerned in Clarkson's touch, along with the aversion that protected her once abused body. She found every part of her focusing on where his hand lay against her waist and longed for it to edge upwards to her breast, or lower, to other parts that had somehow come back to life. She wanted him to kiss her, to take her. She longed to call out his name to that beautiful French sun, stroke his face, his back, all of him as he filled her.

Yes, death was at their door, but that was one thing she could say about war: it made you appreciate the moment you were in, because any one of them could be the last you lived.

And she could honestly say that if moments could be measured, it was the sweetest of life's offerings to wait in sensual anticipation for possibly the greatest of its pleasures.

The rain came. It fell in great sheets, settling in and making the dirt soft beneath their boots.

They marched along, hardened now, no longer eager young men in search of adventure. This part of the giant was forever damaged; sections of him sent off to fight in the desert, other sections falling to dust on the now silent hillsides of Gallipoli, and then this section. The ones sent to France. The fractured Anzacs. The veterans.

They watched the new recruits pass by and tipped their hats, making their jokes. Knowing that the door to death was open before their young brothers, sent off to battle as green as the fields around them. They held no faith in the British commanders who directed their fate, who had butchered their mates in Turkey. What would they do to protect them here in France, now against German tanks and enemies in the sky?

The French roads led them on like veins of blood pumping towards the great beast's heart. It drew their life force in, directing where they would expend it.

Determining where it would take their youth, their strength and their courage and crush it into the earth to win this war.

Clarkson washed his face and hung the little towel over the rail, unwilling to look in the mirror. He didn't want to judge the man who lived there. He didn't need to consider the consequences of what he was about to do because his past and future selves would never understand what the present man needed.

He needed to feel alive, and right now Rose made him feel that more than any other person on earth.

He closed the door softly, watching her in profile as she looked out behind the curtains then turned and met his gaze. Perhaps it was way the light filtered through her blouse as she undid the buttons, outlining the curve of her breast. Or perhaps it was the way she didn't smile, but undid her skirt instead, letting it drop to the floor with her undergarments as she lifted her now bare legs out and stepped forward, dragging the rest of her underthings over her head and standing at last, naked, unapologetic and proud. Or perhaps it was the lift of her chin as she met him squarely and walked over, her body lush and beckoning. Whatever it was he lost control, forgetting his intention of taking things slowly, and devoured her mouth, her breasts and kissing that maddening spot behind her ear. She clutched at his clothes, undressing him as they fell onto the bed.

He took her quickly, her cries spurring him on; their passion burned their skin and filled their senses. He felt her name draw from his throat as the intensity exploded and he climaxed within her, unable to stop, drawing himself to and fro. She rolled him onto his back and traced his arms and shoulders with her mouth and lower, down his stomach, and soon he was ready again. Rose took control this time, riding on top and finding her passion in full force. Soon it was her turn to cry out and she clenched and shuddered over and over as he drove hard and fast, grabbing her firmly and joining her.

It was some time later, as they lay naked and sprawled, his hand tracing circles on her breasts, when he finally spoke. 'I can never give you up now.'

Strange that he should choose the same words that Gregory had once used at Greenshades, Rose mused, and strange how different they made her feel when she felt the same way.

Twenty-seven

Bolougne, 23 July 1916

Twenty-three days. Twenty-three days and twenty-three nights that were distinguished by light and dark and little else. Man after man, torn, ripped. Pale and dying. Alive and tortured with pain. Dead.

The town was filled to capacity, as was Calais, and still they came. Later 'the Somme' would be a name synonymous with loss as they came to know the true extent of the cost. Hundreds of thousands more would die and many more would be wounded, but for now great chunks of the glorious British army lay in shattered threads on the fields of France. Some were sent mad from the terror of the constant rain of shells – bombardments so severe news reports told they could be heard from England. Others were victims of a new torment: poison gas. One young man clung to Emma the whole way in the ambulance, shaking and in shock, constantly crying out his poor mate's name, only to die as they reached Boulogne. Others were stretchered into hospitals only for doctors to find them already cold on the table. Often they never found out which injury killed them.

The new Australian troops had been thrown to the slaughter at Fromelles, a woefully misjudged attack that left many of them exposed in open fields at the mercy of German machine guns. Five thousand casualties and no ground taken. Rose knew she would never be able to wipe the images of stilled young faces and near-new uniforms from her mind.

She'd stopped being able to eat, being able to sleep. Rose was living a nightmare that had rudely interrupted her beautiful dream, and what little time she had to think of Clarkson was shared with duty now as she hurtled along towards more mutilation and death. Brief stolen moments of fear as she scanned the skies as she drove, searching for his plane, in constant dread of death streams lining the blue.

He was caught just as she was in an exploded world, the beasts locked in ferocious battle now, teeth bared and tearing in bloody madness.

Still, somehow he had managed to send her a message. Just a small box with a single chess piece inside. Someone would sit to play one day and wonder where on earth the queen had got to.

She was pulling into the station, returning with more wounded from the front with Emma and Beatrice, when Private Ben Hill ran towards them.

'It's Pozières. Heavy losses. We need to get up there now.'

The girls didn't comment, just helped unload in practised haste and jumped back in with Ben, heading towards the French village in silence. After Fromelles they dreaded what carnage they would find.

Clarkson searched the late-morning sky as Captain Roger Standing came up behind him. 'He's down.'

Clarkson looked to the ground, forcing emotions away as he struggled to accept it.

'Major says you're not to go up for a few hours. Says he knows you're on no sleep for days and he needs you alert,' he continued, clearing his throat as his own eyes filled. 'Try and get some rest, Clarkson. There's nothing else we can do now.'

Clarkson stared at the plumes of smoke that billowed on the horizon. 'He may still be alive.'

Standing nodded, patting Clarkson's shoulder before moving back to barracks and leaving him to his thoughts. Rookie's face imprinted itself on his mind; the image of him waving, his smile enormous beneath his goggles as he and Rose watched him fly over them that day.

He shook his head and strode towards his car. Damn doing nothing and damn sleeping. Rookie could be there, lying in the fields near Pozières, waiting for someone to find him and take him to the clearing station. To where Rose most likely was.

Gregory flattened himself against the wall, heaving. Why the hell had they chosen his regiment, the British 17th Warwickshire, to support these bloody mad Australians? They fought wars like they did everything else. Rash, undisciplined and reckless.

A bomb exploded nearby and he saw Second Lieutenant Pankhurst's body fly past, landing in a lifeless heap in the rubble, a great gash across his neck and chest. Stupid fool, he thought, angry and repulsed at the same time. How had they got so bloody close? Why had he listened to Pankhurst when he'd suggested cutting through this part of the village? Gregory's heart pounded and he decided there was only one thing for it.

'Retreat!' He called to his party.

'But, Captain– '

'You heard me, move back!' Gregory yelled. He'd done everything he could to stay alive in this damn war and he wasn't about to die now.

Clarkson pulled over, trying to take in the sheer scale of the wounded and the desperate efforts of those trying to save them at the clearing station. Hundreds of maimed men, perhaps thousands. All was in constant flux: stretchers, ambulances, white cotton covered in blood. Dead bodies. A savage scramble for life under deafening shelling that promised more death.

He drove around it, scanning the fields nearby, hoping for some sign of Rookie's plane. There was nothing. Only farmland littered with the incongruous articles of war. He parked the car, unable to progress any further, and made his way across to the front of the station, where the men were being stretchered in from aid posts. And there among it all, checking each passing casualty, issuing instructions and covered in the blood of her boys, was his Rose.

The bombs were echoing deep in her core. Rose well understood how the men continued to shake like leaves after days of it crashing through their nerves. The wounded kept coming, some not even on stretchers, just carried, often by other wounded.

'Take him to the right and bandage that gash hard, here.' She pointed where the blood continued to pour out from the man's shin, knowing he would likely lose his leg.

Cut, burned, gassed, shot. It came in a blur as she worked.

Clarkson.

Everything else didn't seem real then, like she was standing inside one of her own dreams, knowing she would wake up. He was here. Something was whole and alive. Death wasn't clutching at him. Not yet.

He came and took the corner of the next stretcher, winking at her and giving her his slow dazzling smile. Rose smiled back and, somehow, it was all she needed.

They worked together, the tall pilot and the redheaded ambulance driver, doing what they could to hold the lifeblood inside the Australians that afternoon. It wasn't what either of them would ever have imagined they would choose to do – bear witness to atrocity and gruesome suffering for hours on end. But there was nowhere else either of them would have chosen to be. The beasts had sliced with their claws and ripped great chunks of flesh in a frenzy of killing and the giant lay bleeding, torn and decimated at their feet. They would do whatever it took to save the pieces that were left.

'Pilot. There's a pilot,' called one voice from a stretcher near Clarkson.

'That's right, fella. I'm a pilot,' Clarkson shouted back, turning towards him.

'Pilot. Like you,' the man called out, coughing. 'In the field. Other side of farmhouse. Plane went down…hours ago.'

'How do you know?' Clarkson went to him and clutched the man's hand.

'Watched him. We was…trapped all day…so I watched. He is…moving.' The man coughed again, grasped at Clarkson, then managed to point to the east. 'He's alive.'

Clarkson followed the man's pointed finger and looked out to a farmhouse that obscured much of the field beyond. He stared for a moment, seeing what he had to do.

'What is it?' Rose called over the noise. Clarkson grabbed a few bandages and supplies, throwing them in a bag before going over to her. 'It's Rookie. He's down. I think…I think he is still alive.' He paused to grab her shoulders and kiss her briefly. 'I have to go, my love.'

He gave her one last look before running out of the station and towards the line of trees that led to the farmhouse.

'You can't go into the battle area,' said Beatrice, watching Rose from nearby.

Rose looked around her as she finished bandaging the soldier's arm she had been tending. 'It's quietened down for now.'

Beatrice surveyed the area and realised it was true. There was a lull. She turned back to argue further but Rose was already gone.

Gregory hunched further into the stall. The animals were well gone but the place stank of manure. Still, it was the best option he had for now, trapped in this sector as they were.

Curse Pankhurst and his stupidity.

'Messenger!' called his young lieutenant, Harris.

'Captain,' panted the man as he arrived at the barn. 'At last! Pardon, sir. Message from HQ. They want you to report back. Leave Pankhurst in command, sir.'

'Pankhurst's dead,' Gregory informed him, sizing up what was left of his party. 'Harris,' he called, 'take over.'

The young lieutenant looked set to protest at being left in the barn, in charge of a band of terrified men under a raining hail of bombing, but Gregory wasted no time on that. He was getting out.

'Rookie,' Clarkson said. 'It's me.'

The sun was crimson behind the heavy clouds and Rookie stared at him, his breathing sharp and short.

'Clarkson?'

'It's me, mate. I'm here.' Clarkson tried not to let the tears slide down his cheeks. He'd seen enough death to know that he was too late.

'The Jerries…' Rookie said, his young body shaking with the pound of each explosion.

Clarkson shook his head. 'They can't see you here, mate. You chose a good field to crash in.' Looking around him, he acknowledged it was true. The crash site was in a valley and only visible from the farmhouse.

'Rose,' Rookie said, looking over his shoulder.

'She's…'

'…here.'

Clarkson turned in surprise as Rose crouched next to him. Rookie tried to smile at her then turned his eyes back to Clarkson. '…I got one…a Jerry. Grandfather…owes me a car…'

The blood trickled from the side of his mouth and Rose wiped it away with her apron as Rookie drew his last breath. She closed his eyes and Clarkson allowed himself his first tears of the war.

He was running. The messenger had been hit as the bombs continued in endless succession and he now ran alone. Gregory fell into the cover of the tree line that ran along a farm near the village and followed them along. Hunted. Afraid. Furious. Pressing himself against a large trunk he paused to heave air back into his lungs, watching the red sun set behind a curtain of black smoke.

This was all because of his wife. If he hadn't needed to stay in England to hunt for Rose he would have gone back to damnable Australia to his house in Melbourne to wait out the war. He never would have been forced by his mother to take this commission. He never would have been made to change his carefully planned life.

He never would have lost his child.

Gregory watched as a woman and a man crossed the field below, walking away from plane wreckage. The pilot seemed to have survived. A tall man. Vaguely familiar. And the woman… not unlike the red-haired slut he'd married.

Gregory's entire being froze as the hatred ran through him like iced water.

Rose. With her lover, Clarkson, after all. Walking across before him through the middle of the war. In his sights at last.

He lifted his gun as they reached the rise and took aim.

I told you I would never let you go.

Clarkson didn't hear the shot in the noise of the artillery, he only saw her fall, stumbling backwards and holding her stomach where a scarlet stain spread. As he turned to catch her the bullet in his back drove him straight into her arms.

'Captain!'

Gregory turned as he headed past the farmhouse, gritting his teeth as a major called him over.

'Yes, sir?'

'Get these men over to the right, near the second house. We need to take out that gunner.' He pointed out the objectives as he shouted his instructions, pressing himself against the stone as a bomb exploded nearby.

'I have to report to HQ– '

'HQ can wait!' The major yelled, pulling his gun around and taking aim. 'Go!' He waved his arm and the lot of them went, Gregory forced to go with them.

The village was by now reduced to half-shells of buildings and rubble and Gregory ran and weaved his way, losing sight of the men almost immediately in the dust. He threw himself behind a broken wall, the explosions around him shaking it as it crumbled further.

She was dead. There was no time to relish the satisfaction as the hell around him flashed in white explosion after explosion, jolting him again and again. A severed arm landed on him and he recoiled, throwing it off in horror. *Enough.*

He ran again, away from the men, away from the explosions, away from the war. This time he didn't pause.

The machine gun shot him in the back and his last awareness was of grim satisfaction. At least she was denied life too.

He felt her heart growing weaker as he laid his head against her breast, his own breath shallow and ragged. She was still warm and soft and it seemed impossible that she would ever be otherwise. He managed to lift his hand and hold hers, forcing himself to roll onto the ground to ease his weight upon her. It cost him. The pain shot through his back and for a moment he thought he was already dead as the white blinded his vision. Then she spoke and his entire being focused on her words as she drew him back to consciousness.

'Stay with me.'

'I told you before, I could never…leave you now.'

'You said never give me up.'

'Did I?' He paused to find breath enough for words. 'Not my choice.'

'What's that…supposed to mean?'

'I don't own you…can't give you up. Your choice who you give yourself to.'

She smiled, applying what little strength she had left to squeezing his hand. 'I give…to you.'

He felt the white coming closer. 'When can I seal the deal… with a kiss?'

She smiled again. 'Typical man.'

Beatrice packed the last of the wounded that could be moved, glad of the morning light at last. The sunrise would have been glorious if not for the constant plumes blocking its beauty, denying the wretched souls here even that comfort.

She scanned the line of trees, wondering desperately where Rose and Clarkson were. Had they stayed near the plane all night?

She paused, focusing on something in the nearby field in the strange orange light, then turned to Ben. 'What's that?'

'Where?' He squinted.

'Just near the rise…'

They ran, staying close to the treeline, then across the rise to the flash of white apron she'd seen in the morning glow.

There were two bodies.

Drawing closer she recognised one was a woman, and her steps faltered as she saw a sight that would remain with her for the rest of her days.

Redsped and her captain lay pale against the earth, their hands in each other's palms as they both stared sightlessly beyond the clouds of death and into the dawn of a new day.

They were buried together, two little white crosses side by side on a green patch of earth in France. In a seaside town nearby a little girl stood at the gate and wondered why her mother didn't come as her great aunt took her hand, telling her they were about to go on a big ship to a wonderful land far, far away.

Twenty-eight

Highview, August 1916

Her back ached and she stretched upwards, holding her bulging stomach and yawning. The doctor said it wouldn't be long now and Veronica certainly hoped so as she pulled back the curtains, looking for Pattie, who'd said she would visit this morning. It would be a cheerful distraction from the monotony and boredom of her life at the moment. Sitting about feeling useless and fat was hard to get used to after her busy life as a nurse.

She sighed, walking out onto the verandah. Spring was set to arrive at Highview. The air was thick with the last of the wattle and the jasmine seemed ready to burst from its purple sockets. She picked one early bloom and inhaled the sweet scent. Maybe she should name the baby after a flower if it was a girl, regretting the thought as Rose's face flashed through her mind.

They'd heard the news just two days earlier and the story was starting to filter through in pieces of just what had happened to her over the past few years. It had surprised Veronica at first to hear that she was working with the wounded, but then she remembered that day when she'd been bitten by the snake and the way Rose had handled things. She'd always felt there was more to Rose after that and the role of ambulance driver suited her well in light of that memory.

Despite the way Rose had treated her, and Jack of course, Veronica still felt sorrow at her passing. Her heart went out to Mildred and George, who'd lost their only daughter and were, by all accounts, devastated. Then there was poor Iggy who had always been a devoted brother to Rose and now had to hear of her passing in a trench somewhere on the other side of the world. To top it all off no one knew the whereabouts of Gregory. Apparently he was missing in action in Pozières. Hearing they'd been in France at the same time, Veronica hoped they'd been able to reconcile, aware that there had been 'problems' via Mildred.

Wherever he was, she was glad Gregory was spared having to deal with her passing for now.

During war, ignorance truly was bliss.

And then there was the little girl, Elizabeth. George's sister Joelene had sent a telegram stating she had been looking after her in France and was bringing her home on the first available ship to Australia. Stroking her hand softly against the baby in her own womb Veronica felt keenly the loneliness of a small child in the middle of a vast ocean, leaving her mother behind forever and possibly her father too as she headed towards a strange land.

The sound of the Sunbeam coming up the drive and Pattie's excited call roused her and she turned to see her arriving with her mother and May. Veronica walked towards them her arms outstretched to hold her niece who clapped her hands at the sight of her, saying, 'Wa! Wa!'

'Auntie Wa can't pick you up today, darling.' Alice held her granddaughter and gave Veronica a kiss on the cheek, reprimanding her gently. 'No heavy lifting, remember? How are you, dear? Is Catherine about?'

'Inside and knitting.' Veronica followed them up the stairs as Pattie linked her arm through hers.

'When's this nephew of mine arriving? Good Lord, you're waddling like a duck! It's not a good sign. The suspense is killing me as to whether he'll have webbed toes or not like his father.'

'He does not have webbed toes!'

'Yes he does: the little pinkie is all meshed up against the next one. I suppose I should have warned you that you were marrying a duck-man but I selfishly wanted you as my sister.'

Veronica laughed, feeling instantly cheered by Pattie's arrival. 'I don't really know that it's a boy…'

'Of course you do,' she said airily. 'Now, we just have to get Clarkson home so I can get busy cooking him a chum. He'll need someone to practise cricket with.'

They took tea with their mothers in the parlour as May entertained them all with her baby discoveries, including some 'sooz' (shoes), a 'sushun' (cushion) and of course, the perfectly clear 'Cake!' The conversation turned to Rose and Alice shook her head sadly as she told them further news.

'Mildred said one of Rose's friends had written to her, expressing her condolences and telling her how well loved Rose was over there. Apparently they called her Redsped because she was the fastest ambulance driver they had. And she also mentioned Rose had an Australian friend who often visited and was killed at the same time. They were collecting wounded from the front line when they died. Stray shots I suppose…Anyway it's all terribly sad, although Mildred said it's a comfort to hear that she had friends over there who cared about her.' They all nodded quietly, imagining this other Rose, tearing along in an ambulance with her friend only to meet their own deaths.

'I wonder if it was anyone we knew?' Catherine said after a moment.

'Mildred said she was going to write back to this girl, Beatrice is her name I think, and ask if she knows the friend's name and any other information she had on her life over there. Rose didn't talk about it in her letters for fear of Gregory finding out where they were. She was quite adamant he not know anything.'

'I wonder what happened to them? They seemed a perfect match,' Veronica pondered, deciding not to elaborate on some of the less savoury ways in which that was true. Not so Pattie.

'Both snakes in the grass if we're honest,' she blurted.

'Pattie!' gasped her mother.

'I was being honest!'

'Honesty doesn't necessitate speaking ill of the dead.'

'Doesn't necessitate reinventing their characters either,' mumbled Pattie as she sat on the floor with May, rolling a little ball to her and smiling as she grasped it with her chubby hands and rolled it back. There was a knock at the door and they heard Eileen go to answer it as May grabbed the ball and placed it in a shoe, pushing it about like a little train and saying, 'Choo choo.'

Veronica was sipping her tea and smiling at them when her mother stood up, dropping her napkin to the ground. Following Catherine's gaze to the doorway she felt her face drain of blood. Alice placed her cup down very carefully, hardly daring to look up at Father Francis, who stood holding the most dreaded of wartime correspondence. A telegram.

Veronica held her breath, following the priest's eyes as he searched the room. They came to rest on Pattie.

She was yet to notice him as she reached under the couch for May's ball.

'Patricia...'

Pattie turned at the priest's voice, standing slowly as the ball slipped from her fingers.

The smile faded from her face, not to return for many months, as she watched him move towards her in his long black robes, like the spectre of death holding out her fate in an envelope that she backed away from. Veronica stood and held her shoulder as Catherine took the telegram and opened it. Her hands shook as she read the words in a blur and Pattie's eyes pleaded with the priest before swinging to Alice, who simply shook her head and began to cry.

Pattie fell onto the floor screaming in pain, the sound more terrible than any Veronica had ever heard. The priest muttered to the others and Veronica vaguely registered the words 'loss', 'Clarkson' and 'line of duty'. Alice collapsed next to her daughter, rocking her to and fro, trying to stem the pain and direct it into her own flesh as her daughter's thin shoulders hunched in agony against her.

And throughout it all, May held out her ball and wondered why Mummy didn't want to play anymore.

They all wore black at mass that Sunday and Veronica watched her friend closely as she placed a wreath upon the altar, her face drawn, dark circles under eyes that couldn't seem to produce any more tears. Next came the Dwyers, Mildred appearing far older than her forty-nine years, holding tight to George as they laid a wreath for Rose and Father Francis offered up a special prayer for the fallen. He spoke of the news that the Australians had taken Pozières in the end, showing enormous courage against impossible odds, and how the victory might change the fate of the war in France. Of the never-ending hope for peace. But the price seemed too high to many in the church that day.

The congregation headed back to the O'Shays' for tea and in hushed tones they moved together, sharing their grief. Veronica served cakes and answered questions about her brothers and Jack as she searched the crowd for Pattie, finally spying her down by the fence, looking out at the fields. She made her way awkwardly to her side and placed her arm about her waist, dropping her head against her shoulder.

'Love you,' she said simply. Pattie leant her head against hers and they watched the new calves seek their mothers in the nursing field.

'I suppose this is it. No funeral. Nothing else to do.' Pattie shrugged helplessly. 'Funny thing is I keep expecting him to walk in and say it was a mistake. Then I think maybe it's just a dream and I'll wake up soon. But I don't. I'm beginning to think it isn't a mistake and it isn't a dream. And he...he's never coming back...' She turned and held Veronica's hands. 'I know I sound crazy but I need you to tell me. Is it real? Did this really happen?'

Veronica nodded and held her friend, who found fresh tears after all. 'Yes, darling, it's real. Terribly real...I'm so sorry.'

Pattie cried for a while, then pulled away, wiping at her face. 'So now I'm just another skinny spinster.' She tried to smile. 'Or should I say whining widow.' Her face crumpled again and she apologised as Veronica held her stomach and frowned. 'Sorry. I'll be all right in a minute.'

'You'd better be. I don't have much use for a skinny spinster or a whining widow, but I am in need of my sister-in-law.'

'To keep my brother in line?' She sniffed.

'No, to help me have this baby. I think my waters just broke.'

The next morning a wail broke over the house as Peter Clarkson Murphy entered the world and no one gave him more cuddles than his aunt Pattie.

Twenty-nine

Beersheba, Palestine, 31 October 1917

It was the flies that got to him. On his food, his face, his ears, cloistered about the dead and annoying the horses, constant and clinging. After nearly two years in the Middle East he'd decided he'd never complain about the flies in Australia again, not after this. It had become a game to them to try and eat their food before a certain number of flies landed on it. Iggy held the record, managing to land only two in his mouth during lunch one day. Some of the men had given up on the 'blowies' and ate them along with the food, figuring it all tasted about the same.

They were waiting for yet another battle, scattered about in small groups across the desert to deter attacks from the air. The horses were thirsty and Jack walked over to pat Tilley and reassure her, impatient to make a move as the punishing sun bore down on yet another dry, dusty afternoon. She pushed her head against him and he talked to her softly, her large eyes trusting as he ran his hand along the pelt of her nose.

A group passed nearby and they squinted and saw they were Turkish prisoners being led away.

Simmo immediately leapt up and began shouting, 'Go back an fight yer bastards!' baring his backside and whistling loudly. They laughed and Jack shook his head as Simmo waved his bottom in the air. 'Tell 'em Australia sent ya!'

Jack gave Tilley one last pat before settling back down and placing his hat over his eyes, moving off to his favourite place: Vera. How he missed her, the lightness of her smile, the everyday joy she exuded, the gentle way she had about her when someone needed nurturing. And her body. Oh how he missed that. He felt he could trace every curve in his mind's eye down to the last inch, although he supposed it was different now in parts. More rounded. He smiled at the thought, looking forward to finding out, then sighed. If he ever got out of this blasted desert. He couldn't seem to remember a time when he wasn't stinking and filthy, the dust in every inch of his clothing and person. Then again he supposed he should be thankful. He could be waist-deep in mud like the poor sods in France. He shuddered to think of living in those trenches.

Something else bothered him though, more than the flies and the dust and the heat. It had continued to grow since Gallipoli, the uneasy feeling that he'd changed here. He'd noticed it in some of the others too, even Iggy. They'd become truly hardened. Once upon a time the sight of a dead man would have turned his stomach, but now he barely noticed the corpses lining the fields of battle. The unthinkable act of burying a bayonet in a man's heart was everyday work. And he didn't even register the screams of the dying and wounded, blocking them out as expected noise.

Not that he enjoyed it. He hated it, all of it. And he hated what it had turned him into.

Problem was, he didn't know how he was ever going to turn back into himself again. Into Jack Murphy. He was 'Lieutenant' or 'Murph' or 'cobber'. Jack Murphy was an ordinary man, not a digger. As much as he lived for the day, he didn't know how he would be able to handle going home. They wouldn't understand; how could they? Even Veronica, for all she had seen, would never have to live with becoming part of the killing. He felt unclean, like the stench of slaying men could never leave him now, sometimes gazing at the blood on his hands and feeling that it forever stained his skin. Only his brothers here understood, and he thanked God that Iggy was with him. Somehow, having a mate going through the same thing made him feel he could face home again.

It was hours later when he opened his eyes, surprised he'd managed to doze off for a while, and he watched Iggy thoughtfully stroking Ebony and staring out across to where they knew their usual division, the 1st, were fighting. He, Iggy and Simmo had been pulled in to the 4th Division two days ago and Jack wondered why they had been picked. With Simmo's recent promotion, perhaps General Chauvel felt he needed more experienced officers for this part of his attack. Jack laughed inwardly, thinking of Simmo's backside waving antics, wondering what Chauvel would make of that particular brand of leadership.

The signal came and Jack roused himself, mounting with the others as they re-formed the line, wondering why they were bothering as the afternoon wore on.

An hour and a half later they were still waiting as the horses flicked their tails, smelling the water in the nearby town of Beersheba. What was Chauvel up to? They had a great deal of faith in their Australian leader but this seemed a strange move. Why hold them there, waiting, so late in the day?

Then the instructions rang clear down the line. They were ordered to draw their bayonets like swords for a mounted charge. The Light Horse were to break through to Beersheba, secure the wells and take prisoners. On horseback. Jack exchanged glances with Iggy. It was unheard of for mounted cavalry to stay on horseback and charge and they knew Chauvel was taking a great gamble based on the faith he had in the abilities of his men.

Jack wondered if this was it. Was this the day he would die, here in this hated desert, a million miles from home, on a suicide charge towards a city of enemies, hoisting bayonets against machine guns?

Backs straightened along the line and they held their mounts firm, bracing themselves. Jack felt the sweat of his palms against the leather as the call came.

'Go straight at it.'

They began at a trot, fanning out, then leapt forward and seized the only weapons they had, speed and surprise. Jack felt the fear flooding through him and harnessed it as determination, urging Tilley on and hoisting his makeshift sword. She flew across the desert next to Ebony, the need for water adding to her speed as the pounding of hooves beat a thundering drum in the burning afternoon light. Machine-gun fire met them and men and horses fell. Flashes of Gallipoli assaulted his memory, but he pushed the images of massacre out of his mind and forced himself to keep on riding. They were still falling but somehow less so. What was Johnny Turk up to? The trenches were near and he realised they were actually going to make it. It was a blur. His bayonet flashed and met flesh and Tilley swung about as they moved as one. He pushed through, Iggy still alongside, and they slashed and turned, watching the Turks scramble to recover from the shock of hundreds of Australians appearing out of the dust and bearing down on them at once, like giants towering above them, orange steel in the sun.

Some surrendered at once, others fought bravely, and soon the sudden chaos was just as suddenly over and the bewildered Turks had lost the stronghold of Beersheba at the hands of just a few hundred Australian Light Horsemen. Turkish losses were heavy and the Australians took over seven hundred prisoners with only thirty-one of their own dead.

But every number holds a precious life.

Jack found Iggy crying, pinned beneath Ebony. The once fastest horse in northern Sydney had taken a fatal shot from a Turkish bullet. Iggy's leg was crushed, but his tears of agony were for far more than the physical pain. Jack pulled him free and supported him as he struggled to pat his loyal mount one last time. When they turned, it was to see a stretcher pass by, Simmo's enormous form sprawled across it, stilled at last by the enemy's sword. They heard later he took on several men at once and was caught from behind.

The horses drank their fill as the ancient city gave in to the night, and slept in the hands of new rulers for the first time in centuries, while on her outskirts the shovels pierced the land and buried those who also slept, but would never wake.

Mick came but Tom chose to continue working with Iggy and the other wounded under the giant red cross marking the mobile hospital from the air. The sky was clear as usual and the sky turned a dusky pink, staining the dark into light as the day dawned on those who still survived this desert war.

Jack and Mick stood together, watching them hammer the white crosses above the fallen and thinking about their mate Simmo, who would never again entertain them or make them laugh, nor delight them with his amazing resourcefulness. The large man with his even larger heart was gone, along with so many others from home. Jack felt his sorrow border on desperation as he stared at the cross that held so few words for such a man. How he resented the fools who'd sent them all there, the men in boardrooms and mansions and castles who played with their lives, poring over their big maps then sipping their whisky from their crystal glasses. He felt a stab of grief and sent it straight to God as the bugler played the last post. *Please, let it end.*

The burial over, they walked back together, the sun beginning to burn once again.

'Jeez, I'm starving. What shall it be, bully beef or flies for breakfast?' Jack sighed.

'Actually I've got high hopes for some eggs now we've taken the town. Saw some chickens running about this morning.'

'As long as it wasn't human chicks you were looking at. They get a bit funny about their women around here, Casanova.'

Mick laughed. 'Hey, I'll be too busy keeping Tom out of trouble to be sweet-talking in this town. I wonder if you can get arrested for being too friendly?'

'Tomfoolery perhaps?'

Mick laughed again before squinting against the sun at an approaching plane.

'What the hell…?'

The single German plane was low and flying towards the hospital and Mick and Jack watched in horror as the impossible happened.

People scattered as the bomb dropped and blew the red cross across the desert, sending debris flying in a massive black cloud. Men ran out of the conflagration, their bodies on fire as the plumes rose like the gates of hell behind them. His senses assaulted, Jack found himself, after almost three years of war, frozen in shock for the first time.

Mick took off at a sprint, screaming orders as he searched frantically for survivors in the chaos, however Jack still couldn't seem to move as he watched the appalling scene unfold, almost as if he were watching something make-believe. It was too terrible to be real as injured men tried to crawl away, their clothing and skin and hair in flames. Then he saw that one of them was Iggy and something clicked. He ran to pull him free and soon joined the others in a desperate race to stay the hand of death.

Then it was done. The dead lay and the living writhed and a terrible sound rent the air.

Jack turned to see his brothers-in-law lying in the morning sun, Mick screaming in pain not from his severely burned leg but for the charred form of his beloved brother, Tom, dead in his arms.

That afternoon the sun's final journey ended as it had begun: in burial. The desert had taken another life, the most unjust casualty of all, because this was a life that had been dedicated to saving others, in more ways than one. A man who made the intolerable duty of war bearable for all who knew him, salvaging their sanity along with limbs and lives. The one person who kept them going was now gone, and in their darkest hour, when they needed him the most.

Departed this world on the feast of All Hallows read a little makeshift plaque near the graves. All Hallows. All Souls.

Jack looked at the words, feeling emptied of faith. His soul was surely damned, because as he stared at the grave of the man who was, in every way, his own brother, the final piece of pain tore within. He knew all his fears had been well founded, for now he truly knew what it was to hate.

Thirty

Circular Quay, Sydney, June 1919

Jack leant against the rail, watching the harbour as the boats moved about in the early morning light and breathing the cold air in deeply. He'd forgotten just how beautiful it was with its golden beaches and bushland edging the city. It didn't seem possible that after nearly five long years he was finally coming home and, as he waited for them to dock, he re-read Veronica's last letter again, drawing her closer in anticipation to pass the time.

Dear Jack,

Pete is finally asleep and I've got some time to write a proper letter without him grabbing at the ink. My apologies for the mess he made of the last one! Your son is a curious little chap as you can see.

Firstly, I want you to know I am so proud of your promotion, MAJOR Murphy. Does that make me Mrs Major Murphy? That sounds terribly official. I only wish it didn't come with another commission. Surely the Egyptian revolt can be handled by the English at this point.

I want you home and I don't care how unpatriotic that sounds!

Speaking of appointments, I'm happy to report that Mick got his. He is now working with Dr Dwyer as a specialist in artificial limbs. Little May is fascinated by the arms and legs and sits up next to Mick, helping him design them. She loves making things and drawing and he doesn't seem to mind at all, although she has drawn quite a few animal legs instead of human ones in her designs. I enclose a few to give you a chuckle.

Mick's first triumph is the new foot he helped design for Iggy, who says he's finding riding much easier now. He has a new mare called Beersheba, or Sheba for short. He told me to tell you that she loves her food so much he really should have just gone ahead and called her Simmo, but that won't do of course, what with baby Simon already having that honour. She's actually getting quite fat but I'm sure he'll exercise it off her. I'm glad to report he is playing piano again. I thought he might have given it away after Helena died but he has got back on with things now. He amazes me with how brave he is: losing a foot, then marrying his nurse, only to lose her in childbirth...well, that's an enormous amount for any man to handle. Fortunately little Simon is so very easy and Mildred is giving him a good smothering, as you can imagine.

Mick's leg still bothers him but he gets around all right. It almost hurts me to look at the scars – burns are such nasty things. Still, he says he'd rather a limp than a missing appendage any day and counts himself pretty lucky, especially where he is working. I'm glad he has something to keep him busy. I know he is missing Tom something awful, but then again so are we all. Our dearest boy.

My parents have planted a row of jacaranda trees along our road in his memory and Mother says one day the flowers will be so bright he'll see them from heaven. I always cry when she says things like that. It is so hard for her that her brother and son both died in an attack on a field hospital. I think she finds that fact crueller than anything else, that such injustice could curse her twice. Still, it hasn't stopped her working at the orphanage with Alice and moving on with life, but there is a sadness in her face I don't think will ever go away.

I'm sorry, my darling. Here I am writing a letter supposed to cheer you up and all I'm doing is telling you of our grief. I'd tear it up but goodness knows I'd better not. Pete may not let me have another chance today and I want to get down to the post office before it closes for the weekend.

To answer your last question, no, the Dwyers still haven't been able to find Elizabeth. It's as if she's fallen off the face of the earth. I feel so sorry for Mildred. She sat down at the Quay right up until recently and the ships kept on coming but never with her granddaughter.

At least she's stopped doing that. It was terribly sad. They have searched under Elizabeth Chambers, Elizabeth Dwyer, even Elizabeth Rose but there is no trace. The aunt has seemingly disappeared too: no Joelene Pascal or Joelene Dwyer. No one travelling and no reported deaths at sea. Joelene's son was killed in the Somme so no leads there. Iggy thinks that Joelene was probably travelling under an alias to hide Elizabeth from Gregory and I suppose that's the only explanation, only where are they now? With Gregory confirmed KIA we will probably never know, but it's all very strange.

Anyway, my dearest heart, I will post this off, but not before I tell you how much I long for you to come home to me. Every day you are in my thoughts and every night I kiss your photo before I fall asleep and put it under my pillow to try to dream of you.

Stay safe and I'll keep on praying that you'll be home soon, my darling,

Your loving wife, Vera

Jack folded the letter, putting it back in his pocket in his old lucky tin. The day had finally come. No more waiting and holding letters and photos instead of his beloved ones. They didn't know it yet, but today he would meet his son and today he would hold his wife.

He had survived the war.

She woke early that day and brushed her hair, checking on Pete, who was sleeping soundly, clutching his bear.

'Daddy is coming home today, baby,' she whispered, kissing his soft head, before dressing and quietly moving out into the kitchen. Eileen was there boiling water for breakfast tea and looked up at her in surprise. 'What are you doing up at this hour, miss?'

'Heading in to the city. Keep a close eye on Pete for me, won't you? And please make sure you bake a cake for dinner.'

She winked at her, then, humming to herself as she put on her new velvet hat, ran happily out the door past the bemused housekeeper.

She bounced along in the new car she had purchased the previous month and marvelled again at the freedom of driving. Iggy had been teaching her every day and she was rather proud of her progress. By the time she parked at the Quay she had moved from feeling excited to deliciously nervous. Jack was coming home. Maybe he was already there.

Veronica was early, she knew, but she didn't want to take any chances. His latest letter was dated three weeks earlier from his last port and, somehow, the feeling was so strong that he would come today she had to sit at the Quay. There were no other transport ships due this week and waiting at home just wouldn't do. This was his boat, surely, and she wouldn't accept one more minute of separation than she had to. Smoothing her new turquoise jacket and straightening the white blouse beneath it, she settled in to wait.

It was late morning when the ship finally docked and she watched it impatiently, scanning the decks. There weren't as many people about as she'd thought there would be, but then again no one ever knew just what time these last ships would arrive. Most families figured it was easier to just see their loved ones when they walked up the path. But not Veronica.

She searched the faces as they walked down the gangway, looking for him, certain he would be among them. They were alike, these experienced soldiers: thin, sunburned, worn. The crisp uniforms they had once donned were long gone and they ambled rather than marched now in faded greens. Man after man they came and still no sign of him. Not another week of waiting. Please God. She moved closer, focusing on each one until at last, she finally recognised a familiar gait. He was shaking hands with another officer and several of the men saluted him as he turned to walk down. Then he saw her. The space between them contracted, their steps too slow as the short distance that ended the years of separation finally closed, and she was in his arms.

He kissed her long and hard, uncaring of the amused glances of the men or the stares of passers-by and she clung to him, joyful tears escaping.

'How did you know?' he finally said, holding her face and drinking in the sight of her.

'I willed you home.' She smiled, and he kissed her again before grabbing her hand to walk through the crowd. 'Wait,' she said, taking off his hat, 'the army doesn't own you anymore.' He laughed as she stood on tiptoe and kissed his cheek, wrapping his arm about her.

As they left the wharf Jack took one last glance behind him and, looking at the sea of diggers melting into their homeland, he hoped to God it was true.

Part Four

Thirty-one

Beecroft, September 1929

Katie ran across the paddock as quickly as she could with her large basket in hand, the cotton skirt light against her legs. She relished the feeling of spring arriving at last, her arms bared and her hat dangling against her long dark hair, feeling particularly excited that morning at the prospect of the day ahead. May said they were going to bake bread in the dug-out termites' nest over at Nana and Pop's, down by the creek, and Eileen had set an extra loaf to rise overnight for her to take along. She was looking forward to watching it cook, then spreading out her little tablecloth and coating the delicious pieces with the butter Mum had packed for her in her very own pot, along with another tiny pot of jam.

Even Pete was excited, stuffing his pack with other things he planned to 'cook' in there, including some potatoes, an old jumper and a pile of his wooden soldiers.

She hoped Simon was coming too. His grandmother often didn't let him play outside, making him stay indoors even on sunny days, saying it was either too hot or too windy or too something else. She was even stricter since Simon's Pop had died.

Katie heard her daddy say Nana Dwyer was 'too damn stuffy', adding 'the boy needs some blasted air'. Her mum told her dad to keep his voice down whenever he used those funny words he learned in the war, which Katie supposed were trapped inside his whisky bottles, because he only ever said them when he drank whisky.

She knew Simon's dad was a famous piano player who travelled a lot, so his nana looked after him most of the time because his mum had died when he was born. Katie thought that was very sad because mummies were the best people in the world, especially hers.

Pete bounced past her on Bonkers, their mule, whooping at the top of his voice, and she called out to him to lift her up, but he either didn't hear or didn't want to stop and she sighed, trotting along behind him. Pity the new baby was a boy too.

Ten minutes later she reached the creek and was pleased to see Simon had turned up today.

Pete was already busy investigating inside the makeshift stove, stoking the fire her Pop had made for them earlier.

'Don't leave the poker in there; it will get too hot, and you'd better stand back or you might get burned from an ember jumping out. Careful!' May bossed him about, acting very important. Pop had put her in charge and Pete didn't like that much. He was under strict instructions to listen to everything she said or else Dad was going to make him stay indoors tomorrow and miss the cake stall after mass as well as the cricket. Pete loved watching the cricket. He'd been practising all winter and hoped to start playing soon, now that he was thirteen. She was turning six and she wanted her birthday cake to be pink with a rose in the middle. Pete's had been green.

'What's that? Don't you even think about putting that in there.' May pointed at the old jumper.

'Come on, May. It'll just smoke up a bit. I thought you might like to do a little dance for us like those Indians do while I make some signals. Get some rain in,' he suggested, rolling the jumper into a tight ball. Katie wrinkled up her nose. It smelled like mothballs.

'Put it away Peter Murphy or I'll tell your mother!'

Pete pulled a face then stuffed the jumper back in his bag, taking out the potatoes instead.

'How 'bout these then? You can't object to actual food.'

May sighed. 'All right, but only after we bake the bread. Have you got your loaf, Katie-bird?' She smiled at her as Katie very carefully unwrapped it and brought it over. They all watched as May put the bread in to cook, the embers burning nicely under the black tray, then May produced a breadboard and she and Pete sliced up the potatoes.

'Pity we haven't got any butter.' May frowned and Katie jumped up and went to her basket, holding out her pots.

'I've got some!'

May told her she was a clever girl to think of bringing it and Katie, encouraged by her success, spread out her tablecloth on the ground and placed the jam pot in the centre, earning another smile from May and praise from Simon.

'Quite a home-maker, our Kate!'

She felt very pleased about that comment. One day she hoped Simon and she would get married and she could bake her own bread in her own oven for him and he could play her lovely songs on the piano. She was sure he was going to be famous like his dad. She just hoped he didn't meet someone else before she grew up; after all he was five years older than her.

She could smell the fresh-baked bread and May took out the loaf, letting them eat while it was still nice and hot, with melted butter and jam. The potatoes baked to a delicious golden brown and soon they ate all of those too. Katie decided Pete had been right about that idea.

'Come and get some water with me, Katie,' Simon suggested and she followed him down to the creek to fill the bottles.

'Why are there always dragonflies down here?' she asked him, watching as one hovered nearby.

'They like water 'cos their babies live in it. Why? You scared of them?'

'Oh no, I think they look like fairies.' She watched the little rainbows on its wing, then ventured to ask, 'Are they fairies, Simon?'

'Nuh. Dad says they're just insects and they're pretty ugly too. I saw one through his microscope. They look like monsters up close.' He screwed up his nose, trying to see it properly through his spectacles. 'See? Six legs.'

She leant over and squinted. 'I don't think it's ugly. I think it's beautiful.'

'Nuh, it's ugly. So's the praying mantis. Dad reckons he should pray to be less of an ugly-looking mug.' Simon grinned at her.

She giggled. Simon knew so many things. She wished her dad had a microscope. Still, she knew she was very lucky because she still had two grandfathers. Simon had only ever known one.

She knew he was sad that his Pop was in heaven now but Mummy said he wouldn't be too lonely because his daughter lived there as well. Her name was Rose so Katie supposed she must have been very pretty.

She was glad her grandfathers weren't in heaven yet. Da played the violin and held wonderful parties and Pop made toys, plus he had an apple orchard nearby which was filled with flowers at the moment.

'Can we go and see the orchard after?' She jumped up, splashing a bit of water on her skirt.

'What do you want to go over there for? There's no apples this time of year.' He picked up the bottles and started walking.

'It's so pretty.' She sighed dreamily as she skipped along next to him.

Looking down at her, he shook his head. 'You really are a girl, you know that?'

'Yes.' She was confused. 'What else am I supposed to be?'

He didn't answer because an angry voice – her dad's – reached their ears.

'Get home. Home!' he roared at Pete, who ran across the field, her dad marching after him.

May was crying and they hurried towards her.

'What happened?' Simon asked.

'Nothing. Take Katie home. Actually, don't...Bring her up to my house.' She was packing the picnic away sniffing and Katie went over to put her arms about her.

'Don't cry, May,' she whispered, starting to cry herself.

'I'm all right Katie-bird.'

But Katie knew she wasn't. 'Why was he so angry?'

May cried hard then and told them. 'Pete...Pete put some soldiers in the fire. I was cleaning up and I didn't see him and then... his dad came and saw them burning and...got really angry and yelled at him and...and hit him...'

'Daddy hit Pete?' Katie was horrified. He got cross sometimes, especially when he drank the whisky, but he never hit them.

'It's all right, darling, I'm sure he didn't mean to. He slipped I think.'

Katie knew May was lying and felt very sad as they made their way across the field.

Simon kicked at a tuft of grass. 'I'm going to cop it too. I didn't tell Nana we were playing with the ant oven. She never would have let me come. And now she'll hear about this for sure.'

'Maybe Daddy won't tell anyone,' Katie suggested helpfully, but they knew that he would.

'Well, if this is your last day of freedom for a while let's make the most of it,' May decided. 'What do you want to do?'

Simon stopped and looked at Katie. 'I hear the blossom trees are very pretty in the orchard. How about a climb?'

Katie ran as fast as her little legs would take her to the orchard as the others followed.

'Pretty trees, huh?' May teased. Simon shrugged in his way, laughing as she added: 'Girl.'

Veronica saw her son as he ran home across the paddock, his fair hair bright in the sun. Something was up. Then she saw Jack following at a distance and knew something was definitely wrong. She could feel his anger from where she was sitting.

'What happened?' she demanded as soon as Pete reached the verandah.

'Nothing,' he mumbled, trying to walk past, but she held his arms and turned him to face her.

His face had a nasty red welt across it and she gasped. 'Did you fall over?'

'Just leave it, Mum.' He shoved onwards, walking through the door and into his room, trying not to cry as he went.

She waited for Jack, her arms crossed nervously. 'What happened to Pete?'

'That boy has no respect!' he spat, slamming into the house and pouring himself a drink. 'I've a good mind to send him away to military school. Teach him some discipline.' She watched him as he threw back the whisky and poured another, but said nothing.

'You know what he did? Remember those soldiers Dad made for him when he was a little tyke? Hand carved? He burned them in that damn ant oven! Threw them in to see what it would look like. Well I know what it looks like goddamnit and let me tell you, it isn't much fun to watch. Absolutely no respect for what diggers did for this country. Where is he? I haven't finished with him yet!'

She closed the door behind her and stood to face him. 'He's just a boy, Jack. Calm down now. They were just toys to him.'

'They w'more than toys. Dad carved them himself. They were bloody Light Horse...had the hats and all.' He downed his drink again.

Veronica was torn between sympathy for Jack, who was obviously remembering the terrible day he saw Tom die, and the anger she felt over her son being hit.

'Where's he bloody gone?'

'He's nursing a swollen face, which I take it you gave him.'

'Don't tell me how to raise my sons, Vera,' he warned her darkly. 'This is between me and the boy. I'm going to teach him how to act like a man and show respect to men who've been to war.'

'What? You're going to take him down to the fields and shoot things, are you? Shoot him?'

'Shut y'mouth!' He swung his arm to slap her but she held his hand.

'No. You don't,' she warned, shaking. '*You don't.*'

He stared at his hand then back at her, crumbling as he realised what he'd been about to do. 'Oh God. Oh God, Vera, I'm so sorry…'

She let his hand drop. 'You will be if you ever hit my sons again. Or Katie. Or me. The war is over, Jack. Don't make another one here.'

He stared at the door long after she'd left, turning to fill his glass. That was the problem.

The war wasn't over at all. Not for him.

Veronica couldn't sleep and it wasn't because of the baby. Little James slept peacefully in his cot as she stole out onto the verandah and watched the moon rise. The home they had built next to Highview might have been a paddock away but she swore she could hear her father's snores as she gazed over at her former home, wishing she could go and crawl up in her old bed and tell her mother all her woes.

Hugging her arms to herself, she wondered how it had ever got this bad.

It had been wonderful at first, when he'd come home and they'd had a life together at last. Gone was the constant threat of being ripped apart, gone was the endless waiting and gone was the heartache she'd felt every day she was away from him. They made love every night and sometimes in the morning too before he headed off to work. He drove in and out, the ownership of an automobile making it possible for him to live at home during the week as well, in the beautiful house they had built between their parents' farms. They had painted it themselves, choosing cream and light blue, and little Pete enjoyed stirring the tins for Daddy, entranced by the coloured paint he called 'funny mud'.

Then, as life settled back down, he started staying in town occasionally, telling her he had to work late. She didn't mind too much, spending the time with Pete whom she felt she'd been neglecting a bit anyway. But then she fell pregnant and he started staying in for days at a time. She tried to tell herself it wasn't because he didn't want another baby, after all he was managing the business end of things for both their families now, but she wondered. He was very proud of his son but he hadn't found much time for him, falling straight back into business and the commitments of his former life. Fatherhood had not caught his full attention.

Then she woke up one morning with terrible cramps and, within a day, knew the baby was lost.

Devastated, she sent him a telegram and waited for him to come, but the days came and went and still there was no sign of him. Finally she took matters into her own hands, driving into the city and walking to his office. Never actually having been to his work before, she was surprised by how young and pretty his secretary Susan was, and how uncomfortable she became when Veronica asked about Jack's whereabouts. Suspicious, Veronica went across the street to wait in a teahouse and, sure enough, Jack came swaying down the street and straight up the stairs to the apartment he kept above his office. Drunk. Not that she was surprised that he was drinking; she'd expected he was indulging too much, given his constant stays in the city. It was more that fact that he was drunk at eleven o'clock in the morning that irked her. And that he hadn't bothered to come home in five days, despite the fact she'd just lost their baby.

Something shifted inside Veronica that day. She was done with turning a blind eye and pretending they didn't have a problem and she decided that when he finally did turn up at home, sober and sore, she would sit down and tell him exactly what she thought. The next day he did just that and she sat, wearing a black dress, her hair pulled back, waiting for him in the parlour.

'Hello, darling. I'm so sorry I . . .' he began, bending to kiss her, but she pulled back and he looked at her in surprise. 'What's this? Oh love, I am so terribly sorry. Truly. How are you feeling?'

She smoothed her skirt and gestured to the other chair. 'I'd like to have a word with you, if you don't mind, please.' He sat, somewhat reluctant, and she cleared her throat, forcing her tears down. 'I came to see you in town yesterday; I don't know if your secretary told you.' He nodded slightly and she continued. 'She's very pretty by the way.'

'Is that what this is about? Because if it is you have no worries on that score…'

'No. I'm hardly that pathetic, I would think. I saw you walking down the street…actually when I say walking it was more like a stumble, you were so drunk.'

'Oh come on, Vera, can't a man have a drink? I think I've earned the right– '

'Not at eleven in the morning when he should be at work, no. And not when his wife has lost…' she paused to compose herself '…lost a baby. The pub is hardly the choice a man should be making at such a time, wouldn't you agree?'

He jumped up and walked about the room. 'For God's sake, Vera, I told you I'd been working. I can't exactly say no to an associate if he wants to wet the whistle no matter what time it is. That's part of business.'

'And who is it that you can't say no to at home in the afternoon?'

He paused at that, then rounded on her angrily.

'*You*! Do this, do that! Look at the baby, visit your parents, ask Pattie for dinner, do you like these curtains, hold the bloody knitting wool! A man needs a blasted drink in this…this woman's world!' He threw his arms out, encompassing the room, and placed them on his hips.

'It's your home too.' She felt her anger building and calmed herself down, taking a deep breath. 'It's your home too.' She stood and walked over to him. 'I know you're used to living with men after these past years and this is…hard to adjust to, but you need to be here to make it yours. Your son needs you too. It's supposed to be a family home, not a woman's world.' She held his hand. 'I need to know you're not going to let me down like this again, Jack. I needed you and you weren't there. You're the last person I thought would ever do that.'

He looked down guiltily. 'I meant to come, Vera. I really did. I just…'

'What? Jack, tell me what's troubling you, please. Even when you're here you're… somewhere else. How can I help you if you don't tell me what's wrong?' She put her arms about him, holding him close, and for a moment she thought he was going to let her in, but then he stepped away and walked to the door, avoiding her eyes.

'I'm just finding work tiring, that's all. Better check on the horses before dinner. I'll see you in a bit.'

And so it had continued over the years. There had been happier times, times when he tried for a while, coming home at night and avoiding the bottle. He was silent and she knew it cost him, but after a while he would take to playing with Pete and the new light of his life, little Katie. She cherished these precious times and the nights of lovemaking that followed, but they were always short lived, as the dreams tore him awake and he took to the bottle again to send the memories to deeper places. Then he would be back to staying in town during the week, coming home on weekends to a blur of dinner parties, cricket, church and visiting, before taking off again. She had little time to talk to him and she suspected that was the way he liked it.

Her only clue to the demons that tormented him was the words he called out in his sleep in the dead of night, when he couldn't guard his tongue; he was back fighting the enemy and calling out warnings to his mates. He often called out that someone was aiming for the cross, thrashing about and yelling for them not to. Other times he cried for Tilley, begging to be allowed to take her home. Veronica knew that very few were able to bring their mounts home, and that most of the men chose to shoot their horses rather than leave them to be mistreated. He never told her what happened to Tilley and she couldn't bear to ask.

But his worst nightmare seemed to be about a man's face, and he sobbed the same words repeatedly in his sleep. 'Don't look at me, close your eyes.' This had grown louder and more heated in recent months; hence her constant exhaustion whenever he was home. Perhaps it had something to do with the way baby James watched him so solemnly, his gaze following his father whenever he was around, which seemed to unnerve Jack, prompting him to say more than once, 'He seems to know something about me.'

She still loved him. Deeply. But the Jack she knew was buried inside him somewhere and she had to live with an imposter day after day. It frightened her to think he would never resurface, especially tonight. For all he suffered he'd never lashed out and hit any of them before.

Veronica stared out across the pale silver fields, her mind filling with images of burning soldiers. Tom dying in agony. She flinched, pushing away the horror. It was bad enough to imagine, let alone witness. Her heart ached for Jack, forced to carry it. How deeply he'd reacted to the burning toys allowed some small light onto the depth of his pain and hinted at the other dark secrets that lay within her wounded husband, imprisoning the kind man at his centre.

And he was wounded. He carried wounds as debilitating as Mick's burned leg and Iggy's missing foot, because to the rest of the world he appeared healthy and whole. He was one of the 'fortunate ones' who, despite being there from Gallipoli until the very end, somehow exited the war without a scratch.

They couldn't see the scars but she felt their presence. Every single day.

Lines of pink were staining the sky by the time Veronica had stirred from her reverie and made herself a cup of tea, returning to the verandah to sip it and watch the sun rise alone. Perhaps it would bask into her heart and heal it a little, as nature always had done. But the heralding song of the kookaburras was joined by the sound of hooves and she looked across to see Iggy arriving.

'Rare time for yourself?' he asked, smiling down at her from Sheba.

'Very rare.' She smiled back, glad to see him. Somehow he always found a way to make her feel better about things with his gentle ways.

'I figured you might be up.'

Veronica didn't respond. Iggy knew she always rose early when she was troubled and undoubtedly Simon had told his father of the previous day's events.

'Want to go for a ride?'

She did. Iggy helped her saddle up her new horse Kelly and they set off together, urging the mares into a canter across the fields towards the dam, circling them under the stand of gum trees.

He didn't try to talk about Jack and she was glad. Iggy knew him probably as well as she did and they both knew Jack wanted to fight his battles alone.

'How's Mildred doing?' Veronica thought to ask as they paused for the horses to drink.

Iggy patted Sheba and shrugged. 'Getting used to things, I suppose. Simon's good for her. Having a miniature version of me to fuss over keeps her busy.'

'And how about you?'

He considered that for a moment, his brown eyes clouding. 'Mixed feelings. I was never quite the son he wanted, but he was different after Rose died. A bit softer, you might say. Even came to my last concert, which was kind of nice.'

'I'm sure he was proud of you. How could he not be, Maestro?'

'That's a conductor, Vera,' he said, starting to chuckle.

'Well I'm sure you could do that too if you put your mind to it,' she said, smiling back.

'Just glad I had a good nurse in Egypt so I can play at all.'

'A good doctor!' she protested. 'I just changed the bandages.'

'You did a lot more than that,' he said, serious now.

They rode back in silence, each thoughtful. It was only when they got to the stables and she was unsaddling Kelly that he looked at her a little oddly, seeming to have something he wanted to say.

'What is it?' she asked.

He reached down and plucked a gum blossom from her braid.

'You've flowers in your hair,' he said.

She watched in confusion as he then turned and rode away. He hadn't even said goodbye.

Thirty-two

October 1929

'Surprise!' Mick laughed as he and Iggy entered the room. Pattie and the children had strewn the place with decorations, including a large comical drawing May had done in ink, echoing her late father's talent. It was a picture of Mick with a horse leading him to a trough, reading *You can lead a man to water but you can't make him happy to have grey whiskers!*

'What grey whiskers? That's an outrage!' he protested, pointing at the offending image in the picture and stroking his own new moustache, pretending to be insulted.

'Dose ones!' Katie pointed.

'Come here, you wretched girls!' He stomped after Katie and May, who ran giggling about the room, before stopping in front of the drinks cabinet. 'They make fun of a poor old cripple and all you lot do about it is stand about laughing! You could at least offer a man a drink!'

Pattie poured him one and handed to him with a little curtsey. 'Your drink, Sir Whiskers.'

Mick burst out laughing. 'Thank you, o-leggy one,' he replied, kissing her hand.

Veronica laughed too as Pattie actually blushed.

It was the first time they'd sat together for a meal since Mick had returned from Florence, where he'd spoken at a variety of medical conferences, and the whole family plied him with questions over dinner. Veronica sat back enjoying the stories and marvelling at the descriptions of the river, the cathedral and, of course, the art.

'And how was David?' asked Iggy.

'By all appearances I would say…cold,' replied Mick, to everyone's amusement.

Pattie raised her hand. 'I'm helping to organise a fundraiser for the Red Cross, an art show actually,' she announced. 'I'm looking for volunteers to pose for some classes…'

'Well, it goes without saying they'll want me,' said Kevin dramatically. Veronica giggled at her father as he struck a few imaginary poses.

'I would have imagined they'd all be asking for you,' Veronica heard Mick murmur across to Pattie. Watching her blush for the second time that night, Veronica wondered what had got into her.

After dinner it felt like old times as Kevin took out the fiddle and Iggy played the piano, inviting Pattie to sing after noticing Jack looked a little the worse for wear. He'd drunk steadily through the meal.

She chose 'I Want to Be Loved Be You', pausing before starting.

'Hmmm, let me see. I think this song calls for some back-up vocals by a fair maiden. Why, Mrs Whiskers,' she exclaimed as she popped her hat on Mick's head and wrapped him in a shawl, 'I do believe you're the very lass I'm looking for.'

Mick grinned, pouting his lips, batting his eyelids and 'boop-boop-be-do-ing' in all the right places. Veronica smiled as she watched, feeling glad to see them both joking around.

They're good for each other, those two, she thought before something else halted her musings, something that gave her a familiar stab of pain. Jack was stumbling forward and her stomach lurched as he interrupted them.

'Nuh, nuh…I want t'sing a real song…play "Australia Will Be There"…one f'the boys eh, Igs?' He leant in a bit too far and Pattie held him.

'Careful now.'

'I'm arright. Come on, Igs! Whatcha waiting for?'

Iggy played and Jack lost the words, telling him to start again, and Veronica knew she had to step in. She picked up their coats and smiled at them all, forcing a laugh as she approached him.

'Yes, I know, dear, it's been a while since we sang that one. Come on, let's have a nightcap at home. I think it's getting a bit late…'

'Nonsense! S'fine! Iggy, play summin' else. Play "Danny Boy",' he slurred, pushing away from her, causing her to collide with a chair. Pete rose, his thirteen-year-old fists clenching.

'I think I need a breather,' Iggy announced, sliding his stool back and moving his leg to stand. 'Come for a smoke, Jack?' He clapped him on the shoulder and Jack relented, stumbling with him outside. Mick took Pete discreetly out the other door to 'show him the new car' and calm him down and everyone busied themselves about the room, making small talk. They were trying not to embarrass her but Veronica just wished she could run away from their sympathy and concern; she was too ashamed even to look at them. Instead she sat back down, putting the coats aside, and waited.

'How about a tune from you, Simon?' Pattie said brightly.

He shook his head.

'Come on! Surely you know something I could sing. What have you been learning?' He bit his lip nervously then, with an encouraging pull from Katie, he rose from his chair and sat at the keys.

'Well I do know this one,' he said, playing the introduction. Pattie perched herself on the piano, her long legs crossed, and swung her hair over one shoulder in a dramatic pose causing Katie and May to giggle and Mick to whistle and applaud as he and Pete returned to the room. Then she began to sing and the words washed over them as Pattie's sweet voice caressed the tune, enriched by a note of yearning as she forgot to make fun and the words touched her heart.

'Oh how I need someone to watch over me,' she sang as her eyes found Mick's. His earlier smile was absent, replaced by something else. Veronica realised to her amazement it was longing.

Mick reached up and held her waist as she slipped off the piano, never taking his eyes from hers until Katie giggled once more and the spell was broken.

'Cake, anyone?' Catherine said smoothly, leading the children out, the adults following, all except Pattie and Mick.

Veronica cast a quick glance their way and felt a pang of memory: the two of them seemed oblivious to everyone else, obviously just waiting for the chance to be alone. She remembered those feelings, long ago, before the war took its hold on her Jack. Closing the door quietly she decided she was not feeling up to facing her family, so she slipped through the side door and went out to the back through the kitchen. She walked along the fence to the nursery paddock as she'd done over thirteen years earlier, on the day of the mass, when she'd stood there with Pattie.

The day Pete was born.

She thought about Pattie's grief and her new happiness and felt a deep sense of gratitude that she could find a second chance at love. And her dear, dear brother. If anyone deserved Pattie it was Mick. Instead of giving in to his own despair he'd dedicated his life to the veterans, bringing hope to everyone else as they watched a fellow cripple defy the tag and its implications. But the laughter had been missing. Veronica could see that Pattie was bringing it back, helping to fill the enormous hole left in Mick after Tom's death. Mick likewise was filling some of the emptiness left in Pattie's heart when Clarkson died. Much like his cousin he was capable, dashing, larger than life, and she realised that Pattie positively glowed under his adoring gaze.

She wondered how long Mick had been in love with her and, looking back, realised he'd written to Pattie more than anyone else in the past few months and, come to think on it, hadn't taken his eyes off her all afternoon. As for Pattie, Veronica mused, it was anyone's guess, although she had been very excited about this party, constantly chatting about it and wearing her new red dress for the occasion. Veronica had just thought she was finally getting sick of greys and blacks after all these years, never guessing there was another reason for it. Especially not a male reason.

She wondered if the laughter would ever come back into her relationship. It was the thing she missed the most, those moments shared when nothing seemed impossible as long as they had each other. Back when there was hope inside her husband.

Lost in her thoughts, she jumped as Iggy spoke nearby.

'Thinking of adding to your brood, little mother?'

Veronica gave him a look of welcome then shrugged, taking in the new calves suckling on their milk. 'If only it were that simple. I think we humans have outsmarted ourselves sometimes.'

'How so?' He came to stand beside her, rolling a cigarette.

'Oh we get caught up in the complications. Too busy being clever, not enough time spent just existing. I think the cows have it.' She tried to smile but didn't quite manage it.

'*He who makes a beast of himself gets rid of the pain of being a man*,' Iggy quoted.

She let out a short laugh at that. 'Yes perhaps we do imitate the beasts sometimes, though we do a poor job of it.' She turned to face him. 'Who said that? Shakespeare?'

'Yes, good old Bill. Had all the answers but still lived a man's life after all.' Iggy glanced at her. 'He had a son you know, Hamlet, but the poor little mite died. He never recovered, so they say. Too much death…it can make life too hard, even for the most excellent of men.' He paused, lighting his cigarette.

'And what about you? You've faced too much yet here you are…successful, functioning, happy. How is it you have escaped?'

'Oh I wouldn't say I have, Vera. We all have our secret sorrows.' He smiled, adding, 'Except Tom. Now there was a man who seemed to hold all the answers.'

'Yes, the good die young,' she said. 'I never thought I'd hear Mick laugh like that again but now…'

'He seems to have finally worked out that the perfect girl is right under his nose. Blind Freddie saw that one years ago.'

'How did I not know about it then?' she said. 'Lord I must have my head in the sand half the time. When did you figure it out?'

'A man doesn't go through a war with another man without learning a few home truths about him,' he said, dragging on his cigarette. 'Not too many secrets that you can hide from each other.'

'Did you hide yours?' she asked, shaking out her hair, which was coming loose in the wind that promised rain, and pinning it back up again.

'Not very successfully,' he admitted, watching her. 'Mick knows me well but Jack even better. He knows pretty much everything about me. That I hate sand but I like the sun, that I cried like a baby over my horse, that I was so hungry in the desert I killed and ate a lizard, that I once let a girl dress me up in skirts and a wig so I could win a bet…'

She giggled at that.

'That I'm in love with his wife.' Veronica felt the air leave her.

'Always have been,' he said softly. The wind carried the words and she felt them touch her, bringing tears to her eyes in the afternoon light as the storm clouds rumbled towards them. 'Everything about you,' he continued, seeming unable to stop. 'The way you are with your family, the kind things you do for other people, for your children...and yet you still find time for the orphanage, for God's sake. What is that? It's torture,' his eyes bored into hers, 'to love someone who is an angel, because no one can ever compare to her. My wife...my wife was a good woman and we were happy enough for that short time but she deserved more than me because I could never give her everything. Not when so much of me belongs to you.' He moved to stand close.

'I love you, Vera. Every beautiful inch of you; every part. And I...I want you. I know I can never have you and neither of us could ever do that to Jack, despite what he's done. Besides, I'm just a cripple– '

'Don't ever say that.'

' –and I shouldn't even be telling you: I know that too. But I just need to, before we grow old and it's dead and buried with us, Vera. Just this once. I love you, Veronica. I love you. And although I can never be with you, I just...had to say it.'

He held her face as if to kiss her, then dropped his hands as she shook her head, tears falling.

'I...I'm not worthy of this. I'm not this perfect person...'

'Don't. Don't tell me who you think you are,' he whispered. 'You're an angel to me.' She tore her eyes from his handsome, earnest face and looked down, ashamed to realise she actually wanted to kiss him. What perfect angel thinks such thoughts?

'Do me one favour?' he pleaded. 'Bring him back to us. It's bad enough not being able to love you, but it's worse when he's doing such a poor job of it.'

'Iggy,' she cried out as he limped away and he stopped. 'I...I love you too. I just can't...love you.'

'I know.' He didn't turn, his back hunched against the rain that had started to fall as he left.

Veronica turned her face to its lashing, her hot tears mingling with the cool. The cattle called to their calves nearby, and she felt keenly the pain of man.

The sun rose behind a wet and grey world next morning and, parting the curtains, she saw her husband wielding the axe in the rain. She guessed he was venting the shame he felt from the night before, when he had to be half carried home by his father and Mick. What good did it do? She sighed. The shame was never enough to stop him from doing it again.

Lying back down she thought of Iggy, allowing herself to imagine a different ending to last evening. She pictured him taking her to his bed, kissing her, holding her, unleashing years of longing, his talented fingers stroking her body, his face above hers. Yet, try as she might, she couldn't bring herself to stay there, feeling disloyal to Jack to be thinking such things, even though she knew he probably didn't deserve loyalty. She wondered if he was taking women to his bed when he was in town; after all they rarely made love any more, mostly because he was hardly there and then, when he was, because he was too drunk. Or she was too hurt for anything to eventuate. She hated the thought that he might.

Sighing, she gave up on her fantasising and went out to the kitchen where Eileen had set up breakfast before heading back over to Highview to do the same. Soon the children would be up and the house would be filled with chaos until Millie arrived to help her with James while she got the other two off to school. Hopefully Jack would be gone before then. His temper was always frayed when he was nursing a hangover and she didn't want to give him any opportunity to take it out on the children. As it was he'd been threatening military school for Pete with greater regularity these past months and the last thing she wanted was for her son to be separated from her right now.

Pouring the tea, she picked up the local newspaper, reading the headline that Cowpasture Lane was to be renamed. It was to be called Gallipoli Street '*in acknowledgement of our brave men, who served with honour. Lest we forget*'.

Veronica stood and looked out the window, the rain distorting her view of Jack as he swung the axe, then out to the road beyond. She looked at the homes along the lane, the Dwyers, the Murphys, Highview, and thought of the tears shed by the families who lived there. They hardly needed to bother with the name. Tracing the path of the road on the pane with her fingertips, she mused that it was already their address, carved into every family that lived there. Gallipoli marked the beginning of a road they couldn't seem to leave as they struggled along, dragging the memories behind them.

Lest we forget? How about lest we remember? she thought bitterly, for if Jack could only forget, they might stand a chance at happiness.

Jack wielded the axe, splitting the logs with precision, noting to himself that at least he could say he was good with a blade these days. Too good. It felt freeing somehow to do something physical rather than sit inside his head as he usually did, worrying that he'd get stuck in the room in there where the dark thoughts plagued him. He wished with all his soul that the room could be blown away and his mind cleared of it forever, but the door continually creaked open and he battled with two choices as to how to close it: fix it shut or block it out. Fixing it required facing what was in there, which he couldn't seem to do, so he blocked it out with work, socialising, his family, even manual labour like now.

Inevitably, though, it would require the bottle to lock the doors back in place.

He had become its slave, trapped in a cycle he could not break, and all because the room held a terrible secret he could not share: he was a killer, a beast, a machine designed to end life. Dozens of men were dead at his hands, hands that were now asked to hold babies and sign cheques, drive a handsome car, make the sign of the cross at mass and hold a pretty wife. But they were killer's hands.

People applauded him, threw streamers on Anzac Day and cheered. Captain Jack Murphy, the hero. Glorified remnants lay under the bed in a box, decorations of war; medals from battle and his Captain stripes placed inside the old tin with the bullet dent that saved his life. Often Jack took out that box, laying out the contents that were wrapped in a commemorative silk scarf the Australians had each been given by King George. Trinkets of death, representations of bravery that only caused him shame and self-disgust. Blood traced into the fibres of each one.

These people around him, in the cheering crowds, in the restaurants, the streets, the church; if they'd seen what he had done, what these hands were capable of…no, he could not face it. The memories of what he had wrought and the realisation of what it made him were too much to bear. He couldn't sit through the images in his mind and try to accept them. There was no acceptance, no relief to be had. He was a killer. And worse, he had wanted to kill in the end. After what they did to Tom.

He didn't deserve to live this life.

And when his youngest child watched him it was as if this most innocent of all beings knew the truth. They say babies know someone's true nature. Little James knew what was held only in that room and in his dreams, and the truth reflected in his son's dark-blue eyes made him wish he was lying under a cross in the desert.

Why had God spared him only to suffer this unbearable paradox? To live a life that was perfect in every way with the most imperfect of souls. He floated in and out of it, finding himself in places without knowing how he'd arrived. The office, the apartment, home, the car. People had conversations around him and it was all he could do not to scream at them to shut their mouths and end the pointless words that poured from them. The price of an apple, the length of a skirt. Life was about living or dying, not about these inane details. How was it that the world had moved on? Only the other diggers understood, walking ghost lives too. He saw them in the streets, many of them drifting now, unable to work or relate to this strange, irrelevant existence, and he would stop and buy them a meal or, more often than not, a drink. The Anzacs. Such a noble word. But the lives they led now, for all the glorious rhetoric, were empty. Many of those who'd survived were barely alive, fighting their last and greatest battle every day, suicide beckoning them to surrender.

And so he swung the axe and split the wood and tried not to think too much about the other blades he had swung and the marks they had left. He especially tried not to think about the woman standing at the window, whom he loved so much yet couldn't seem to stop destroying, nor the sons, one whose resentment was growing each day, the other whose eyes saw straight through him. And he tried not to think of his little daughter, who still believed in her daddy, yet whose faith in him would soon turn to disappointment, just like her mother.

Thirty-three

30 October 1929

Veronica watched the car approach that Wednesday morning and, to her surprise, saw it was Jack. What on earth was he doing back at eleven-thirty? Up until yesterday he'd been coming home every night these past few weeks, admittedly very late, but as yet choosing not to stay in town since the night of Mick's birthday. Things were the same between them but she knew he was wrestling with himself on a different level now, trying to confront something within but unable to find a way through. He'd apologised that morning when he'd split the wood in the rain, only a few words, but heartfelt, and she knew he was sorry; but sorry didn't change things. Neither did coming home to sleep, really. What she wanted was for him to let her in to help him fight, but he still chose to struggle alone while she waited on the fringes, loyal, frustrated and ineffectual.

She checked on the sleeping James before walking out to greet him, guessing he wanted to explain why he hadn't come home the previous night but becoming worried when he didn't get out of the car.

'What's wrong?' She found his eyes, emptier than she'd ever seen them, and her heart went out to him as he stared at the windscreen, which was spotting with rain.

'There's been…a problem.' His voice cracked and she ran around to the other side, sitting herself next to him, holding his hands.

'I know, my darling, but I am here for you, and whatever it takes– '

'No, love.' He squeezed her palm, a flicker of gratitude there, but then it was gone as the words were uttered that he seemed hardly able to bear. 'Wall Street…the stock market, it's crashed. All of our stock is…worthless. I've been up all night. It's just…it's gone.' He shrugged in a helpless, disbelieving way and she stared at him in shock.

'But what about…? But we still have the factories…'

'It will all need to be sold. We've been through the books again and again. All the workers are being told in Queensland today and I…I suppose I'll tell our staff this afternoon. We're closing down, love. There's nothing else I can do.' He sat looking at the fields, at the blossom trees in late bloom, as it began to rain in earnest.

'What about Mum and Dad's stock?'

He shook his head, fighting tears. 'It's all gone. Everyone's stock. It's not worth anything. We'll have to sell off most of the cattle too. And let go of the help.'

'Can we keep the land?'

'Yes,' he said and she breathed a sigh of relief, 'but not much else. The cars will have to go. I'm…I'm so sorry…if I'd only known…my mind hasn't been on the job, I know…'

'No. We're not doing this.' She gripped his hand tighter. 'Stop blaming yourself. You said the New York market? It appears to me that it was a much bigger problem than anything you could have controlled.'

'Yes, well, everyone is in the same boat. Those poor buggers out there won't know what hit them. It's going to be a huge mess,' he admitted.

'So, the way I see it, you did exactly what everyone else would have done and it was certainly not your fault.'

He looked across at her, her chin jutting out, loyalty in every word, and he shook his head. 'How can you stand by me, Vera?'

'Because I love you, remember? And you know I mean it. I'm a terrible liar.' She managed a smile.

'But I'm a failure, on top of everything else…both of our families stand to lose the lot. Because of me.' His head fell into his hand as he rubbed at his drawn face, the lines stark against his skin. For a man in his thirties he looked far beyond his years. But all she saw was suffering.

'No. Because the stock market crashed. You are not to blame so stop this nonsense right now, Jack Murphy. It is not your fault, do you hear me?' She turned his face towards her and stroked back his still thick dark hair, now flecked with grey. 'You can do this. We can do this. We'll…we'll eat rabbit and wild honey, pick the apples and milk the cow. I'll be right beside you all the way. I'm not afraid to work hard, Jack, and I can live without servants and fancy cars…but I can't live without you, do you understand?'

He shook his head. 'You're all better off without me… I wish I'd ended up dead and buried…'

Veronica slammed her hand against the dashboard. 'Don't you dare! Don't you even say it! To think of all my prayers! And all those men who didn't make it and would have given anything to have what you have now. What is it you can't bear? Is it me? The children? What is so terrible about this life we've given you? Is there someone else? Don't you…don't you love us? For God's sake, Jack, just tell me. There's nothing else to lose now.'

'Of course there's no one else. It isn't because of you and the kids, how could it be…?' He stopped and she waited, unwilling to let it go. Not this time.

'Just tell me what it is then!' she said again.

'But I…'

'Just bloody talk, Jack!'

He stared at her in surprise. 'I…I wanted to tell you…there were things that happened, things that if you knew I'm afraid you couldn't possibly love me anymore,' he said falteringly.

'It's impossible for me not to love you, you bloody idiot of a man. Go on.'

The words were coming reluctantly, but he was actually forcing himself onwards. Veronica felt like she was pulling in a prize fish that was only just on the hook.

'I was there a long time, you know. I…I killed a lot of men and their faces became nothing to me somehow. I stopped caring. But now I can't stop seeing them…especially their eyes as the life…left them…and…and I can't understand how I did those things. Some of the stuff I saw. Tom…when I saw what they did,' he choked, forcing himself on, '…it...it made me so angry. After that I…I wanted to kill them. I wanted to kill, do you hear me? Do you love that man?'

His eyes were red and his face twisted in agony, but she blessed his bravery as he fought his way out against the greatest enemy he had ever faced: his own guilt.

'More than ever.' The tears began to fall and she smiled through them as he reached up and touched one.

'I'm damned, Vera. A condemned man before God. Thou shalt not kill, remember? I'm not fit to walk along the street and pretend to be anything else. I'm…unworthy to live with good people, especially you. I love you so much…and the children. How can I be a husband and father to innocents when I am a monster? *A murderer*?' He forced the last.

'You're not the monster.' She shook her head. 'War is the monster. Do you think I didn't hate when they killed our Tom,' she held back a sob at the thought of him in torment, 'and I saw Mick and Iggy maimed and…and Clarkson? They shot my cousin dead, leaving my best friend a widow! Do you think I didn't want to pick up a sword when I saw what they did to all of those young bodies in the hospitals? *I hated them too. I wanted to kill too.*' She said it slowly, emphasising every word. 'We are human,' she said, taking his hand. 'God knows that. What, did you think I didn't know what you had to do and what you must have felt? For pity's sake, what do you think I was doing over there? Dabbing at paper cuts? I'll wager I saw more death than you! And just because I didn't wield the swords or shoot the guns doesn't mean I was any the less responsible. Your country sent you to war to kill. It sent me to war to stitch them back up. Let's face it, I probably killed more men than you by helping save them then sending them back!'

He shook his head. 'But it was at my hands. I killed. Me.'

She thought about that for a moment. 'Well, you might have been the hands but the government was the brain…and the people…well, they were probably the heart and everyone else…I don't know, parts of the whole body. We all killed. The war made anything else impossible. Kill or be killed. War forces us to commit murder, to stop it coming here. War makes us hate and enjoy revenge. But don't give war this. Don't give them us.'

'But I still did it...'

'Yes. You did. But your only other choice was to die.'

'But I wanted to kill them...'

'How could you not, after what you went through?'

Jack was silent for a moment, staring at the windshield as the rain blurred the outside world. 'So what does that make me?'

She searched for the right word, finding it suddenly. 'A survivor.'

'I don't deserve to have survived...'

Veronica kissed his fingers, shaking her head. 'Remember when you asked me to marry you? When you said I deserved to have children and grandchildren and be loved?' She moved into his arms, holding her ear close to his chest. 'That's how I feel about you. *You do deserve survival.* You do,' she squeezed him as close to her as she could. 'Just because you had to kill doesn't mean you don't deserve to live. Please, Jack. Please. Come back to me.'

His heart beat strongly against her and she heard the words reverberate as he finally spoke. 'But we'll have nothing.'

She raised her face to his. 'Do you really believe that?'

He stared into her eyes and she saw the answer dawn. Jack stroked back her hair, shaking his head. 'No.'

'No,' she confirmed, loving him. She smiled and finally, beautifully, he smiled back and leant forward, kissing her tenderly.

The weather pelted against the soon-to-be-sold car as they made love in it for the first and last time, and afterwards, as Veronica ran back up to the house to check on James, Jack opened the car door and stood, stretching his arms out to the rain. They had lost everything, and in doing so he had found himself forced to the cliff's very edge. No more pretending. Time to fall or jump. So he'd jumped, and somehow he was free. Not perfect, not without scars, but the truth had been released and the most beautiful soul in the world accepted it. And if she could, maybe he could too.

Jack went into his mind and visited the room. The door was wide open and for the first time, he let it be.

Part Five

Thirty-four

St Reuben's Convent, country New South Wales, March 1937

They ran across the gardens, their long uniforms flapping awkwardly as they crunched through the leaves of the liquid amber trees outside the convent.

'Come on,' Theresa panted, taking the stairs two at a time, urging Missy onwards. Mother Superior didn't tolerate tardiness.

They arrived outside her office and straightened their uniforms and hair, composing themselves before knocking. Theresa was nervous. Nothing good ever came from being summoned by Mother Superior.

'Enter,' said the much-feared voice.

Missy raised worried eyes to Theresa, who took her hand briefly, squeezing it. 'We'll be all right,' she whispered, letting go to push into the room. Missy followed her.

Mother Superior sat behind the large desk, looking up at them from beneath her spectacles, her watery eyes pinning them. Theresa felt as if she were ten years old and about to get into trouble for stealing plums from next door's tree and shifted nervously, feeling the tension emanating from Missy, who stood stiffly beside her.

'Sit,' ordered the nun and they did so automatically, perching themselves on the edges of the hard wooden chairs. She watched them for a moment before firing a question. 'You've finished the night shift, I take it?'

'Yes, Mother,' Theresa said. 'Just now.'

Mother Superior shifted her gaze to Missy. 'You were late.'

'Yes, Mother,' Missy said, looking to Theresa for help. 'The matron wanted us to– '

'Do not blame others for your mistakes, Bernadette. Contrition and a constant focus on improving oneself is all that God asks.'

'Yes, Mother,' said Missy, squirming.

They waited as the nun tapped her fingers against some paperwork in front of her and Theresa tried to make out the words upside down.

'I have good news for you two girls,' Mother Superior said suddenly, flashing a smile so small and brief they thought they'd imagined it. 'I've had word from the bishop and he has agreed to allow you both a rare and exciting opportunity. Two posts have become available with Father Burnett, who as you know is working in the Congo as a missionary with some of our sisters. You're familiar with his regular reports in the Parish News?' They nodded and Theresa had a sinking feeling.

'Father O'Brien and I have managed to pull a few strings and, as soon as you take your vows of course, you are granted permission to join them. I know this is sudden but I'm sure you'll feel enormous relief that the good Lord has provided for you.' Her voice prattled on as she went through the details of their entry into the order and they listened in silence, hardly believing what they heard until finally she asked them a question, rousing them out of their shock. 'What names will you be taking?'

'Names?' Missy echoed.

'Yes, girl, you'll need to consider which name you will adopt. Here, take my book of saints with you. You can decide that later. I can't tell you how pleased I am that you've been blessed in this way. Goodness knows I didn't know what would become of you at this age, but there you are. A good lesson in trusting God will provide. Do you have any questions?'

'No, Mother Superior,' they both murmured automatically before finding themselves excused.

Walking back down the stairs and out into the fresh air, Missy turned to Theresa, her emotions erupting.

'Nuns? *I don't want to be a nun*! And in the jungle? With the leeches? Oh God…Theresa, why are they making us do this?'

'I don't know. I suppose they think we're spinsters now at the grand old age of twenty-two,' she said, kicking at the leaves as they walked. 'They probably figure if we're not going to fulfil our Christian duty as mothers and wives, we need to serve God elsewhere.'

'It's not our fault! How were we ever supposed to meet anybody here?'

Theresa couldn't have agreed more. The country town they lived in only had a limited number of eligible bachelors and most of them had been snapped up by girls with 'family'. Poor orphan girls were not marriage material. Of course that hadn't stopped the boys pursuing them for other reasons and Theresa had had to drag Missy out of precarious situations on more than one occasion. Somehow the time had come and gone and their opportunity for husbands with it.

'There must be a way out of this.' Theresa furrowed her brow, thinking hard.

'Let's run away! They can't make us live in the Congo. It's… it's undemocratic!'

Theresa gave a little snort of laughter. Missy really should be on stage, as she so dearly wished to be; she was very dramatic. 'Of course, but without any money how are we going to go anywhere? And if we refuse we may lose our places at the hospital as well. Then what? Live on the street?'

Missy began to cry, wailing about giant snakes and cannibals until they reached their dorm rooms in the hospital. Theresa tried to comfort her.

'There, there, Missy,' she soothed, 'I'll figure something out. There must be a way.' Missy threw herself on the bed and Theresa watched her thoughtfully. She was the closest person to her in the whole world, their fates having collided the day Missy arrived at St Reuben's at the age of eight, having lost both parents to illness in the space of a month. Small and frightened, Missy had latched on to Theresa who was strong, resourceful and, for some reason, immediately protective of this new girl. She wouldn't allow anyone else to hold Missy when she cried or say unkind words about her skinny frame and boggled eyes.

Looking at her now, it was hard to imagine that the scrap of a girl was the same person. Bernadette 'Missy' Garcia had blossomed into a shapely woman with glossy brown curls, and her enormous brown eyes had lost their stricken appearance and were now her greatest feature. Theresa knew she would be a hit on stage, if only she had the chance.

She strengthened her resolve. Theresa had never let anyone take advantage of Missy if she could prevent it and she wasn't about to let that change now.

She worked through the situation over and again in her head, knowing she would have to use all of her wits and strength to battle the mighty force that was the Catholic Church in this town. Most of the townspeople paid more mind to Father O'Brien and Mother Superior than to the politicians or the police. It would be a difficult task indeed to gain sympathy or quarter. No, their only hope was escape, but how to do it on their paltry nurses wages, most of which the Church found ways of filtering back to their coffers?

'We need money,' she said decisively. 'Come on: let's think. What are we good at? You can sing…'

'Maybe we could join the circus,' Missy mumbled into the pillow.

A knock came to their door and Theresa opened it. 'Sister Carmel,' she said in surprise.

'Good morning, Theresa, Bernadette. I wonder if I might have a moment?' said the elderly nun, her face a pattern of wrinkles in its white habit frame.

'Of course,' Theresa said, standing back to allow her in.

She stood in the small room, taking in the austere furnishings that Theresa had tried to soften with bright crocheted blankets and the watercolours Missy had produced over the years.

'It's a cosy little nest you've made here, isn't it?' She smiled at Theresa, the lines around her bespectacled eyes falling into rows from the many thousands of such smiles she had bestowed during her life. Theresa couldn't help but return it. This nun was the only one who had ever shown them true kindness during their harsh upbringing. She and Missy had always adored her, and had missed her since she'd retired.

'Please, Sister, have a seat,' Missy said, settling her gently into a chair by the windowsill.

Sister Carmel thanked her and looked out at the hospital wall opposite.

'A pity the wall sits here but I see the good Lord has blessed you with a rhododendron tree. Must be lovely for you in spring.'

'Yes, we look forward to it each year,' Theresa said, nodding towards the thick green leaves that relieved their bland view and wondering at the timing of Sister Carmel's arrival.

'I've heard of your commissions,' Sister Carmel said, turning back towards them, confirming Theresa's suspicions. Their old friend didn't leave the convent very often anymore, so she'd known there would be a particular reason for this visit. 'And what do you make of it?' Her still-shrewd eyes were on Missy.

'I am…That is to say I feel…it is probably my duty, I suppose. To do God's work,' Missy hedged. 'If I must fight through the jungle for the Lord then I suppose that's my calling.'

Sister Carmel's eyes twinkled at her. 'I don't believe you actually have to become a female Tarzan, my dear,' she said. 'I've seen him at the pictures,' she confided. 'Quite entertaining, I must say, but hardly what this work would involve. It will be more teaching and nursing work and the like. The villages are very primitive but quite settled. Terribly hot though, I hear say,' she nodded, fanning her face at the thought. 'But there's a bit more to it than that, isn't there, my dears?'

'Yes, Sister.'

'Do you feel ready to take your vows and become a bride of Christ?'

Both girls stared at her and Missy finally blurted out the truth. 'No. I mean, no offence, sister, but I…I don't.'

Sister Carmel nodded slowly. 'And you, Theresa?'

'Nor I, Sister. It is not what I would choose,' she replied honestly.

The old nun looked down to her pocket and slowly took out a letter.

'I wrote this to you, then I decided I'd really rather come and see you myself to explain…' She paused, holding the envelope in her lap and seeming to search for words. 'I know you won't mind me telling you this in front of Missy, Theresa. Heaven knows you would run and tell her what I'm about to say anyway. Never could keep you two apart.'

Theresa stared at the letter then back at the nun.

'When you take your vows you give up your claims to all your worldly possessions, child and…well, I'm not sure if anyone has ever told you that you had quite a few things when you came to us.'

'Things?' Theresa repeated.

'Yes. The clothes were given away but there were other objects you may not be…keen to give up easily. Father O'Brien has them safely locked up, and I'm sure he will tell you about them before the ceremony, but I'm afraid you will feel that by then it is too late to change your mind.'

Theresa let that information soak in for a moment. 'Or perhaps never tell me at all.'

Sister Carmel cast her eyes down and tapped at the letter. 'I've prayed on this matter and I must do what is right,' she whispered. 'I cannot watch you follow a religious vocation without knowing you have other choices in life.'

'Won't you be in trouble for telling me?' Theresa asked, knowing the answer.

Sister Carmel lifted her gaze and it was soft with affection. 'Never you mind about that.' She stood shakily and handed her the letter. 'Vocation is a calling, girls, not a command.' She walked to the door, turning to Theresa before she left. 'Ask for your possessions, child, then decide what you want in life. I'm sure that is what your grandmother would have wanted.'

Missy followed the old nun out to help her down the stairs, giving Theresa a moment to open the envelope and read the few lines contained within. It was a simple letter, written in the old nun's hand, summarising the words she had just spoken and ending with Sister Carmel's typical kindness:

I put these things away for you many years ago on your grandmother's behalf and if nothing else you deserve to hold these traces of her love. May God bless you and guide you always.

Her grandmother. How Theresa had wondered about her and then to find out after all these years that there were possessions, things that belonged to her, was too exciting to believe. And then there was another emotion. There was anger. She walked to the window and clenched her fists. How dare they withhold this from her? It should have been given to her when she'd turned twenty-one and she knew full well that they were probably planning not to tell her. Father O'Brien had always been inclined to recruit the orphan 'graduates' into the church, seeing it as a bounty provided by God. She wondered how many nuns and priests he'd procured in this way. Well, not her! And not Missy either. If this grandmother of hers had left her anything valuable she'd sell it and buy tickets to Sydney where they could fulfil Missy's greatest dream of taking to the stage and start living at last.

Mother Superior may well say 'God will provide' but it was Sister Carmel who had proven it to be true.

Theresa stared at Father O'Brien's door. Next to this dreaded office Mother Superior's seemed like a picnic spot. She raised her hand, determined not to be intimidated by him, and knocked, trying to still her racing heart rate.

'Enter.'

The priest finished what he had been writing and looked up at Theresa in mild surprise.

'What is it, Theresa?'

'I wonder if I might have a word, Father,' she said, trying to inject an air of confidence into her tone.

'Take a seat,' he instructed, sitting back and looking rather impatient. 'Although I haven't long, so you'd best be brief. I expect you've come to tell me of your decision to take your vows.'

Theresa decided she might as well just come out with it then. 'No Father…I've come for my possessions.'

She saw a flicker of surprise that he quickly masked.

'Who told you there are possessions held for you?' he asked coldly, remaining behind the enormous desk, his fingers pointed upwards together in a small tent.

'Aren't there?'

Father O'Brien seemed to wrestle with himself before replying. 'For what purpose would you seek to sort through a trifle of possessions?'

'Please, Father, it would be of comfort to have them.'

He narrowed his eyes, replying in a dismissive tone, 'Comfort comes from prayer, Theresa. I cannot allow you to squander your soul on seeking a material life when a life of servitude and redemption awaits.'

'Yes, Father, but I believe it is my soul to squander or otherwise, and as a legal adult I am entitled to have my grandmother's things, as little as they may be.' She stared him down, quaking internally but determined to fight for herself and Missy.

'The Lord has spoken to us on the issue of piety many times, Theresa. Have you forgotten your namesake?'

Theresa reached up and touched the medal about her neck. The nuns had told her she'd been wearing it when she arrived. It was St Therese of Avila.

'She spoke of the way to perfection, and lived a life serving God through poverty and prayer. Would you throw away this opportunity to live spiritually?' He leant forward, casting what he knew was his ace upon the table. 'What would you rather, the comfort and safety of your family here in the church or the coldness of life in a world waiting to take advantage of an innocent such as yourself? Come now, Theresa, let us have no more talk of such nonsense. *Render unto Caesar the things that are Caesar's and to God the things that are God's.* Think no more upon worldly things, my child.' He rose, considering the subject closed.

'You say they are but a trifle of possessions, so why do you fear they will lead me to a material life?'

He glared at her, unused to people arguing with him. 'Even a trickle can run to a stream. What if you take these things and buy a small amount of shelter or clothing. What then? The flesh is weak and easily seduced, particularly for women, who haven't sufficient sense when it comes to the practicalities of survival. I cannot allow you to be vulnerable upon the streets.'

Anger flooded her face. 'I have the sense God gave me. As you say, St Therese lived a life for God – in fact she started her own religious order and it seems to me she had a firm grip on the practicalities of survival, even if she was *just* a woman.'

Father O'Brien's cheeks turned red and he spat his words back. 'St Therese was blessed. There were miracles that shaped her life that you cannot possibly compare to your own! She was a saint– '

'Yes, but she was simply a woman once– '

'Enough! I will pray upon the matter.' He flung up his hands and sat back down but she remained where she was and responded in a clear voice.

'Then I shall wait.'

Twenty minutes later she walked out of the presbytery and down the street to the hospital, stunned at her victory but not daring to look inside the deliciously large box until she and Missy had safely locked their door and sat down. Running up the stairs and along to their room she saw Missy waiting, her eyes so wide at the sight of the box that Theresa burst out laughing, telling her to be careful or they might fall out. They placed it carefully between them on the bed and Theresa paused for a moment to savour the wonderful anticipation. It was like opening an incredible Christmas present and, even though it was March and Missy wasn't technically her family and her grandmother wasn't actually alive, this felt like her very first family Christmas.

She'd witnessed a real family Christmas once, at a beautiful house where Sister Carmel had taken her and Missy to join her cousin's charges, some other orphans from northern Sydney. It had felt like a wonderful dream as they'd lived like rich children from a privileged world for one whole day.

But now it wasn't someone else's family. It was hers.

She opened the lid and they saw that each item had been carefully wrapped in tissue paper. Theresa imagined it had been Sister Carmel who'd taken such care with them. Then she noticed a large envelope to one side and drew it out, opening it to find a registration form, filled out when she'd arrived back in 1916. They read it together, incredulous Theresa had never been shown it before.

Date: 21st of November, 1916
Child's name: Theresa Jones
Parents: Deceased
Next of kin: Unknown
Hair: Blonde
Eyes: Brown
Date of birth: 4th of June, 1914
Age: Two years, five months

Documentation: Ticket of passage of child and grandmother confirms name, age and parents' deaths.

Comments: Grandmother, Georgina Jones, aged fifty-nine, died mid voyage of a suspected heart attack. Child was not claimed upon arrival. Attempt to contact next of kin at registration address returned to sender.

Then, in a different handwriting, there was an additional comment. *Child speaks some words in French.*

Theresa stared at the words, desperately turning the page over for further clues, but that was all there was.

Missy gaped at her. 'French?'

Theresa knew she had come off a ship and been taken to the orphanage after the death of her grandmother, but she had never been told she'd spoken French, only that the ship had sailed from London. She'd always assumed she was English.

'Perhaps there are more clues in the box,' Missy said hopefully and they began to unwrap each item eagerly.

One by one the precious treasures were revealed: a silk scarf, a bottle of French perfume, some soft cashmere gloves, a hand-embroidered child's blanket and a large carved jewellery box. It was the last that caused the most excitement and the two exchanged glances before Theresa lifted the lid to reveal the contents inside. It was strangely almost empty, save four items: a gold ring, a heavy and very ornate gold watch, a string of pearls and a photograph. She picked up the photograph and stared at it as the image of her baby self smiled back, her face covered in what appeared to be chocolate, the medal shining about her neck. So I had it even then, she thought, holding it. It must have been from her mother. Theresa felt tears prick at her eyes. She had never seen a photo of herself as a child before. Tracing the image, she felt an aching sense of grief for the little girl in the picture who had no inkling what harsh days lay ahead.

'Is there anything written on the back?' Missy asked, but it was blank. They searched the contents again but there were no other clues as to her family, or her history.

'It's almost as if she was trying to make sure no one knew anything about me,' Theresa finally sighed.

'Look!' Missy pointed to the corner of the blanket and they read the initials in confusion. *EC.*

'Perhaps it was second hand.'

Theresa shook her head. 'No. Not this dame,' she said, holding up the pearls. 'She really was trying to hide me. She didn't even use our real address.'

'EC. I wonder what your name was. Enid? Elizabeth? Elspeth?'

She held the holy medal, guessing her grandmother had used it for inspiration for an alias. 'It doesn't matter. I'm Theresa now.'

'Erica?'

'I guess we'll never know.' Theresa shrugged sadly. 'So,' she brightened up and looked into the box, 'what do we sell and what do we keep? We'll need money for train tickets, the first month's rent and some clothes of course. Can't go to Sydney looking like a couple of hobos...What is it, Missy?'

She had begun to cry. 'You mean we are really going?'

'We certainly are, and you can sing and dance to your heart's content! Unless you'd rather live in the jungle with the leeches... Personally I'm betting there will be leeches in the city too, big male ones, but I'm sure we'll be smart enough to recognise them when they come along.'

Missy laughed and they hugged each other over the box that might not have held all the answers to the past, but certainly held the ones to the present.

Thirty-five

Kings Cross, Sydney, September 1939

Missy and Theresa were late for work as they tied the straps on their shoes and rushed out of their flat. Not that they ever called it a flat as such, it being not much more than a room with two beds, a stove and a wardrobe with a bathroom on the side; they just called it home, and lovingly so. It might have been tiny but they well used to small living quarters and besides, it was theirs, and that was all that mattered.

It had been two and a half years since they'd moved to the big city after their rebellion against the church. Theresa often looked back on those few days in wonder, still marvelling at the drastic turn her life had taken. Holding her medal she offered up a quick prayer to St Therese before running along with her handbag swinging.

'If only Mother Superior could see us now!' Missy laughed, flashing her new costume at her before tying her coat tight.

If only she could indeed, Theresa mused, thankful they were now well away from the nun's penetrating gaze. She shuddered to think how she and Father O'Brien would judge them now.

The bright lights welcomed them as they jumped off the bus and ran down the street, giggling as Harry and Rick called after them, their heels tapping against the bitumen.

'Just a quick drink before work!'

'No, we'll be late!' Theresa called back as Rick began to sing along with the wireless coming out of a terrace window, running after them.

'*You must have been a beautiful baby*,' he caught up with them, swinging from the pole in front of her, '*'cos baby look at you now!*'

'Stop it, you silly man!' She laughed at him. 'Missy and I have a show in half an hour.'

'Any free tickets for a fella who's dizzy for a dame?' he implored, catching her hand.

'No, not for the likes of you,' she teased, 'and since when did you become an American?'

He stroked her palm. 'Since they say all the best lines in the movies to capture a sheila's heart.' He grinned at her, stealing a kiss. They'd been seeing each other for a few months now and Missy had been stepping out with his friend Harry. Secretly Theresa felt she was falling in love for the first time.

'Catch ya after the show then?' He nuzzled her ear and she giggled again.

'Shhh!' Missy waved her hands. 'There's going to be a message from the Prime Minister.'

People stopped alongside as they stood still in the street to listen, a stiff breeze filling the pause until Robert Menzies' voice washed over them.

'Fellow Australians. It is my melancholy duty to inform you officially that in consequence of a persistence by Germany in her invasion of Poland, Great Britain has declared war upon her and that, as a result, Australia is also at war. No harder task can fall to the lot of a democratic leader than to make such an announcement...'

Theresa stood frozen. Surely it wasn't possible, she thought, the same sentiment echoing on the faces around her.

'…we are therefore, as a great family of nations, involved in a struggle which we must at all costs win and which we believe in our hearts we will win.'

So there really was going to be another war after all. How could the world fall into conflict again so soon? Theresa saw the defeated slump of an older man, perhaps a veteran, and wondered if he had sons to send. A woman with a pram lifted the baby out and held it, brushing at her tears. Then Missy caught Theresa's gaze with large worried eyes.

'Strewth,' said Rick, 'well that's it for me then.'

'Will you join up?' Theresa asked, fear clawing at her.

'Course I will. Did ya hear that, Harry?'

'Yeah I heard. Guess my old man'll be happy I've got a job at least. Hey, gorgeous.' He put his arm around Missy who allowed him a kiss, her eyes full of tears. 'Come on, we'll make short work of the bastards. Everyone knows Aussies are the best fighters around, eh, Rick?'

'Too right!' Rick slapped Harry on the back.

Theresa watched them, feeling sick. Why were men always so ruled by their lusts? Lust for fighting, lust for women, lust for drinking and gambling. Mother Superior had been right about that much all those years.

'Come on, Missy, we have to go.' Theresa grabbed her arm and they ran down the street, agreeing to meet the fellas afterwards to 'celebrate'.

Arriving at the nightclub, they unbuttoned their coats quickly. They had become used to the scantiness of the costumes over time, acknowledging that it was the norm here in the Cross, but at first they had felt naked and sinful. Even the underthings they'd worn as nurses covered more than these concoctions. But the pay was good, more than nursing anyhow, and they had to start somewhere in the industry if Missy was going to be a success.

They hoped Mac hadn't noticed how late they were. He had. Rounding through the door he loomed above them and Missy began to tremble next to Theresa.

'Mac' or Gerome McDougall was a much-feared man in Kings Cross and with good reason. He shoved them both back, pointing his cigar at them over his large protruding belly.

'What the fuck kind of time d'ye call this?' They flinched at the use of the word they definitely hadn't got used to. The son of Scottish migrants, he had all of his father's temper as well as his reputation for being a 'hard' man, earning four consecutive boxing titles before turning to nightclub ownership.

'I'm sorry, Mr McDougall. It was all my fault. The radio…they announced that we are at w-war– ' Missy stammered.

'And what's that t'do with you, y'useless baggage? Get on out there and tell Clements I said t'dock yer pay.' Theresa moved to follow but he held one arm across the doorway, blocking her way.

'Not finished with ye yet, Princess.' His face contorted into a lascivious leer as he swept his gaze down, taking in her spangled low-cut top and sequined shorts that she wore for that night's new theme, 'Aladdin's Dream'.

'Rocco's been asking after ye. Seems to have taken a bit of a shine. Pay him some special attention tonight and I might throw in a bit extra in ye pay.'

'Yes sir.' She moved to walk on but he stopped her again.

'And if he's wantin' to take ye upstairs just nod me way and I'll fix ye up.'

'I told you before, sir, I don't do upstairs.' She felt her palms begin to sweat as he leant in closer, his cigar-ridden breath nauseating her.

'And I told ye to do as y' told if ye want to keep y' job,' he breathed.

'In that case I quit.' She met his gaze squarely.

'Is that so? Well I hope ye friend feels the same way, 'cos ye'll both be out.'

Theresa paused. Missy wanted to keep this job, she knew. It had taken a while to learn how to dance and sing the songs and they'd only been working a few months in this club, which was a big step up from the waitressing they'd done in the early months. She'd quickly come to realise being a showgirl really wasn't for her, but Missy was in her element on stage, her sweet face alight beneath her brown curls. The crowd adored her and she doubted Mac would make good on his threat, especially since Missy had been performing a new popular solo these past few weeks. Then again he had such a hot temper it was difficult to know. She would hate to shatter Missy's hopes.

Maybe Rocco wouldn't ask to go upstairs. Maybe he just wanted some company.

'Think about it.' Mac dropped his arm, slapping her behind as she left. She almost turned and slapped him back but thought better of it. Rocco was sitting with his cronies and she waved over at him before taking the stage next to Missy, performing the dancing and singing as best she could as her mind raced.

An hour later she was beginning to panic as Rocco pulled her into his lap just as Missy took her place behind the microphone.

His hand grazed across Theresa's chest as he leant in to whisper the words she'd been dreading whilst Missy's words entertained the room.

'Oh-la-la!' sang Missy.

'Oh honey, I can't tonight, but Scarlett's free and she'll take real good care of you, if you know what I mean.' She winked. 'I'll just go and get her.'

'I didn't say I wanted Scarlett the harlot, I said I wanted you.' He stood and dragged her with him, diving his hand inside her top and she pulled back, slapping him across the face. Mayhem exploded as he stumbled back onto a table, spilling the contents on a very drunk group of bohemian-looking men, who lurched out of their chairs, fists flying. Theresa ducked across the room and grabbed Missy off the stage, pulling her through the crowd as chairs flew, making it outside just in time for Mac to come storming out the other door, narrowly missing them.

'You'll be sorry for this y'bitches!' he yelled, panting, but they were well down the street by then, still in their costumes, earning catcalls of approval from passers-by. They ran around the corner and down the street to where they knew Rick and Harry lived, running up the stairs, and pounding on the door before falling into their arms, crying.

'I don't know what I'm going to do now,' Theresa sighed later, after a sniffling Missy had been kissed better by Harry, who had since taken her to his bed. Theresa hoped she was being careful. They'd been lovers for a few weeks and Theresa had given her strict instructions on how to avoid getting pregnant after asking a few discreet questions of Scarlett at the club. Once she would have found it impossible to believe that Missy would even contemplate sex before marriage, but here, where it was so commonplace, it didn't seem the gigantic sin it once had.

'I wish I could just stay right here.' She curled up against Rick, sighing.

'So marry me an' live happily ever after.' He swung her onto her back and she looked at him in surprise. Then she laughed.

'Don't joke. I've lost my job now and I doubt I'll be getting another one easily once Mac has made my name mud,' she said, pulling a face. She had already used up nearly all the money from the sale of her grandmother's ring. She'd hate to have to sell the pearls or the watch.

'Who says I'm joking?' His face turned serious then as his eyes roamed down her body, taking in every detail revealed by her costume. 'Y'know I love ya, an' I'm about t' join the army and make a quid. How 'bout it? Let me take care of ya.'

'When? On leave? Or are you planning on knocking me up before you go and get killed and getting me a pension?' She was serious too now and he reached up and stroked her neck, his fingers moving downwards.

'I'll come back. Promise. And we'll move out to the country, to where me family is. Have lots of little tykes and I'll getcha a nice little cottage where ya can cook me Sunday roasts and knit me jumpers…' He leant in and kissed her and she melted in to him. 'I'll plant ya a nice rose garden and the kids can play footy in the backyard…raise a little family of champions all in a row…'

A family. How she'd always longed for it. 'What about Missy?'

'She an' Harry can live next door. We'll start a whole footy team!'

Theresa laughed, imagining herself and Missy, living side by side. Raising their families together.

'Come to bed, love,' he whispered.

'No…I want to wait…'

He kissed her again and stroked his hand further down and she gasped. 'Come on.'

Rick picked her up and carried her into the room, like a groom over the threshold, and she giggled, giving in at last as he lay her down. Their bodies entwined in the moonlight that bathed them through the window as Theresa felt the sweetness of touch for the first time in her twenty-five years. Afterwards, as they lay together, he offered her a cigarette and they watched the little trails curl into the silvered night.

'I didn't know you were a virgin,' he finally said. 'I woulda thought…'

'I didn't seem to find the time. Or the man. Until now.' She smiled over at him. 'Yes, by the way.'

'Yes what?'

'I'll marry you.'

The next morning it poured rain and Theresa reached out for Rick to find he was already up.

She put on her clothes, looking forward to seeing him, but walking out into the other room she found only Missy, sitting huddled on the lounge and holding a note, the previous night's make up running down her face.

'What is it?'

'They've run off to join the war.' She handed Theresa the sodden piece of paper. 'And the landlord's been. Seems they left us the bill for three weeks' rent.'

Theresa looked down at her skimpy outfit and thought of the stain on the sheets: it would wash away, but she knew at that moment the stain in her heart would remain as she collapsed onto the chair.

'Seems like we found ourselves a couple of big leeches after all,' she tried to joke, hiding the pain that threatened to overwhelm her. She thought about his offer to marry her last night and felt a wave of hurt as the betrayal registered in full. He'd tricked her by offering her the one thing he knew she couldn't resist: a family. Despite all the caution, all the waiting, all the warnings, she'd fallen for a conman in the end and lost her soul to the sins of the city. Father O'Brien had been right about her and she felt ashamed of what she'd become. Was this what her grandmother's ring had bought her?

'What are we going to do?' Missy sniffed, staring at the note.

'I don't know about you but I could really use a cup of tea.'

They sat on the little verandah of their runaway lovers' flat in Kings Cross, overlooking the artists, the showgirls, the writers and the businessmen as they passed by in the rain.

Theresa and Missy slouched in their matching spangled outfits and drank tea and smoked.

'Look at us.' Missy flicked at a glittery tassel. 'We've really become one of them now, haven't we? Fallen women.'

'Seduced but not conquered,' Theresa reminded her, feeling some of her familiar resolve return. It was true. They might have been foolish but they hadn't betrayed themselves completely. Their newly acquired state of unemployment was testament to that.

'It's just that it's another world here, isn't it?' Missy sighed, watching a man in a suit carrying a large feathered hat, a tiny dog trotting behind him in a glittery vest.

Theresa gave a short little laugh. 'The question is who does belong here?'

'I guess I do,' Missy said thoughtfully after a while. 'In Kings Cross anything is possible.' She turned to watch a crowd of young men as they sang their way home after an all-night celebration. 'In a funny way it makes me feel that there is hope; that you don't have to conform and do everything that is expected of you. It's… freeing.'

Theresa dragged on her cigarette. 'Unless you get trapped. And trouble is it's turning me into someone I don't want to be.'

'There'll be other fellas.'

'No, it's not that,' Theresa shook her head, her damp hair sticking to her cheek, 'I…I don't enjoy it, Missy. The stage, the club. I just feel…on display or something.'

'But isn't that the point?'

'Well yes, but that's the problem. I just don't like the way it makes me feel. When…when Rocco grabbed at me last night I panicked, but later I realised he's no worse than a lot of them and it will keep on happening if I work as a dancer. Men see me in a certain way. I guess I look like I would…do that…and I know it's just a stepping stone until we get into bigger things, but I think if I keep doing that I'll...' she searched for the right words '...I'll just lose myself.'

'What are you saying?' Missy asked nervously.

'Missy, it isn't for me. If there's one thing I've learned here it's that we do have choices now and we are free and this...this isn't my choice.'

Just then the landlord arrived and Theresa and Missy hurriedly donned coats they found in the wardrobe and walked him the few blocks to their flat, paying him the owed rent rather than risking arrest. Missy saw him out and returned to find Theresa packing her belongings into a suitcase, leaving her costumes behind as she went.

'What are you doing?' Missy watched her fearfully.

Theresa didn't answer, collecting her thoughts then turning and handing Missy the key along with a small box.

'What is this?' she asked, beginning to cry as Theresa donned the jacket of her only suit.

'Just something to get you by until you get another job. A much better job,' she replied, unable to look at her face.

'Where are you going?'

'Missy, it's over for me. I just can't do it anymore.'

'But...but what will you do?'

'As much as I hate to admit it, I really rather liked nursing, believe it or not, and I think...Well I just think it's time to choose what I really want. I'll be needed.'

'You want to...to go to war?'

'Well if no one volunteers to patch up all the fool men determined to get themselves shot...' She tapered off as she noted Missy's devastated expression. She was her only true friend and the only family she had ever known. Theresa didn't know how she would be able to leave her, but she knew the time had come.

'I'm coming with you.'

'No. I want you to stay and fulfil your dream. Performing is all you've ever wanted to do and I couldn't bear to stand in your way.'

'But…but this is so sudden. Stay and talk about it at least…'

'Missy, it's better this way. If we talk about it you'll end up coming with me or I'll end up staying and one of us will always be giving up what she wants for the other. There's nothing here for me…except you. It'll just be for a short while, then we can each settle down with a non-leech and raise kids next door to each other, all right? Oh, come here!'

Missy fell into her arms. 'But I'll miss you,' she sobbed.

'I'll miss you,' Theresa whispered brokenly, holding her tight. They sobbed together, the pain of separation unbearable, before Theresa finally pulled away, heading out the door. 'I'll write to you all the time,' she promised, walking backwards to soak up the memory of her dear friend's face one last time before they parted.

'I love you!' Missy called after her.

'I love you too!'

Missy watched until Theresa had disappeared from sight then went inside and slumped down onto the bed, not knowing what to do next. Looking down at her hands she realised she was still holding the little box Theresa had given her and, sniffing against her tears, opened it to find the string of pearls inside. Closing it slowly she made a promise to herself.

No matter what happened, she would never, ever sell them.

Thirty-six

Beecroft, December 1939

Pete took to the crease, pulling his cap low, watching Wally Collins marking his run-off carefully. Definitely short. Sure enough Wally bowled a short delivery and the crowd let out a cheer as the ball swept the ground for four. He laughed as his little brother James let out a whoop from the stands and his father waved his way, the crowd from Gallipoli Street clapping enthusiastically, taking up half of the pavilion. Even his grandmothers had come for once, along with his mother and Aunt Pattie, and he felt his attention waver momentarily before refocusing and pulling the ball to the left for another two. It was his last game before he left and he'd chosen to rejoin his old team for one final show; he was savouring every minute at his home ground. He'd already retired his cap from the New South Wales team, temporarily he hoped, until he returned from the war. The ball flew to the boundary as Wally scratched his head amid the excited cheers. Pete was determined to enjoy this and put all thoughts of the next few weeks out of his mind. They would come soon enough.

Drinks were called and Pete joined the players as they went over to the pavilion to rowdy applause, laughing as his father and Uncle Iggy instigated a chant: 'Mu-r-phy!'

'Over here!' called May, who'd set up refreshments with Katie.

'What on earth have you been up to now?' He laughed at the sight of her. Her bike trousers and shirt were covered in a large ink-splotched apron.

'What? I'm preparing food,' she declared, wiping her hands against it. 'Now hush up or I won't let you have any.'

'Nice looking cakes,' remarked one of his mates, Larry Naismith, nudging his brother Vince and giving May an appreciative smile as he took a slice. Even in her usual disastrous state, May still got plenty of attention. It took more than a boyish haircut and wild fashion choices to hide a stunning face and figure like hers. She rewarded Larry with a flash of her dimples and he held the cake in mid-air, staring while his brother laughed.

'Knock it off,' Pete cuffed him. 'What have we got here, Katie-bird?' His little sister paused as she worked alongside May.

'Lamingtons, sandwiches and apple tartlets,' she answered, surveying the array of baking they'd laid out on the table. 'And Anzac biscuits of course.' She smiled at him but he saw the sadness in her eyes.

Pete gave her a wink. 'Thanks. Hey, move back, you lot. Brothers and cousins first.' He seemed to be pushing back a tide of admirers around the table and a fair share of them were there for Katie too. At sweet sixteen, she was the spitting image of his mother, save her long dark hair, and with her kindness and gentle ways fellas were always falling all over her. Not that she could care less, he noted to himself, watching Katie carefully pour Simon a cup of tea and place it before him. She'd only ever had eyes for their lifelong mate, who was completely oblivious to her feelings. With his head usually stuck in a book, Simon probably wouldn't pick up on the fact unless Katie knocked him over the head with it and, considering she was the most ladylike little miss in Sydney, that didn't seem likely to happen any time soon.

The afternoon wore on and Pete made a century for the team, although the way the Gallipoli Street crowd cheered he felt it might as well have been for New South Wales.

It was a happy convoy of cars that headed for home, Pete driving the old Sunbeam with Simon alongside and his little brother James in the back. May tore along on her motorcycle in front, Katie wedged into the tandem seat alongside. How May talked his sister into riding in that contraption he never knew, although Katie always had followed her about like an adoring puppy.

Pete laughed as Simon and James sang the victory song once more, relishing the journey. It would be last time he would drive the Sunbeam for a long time and he flew her along in a final farewell. The beautiful car was reminiscent of a more affluent time in their parents' lives. Things were certainly better now than a few years back, when they nearly lost everything, but it had been a slow recovery and there certainly wasn't much left over to buy expensive motorcars. Pete didn't care. He loved this old car and looked after it meticulously, knowing that his aunt Pattie had been a bit torn when she'd given it to him for his twenty-first birthday.

They arrived at Highview and made their way along the fence, where a brilliant row of purple flowers stirred from the treetops of the jacarandas. Pete knew they were a living tribute to his uncle Tom and thoughts of war intruded on him once more as they turned into the gate and made their way up the drive.

'Aunt Pattie!' called James, running towards her. 'Can we go and check the traps?'

'I was just waiting for you to arrive to do that very thing!' she replied and they went off together to the creek to check the crayfish traps they'd been working on all week.

James was constantly on the lookout for something to do and Aunt Pattie always had an idea up her sleeve, having spent so many years learning about tools and carpentry from her father in his remarkable shed. His parents often shook their heads at the way the two of them would occupy themselves building carts, designing forts and inventing all manner of contraptions, all destined to be the next, best thing.

Once they'd even tried capturing a black snake from under the house with a marvellous invention they called the 'Snake Snatcher' (which Pattie later acknowledged she really hadn't thought all the way through). It caught the snake well enough but made it such a cosy little home it wouldn't come out; and coaxing it was a dangerous undertaking. In the end they'd opened the hatch and left a dead mouse out, though the snake must have had enough by then. The two were seen flying across the paddock, Pattie moving remarkably quickly for a woman in her forties, both yelling 'Snake's out!' Veronica had been twitchy for the next few days, constantly on the lookout for a non-caught and now very annoyed reptile.

But Pete knew his mother didn't mind. Pattie had a special soft spot for each of them. May was of course her living reminder of Uncle Clarkson, Katie a miniature of Veronica and therefore incapable of ever doing anything wrong, and James was her baby. He'd come along a little before Pattie and Mick had married and, as they were never blessed with children, Pattie seemed to see him as hers, especially as he was so much like her.

He knew all of this because Pattie kept a very special spot in her heart for him too. Pete was her comfort. He'd been born at the very worst time in her life and she seemed to consider him some kind of sign from God that things would get better. He knew whatever happened, Aunt Pattie would be there for him, Peter 'Clarkson' Murphy, just as she was for all of them.

Pete sighed, trying to break himself out of his reverie. One by one he was saying goodbye to them all in his mind, he knew that, but he was really just putting off the inevitable. Sooner or later he was going to have to say goodbye to his parents.

The sun beat down as Pete leant against the car, absorbing Highview one last time. How he would miss it. The verandah needed a fresh coat of paint and the garden was far from the manicured glory he remembered as a child, but his grandparents had kept it well tended. There was an air of grace about the place that welcomed people in. Despite the frayed edges, it radiated the quiet elegance of his grandmother and the hospitality of his grandfather. The latter was already bringing out drinks for the family as they arrived, placing them in the wooden ice tub his aunt Pattie and James had built next to the side table under the parlour window. A little too ambitious and not altogether practical in size (Mick had proven the point one day by lying down inside it) the ice tub was nevertheless a wonder of ingenuity and Pattie and James were inordinately proud of it.

Eileen, along with her husband Nigel, had stayed with them through the lean years and she gave Pete a sad little wave as she laid out plates and arranged sandwiches before turning for inside, dabbing at her eyes with her handkerchief. Pete waved back then turned at the sound of footsteps on the drive to see his father Jack walking towards him. Stomach churning, he swung his gaze to the paddock next door and his parents' house, the cream and blue of his childhood home cheerfully set against the green of the rise, and waited.

'Good game, son. Nice way to finish your season.' His dad walked over and clasped his hand. 'Not that you can really call four weeks a season. You'd think they'd have the decency to work the war in with our cricket.' He leant against the car with Pete, following his gaze. 'Saying goodbye to the house?'

'I can still remember when we first painted it.' He smiled. 'I thought the paint was blue mud.' They laughed and looked across together at the neighbourhood, the winding road of Gallipoli Street linking the families that had been through so much together and now sat on the precipice of war once again.

'I feel like I can see my whole life from up here,' Pete said, 'not that I've done much with it.'

'Oh I don't know. A law degree, a New South Wales cap… you've hardly been idle.'

'No, I mean what I've seen. I guess I've lived a pretty sheltered life.' He paused, looking at the road as the Dwyers approached at a distance and took a deep breath, finding the words that were so difficult to say. 'I tried to pray at mass but I felt like a hypocrite, asking God to forgive me for sins I was about to commit. I...I remember what happened to you, Dad. What if I can't cope with it?' His voice shook slightly and he pulled back his shoulders, trying not to appear weak.

Jack watched him, seeming to contemplate his answer. 'You know, when I went off to war I had no idea what to expect. I think I figured it would be difficult, you know. You'd have to stuff cannons and capture prisoners. I suppose I knew I'd be shooting at people. But nothing prepared me…' He paused, clearing his throat. 'Nothing prepared me for the reality.'

'But you ended up a war *hero* Dad. I just…I don't want to let people down,' Pete admitted.

'You'd never be doing that, son.'

'How do you know?' Pete waited, needing the answer.

'Because you do know what to expect. You won't be ignorant like me. You know you'll be dealing with death and you know it could be for a long time. I didn't. I was completely unprepared, but you're not.'

'That doesn't necessarily mean I'll be able to handle it.'

'Well, you're going in with your eyes open and that's a pretty big step towards handling it, don't you think?'

Pete shrugged. 'I hope so.'

'I want you to remember something, son,' Jack said, standing in front of him, 'and this is the best advice I can give you because it isn't mine, it's your mother's. No matter what happens, no matter what you have to see or what you have to do, it is war that forces you to do it. It's not your fault that you have to fight... it's just...'

'My duty, I know. I'll do my best...I mean I'll do my *duty*. It's not that I'm afraid...'

Jack sighed. ''Course you are. So am I...bloody terrified truth be told.'

Pete forced a shaky smile, and Jack held his shoulder for a moment. 'It's a job, mate. They are sending you in to do a *job*: to stop war coming here.' He gestured out at the homes before them. 'You didn't cause it, you didn't ask for it and God knows you don't want to do it, but you're going anyway, to protect all of us. That's real bravery. Especially when you know what...well, what I was like for a long while there.'

'I'm going to have to kill people...'

Jack held his eyes, unflinching. 'Yes, you are. But that's war. That's the job. Don't confuse it with...well anything else.'

Pete nodded slowly, trying to absorb the weight of his father's words, knowing he would need them. 'How does it come down to this?'

Jack sighed, leaning back against the car with him once more. 'I don't know, mate. Maybe if the politicians spent a day in the trenches there wouldn't be any wars.'

They stood side-by-side, watching family and friends come together for one last time, and Pete knew it was a scene he would replay over and again. The last day before it all changed.

Because things would change, that much he knew. War changed everything.

Veronica watched them through the window, her heart aching for them both: her son, about to leave home and face what had nearly broken his father; and her husband, watching him go.

She turned around to the calls of a mud-splattered James, who had come to find her.

'Look, Mum! Crayfish!' He thrust the trap at her in excitement and she pulled away as the slimy creatures were shoved in her face.

'Goodness!'

'Pattie said we can make a 'quarium for them. Can I keep them?'

'Well…'

'Thanks, Mum!' She was enveloped in a squash of boy and slime before he rushed off again, calling back over his shoulder.

'I'm gunna call the big one Pete!'

She watched him go and prayed that when he came of age there would be no wars to send him to.

Thirty-seven

Circular Quay, January 1942

Simon watched Katie approach as she ignored the wolf whistles of some soldiers walking by. He smiled at the sight of her, feeling rather self-conscious that this beautiful nineteen-year-old was having lunch with him, a twenty-four-year-old man not even in uniform.

'Hello, Katie-bird,' he said, standing up and giving her a kiss on the cheek. 'You're looking very summery.'

She gave him a little pose. 'I copied Katharine Hepburn,' she said, holding her hand at the tiny waist of the rose-pink dress and smiling at him from beneath the wide-brimmed white hat. Simon found himself staring and immediately snapped himself out of it, pulling back a chair for her.

'Well I'm sure she never looked as nice as you,' he said, trying to be suave but blushing profusely. He was terrible at compliments. Fortunately it was Katie and she never seemed to notice when he tripped over himself.

The waiter came and they ordered, both deciding on the fish.

'Have you got long?'

'Oh, about an hour,' he confirmed. 'I have to get back and sort out the problem with these transmitters.'

Katie tilted her head. 'I really don't know how you do it,' she said, fixing him with one of her curious, contemplative looks. 'I think I'd go mad working on little wires all day and half the night. It would make my head spin.'

'Well, they're not things you'd like to cross incorrectly.'

'No. Fortunately for the army they have someone like you who can do it. Mum told me you've been made head of development.'

'Well, yes. It's just a glorified title really– '

'Nonsense. Dad always says intelligence wins wars– '

'And stupidity causes them. My dad says the same thing,' he finished, smiling.

'Well I think they are quite correct.' She smiled back. 'Our boys all need radios and transmitters just as much as they need guns. And clever men like you to make them work.'

'Pity it doesn't come with a uniform,' he said quietly, then wished he hadn't. She didn't need to know about all of that.

'Well if it did you'd have lots of bars on your sleeve, that's for sure,' she said loyally. 'Now, guess what I've got in my purse?'

She pulled out a newly arrived letter from Pete and they read through it as they ate.

Dear Mum and Dad,

Well, it's Christmas Eve and I'm thinking of you all, gathered at Greenshades and dressing up for the singalong. I'll bet the house is filled with the smell of ham and turkey. It's enough to make my mouth water just thinking about it.

It is very quiet here now compared to battles we've been through in Libya, Greece and Crete. It was madness at first, of course, but now we are twiddling our thumbs in Syria and waiting each day to hear when we can come back to defend home. It's hard to understand why the politicians and generals are taking so long now that the Japs are on the rampage. Wasn't Pearl Harbor enough? We feel like a bunch of nursemaids here, holding things as we are. They seem to know nothing about war. Maybe we should get them all to come spend some time in the trenches, eh Dad? Maybe then they would see that we need to come home and finish things off and put an end to the whole thing.

Katie paused, looking out at the boats nearby. 'I wish they would come home. Why on earth are they keeping our soldiers on the other side of the world?'

Simon shrugged. 'The English politicians don't always take the Australian politicians seriously. Luckily the Americans do. They're on their way, don't worry,' he assured her. Katie nodded at him, still frowning, then continued reading.

You might not think it but it is bitterly cold here. Tell May I loved the scarf, even though it does have an ink blotch or two, and I wear it every day. As for the news that Pete the Crayfish Number 4 has kicked the bucket, I think it may be time for James to investigate new pets for his 'quarium'. Katie, what I wouldn't give for some of your biscuits and cakes right now. I wish they could make the journey. Tell Simon to eat my share while I'm gone. He could use some fattening up.

They laughed at that. 'Hey, I'm doing my best right now,' he protested, patting his slender belly.

I can hear the fellows singing 'Good King Wenceslas' next door and I think I'll go and join them, although they are doing a woeful job of it compared to you, Dad. Wish you were here right now to show them how it's done.

Mum, I miss you every day.
Keep safe and keep me in your prayers,
Your loving son,
Pete

Katie wiped at a tear and Simon looked down, missing his friend.

'Well, at least he's out of the fighting for now,' she said.

He nodded, looking up at her lovely face and wishing he could bring her brother home. Just then a woman came over to their table and Simon looked up in surprise as she handed something to him. She was gone before he had time to hide the white feather from Katie's eyes.

Thirty-eight

Kokoda Track, New Guinea, November 1942

Pete pulled his foot out of the mud and dragged it over the next log, wiping at the sweat that ran continuously into his eyes. The 'Golden Stairs' seemed to go on forever and he tried not to look up at how much further he had to go, knowing it would make him feel even worse, if that was possible. Not that he complained. Nobody did, not even the walking injured, who were a constant stream towards the hospital, most of them suffering gunshot wounds. He overheard one digger further up objecting that he could walk and to 'give some other poor blighter the royal treatment'. Passing him by Pete saw the man's mutilated leg and understood why the stretcher-bearers were insisting he be carried. The stretchers themselves were ingenious things, consisting of two blankets tied to two long poles and carried at each end by 'Fuzzy Wuzzy Angels'. These native men were perhaps the most selfless people Pete had ever met, often sleeping four a side next to their charges, tending to their every need and going without food to give the soldiers something to eat. And the smiles! So wide and kind it gave more comfort than anything else as they gently carried the men barefoot through the mud and across the mountains.

It began to rain again and Pete struggled on, telling himself the same thing he always did at such times: it will end. The jungle was thick along the track and the constant threat of an invisible enemy made the trek a nerve-racking experience as well as an exhausting one, but he followed Simon's footsteps and pressed on, figuring he'd call a break for lunch soon. His promotion to lieutenant had given him that right at least.

'How goes it there, Slimey?' he called ahead.

'Living up to my new name,' Simon called back and Pete chuckled. It was such a lift having him there, although he was furious about the reason. What a waste it was to take a brilliant telecommunications expert like Simon and stick him here in the mud. All because people were ignorant of what bravery really was.

Pete had received the shock of his life when Simon had turned up one day, casually strolling over in the mess tent in Port Moresby and sitting down next to him, his dinner in hand. Now it just felt like he'd always been there.

Katie's most recent letter had been more agonised; she begged Pete not only to look after himself but to keep her future husband alive. Pete had written back, suggesting that if she would only let Simon in on his status he'd probably feel he had more to live for. He looked forward to the next mail immensely.

Pete decided to call for lunch and they slumped exhausted to one side of the track, clutching at their canteens thirstily and pulling out their rations.

'Bloody bastards,' Simon muttered, pulling off the leeches that clung to his ankles, reminding Pete to do the same. Sully approached, introducing him to a new recruit who had just arrived in New Guinea and had been assigned to their battalion, the 16th.

'May I introduce Dominic Carson. Dom's just arrived from Sydney town for a bit of a tropical adventure. Dom, this is Lieutenant Pete Murphy.'

'Private,' Pete acknowledged, shaking his hand, apologising as a leech landed in Dom's palm.

'Ah, I see y'enjoying the wildlife. Plenty more fun in store for ya there. Personally I'm fond of the mozzies myself. Blood-sucking vampires,' Sully slapped at one on his back.

'Just joined up, Dom?' Pete asked, biting into a banana passed down the line by the natives.

'Yeah; haven't seen a Jap yet,' Dom said.

The others laughed and he looked at them in confusion.

'That's because they're invisible mate. Ya wouldn't see 'im if they were three feet in front of ya and had legs like Betty Grable,' Sully informed him.

They were on their way to reinforce the 7th Division and Pete assured him the Japanese would certainly be making their presence known when they got there, if not before.

'I heard that the Japs are on the run. Maybe we won't be in any fighting,' Dom suggested.

'Bullshit,' Sully told him. 'The powers that be want ya to believe that but the truth is they're everywhere in this bloody jungle, and as mad as cut snakes. They'd rather swallow their own swords than retreat.'

Pete stretched out his aching legs, squinting against the scorching sun as it began to peer out from behind the dark clouds. 'It's all about hearing the enemy in this jungle. Can't see a bloody thing.'

'Not like those bastard krauts. They like to announce their presence by blasting ya eardrums to kingdom come,' Sully said, biting into an orange.

Dom nodded, looking from one to the other. 'I heard their bombing raids were brutal.'

'I'm deaf as a post between you'n'me and the gate but still the most handsome bugger 'round these parts,' Sully stretched to his full five feet eight and grinned. 'But God, I'm as dry as a bull's bum going backwards up a hill, which incidentally is what Slimey here looks like most days. Hey! Pass the water down,' he called, moving along the stairs.

Pete and Simon laughed as Sully called out a few other choice remarks down the line, mostly amusing insults about the various physical traits of his mates who threw back colourful ones of their own.

'Keep it down you lot,' Pete ordered, but he was grinning.

'Don't worry too much, Dom,' Simon reassured the young man as he gathered his things.

'They're a different kettle of fish these Japs but we've got the angels on our side so we'll get there in the end,' Pete added, nodding at one of the natives as he passed. 'You'll still get your fight though, I guarantee it.'

He signalled that lunch was over and they rose to continue their trek, the sun now blazing. Several large butterflies had appeared with it and Pete mused that, even here, life went on, despite the foolish humans seeking to destroy it.

Theresa pushed the damp strands of hair back under her cap and washed her hands, readying herself for the next patient. Another soldier with another bullet in his young body was brought in the operating tent and she went to stand beside Dr Kindred. She knew the latter was exhausted but wouldn't say.

This soldier looked very young indeed, probably only just eighteen. His freckles were stark against the paleness of his skin and looking at his leg she could understand why. They worked together, managing to save it, and the boy clung to the doctor's hand afterwards. The morphine was making him drowsy but he got the words out clearly.

'Thank you. You've...just given me a normal life.'

She pondered those words later as she cut bandages and sterilised instruments. How normal a life could any of them hope to live after this? Sighing, she took a rare break, and sat down to re-read Missy's letter over a cup of tea.

Dear Theresa,

I hope this letter finds you well. Actually I'll be pleased if it just finds you! I can't believe you've ended up in the jungle after all. I have images of you in my mind living in a treehouse and swinging about on vines but I think that's because of my new job. Brace yourself. I've been given a walk on part in a Tarzan movie! Can you believe it? Imagine what Sister Carmel would say. Terry, my new manager, managed to get it for me today and I couldn't wait to get home and write to you to let you know the good news. It's not until November but that should give me plenty of time to settle in a bit more.

The job in the nightclub is good. I sing a duet with another girl called Dottie and it always gets a laugh because we wear costumes that are women's clothes on one side and men's on the other, and we have to sing in low voices for the men's bit and high voices for the women's. I hope I explained that all right. It's a bit difficult to describe. I know, I'll include a picture. Anyway, Hollywood is everything I thought it would be and more, although it's very expensive, especially with the war on. I'm sharing a flat with a few other girls from the club and it's pretty crowded and ridiculously priced but guess what? We can see the Hollywood sign from our balcony and, even more exciting, we have a pool! Some marines came over on Sunday and we had a pool party. I drank too much champagne and ended up kissing a guy called Bobby who was very keen and asked for a picture because he said he needed to look at my face every day for inspiration. He also said he wants to write to me. We'll see if he does. How is your hair coping in the humidity? I'll bet it's curly. No need for rollers there! Anyway I'll finish this up and get it out in the evening post. Missing you more than words can say.

Love always

Your Missy

PS Terry's given me a stage name: Missy Mayfair. What do you think?

Theresa held up the picture and smiled. Missy looked happy and Theresa figured her grandmother's pearls had been put to better use than the ring, although without the ring they never would have found their independence in the first place. She supposed both items had brought happiness in the end for Missy. For her part she couldn't say she was happy exactly. How could anyone be, surrounded by so much suffering and living in such unbearable conditions? Queensland had been bad enough but these last weeks up in the jungle were a whole new level of uncomfortable, the air clinging to her like a thick, saturated blanket, but the work drove her onwards.

Walking over to the door she watched the rain clear, and the thick foliage sparkled under the sunlight in a million shades of green, sending the birds into chorus as they chattered excitedly to each other in the treetops. She had found something here that she didn't expect. She had found herself. It was as if she was always destined to work in a crisis situation, tending to the wounded and remaining level headed. She was good at it, so good in fact that Dr Kindred had told her he thought she would make an excellent doctor; she had taken that little seed on board. It grew as each day passed and she had recently decided that when the war was over she would do just that, helping to pay for her education by selling the most valuable item her grandmother had left her: the gold watch.

She knew she would also have to work nights to make up the difference but that was fine, she'd always worked hard, and meanwhile she was under the excellent tutelage of Dr Kindred, who didn't mind talking her through procedures on occasion. They made a good team: the two of them, the other nurse Daphne and 'Two-Bob', the orderlies, native twin brothers who for some reason both referred to themselves as Bob and quickly earned the collective nickname from their Australian patients. Together they were making some kind of makeshift home of their little hospital, dedicating most of their waking hours to the wounded.

Explosions echoed through the valley and Theresa was roused from her thoughts, ending her break and moving back over to the operating theatre. It reminded her of one truth that was unavoidable here: they were never short of patients.

'It's from Katie,' Simon said, turning over the letter in his hand as the other mail was given out.

'Read it out loud, Slime. I could use some cheering up.' Pete leant back in gleeful anticipation, wondering if she'd done the deed and 'fessed up' at last.

Dear Simon,

I hope you are still well. It must be dreadful for you up there in the tropics. Your grandmother seems more worried about you being too hot than anything else, constantly telling me that she's of a good mind to ring those responsible and tell them to move the war out of that 'perishable heat'. She seems to think the sun is your greatest threat, never mind the Japanese.

They both laughed at that.

We are all well here. May has heard from your mate Larry Naismith on quite a regular basis and she actually gets a bit fidgety when his name comes up, which is funny to see. She was terribly upset when news came of him being injured but he is recovering well now in Brisbane, although his back will have a nasty scar. Vince is still missing in action though. I feel so sorry for their parents.

James said to tell you boys to use the sap from rubber leaves and rub it on your skin to deter the mosquitoes, although I don't know how reliable his source is.

'That would be like pasting yourself in glue! Mozzies would stick to you permanently!' Simon grinned over at Pete before continuing.

Simon there's something I need to tell you and it's been playing on my mind as to whether or not to do so, especially as I don't know your feelings.

Simon stopped reading aloud and Pete watched with interest as he began to blush. He finished the page and turned it over quickly, fumbling, and Pete sent out a silent congratulations to Katie for her courage.

'Why did you stop?' he asked innocently.

'Hmm? Oh it's nothing…it's just she…oh bugger me!' His mouth dropped open as he read the last few lines. Pete laughed as Simon's eyes reached his.

'You knew?'

'Everyone bloody knows, you dill. So what do you say? Have I got a brother-in-law?'

'But why me? A girl like that…she could have anybody.' Simon stared at the photo she'd sent along with the letter.

'She doesn't want just anybody. She wants you.'

'But why?'

'She's had a thing for you her whole life. Surely you noticed?'

Simon looked at him as if he'd grown an extra head. 'She has?'

Pete laughed again and Sully slid over.

'What's the lark?'

'Slimey's just received a proposal,' Pete grinned, 'although he hasn't said yes or no as yet.'

'If it's you I vote no,' Sully declared, reading over his shoulder. '*I feel like a moth drawn to the flame*...come on give us a squiz. Is this her? Holy smokes, she's a good sort too. But a few sandwiches short of the picnic, I'm guessing?'

'Watch out, that's my sister you're talking about.' Pete grabbed the picture.

'Ya sister? Well, we won't hold that against her. So what's y'answer, Slime?'

He looked at them both and his face split into an enormous smile. 'God yes!'

Sully clapped him on the back and Pete leant over and gave him back the picture.

'A moth eh?'

Simon turned even pinker and mumbled something about there being no bloody privacy, but he was still smiling.

It was the happiest Pete had felt in a long while but he didn't have time to savour it as he looked at his watch and realised they needed to get moving again, calling out the order. Simon got to his feet slowly, looking somewhat dazed, and Pete thought he might have imagined it but he could have sworn he saw Simon kiss the photo before putting it carefully in his pocket.

Thirty-nine

They were cut off. Pete didn't know how it had happened but they were scattered and in shreds, reeling from the viciousness of the attack, and he was stranded with a handful of others in a narrow gully that was thick with mud and mosquitoes.

'Have you seen Slime?' he whispered to Sully as they lay awkwardly against the slope, aware that the Japanese were moving in front. Sully shook his head and Pete scanned as best he could in the moonlight. It was damp and they gripped the forest floor, biding their time, waiting for something to happen. It did. Gunfire rang out and Pete decided to use the noise as cover, moving back into the trees and hoping they weren't about to bump into more Japs at the rear. Finally they found a cave and hid inside, Pete signalling that he would take first watch. Not that it mattered.

The night glinted in silver and black, every drop of water sending the smallest of movements to grate upon their nerves, each nodding leaf a potential lapse in stealth from the silent enemy they had so come to fear. A cacophony began: the jungle spoke in millions of mysterious languages as the insects and animals explored their nocturnal world, oblivious. But the men didn't talk. They barely dared breathe let alone sleep as they waited for the sun to finally rise so they could make sense of their situation. When it did they were no better off. The foliage was incredibly thick and Pete realised they would have to go at it blind, relying on their hearing for detection of the enemy.

When they walked into gunfire it seemed the old joke was true. The Japs really were invisible.

His heart was leaping in his chest as he heaved great draughts of air into his straining lungs. Flattened against the tree, he illogically feared they could hear its drumming above the roar of combat. Pete closed his eyes, the words of a lifetime of prayer failing him, and he found only one word echoed over and over in a desperate plea.

Please. Please. Please.

Images of Sully falling next to him moments before, with sightless eyes and blood-soaked chest, flashed in his mind as the gunfire began to pause and splutter in shorter bursts. The thick jungle gradually fell silent and Pete knew he had to move before they came through to finish off the dying. He stepped over the bloodied leg of Dominic Carson, bending down to check if he was alive, only to stare into a face almost unrecognisable in death. Emptied of expression, Dom was truly gone from this world and left only a pale imitation of himself behind. Pete forced the guilt away; this boy had died under his command.

It's war.

He grabbed Dom's wallet and wristwatch and moved on, his heart beating an unbearable rhythm of fear, paining within his ribs until he finally reached the creek. He wondered how many others had made it out and whether or not they were already on the other side as he cautiously crept across. The water was shockingly cold against his overheated skin.

'Pete!'

Startled, he turned to see Simon on the other side waving him over, watching his back. He scrambled then, landing beside him in the thick undergrowth as they stared at each other with a mixture of relief and surprise, but it was short lived. Gunfire exploded from the other side and they ran, their exhausted legs hurling them forward through the blinding green, their boots tearing at the muddy slopes.

He had no idea how long it was until he finally fell, and realised that the gunfire was far behind. And he had no idea how far back it was that Simon must have been shot and he'd run on oblivious, leaving him alone, lost in the middle of an impossible battlefield at the mercy of whoever stumbled across him first.

And he had no idea how long he would lie there until the gaping hole in his back spilled enough blood into this hungry, unforgiving animal, and he became just another part of the rich brown mud that gave it life.

Pete stared up at the canopy, a space in between the thick eaves framing a view of the sky. He drifted out of consciousness, reflecting that it was comforting somehow that it stayed with you no matter where you were, this calm, clear, endless blue with its armies of slow-marching clouds. It had been months since he'd looked up and noticed it, the giant dome that covered them all.

As the armies gathered in grey mass he slipped into nothingness, wondering how the sky looked above Gallipoli Street, and if it would rain there too when the telegram came to tell them he was gone.

Veronica woke in a sweat and Jack stirred.

'What's wrong?' he asked drowsily.

'Nothing…go back to sleep.'

She rose out of bed shakily and went out onto the verandah, her head pounding.

'What is it?' Jack came up beside her, wrapping her in his arms as the moonlight lit the fields around them.

'It's Pete. I…I dreamt he'd been hurt.'

'Well, my darling, that's understandable…'

She nodded, wiping at her tears. 'I suppose. It just seemed so… so real.'

He smoothed her hair and kissed her cheek, holding her close. 'Problem is it is real for us. We don't have to imagine what it's like.'

'I wish I didn't know,' she whispered.

'Me too.'

They stood together and stared out into the night, their hearts stretching across the miles to a jungle far away to the north, holding on to one another as they prayed for their son.

Forty

Field Hospital, New Guinea

Theresa shook her head, trying to stay awake as she bathed his face. This one had lost a lot of blood and it was still touch and go. He and the other fellow were the only survivors of the ambush though both of them had been shot. She couldn't say for sure at this point whether either would make it. Looking over at the one who wore spectacles she noticed his colour was at least good. He had been shot in the chest but Dr Kindred had managed to get the shrapnel out and, as long as he didn't get a post-operative infection, his chances weren't too bad.

He stirred and she went over to him as he opened his eyes briefly, disoriented.

'It's all right,' she said quietly, feeling that she recognised him for a moment, then realised it was just that his eyes were the same colour as hers, a very dark brown. He closed them again and she waited until he slept, then moved back to the fair-haired man.

The gunshot had been removed from his back but he had a perforated lung and was weak from lying so long and bleeding out. The natives had found him in a dark pool and she feared he wouldn't make the night. He looked to be in his mid-twenties, his handsome face pale against the sheets. She sighed, realising she was admiring a possibly dying soldier and thinking how pathetic it was that this was the only way she got to meet men these days. There weren't too many pool parties going on around here.

Theresa settled herself between their beds and prepared herself for a long vigil, praying they would both make it.

It was sunrise when the blond man finally stirred and to her enormous relief opened his eyes.

'Welcome back.' She smiled. His eyes were as blue as the midday sky.

He seemed to try to focus but closed them again and Theresa smoothed his forehead, continuing to wait. Willing them back open.

'Am…I…dead?' Pete asked, looking at the woman's beautiful face bathed in morning light and wondering if she was an apparition.

'No, Lieutenant Murphy, you are alive. Someone must be looking after you up there though.' She took his wrist and checked his pulse as he continued to stare at her.

'You'll…do.'

She patted his arm and asked him if he was hungry.

'Thirsty.'

She poured him some water and lifted his head slightly to drink as he watched her every move, trying to force his eyes to stay open, but failing. As he fell into the black again his last thought was that she looked vaguely familiar.

When he awoke again she was gone, but someone else was mumbling from the next bed and it was a voice he'd feared he'd never hear again.

'What's a man got to do to get some bloody rubber leaves around here?' Pete heard slapping as the man searched for the offending mosquito.

'Like moths…to the flame.'

Simon swung his gaze. 'You're awake.'

'Seem…to be.'

'Last time I saw you, you were busy getting shot. How'd you learn to run like that with a bullet in your back?'

'Cricket. Strict…coach.'

Simon laughed, his eyes filling as he looked at his closest friend, soon to be brother, and almost lost to them forever. 'I think we might have to retire hurt.'

Pete smiled. 'Wait…for drinks.'

'My shout, Turps.'

'Turps is it? And here I was thinking you looked like a gentleman.' Theresa had appeared carrying her medicine tray and Pete's head turned slightly at the sound of her voice. 'How are you feeling?' She felt his forehead as his eyes shut for a moment.

'Good,' he lied, trying to force as much clarity and strength into the word as possible.

'Hmm,' she said. 'Take these.' He swallowed his pills dutifully as she held up a needle before injecting it into his arm. He took in every detail of her figure as she straightened his bed and pulled at the blinds in the large bamboo structure that made up the hospital. She was taller than average and willowy with long arms and legs that moved gracefully with every exertion, but she also had curves and his eyes were drawn to those areas in particular as she reached high for the rods.

'Careful you don't strain yourself,' Simon said under his breath and Pete saw his friend watched him with amusement.

'Oh it isn't very difficult, just a bit awkward,' she grunted, pushing the last blind free and tucking a fallen white-blonde curl back into her cap. Pete found himself wishing he could see her without it.

'Now, let's take a look at your dressings.' She was gentle as she did so, and he found himself focused on the scent of her, deciding she carried a mix of honey and lime about her. His mind felt fuddled as he tried to think of something to say and he wondered how much time had passed since he'd been shot.

'Have I…been here…long?' he asked, flinching as she removed a bandage.

'Two days,' she replied. 'Hold still.'

'My mind…feels foggy…'

'I just gave you some morphine to ease the pain. We'll start weaning you off, don't worry. There,' she finished, easing him back down and straightening his sheets. 'Can I get you anything?'

He shook his head, happily drinking in the sight of her again and deciding she was surely the most beautiful woman he had ever seen, but something else was nagging at him.

'Have we met…before?'

Simon gave a cough in the background that she thankfully didn't consider suspicious as she answered him.

'Not that I recall. Now get some more sleep and try not to talk too much.' She patted his chest lightly as she turned away and he closed his eyes, relishing the feeling of her touch before slipping off again.

'Good morning,' she said the next time he opened his eyes, feeling it was almost worth being in hospital if she was the first thing he got to see each day.

'Have you been here…all night?' he asked, noting the blanket draped over her shoulders.

'Favouritism,' Simon said, smiling at her over his spectacles from behind a book before making his blushing way back behind it.

'You should…be getting…your own rest,' he protested. He seemed to be able to manage only a few words at a time before needing to take a shallow breath.

'Oh no, no, I'm fine. You've a letter from home,' she said, looking excited as she placed it in front of him. 'Somebody managed to find you even in the jungle.'

'Probably my…mother…bit witchy…like that,' he said, lifting his hand and holding it weakly, every part of him hurting if he moved. 'You sat up…all night…to tell me that?'

'How about I give you some breakfast then read it to you?' she suggested, ignoring his question and taking the letter from him gently.

'First things first...do you have...a name?'

'Theresa,' she answered as she prepared to feed him. Catholic too, Pete observed, noticing the saint's holy medal about her neck. Perfect.

Pete managed to swallow some banana and porridge, after which Theresa opened the letter.

'It's from your mother,' she confirmed, looking at the bottom.

'Told you,' he said. She gave him a little amused glance then began.

Dear Pete,

I'm writing this to you from down at the creek. Kelly and I decided we needed a bit of air and there's nothing quite like a good ride to clear the senses.

'You have horses?' she asked, pausing in surprise.

'Just for...racing...mostly.' She looked a bit taken aback so he added, 'Not country hicks...we have...cars too.' That didn't seem to reassure her.

I'm dipping my toes as I write and you won't believe it but a crayfish just swam by. I wonder if I should try to catch him and make him Pete the Crayfish number seven?

Theresa raised her eyes. 'Your mother names crayfish after you?'

'Brother.'

'Oh,' she said, continuing, wearing a twitching smile.

Your sister has been checking the post for days and driving me slightly mad until finally this morning the good news arrived, and she burst into the dining room announcing she is marrying Simon. What miracle occurred to make him realise how she felt at last we can only imagine, although I suspect you might have had a hand in this. Matchmaking from the jungles in New Guinea...is there any end to your talents?

'Simon is marrying your sister?' Theresa asked, looking over at the same, who was blushing again.

'I'm as shocked as you are,' Simon confessed.

'Close neighbourhood,' Pete offered.

'I see.' Theresa smiled at Simon before continuing.

Please bring him home safe and yourself included. Your father and Iggy can't wait for the wedding.

Theresa looked up, waiting for an explanation.

'Our dads are best friends. Served in...the Great War together.'

'Close neighbourhood.' She nodded.

'Typical Catholics,' he grinned. 'You…should know,' he added, nodding at her medal. 'Wasn't your…neighbourhood…like that?'

Theresa held it in her fingers. 'I didn't actually have one really,' she said. 'I was raised in an orphanage.'

Pete stared at her in surprise. 'That must… have been…lonely.'

He said it with such kindness that she couldn't deny it. 'Yes, it was really.'

Pete held her eyes with his. 'Whoever your parents were… would have been…very proud…of you.'

Theresa looked suddenly vulnerable, something she immediately hid. 'I have Missy, my best friend. She's my family,' she replied, pulling her shoulders back and reading on.

Dad wants to have it at their place and it promises to be quite a party. Pattie said you'd better get practising for some dance-floor numbers.

'Who's Pattie?' Her head snapped up.

'Aunt,' he said.

'Oh.' Pete watched her face. She sounded jealous, which pleased him enormously. 'Did you think…she was…a stage dancer?'

Theresa blushed and Pete wondered what he'd said wrong. 'I… don't have…any of those…waiting for me…promise.'

'I was a dancer at one stage,' she confessed.

Pete's eyebrows raised and he grinned a little wickedly. 'Looking at those pins…I can…believe that.'

'When have you been looking at my pins?'

Pete glanced down at them then back at her face, stating quite clearly, 'Whenever I can.' Theresa said nothing but there was a look in her eyes that made his mouth go dry.

They were interrupted by the arrival of Two-Bob who nodded and smiled as they carried in the fresh linen to make up the beds.

Theresa folded the letter and handed it to Simon, who promised to finish it for her when they were done.

As she walked away it wasn't hard for Pete to choose what to focus on.

It was mid-morning by the time Simon finished reading the letter to Pete and they each lay, thinking about the contents. The rest of it was mostly about May, who had just returned from Queensland and a visit to Larry Naismith, their old cricket mate and May's now fiancé. Apparently Pattie hadn't been too keen to hand back her daughter's motorcycle upon her return. Pete and Simon had been laughing at the image of her flying along in her old fur hat, scandalising the town.

But the last few lines sobered them again:

I have some sad news to finish with I'm sorry to say. We have found out that Larry's brother Vince has been taken prisoner of war. His poor parents are worried sick and I don't blame them. We hear such stories.

We know there is heavy fighting up there and I'm praying every day. Please come home safe to us my dear, dear boy. Your father and I think of you always.

'Do you think they know…we are injured by now?' Pete asked Simon, hoping they would take the news all right when it came.

'I'm not sure. What do you think, Nurse Theresa?' Simon seemed to have finally mastered the effort of not blushing every time he spoke to her. Theresa obviously had that way about her of making people feel comfortable.

Pete turned at the mention of her name and his heart skipped a beat.

'Yes, they would definitely know. Don't worry, I'll get a telegram off when you are discharged from here, which should be soon I think.'

'You'd better hurry or my nana might turn up and then we'll all be wrapped in mosquito nets and dosed up with cod liver oil,' Simon warned her.

Theresa laughed as she moved some supplies onto a chair.

'Let me help…you,' Pete said.

'No, really, I'm fine. The best help you can give me is getting more rest instead of pushing yourself so hard. What's this I hear about you trying to walk over to the cupboards this morning?'

'I was looking for an apron…so…I could help you serve lunch.'

Theresa laughed again, the sound echoing in the ward, near empty as it was save for him and Simon, who was now pretending to read again.

Pete attempted to prop himself up to look at her more easily, grunting against the tightness in his chest and back, to be rewarded by an excellent view of those pins as she stood on a chair, sorting equipment into the storage cupboard in the corner.

'There's a chessboard...in there. How about...a game later on?' he suggested. She pushed a large box of netting into a corner, shaking her head with a smile at his invitation. 'When do…you get…any time off?'

'What's that?' she threw over her shoulder. 'I can't seem to recall the concept.'

'Time off, you…remember. Doing…something enjoyable…for yourself? With someone…charming and…irresistible?'

She glanced over at him and raised an eyebrow. 'Hmm, I wonder where I could find someone like that?'

'Ready, willing and…able.'

Theresa sent him a look. 'Perhaps willing but hardly ready or able,' she said briskly, moving over to the empty beds. She stripped the sheets as Pete's eyes trailed after her. He loved that she was a good Catholic girl and holding him at bay. It made him even more determined to win her over.

'It's only…a little game of chess…surely you could…spare enough time for that?'

'No.'

'Why not?'

'Because I don't get time off.'

'You get time…to sleep…don't you?' he pressed.

'Rarely,' she replied drily, gathering the sheets into a pile and dumping them in the basket next to a box of fresh limes Two-Bob had gathered for her. He knew now she liked to add lime juice and honey to the sheets, believing it helped ease the men's breathing in the thick tropical air. She did a lot of little things like that for the patients.

'You said…I'll be transferred soon. Just want a little…time… with you.'

She sighed, placing her hands on her hips. 'You don't give up, do you?'

'Psst,' said Simon from across the room. 'I should have warned you earlier, Theresa: he's a lawyer.'

'Is that so?' She raised her eyebrows. 'I suppose that's where the stubbornness comes from?'

'No that comes from cricket. Pete is the opening batsman for New South Wales.'

'Really?'

'Yep. But all the annoying persuasiveness comes courtesy of the law courts,' Simon continued helpfully. Pete decided he really preferred it when Simon was painfully shy.

'How's the book?' he said to him, pointedly.

Theresa gave them both an amused look then addressed Pete. 'You're asking a lot. Time is the most valuable thing I have…' she began, then gave in, sighing at his expression. 'I'll probably finish around nine tomorrow night.'

'Tomorrow,' he repeated, relieved.

'Now get some sleep before I change my mind,' she ordered and he obeyed, offering her a weak salute before she went.

Theresa giggled as she walk outside, then shook her head. What on earth was she doing? Flirting with a sick man, a patient in her care. It was breaking all her personal rules, the honour code she adhered to of serving without thought for self.

'He's a looker,' a voice commented from behind.

Theresa turned to see Daphne smoking on the steps, taking a rare break. She sighed, sat down next to her and took one for herself.

'That he is,' she said. They stared out at the jungle together, flicking ash in silence.

'One in a long, long line, love,' Daphne reminded her.

'I know, I know. He'll be gone in a few days. There's no point,' Theresa shrugged, frowning.

'So why play games?'

Theresa stood, brushing off her skirt before picking up her basket. 'It's only chess.'

'Watch out the queen doesn't lose her head,' Daphne replied, crushing her cigarette into the ground.

Forty-one

The morning was grey and mist-filled as Pete watched the doorway, waiting for the best part of his day to walk in as the rain began to tap the roof in a loud, sudden drum. The tightening in his chest was much better today and Nurse Daphne had him sitting up, propped against several large pillows, to keep his lungs as clear as possible. It allowed him to see around the sides of the shuttered windows to the jungle outside. Today it was full of movement as the wind and rain buffeted the waxy curves of the palm-tree fronds, forcing them to bow and bounce against one another.

'Good morning, men,' Dr Kindred said briskly, striding into the tent, Theresa in tow. 'How's everyone feeling this morning?' He addressed the four patients as one without looking at their faces, busy as he was with scrawling notes on his clipboard and checking charts. Simon and Pete watched as the two new patients were examined first, one fellow with a badly injured foot from a sniper shot and the other with a bandaged eye and shoulder who'd been breathing very heavily all night.

Pete watched Theresa as she removed bandages and applied fresh dressings, mesmerised by the stray white curl that kept escaping onto her lovely neck only to by pushed back up into that damnable cap.

'Sergeant Murphy,' the doctor said brusquely as he arrived at his bed. 'How's the chest feeling today?'

'Much better,' Pete replied.

'Hmmm.' Dr Kindred concurred as he listened to it and examined him. 'A far cry on a few days ago, isn't it? Have you attempted to walk at all yet?'

'Only to fetch my apron.' Pete grinned, winking at Theresa, who turned a delightful shade of pink.

Dr Kindred shot him an amused look and made a few notes. 'Try a few stretches if you can today. Not too much, mind. The nurses will help you. Dwyer, you can get a bit of exercise too. I'll need you as fit as possible for tomorrow.'

'Tomorrow?' Simon queried.

'Transfer party are on their way up. You're being moved to Port Moresby. Who knows? You may even get to go home for a while.'

'Home?' Simon repeated, his face lighting up. Pete's eyes never strayed from Theresa. Was that disappointment he glimpsed?

'Yes, I should think so. Although with the rapid recoveries you're both making they may just send you back into the fight. Try not to look too healthy, won't you?' He gave them both a quick smile then turned to the nurses to issue instructions before striding out once more.

'Theresa?' Pete said, halting her departure. 'Are you…are we still on for chess tonight?'

She seemed to hesitate against the decision but to his relief she nodded. 'Just a quick game.'

He settled back against the pillows as she left, trying to digest the fact that he was leaving her tomorrow, then pushing that thought firmly to the side. Nothing was over until the game had played itself out. He would take this one move at a time.

Pete waiting impatiently, tapping his hand against the chessboard and looking at his watch again. Five minutes to nine. He stared at the doorway then out at the night, willing her to arrive.

The moon moved between the high skidding clouds like a brilliant white pearl dancing with feathery veils, a golden ring surrounding it in a vast halo. A lover's moon. Pete cursed his injuries, wishing he could make love to Theresa in the moonlight, her dark eyes beckoning as he lay her down, like Adam and Eve. Just a man and a woman crying out to the stars, primitive and wild like the jungle itself.

Time was skidding along with those clouds and suddenly he only had tonight to capture her heart. Who knew when he would see her again? Or whether he would? Coming so close to death had made him desperate to live every second and more than anything right now he wanted those seconds, those precious hours of living, to be with her.

He thought about Australia, about going home at last. Pete was shocked to realise that a part of him didn't want to go. As much as he longed to see his family and friends again, he could almost prefer to sit in this stinking bed in this stinking jungle with Theresa. Maybe it was love at first sight, or maybe he was just a cliché: a typical wartime patient with a thing for his nurse. Maybe the jungle had finally sent him mad. But there was something about her, a familiarity that resonated from her eyes; it was like an old truth that she was always going to be the one, as if she were made for him. Impossibly and illogically, it just felt so right.

He turned to the door, willing her to appear again, and this time she did, filling the space, everything around her fading to nothingness. The gramophone from Dr Kindred's quarters nearby filtered 'Moonlight Serenade' across through the trees and Pete felt every note as she moved towards him in the soft light.

She had changed out of her usual nurse's uniform and into a soft white blouse and pants, a yellow cardigan draped casually about her shoulders and her hair freed from its usual cap. It was even softer and fairer than he had imagined and it seemed to Pete to be made of moonlight as she walked towards him.

'You look beautiful,' he said, the words hanging between them.

She sat down on the chair next to the bed and smiled, pulling at the cardigan a little self-consciously. 'Just felt like being comfortable. I haven't worn anything but my uniform for months.'

'I've been wondering what you looked like without it.' He gave her a look that was half longing, half devilish delight, which made her blush and smile in return. Pete decided he would spend the entire time they had tonight trying to recreate that delicious response.

'Black or white?' she said, turning up the lamp and picking up the chessboard, placing it between them on the blanket.

'Lady's choice,' he responded and watched as she picked up the white pawn, moving it two squares forward.

He moved in kind and waited as she frowned, planning her game.

'Who taught you to play?' he asked, watching her fierce concentration in amusement.

'One of the nuns at the orphanage,' she replied, jumping her knight. 'Sister Carmel. Nicest lady in the world but terrifying when armed with a miniature army.'

'Do you remember your parents at all?' he said after a pause.

Theresa shook her head. 'No, I was only about two when I arrived in Australia. No one even knew their names or where I had come from, only that my grandmother had died on our passage over from France during the war.'

'Didn't anyone come to collect you?'

'No. There was no one. No enquiries. Nothing.' She shrugged nonchalantly but Pete glimpsed an old hurt.

'Difficult to solve mysteries during wars,' he offered.

'I didn't even know this much until a few years back,' she admitted, sharing with him the story of finding out about her possessions and how her fate had unfolded. 'If it wasn't for Sister Carmel it's quite obvious that Father O'Brien would have left me in the dark and there I'd be, in the middle of a jungle in an uncomfortable uniform in the tropical heat...hold on. There's something rather familiar about that.' She began to laugh and Pete joined her, coughing a little from the exertion. She immediately handed him a glass of water and he took it, watching her thoughtfully over the rim.

'I suppose there's no escaping it,' she sighed as he drank. 'I'm destined for a life of servitude and penance after all.'

'Why penance?'

She placed the glass back on the table and, picking up her bishop, pointed it his way. 'For defying my betters.'

'On the contrary,' he suggested, following her hand as it placed the bishop on the board. 'I'd say you bettered yourself through defiance.'

Theresa laughed again. 'You really are a lawyer, aren't you?'

They played in companionable silence for a while and Pete stroked his chin as she dramatically took his knight.

'Sister Carmel must have been a better teacher than my dad,' he said.

'Must have been nice though...having that time together, I mean.'

Pete tilted his head, wondering how to explain things. 'It was actually. Helped us to get along better.'

'Hadn't you always?'

He wondered how much to reveal, but then again she was being so open it seemed right somehow. 'No...he found it very hard. After the war.'

Theresa watched him thoughtfully, her brown eyes filled with understanding, and he realised he wanted to tell her everything. A sudden need for confession; a baring of the soul. 'He drank a lot,' Pete admitted, 'and it was a bit rocky between us when I was younger. It changed him when he drank that much. Made him… angry.'

'Ah.' Theresa nodded. 'Well, after what I have seen of war I can't judge anyone too harshly for that. I don't imagine any of us will be the same after this.'

'All the death…' he said quietly.

'And the hate too, I think.' Theresa held the rook, twisting it around in her hand. 'I've had moments here when I hear the priests' words over and again in my head: turn the other cheek, love one another.'

Pete nodded. 'Feels as though we were taught one set of values in church and quite another set out here.'

'Exactly. No one taught us how to achieve that when someone so young is holding your hand and the life is…just…' She shook her head, her eyes filling with tears. 'Just stolen. And I…I hate all the people responsible, you know? And then I hate the Japs, hate them with all my heart, and I think I'm going straight to hell.' She ran her hand across her eyes, the rook still clenched tightly. 'Sorry…'

'Don't be,' he said.

She looked at him, a little embarrassed. 'You must be a good lawyer. You're extracting all kinds of secrets from me tonight.'

'What you see is what you get.' He smiled easily, his gaze becoming serious once more as the lamplights flickered. 'Dad had to figure it all out and Mum helped him of course. She was pretty amazing when I think about it,' he admitted, missing her in a sudden rush. 'I guess seeing him do that gave me hope that it doesn't have to ruin the rest of your life. Plus he told me some good advice and that helps. He said you can't let it make you feel like that. No matter what happens, no matter what you have to see or what you have to do. All of this death...it's to stop it from reaching home. That's war. That's the job.'

'And the hating?'

'It's the war you really hate. And God knows the war deserves to be hated. He won't punish you for that.'

She stared out at the night. 'No, it's not just war...I do hate the Japs. When I hear what they do and see it with my own eyes...'

'No you don't. Not really.'

She looked at him quizzically. 'Don't you?'

'No.'

'Honestly?'

'No,' he said again. 'I mean sure, the politicians are fools and I hate what they're doing...and when I'm getting shot, well... there's no love lost. Could have strangled any one of them when I saw my mates' faces after...you know...' He gestured out at the jungle and shook his head, trying to eradicate the images of Sully and Dom and the recent carnage. 'But after the battles are over and my blood has cooled down a bit that kind of goes away. I've seen dead Germans, dead Italians, dead Brits...we all kind of look the same then. A dead Jap is just another soldier who tried to get out and didn't make it.' He shrugged. 'So I figure they are just like us really. Trying to survive, trying not to look at the faces of their mates when they fall. Wanting to go home to their families. Those blighters out there are going through the same thing as us,' he gestured at the chessboard, 'just on different bloody sides of the game.'

She stared at him in amazement. 'But surely after what you have been through...'

'Same thing they're going through, isn't it? Only none of them have an angel sent to save them.' He smiled at her, feeling his heart contract as he realised how much he actually meant it. To him she was like a pure ray of light that had suddenly appeared at his darkest hour.

'I'm no angel, Pete.'

'Yes you are. Look at your halo,' he teased, lightly touching her hair.

'I'm a fallen one, if that.'

'What great sins have you committed? Hating the enemy? Hating the war? I've told you, God understands.'

'No, it's not just that.'

Theresa paused, looking at his easy expression, his open confident gaze. A man who had been given every advantage and made something of each and every one of them. A man so loved throughout his whole life he could even forgive an enemy trying to kill him. How could someone like him ever comprehend what it was like to have no family, no home? To be left to fend for oneself in the clubs of Kings Cross? To fall for the first conman who promised stability and family. 'You wouldn't understand.'

'Try me.'

She frowned, trying to form the right words. 'You're not like other people…you're different…' she began hesitantly.

'Hey, I'm just a digger, lying in a hospital bed, trying to get to know my beautiful nurse,' he protested charmingly.

'But you're not just a digger. You're the one who is perfect… a golden boy. Lawyer, sportsman, cherished son in a loving family…you have racehorses, for goodness' sake. You're…blessed. I've never met anyone like you.'

'Just because I'm some kind of…golden digger doesn't mean I won't understand you,' he said, taking her hand.

She stared at it for a moment before pulling away, moving the chessboard to the table and straightening his sheets. 'I think it's time for you to rest.'

'Theresa,' he began.

'You're leaving tomorrow,' she reminded him, stilled by his imploring eyes.

'Then stay this last night near me.'

There was no point, she knew, no possible future with this perfect man, but she found herself pulling the chair close anyway, matching his gaze until his eyes closed. Wishing for a life by his side where every night the kind eyes of this golden digger were the last things she saw.

Theresa stood watching with Daphne as they prepared to leave, the natives hoisting the four patients being transferred in their makeshift stretchers. This was it, the way it had to be. Instead of some romantic fairy tale that ended in him sweeping her off on his steed through the jungle, Theresa's fair prince was being carried down a muddy hill and she was going back to blood and pain and death. No happy ending. Not even a farewell kiss.

'Chin up, there's our girl,' Daphne whispered to her, offering the party a cheerful wave.

She pasted a smile on her face and lifted her own hand to Simon and the others, steeling herself to look at Pete one last time. His eyes held everything she was trying to hold back; longing, regret and another emotion, something so intense it lodged in her throat and she ran to him, despite herself. He clasped her hand tight and their lips met briefly with sweet intensity. Then her tears fell as the Fuzzy Wuzzies began to pull him away.

'I will see you again. I will find you,' he promised as her hand slid from his.

'How?'

'Hey I'm the Golden Digger, remember?'

And with the sunlight catching his blond hair and his heart-breaking grin illuminating his handsome features, for that moment in time he was more than an injured soldier on a stretcher. He really was the Golden Digger…and she believed him.

Forty-two

Early December 1942

Theresa woke in a sweat, the sheets twisted, and took a moment to register where she was: New Guinea. It was always her first thought, followed closely by a second: Pete. The flow of patients had been constant and heavy since he'd been transferred, which was at least a distraction for her during the day, but the nights were long and lonely, and made so much worse by the humidity. She kicked at the sheets and stared at the mosquito netting above. How she wished for news of him, not that it was likely – and besides all the mail had dried up. Japanese forces were close by and the job of war was on their doorstep, far outweighing mundane matters such as letters from sweethearts being carried up the trail.

She kicked at the sheet again and decided it was no use, she might as well get up and have a smoke. The night was very clear and the stars blazed in the distinct path of the Milky Way above the trees as she sat on the step and took out a cigarette, listening to the night creatures in song. There was a crack nearby and she wondered what had made the noise. Probably some furry little animal. Or a snake. She wrinkled her nose at the thought, preparing to strike a match, but something made her freeze midway. There was a figure moving along the edge of the trees. A soldier. Her insides clenched in sudden terror. A Japanese soldier. Her heart pumped unbearably in her chest and she watched as he moved towards the supply shed and disappeared inside.

She took her chances.

Treading as softly as she could, but imagining every move she made was deafening, she crept across to Dr Kindred's quarters, feeling her way in the dark. The net around his bed shrouded his face and she wondered how to wake him without him calling out in surprise. To her relief he opened his eyes and gave a start but thankfully, no cry. Theresa placed her finger over her lips then pointed outside, mouthing the word 'Japanese'. He moved quickly and quietly, waking Two-Bob, and the four of them crept back to the nurses' hut and peered out the windows that faced the storage shed, one of the Bobs shouldering a rifle he'd pulled out from under the bed. Daphne was keeping vigil at the hospital and Theresa itched to get over there to warn her and to protect the patients.

They waited in silence and Theresa felt the sweat glide slowly down her back as the agonising seconds ticked by. Finally the soldier emerged, carrying a bag and making his way back along the treeline once more.

Dr Kindred signalled to Two-Bob and they quickly went out to make sure he was alone and definitely gone. After some time they returned and whispered that they couldn't find any trace of him and Theresa slumped in relief against the wall. So much for waking in the middle of the night with hopes a cigarette break would send her back to sleep. She doubted now she would ever rest in this jungle again.

By the time they had all joined Daphne in the hospital the dawn was breaking and with it came the arrival of Australian soldiers, for once not carrying wounded. But they did carry something else: orders for evacuation.

'The Japs are supposed to be retreating but they're fighting the whole bloody way and moving towards this ridge,' reported the young lieutenant. 'You were lucky last night's visitor was probably just some starving bloke on his own. You're sitting ducks.'

Theresa shuddered at the thought.

'Pack your things,' the lieutenant ordered. 'We are leaving now.'

'How far will we go?' Dr Kindred asked.

'How bad are the wounded?'

'They can travel, although two can't walk.'

'We'll stretcher them out. I've got orders to take you right down to the port. You don't want to be round here in the next twenty-four hours. Artillery is set to go.' He walked off issuing orders and Theresa stared at the others.

'You don't have to tell me twice,' Daphne declared, running off to pack. The rest did the same but Theresa was momentarily paralysed, not by fear this time. They were going to the port. Port Moresby. To the last place Pete had been. Then she found her feet too. They didn't have to tell her twice either.

Forty-three

Port Moresby

'I think the jungle might kill us before the bloody Japanese,' Daphne sighed, pushing vines aside to allow Two-Bob to get past with a stretcher.

'Nearly there,' puffed Dr Kindred.

'Might have to kill him if he keeps ruddy well saying that,' Daphne muttered under her breath and Theresa grinned. She didn't care if she turned into a ball of sweat and rolled down the track. She was heading closer to Pete and away from potential midnight raids from the enemy. Let the jungle be as hellish as it liked. She was leaving it.

Fortunately for Daphne, Dr Kindred proved himself right this time and the path started to widen, the road coming into view. They began to make their way along in the open sunshine and Theresa squinted up at the sky, relishing the wide expanse despite the hot sun. A rumble of jeeps approached and the convoy – Americans – stopped, grinning hordes of marines making room for their party, especially keen to sit near the nurses.

'Would you ladies care to join us tonight for some dancing?' asked one eager young lad called Jerome.

'Dancing?' repeated Daphne. 'Last time I saw the port it was caught in the middle of a war.'

'Still is,' another announced, tapping his boots in a little jig on the floor of the truck. 'Doesn't mean we ain't got no feet.'

They all laughed and Theresa figured Port Moresby would probably feel like Paris itself after the backwards life they'd just been living, armies notwithstanding.

An hour later they stood to watch the view unfold. Paris it wasn't, but civilisation was certainly abounding. The streets were alive with trucks and soldiers, Americans and Australians shouting out orders or exchanging banter, occasionally drowned out by the low-flying planes guarding the multitude of boats in the harbour. It was alive with humanity in full-blown activity and the movement and colour flooded Theresa with a sense of security. She squeezed Daphne's shoulder and the latter turned and gave her a look of pure relief from beneath the dirt and sweat that covered her exhausted face.

'Think they have a hairdresser nearby?' she queried, taking off her cap and shaking out her tangled hair. They both laughed.

'Don't know about that but I think I'd trade everything I own for a hot shower.'

They arrived at their quarters in a chorus of cheerful goodbyes and invitations from their rescuers and made straight for the longed-for showers, relishing the incredible luxury of hot water again. Afterwards Theresa slid her feet down inside the clean sheets of her bed and sighed at the delicious feel of it all. She'd never felt so clean and so tired at the same time. They didn't have to report in until the following afternoon so she was allowing herself a second indulgence:

an afternoon nap, planning her search for Pete on the morrow. Even if she had to scour every hospital bed, ship list and building in Port Moresby, she would find something, of that she was sure.

Pete woke in a sweat. He'd been dreaming that the jungle was eating him alive, vines twisting at his legs and arms as he tried to get away. He shook his head clear, figuring it was just that the sheets had pinned him in his sleep, and disentangled himself from the damp mess.

'Wakey wakey!' called out Bluey, his friend from the hospital and now self-appointed social secretary since they'd been moved to rehab. 'Tucker's on.'

'What are you all dressed up for?' Pete asked, rubbing his eyes, noting Bluey's slicked down red hair and ironed shirt.

'Me mate Jono flogged…I mean *found* some beer crates. Reckon I'll go over and join the party. I'd say come too but I figure you'll want to hobnob with the officers now you're leaving us and reclaiming your rightful place with the toffs.'

'I doubt there'll be much beer at the Officers' Mess tonight by the sounds of things,' Pete remarked.

'No idea what ya mean there, sir,' Bluey grinned, 'but come over and slum it with us tonight. Last hurrah, eh?'

'Think I might just have to do that. Too damn hot in here,' he muttered, sitting up and pulling off his saturated undershirt.

'That's what ya get when ya lie about mooning all day.'

'Since when do I ever do that?' Pete objected. He'd actually been trying to keep himself busy, spending a bit of time doing some legal work for the senior officers, but only a few hours here and there. He'd got tired very quickly, especially in the last day or two. Maybe he'd been overdoing it. Maybe saying he was ready for light duties starting tomorrow was a mistake.

'Every time that schmaltzy "Moonlight Serenade" comes on the radio ya get all mopey– '

'I'm not mopey I'm just…hot,' Pete objected, but acknowledged to himself that he had been 'mopey' since he'd arrived in town, especially compared to his usual cheerful self. It was worse now that Simon had been sent home. They'd said Pete was still too weak to join him at the time and he hadn't minded another week or two in New Guinea, as illogical as it sounded. Theresa was closer here. But not close enough. Being away from her was torturous, especially when lying in bed took up a good portion of the day.

'Ya gotta be kiddin'…' Bluey exclaimed as the radio played 'Moonlight Serenade' right on cue. 'Right. Either you're comin' with me or I'm flushing that bloody thing down the crapper. What's it gunna be?'

Half an hour later they walked out into the night and Pete breathed in the warm, moist air. Simon's nana was right. Someone needed to move this bloody war out of the tropics and this perishable heat.

When she awoke it was twilight and Daphne was humming to herself as she brushed her dark hair, looking almost unrecognisable with her curled locks, red lipstick and a crisp, clean uniform. 'Fancy a walk?' She winked.

'Goodness. When did Jane Russell arrive?' Theresa teased.

'About one minute ago and she's waiting for Lana Turner,' she replied, throwing her a lipstick.

'I think Lana is having a quiet night in.'

'To pine the time away thinking about a certain lieutenant? Not tonight she's not. Come on!'

Theresa laughed. Daphne's playfulness was infectious. 'Maybe just some dinner…'

She put on a new uniform, feeling fresh and rested for the first time in many weeks, and let Daphne curl her hair before they headed out together, marvelling at the smells, sounds and sights of a wartime base at night. The air was thick with a sticky sweetness that clung to them: a mixture of sea salt, earth and rain with a good dose of fumes and garbage thrown in. There were uniforms everywhere they looked – marines, infantry, cooks, officers, nurses like them. Some rushed about, intent in purpose, others lazed against the walls and called out as the two women moved through the throng, causing them to laugh more than once. It felt good to just be a girl, Theresa reflected, realising she was actually having a real 'night off' and enjoying the distraction from her constant thoughts of Pete and the war.

They saw light spilling out from one corner building, the music drawing them closer as they peered inside. The rest of the port might be organising a war but this room seemed to be intent on forgetting it. It was loud and raucous, the native band playing over the din as soldiers danced, sang, yelled and laughed, the beer flowing.

'Over here!' beckoned a few of the lads, and Theresa and Daphne recognised some of the marines from the convoy earlier that day. They made their way amid several loud catcalls and appreciative comments, soon finding themselves inundated with drinks and surrounded by admirers.

'This is quite a party.' Theresa laughed with Jerome, the young man they had been talking to on the truck.

'A few crates didn't make it to the Officers' Mess,' he yelled back. 'You can thank the Aussies for that!' he added, pointing to some very cheerful Australians, swaying near the band and singing an enthusiastic, off-key version of 'Ac-cent-tchu-ate the Positive'.

She laughed, drinking the beer she was handed thirstily as the Australians serenaded the room.

'Care to dance?' Jerome asked.

'Why not?' she responded, feeling the effect of the first real drink she'd had in weeks begin to take its pleasantly fuzzy effects. There were roars of approval as they began to jive. Jerome turned out to be a wonderful dancer and her old stage routines came flooding back so she could match him. Daphne and another soldier joined in and, what with the definite shortage of women in the room, they were soon surrounded by would-be partners. As the band began to play 'Boogie Woogie Bugle Boy' they caught each other's eyes and laughed. They'd both forgotten what fun felt like.

'Strewth, what a turn-out,' Bluey exclaimed as they approached the crowded doorway, dozens of soldiers cramming to see the scene inside. 'Come on move aside, move aside, officer in the house.'

A pathway was forced as Bluey pushed and bossed his way in and Pete followed him, distracted by the sight of some marines hooting and singing from atop a pile of crates in the corner.

'What's all the commotion?' He laughed, turning to Bluey just as the scene ahead came into view.

'Cor...' breathed out Bluey in one long exclamation. But Pete couldn't speak. There, on a table, was Theresa, dancing for all she was worth with a grinning marine, flashing the legs that kept him awake at night to the whole room and a long, long way from a small hospital in the middle of the jungle.

Theresa was flying. The music pumped in her veins and her legs kept responding, remembering all those hours on stage.

Jerome picked her up and swung her about and the crowd cheered, handing her drinks, which she drank, and smiles, which she returned.

She laughed with the blur of faces, waving at Daphne who was dancing and cheering too. Everyone was happy. No one was hurt or sad. This was the way life was supposed to be. Everyone smiling. Except that man. That man looked like he'd just been slapped.

The information registered and her steps faltered, slowing her to a standstill.

That man was Pete.

Theresa stood frozen, dropping the drink she'd been holding; it crashed to the table, the noise lost in the din as the throng cheered for more. Jerome stopped too, following her line of vision as the crowd began to realise something was going on with the gorgeous blonde as she stared across the room at a tall Australian officer.

A pathway began to form between them and Pete walked towards her slowly, finally coming to stand in front of her, still staring in shock.

'Pete!' Her face broke into smiles and tears at the same time and she threw herself off the table, into his arms and into his kiss. The room erupted but neither cared or noticed because as soon as their lips met that was all that mattered any more.

'It's a…beudderful thing. Beaudderful,' Bluey was saying as he waltzed on the street with Daphne.

'I loove this tune,' she sighed, pressing her cheek against his shoulder.

'Moonlight Serenade' played from the radio inside; Bluey pulled back to look at her face. 'So do I!' he lied emphatically before kissing her.

Theresa and Pete pulled apart from their long, blissful kissing in an alley nearby and he smiled. 'So do I,' he whispered. 'It's the song that played the night I realised how hopelessly in love with you I was.'

She kissed him softly. 'And I realised I'd fallen in love with a man I'd never see again…which was hopeless…*hic*.'

'Told you I'd find you. I'm the Golden Digger, remember? Blessed? Lucky? All that stuff?' he murmured, kissing her neck.

'Mmm…you didn't find me, I found you.'

'How do you figure that? From what I could see you'd forgotten all about me.'

'I was creating a diversion to…*hic*…attract you to me.'

'Attract every man in Port Moresby more like it,' he muttered, kissing her behind the ear and making her shiver with delight.

'Jealous?'

'Horribly. Don't ever do that to me again.'

'S'jussa little dancing…'

'Hmmm…it seems to me alcohol clouds your judgement as to what is dancing and what is putting on a show.'

'I told you I used to…be on stage…'

'Hmmm…I think we'd better stick to not dancing on tables from now on though, agreed?'

'Agreed!' She smiled, saluting him.

'And while you're in such an agreeable mood, I think I'd better ask you to marry me.'

She gaped at him in surprise before wrapping her arms around him tightly. 'Agreed,' she said, tears filling her eyes.

He kissed her again, laughing as Bluey's voice reached them from the street.

'Who's up for a midnight…schwim…?'

'I'll schwim!' cried Daphne.

'I think we'd better get them home before they catch their deaths.' Pete laughed.

'I don't know…sounds like fun…' Theresa said playfully.

'Temptress.' He grabbed her hand as they walked out of the alley. 'It's way too freezing.'

'What are you talking about? It's so hot. S'always hot here,' she said, yawning.

'It was boiling before but it's got really cold now. Come on, I'll see you home and we can meet for breakfast in the morning and make plans. Agreed?' he said, huddling closer to her, his teeth beginning to chatter.

'Agreed,' she said happily.

'I sure hope you stay this agreeable as a wife.' He grinned.

'Only in the bedroom,' she said, feeling outrageously sexy as she said it.

He stopped walking and took a deep breath. 'There goes any hope of sleeping tonight. Remind me to give you plenty of drinks at our wedding.'

She giggled, realising she was actually more than a little tipsy or she never would have said something like that, especially considering her secret, but also figuring her past didn't matter right now. It was all too perfect an evening. Tomorrow would suffice. Tomorrow she'd tell him everything about herself so there were no secrets, and he would understand because he was the Golden Digger with the golden heart.

They made their way home with Daphne and Bluey, the streets echoing with their laughter, and, when she finally dragged herself away from Pete and his blissful kisses and fell into bed, she did so with the knowledge that life would be better from now on. God had forgiven her all her sins and she'd never be alone again.

He was late. Very late. Theresa checked the clock on the wall against her watch. He'd said outside the hospital at ten. It was half past. Where was he?

'Theresa.'

She turned at the sound of his voice, her smile fading. 'What is it? Oh God...you're sick.'

'Sorry I...just couldn't seem to get up and then...I felt so dizzy walking over here...'

He collapsed and she clung to him, arresting his fall. His face was pasty white and his clothes were soaking wet, fever burning through his body. She cursed herself for having been too drunk to take notice of the telltale signs the night before as she dragged him over to the hospital doors, calling for help.

As she sat by his bedside later she couldn't help feeling that maybe some of her sins weren't quite forgiven yet, especially the one that remained unconfessed. God seemed to have a few more points to make before he was done with her, but surely striking down her fiancé with malaria was being a bit blunt.

Forty-four

Sydney

She watched the pattern of his breathing, the stuttering fall and the rise that was blessedly less shallow than a few days earlier, but still laboured. Theresa patted his chest gently as he slept, glancing over towards the window. They were approaching Sydney at last and she stood and stretched, deciding to see it in all its glory. The bunks in the plane were close together and she checked patients as she went, glad of the comfortable pants nurses were allowed to wear during aerial transit. She hoped she could get transferred to this role after the wedding. It was more rewarding, happier work, bringing the men home, despite their injuries. Helping them to feel warm and comforted even before they hit Australian soil was a great privilege. Assuming Pete would still let her work.

What am I thinking? Since when does a man tell me what to do? She shook her head. It was hardly a normal engagement. She didn't know his opinion on having a working wife any more than he knew she was coming to him minus her virginity. She sighed. There was plenty of time to sort all that out later. Focusing on his survival was all that really mattered after all. She'd been doing the right thing, she told herself.

Gazing at the Harbour Bridge lit by the glorious dawn, Theresa felt the relief catch in her throat. She wished she were bringing every soldier home from war, feeling for all the families whose sons would never come flying in over her shores, safe once again in this glittering, wonderful place.

'Want to watch?' she asked one very young soldier who was nursing a badly injured arm.

She helped him over to the window and they drank in the sight together. The dotted grey-green of the bush among the sandstone and city, the sapphire blue of her waters, where boats bobbed about like little corks in their happy harbour; all were watched over by the great bridge, a reminder to those who visited that Sydney was a place of hope. The graceful arch, built during the desperate years of the Depression, had pulled them all forward to her completion, a metaphor for their collective, ultimate triumph over adversity as the city was united and better times arrived. And so it was, ten years later, that Sydney's arching heart watched over them still, the symbol of hope standing strong during these days of war. A promise that dark days have endings and that good times come once more.

She felt safe and welcomed home as a renewal of strength flowed into her. Here there was an abundance of nurses and doctors, workers and families. Here there was a country to take them and hold them again, a place where the guns were silent and the invisible enemy absent. Here, in this country, she could marry the man she loved, and, when the war was over, have a family with him and live in a real home together.

How extraordinary it seemed that she could ever have felt trapped here when this place had given her every opportunity she could ever desire. Here she was limited only by her own strength – she knew that now, because in Australia they were free. It had taken a great deal for her to realise that and she would never forget it now. No orphanage, no church, no nightclub owner and no war ever really held her fate. The choices were hers to make. Free. With one goal in mind: to get Pete well, for without him even freedom meant nothing at all.

She looked over at her young patient, grateful that this soldier at least was spared from battle for now.

'Got someone waiting for you?' she asked the youth.

'My mum,' he said, trying to hide the tears that had welled in his eyes.

She smiled at him gently. 'I'll bet you're looking forward to her cooking.'

'Sure am. She's promised me some of her banana cake as soon as I get there. And Dad said I can have a beer with him down at the pub. First time,' he said looking excited.

'I'm sure he'll be bursting with pride,' she assured him.

He looked at her shyly. 'Want to come too? I reckon they'll let a good sort like you in the main bar. You look like a pin-up girl.'

She laughed. 'And here I was thinking you were a little innocent. You just save those cheeky comments for girls your own age.'

She helped him back to his bunk then looked over towards Pete. He had woken up and was sending her a look of such tenderness it made her stop for a moment to hold it, soaking it in before she made her way over to him.

'Thought you'd jumped off and left me.' He smiled, holding her hand.

'I can't swim.' She smiled back, smoothing his hair.

'We'll have to do something about that then. I bet you'll look ravishing in a swimsuit,' he whispered hoarsely. He craned his neck to see the view from the window as she gave him some water then lay back weakly. 'Beautiful sight,' he said.

'Funny to think last time I came into this harbour I was just a toddler on a ship, all alone. Not that I remember.'

'Not this time. This time you're coming home to be my wife,' he said proudly and she felt his love engulf her, warm and safe. 'Can't wait to show you off at the big Christmas party at Greenshades. Hope I'm well enough.'

'Greenshades?' Theresa echoed, something tugging at her memory.

'My great-uncle's estate in Wahroonga. Massive joint with a nice pool and tennis courts. They have a Christmas do every year and the nuns bring over the orphans from the parish up that way. It's a big affair, marquee, dancing. You'll enjoy it: lots of singing and carrying on…what's the matter?'

'I…I remember.' She stared at him, stunned.

'Remember what?'

'Greenshades. I…I went there once. As a little girl. Sister Carmel took me because her cousin worked at that orphanage and she decided to take me along.'

He stared at her in surprise. 'Seriously? But that means we would have met once upon a time…and you've met my family too.' He chuckled, shaking his head and kissing her fingers. 'I knew we were meant to be.'

'It was…magical there,' she whispered, still incredulous.

'Yes, it's good fun.' He yawned as he drifted back off. 'Good fun…can't believe you were there. Told you I thought you were familiar when we met.' He squeezed her hand. 'Destiny.'

She watched him fall asleep, processing this new information. So that was the family she would be marrying into. It hardly seemed possible. The one family she'd had a glimpse of: a privileged, wealthy family. A family she had envied from afar and fantasised about, this family would be hers now. She felt slightly sick as the prospect of meeting them loomed closer. All they knew of her so far was whatever Pete had told them in his letters from Port Moresby and a few lines she'd sent in a telegram before the transport journey. She could be anyone on the street to them.

What would they make of her? A girl with no family, little money and no concept of their way of life? And she was two years older than Pete. The list of possible grievances seemed endless. How was she supposed to slot into their world? What if she picked up the wrong fork or said the wrong thing? No, the nuns had been very strict in that regard. She knew she wouldn't disgrace him in manners or etiquette. But there was still the issue of not understanding how to be one of them. She had no idea of how to be in a family or how to handle life as a one of the wealthy. She enjoyed her work and had no intention of becoming a member of the idle rich, chit-chatting about fashion and knitting for the poor orphans. *She was the poor orphan.* For the first time in her life she was actually worried about what people would think of her, seeing herself as falling very short of what they would consider a suitable match for their eldest, marvellous son.

Most of all she dreaded meeting his mother, a woman he seemed to worship. Would she see through her to the frightened little fraud that she was? And what of the issue of her virginity? This Catholic family would be expecting a virginal lady in white and here she was, a soiled dove. She only hoped his mother was as kind and understanding as Pete said she was.

She didn't have long to wait. That night they had just settled into the ward at St Vincent's Hospital, and Theresa sat, pen in hand, writing another telegram for his parents, when there was a knock at the door and a lovely woman in a stylish blue suit and hat entered. Her face broke into a stunning smile that matched her son's as she rushed forward and gathered him in her arms, tears falling.

'I won't ask how you knew.' He laughed as she drew back to study his face and feel his forehead.

Just then a good-looking man arrived and strode across the room to clasp his son close; he was openly crying, pushing at the tears roughly and apologising. 'Sorry, mate. Oh God, it's good to see you.' He laughed at himself.

The three of them sat for a moment and Theresa wondered if she should leave when Pete looked over at her. 'Mum, Dad, this is Theresa,' he said simply, his voice filled with pride.

'How wonderful to meet you,' Veronica said, walking over and taking her into her gentle embrace, much to Theresa's surprise, 'and how beautiful you are. Like a swan, isn't she, Jack? Pete raved on for pages about you but now I see words can't do you justice.' She smiled warmly, from the heart, and Theresa realised her fears over her future mother-in-law were unfounded. This woman was all goodness, just like her son.

'You've cared for our Pete and now here you are, ready to become part of our family. I can't tell you how grateful we were to get your telegram,' Jack said, kissing her cheek and placing his arm around his wife as she nodded tearfully. 'Made such a difference to know you were bringing him home.'

'Yes, so very grateful, dear. What a blessing that you found him again,' she said, studying her face. 'You know it's the strangest thing– '

Just then there was another knock at the door and Simon's face appeared, gaunt but far healthier than the last time Theresa and Pete had seen him.

'Hear there's a thirsty man come back from war.' He grinned and Pete let out a laugh as Simon entered, holding an older lady's hand. 'Nana wouldn't stay away. Wanted to see the survivor of the perishable heat. Here he is, Nana, I told you I wasn't the only one.' Simon shook Pete's hand as Nana Dwyer kissed him and clucked at Simon.

'Now, now, 'tis a sin to make fun of an old lady. For shame.' She shook her finger at them, giggling. 'I was only wanting to see ye for meself, lad. Are ye still feelin' poorly?'

'Far better than I was, although I still have the fevers,' he told her.

Simon let out a low whistle.

'Hush now!' his grandmother admonished, turning as Simon walked over and kissed Theresa.

'Nana, may I introduce Pete's fiancée, Theresa? Theresa, this is my grandmother, Mildred Dwyer– '

But his grandmother had turned white and he leapt forward to catch at her as she pointed at Theresa in shock.

'Saints in heaven...*it's my Rose...*' They all stared at Theresa and Veronica stepped closer, scrutinising her face again.

'Rose...my baby...' Mildred began to cry, her hand over her mouth, her head shaking from side to side. 'You've come back. But how...?'

Theresa didn't know what to do or say. She didn't know what she had expected, certainly not this, but the poor lady looked so distressed she took her hands gently and spoke as she would to a soldier in shock. 'Madam, my name is Theresa, after St Therese. You see? I wear her medal, here, about my neck...I've had it since I was a little girl. I...I think it was from my mother.'

'Your mother?'

'Yes, my mother.' Mildred searched her face and she felt obliged to explain further.

'She...she and my father died when I was a baby. I came here with my grandmother in 1916, only she died too and I was raised an orphan. I have...no family.' She felt herself blush as she announced it to the room. 'My name is Theresa. Theresa Jones.'

Mildred shook her head, taking the medal in her trembling hand and turning it over.

'I gave this…I gave this t' her. Two medals. One for her and one for the baby. I sent it t' ye mother when she…she stayed in France. Before she passed on. We waited for you. We searched. *You…you are Elizabeth.*'

'My…my name is Theresa,' she stammered.

'No, my dear.' Veronica came forward and placed a hand gently on their joined ones. 'Your name is Elizabeth Chambers, née Dwyer, and this…this is your real grandmother.'

She raised her gaze to this woman who clutched at her desperately, her eyes shifting to Simon who stood behind. His eyes. They were the same as hers. He was her cousin. The truth came all at once and hit her with force. *France.*

'EC,' she breathed. '*Elizabeth Chambers.*'

Mildred dissolved into tears and took the beautiful girl into her arms.

The granddaughter she had thought lost to her for all time had been brought back to her by the miracle of the prayers that she had prayed every day since, still wearing the blessing of St Therese sent all those years back. Here to marry Jack's son.

The Lord was merciful indeed.

Forty-five

Highview

The jasmine was thick along the verandah at his grandparents' home and she shielded her eyes from the sun as she took her walk, drinking in its delicious perfume as she went. The white cockatoos glided past, landing on the roof then ambling their way along, looking down at her with curiosity. Much like everyone else, she acknowledged. She looked beyond them, out towards Gallipoli Street. Little wonder this house was named Highview, she thought, standing to take in the scene laid out before her.

She traced her eyes along the row of jacaranda trees towards his parents' blue and cream house on the hill, further along the other side of the street to his other grandparents' house, the Murphys, then finally to her own grandmother's house, the Dwyers. The house she would have been raised in, if only things had been different. To think she could have known him all her life. This perfect, golden man.

She sighed, watching him in the distant field on Kelly. His recovery had been fast these past few weeks – too fast if it meant he would soon be sent back. This was due in no small part to the constant production of dishes from Highview's kitchen, where his two grandmothers, his mother, his aunt and Eileen, their maid, were on a constant mission to fatten him up. So much for the idle rich. These women never stopped!

She enjoyed their company but found she needed time to herself too, unused to cooking much and even more unused these days to being in a close situation with others on a daily basis, especially women. Even at the hospital or the orphanage she'd taken to her own space when she had spare time, whereas here everyone seemed joined at the hip. She didn't know the people they talked about or the dishes they made, and had no part in the memories that were laughed at or insights into the personalities examined. It was hard to get used to.

Not that they excluded her. On the contrary. A more welcoming group of women would be hard to find, especially Pete's mother, to whom she was growing closer every day. His grandmothers had also been very kind. Both still worked for the local orphanage and seemed to see her as an adopted child they could share, making every effort to ensure her transition into their families was as gentle a landing as possible.

His cousin May was a wonderful diversion, popping over to scoot her off on her tandem bike every few days and reminding her to have fun, but it wasn't quite enough. She had only briefly met Katie, who had reminded her enormously of Missy and was currently on her honeymoon with Simon; they were not due back until after Christmas. Their wedding had been a quiet, sudden affair in the end, due to his imminent transfer back to war. Personally Theresa considered that Simon had done more than enough for his country already. She didn't want to lose her only cousin now, not after a whole life spent longing for family.

The men, likewise, were all lovely, even James, the gangly thirteen-year-old (although he blushed every time she entered a room), and his father was kindness itself. It seemed hard to imagine him as Pete said he'd been after the Great War.

But there was one among them of whom she felt wary: there was an element of distrust underscoring her words, and the warmth didn't quite reach her eyes. Not that Pattie didn't believe that she really was Rose's daughter. Everyone could see the likeness, and the production of her great-aunt's watch, the photo of her as a baby that matched one Mildred had at home and the initials on her grandmother's embroidered quilt had been quite enough validation for even the greatest of sceptics. It was something else in Pattie's manner that made Theresa suspect that she hadn't quite won her over. Something wasn't quite right about the older woman's attitude when it came to her mother, Rose. In fact Pete's family in general didn't seem to have a lot to say about her, except that she had saved Veronica's life after she'd been bitten by a snake one day. She loved that story, feeling it brought her mother's persona to life for her. A glimpse of who she was, especially since aside from that there was an odd absence of stories. Sometimes it just seemed as if they hadn't known her all that well. She supposed it was that, or else what they knew they didn't want to share. Hadn't they liked her?

It was this feeling that drove her over to the Dwyers' house on almost a daily basis to spend time with her clinging, coddling, yet completely adorable grandmother. It felt comforting to have her mother's photo on the mantel there and her things in her room still. Theresa loved to sit in that room and visit with her mother's spirit, getting to know her through the traces she left behind. She had fine taste, she decided, discovering drawers of silks and satins and a wardrobe of beautiful dresses, including a gold satin evening dress she was having reworked for the ball at Greenshades in two days' time. Nana had given her all Rose's jewellery too, and she played with each piece, imagining a life where such trinkets were commonplace. Now her life, strangely enough.

Then there was Rose's ambulance patch, a relic of the war sent home to her parents by a friend. It had been a great joy to discover that her mother had been in the Yeomanry and she found it amazing to think that Rose had been a part of those pioneer times for women tending to the wounded. It made her very proud to be her daughter and tied in even more feelings of belonging to the family, especially when added to the fact that her grandfather had been a doctor. She wished she could have known him. It was a strange feeling indeed to hold the patch her mother had once worn, the same red cross of duty Theresa wore herself. Apparently her grandfather had kept this one in his wallet in memory of his daughter. It was sad to hold it, knowing that, but it was comforting at the same time knowing they both wore it with pride and that she shared this family legacy of medical care.

But by far her favourite discovery had been a box of photographs, where she found several images of her mother and this new extended family she was trying to understand. She often sat and stared at one taken the day Pete's uncle Clarkson had arrived with the Sunbeam and the party at Greenshades had gathered around it for a photograph. Her father was in it, to the side, and her mother was pictured standing next to Jack, his arm around her. Funny she wasn't standing next to her father.

And then there was one of her mother with her in France, taken by a street photographer, her face pressed up close against her own, her arms protective in their embrace. This was her greatest of treasures and she kept it in a frame by her mother's bed. She adored that room and would rather have stayed there than in the spare room in the Murphys' house, as lovely as it was.

Her mother's memory felt welcome there. Understood. Loved.

It was there she headed that morning, determining that she would ask more about her father this time. His personality was proving harder to grasp and she thought about the things she would ask her grandmother today, including how her parents met and where they married. Perhaps she would marry in the same church. She would have to decide where to have it soon. Pete's rapid recovery meant their time together was growing ever shorter, as was the growing need for complete honesty, but she put that issue aside for today.

Today was all about Gregory Chambers.

Except for the Greenshades photo there was only one other single shot of her father, with her mother, leaving on the ship for England. Aside from these, and the knowledge that they had both died in France during the war, she had no other information on him. His face held little of hers but she finally knew where her unusual hair colour had come from, thinking it fortunate she had been wearing her nurse's cap the day her grandmother recognised her, otherwise she might still have been in the dark about her heritage.

Her grandmother was beaming when she opened the door, although she immediately fussed before telling her the news. 'Goodness, child. Ye'll burn ye nose to freckles in this sun. I've a lovely surprise: come in, come in.'

Theresa entered the cool room, embracing her grandmother fondly. Mildred patted her face. 'Iggy! She's here!'

A tall man entered the foyer and came over slowly, seeming to drink in the sight of his sister's reincarnation with amazement. He looked a bit like Simon, only older and without glasses, and she stared at his face. He was more like her, she decided, his features much the same as her mother's, and she marvelled again at this newfound world of belonging somewhere.

'So you are found at last…I can't tell you.' The emotion shook him as his voice broke. 'I'm so sorry. She was about your age when I last saw her and you are so much like her…'

He began to cry and Theresa fell into his arms, both weeping for the loss of a mother she was only just beginning to know and a sister he missed so much. He reached over and caught his mother close as she joined in sobbing. He kissed her grey head and choked out words of comfort.

'There now, Ma. She's sent you a sign, Theresa no less. Your prayers were answered.'

Finally they broke apart and Mildred dabbed at her cheeks and left the room, muttering about tea. Iggy sat opposite Theresa, unable to stop staring at her.

'May I...ask you a few things about her? There's so much I don't know.'

He patted her knee and sat back to fill his pipe and calm his nerves, rubbing at his eyes. 'Ask whatever you want, dearest girl. I am from now, and forever more, your most devoted uncle.' He smiled happily at her. 'But first things first: do we call you Elizabeth or Theresa?'

'Theresa.' She smiled back at him. 'I can't imagine myself by any other name now, and seeing as my last name is about to change anyway, I thought I'd otherwise leave things as they are.'

'Right you are. An Elizabeth by any other name is still sweet by me,' he declared, 'as was our Rose of course.' He smiled affectionately, still teary. 'Now, what burning questions do you have for me?'

'Well first of all...what can you tell me about my father?'

'I knew him of course,' he said after a pause, nodding slowly, 'although not very well. They had a somewhat secret courtship in Melbourne before we moved up here. I guess he realised he couldn't live without her because he turned up out of the blue at Greenshades and announced their engagement the very next day. Came as a bit of a shock, to be honest. Ah, here's the tea. Thanks, Ma.'

Mildred set it down and left to fetch the cake.

'But what did he do? What was he like?' she pressed.

He thought about that for a moment, sitting back with his cup. 'He was an importer of cars. Brought that Sunbeam your fiancé drives around in over from England, in fact, for his uncle Clarkson. I suppose you know about him?' She nodded. Theresa had heard the tragic story of Pattie's first husband. 'Gregory was…driven, pardon the pun. A very focused man. Knew what he wanted and went for it.'

'I'm a bit like that,' she admitted.

'Well your mother was too, so you had pretty strong chances there. I imagine it was a very feisty marriage.'

'But they were happy, weren't they?'

'Enough of all that now. Who wants some cake?' Mildred interrupted, casting Iggy a warning look.

'Please. I have lived a life without family, wondering all this time who they were and whatever happened to them. Please, tell me, where they happy? Did they love one another?'

'You are like them, aren't you?' Iggy smiled, and held up his hand at his anxious mother, leaning forward. 'Yes, I believe they were happy, for a while. They married at the local church and whisked themselves off to England so fast we didn't get much time to know him. I supposed they were a good match, but they had a falling out in the end. That's why she went to France to stay with your great-aunt, and joined the Yeomanry. She only wanted the best for you and felt your father was…too possessive. But you need to know, they loved you, both of them, very, very much, and they would be so proud of the woman you've become.'

She turned that information over in her mind. 'Was he searching for me? Is that why they tried to hide my identity?'

'Yes, it certainly seems so.'

'I know now that Aunt Joelene had called herself my grandmother and given false names for the voyage but I haven't understood why. Perhaps she was afraid my father would take me back to England…away from all of you.'

'Yes, I would say that was exactly why. He could be very… stubborn.'

Her grandmother tutted, cutting the cake. 'Aye, she had her reasons.'

'What reasons?'

Iggy looked at his mother but she was pursing her lips so he answered instead. 'Things only they knew. Leave it be: you cannot blame yourself for the choices of others. Suffice to say they loved you and they both wanted you, and here you are where you belong at last, with us.'

She smiled as her grandmother patted her cheek again and felt that much was true. Even after only knowing them this brief time she felt she belonged in that home, with its stories and its ghosts, and with the living members who remained to her: the uncle, the grandmother and the cousin. She was, finally, with family.

Forty-six

Greenshades, Christmas Day 1942

Pattie watched her from the window, her mind in conflict. She supposed the girl couldn't help being who she was but it was still difficult to accept that this person, Rose's daughter, would marry her beloved nephew and become a part of their family. After all that had happened Pattie still couldn't forgive Rose for breaking her brother's heart and nearly ruining her best friend's chances at happiness. Veronica could forgive that easily, and even Jack had fallen under the girl's spell, but Pattie couldn't bring herself to trust Theresa or Elizabeth or whatever they were supposed to call her.

'You have to get past it,' a voice observed from the doorway.

'I know,' she sighed, turning to stretch out her arms as Mick came over and held her. 'Veronica is convinced it's fate. Destiny at work, but I just can't bring myself to trust her. It's like déjà vu. Greenshades, Pete strutting about looking so happy, her putting all the men in a tizz. I'm just waiting for some bozo to walk in the door and announce she's already agreed to marry him and we'll be set.'

He kissed the top of her head. 'Come on now: she's a very different girl. Rose was spoilt rotten and it made her the way she was, but this girl…she's done it tough. She's got kindness in her and she's giving. Look at her down there with the kids. She hasn't forgotten where she's come from or who she is.'

They watched her play with the orphans near the pool and Pattie conceded she was certainly a far less selfish person than Rose; but still, it was difficult to trust a woman who looked like that and she voiced this unworthy thought to Mick.

'I don't know. You're built for sin and I trust you.' He grinned, sliding one hand up her skirt.

'Stop that,' she said, but he didn't, and all conversation about Theresa was over.

Father O'Brien sipped on his tea, bored by the constant fawning of those around him, particularly Father Francis who seemed far too weak a man to handle such a blue ribbon community. What he wouldn't give to take the reins. He'd been contemplating a change. Perhaps his days at St Rueben's should come to a close, he thought to himself, eyeing the surrounding luxury and considering the alternative. Maybe having to spend Christmas recuperating from his operation in Sydney at this parish was a fortuitous situation after all.

'A miracle really. Her family had given up on ever finding her and then there she was, named Theresa no less, standing in the hospital room, engaged to the boy who grew up just across the road,' Father Francis said, continuing the story that had taken a good part of ten minutes and which Father O'Brien had long since lost interest in.

He scanned the lawns instead, ignoring the other priest's drone and watching the children with disinterest as they played games and sports in an array of activity before him. There was a crowd of them gathering at the pool and he leant forward to see what had piqued their particular interest. It was a young woman clad in one of the latest, scandalous swimsuits that were all the rage. She was dancing to a gramophone, long legs kicking in high, practised routines and the orphan girls were trying to imitate her every step. Disgraceful, he thought in disgust.

The young woman turned, pulling off her swimming cap, and Father O'Brien blinked in startled recognition at the flash of white-blonde hair in the sun.

'Ah there she is, the girl I was telling you about,' Father Francis said, peering over to see who or what had taken his interest.

'Theresa Jones.'

'Yes,' said Father Francis, taken aback. 'How do you know her last name?'

Father O'Brien stared across at Theresa, stiff with indignation at the thought that this girl, this disrespectful harlot of a girl, would marry into this prestigious family. 'I know quite a bit about her in fact,' he replied.

'Ah, here's our fellow,' Father Francis said, turning as a tall man crossed the lawn towards them, towel in hand. 'Off for another swim?'

'Yes, Theresa wanted another lesson, although I think she's going in to dress for dinner.' He looked towards her departing figure, disappointed. Father O'Brien's eyes narrowed at the realisation this was Theresa's fiancé, the much admired Lieutenant Peter Murphy.

Peter paused to smile at Father O'Brien politely. 'I don't think I've had the pleasure, Father...'

'O'Brien,' he supplied, shaking Peter's proffered hand.

'Peter Murphy. Welcome to Greenshades,' the young man said, displaying a charming smile along with his manners. 'Are you here to say mass with Father Francis? Two priests and a dozen nuns,' he shook his head, 'we may have to start our own church right here on Aunt Marjorie's lawn.'

A well brought up Catholic boy who was both rich and handsome, Father O'Brien noted. Surely he couldn't know the truth about the girl he was about to marry. He decided it was time to do his Christian duty and enlighten him.

'I was just saying to Father Francis that I am well acquainted with your...uh...fiancée. She was a member of my parish for a long time.'

'Really?' Peter seemed very surprised. 'Well that's wonderful news. I haven't met anyone yet from her home town.'

'No, I wouldn't imagine you had,' Father O'Brien replied. 'I'm quite sure you won't be either, if she has a choice in the matter.' Peter had stopped smiling and was now looking at him with an air of wary confusion, as was Father Francis.

'On the contrary, Theresa is very keen for me to meet her friend Missy...'

'Ah yes, well I tend to cast them both in the same mould. Neither are considered a part of our town anymore, nor the parish, but I'm sure you are well aware of that.'

Father Francis fidgeted with his hat nervously as the other two men faced one another.

'Father O'Brien was it? Yes, I do seem to recall the name now.' Peter's tone was casual but there was a glint of anger surfacing in his eyes. Father O'Brien pushed on regardless.

'I must commend you on your strength of forgiveness. Not many men would have been able to overlook such a past.'

'Surely a convent upbringing, in a town such as yours, is nothing to be ashamed of...' Father Francis interjected, red-faced.

'I wasn't referring to her country days,' Father O'Brien continued, 'it was the life of sin on the streets of Kings Cross that ruined her. But if you can see your way past it, again, I must commend you.'

'You can't possibly be suggesting...surely you can't be serious...' Father Francis was blustering but Peter remained cool, betraying nothing of what he must be feeling.

'I am sure you have been the victim of idle gossip, Father. My fiancée was merely a dancer before the war and I am quite aware of the reasons she had for leaving your parish. I would say she showed great courage and dignity under the circumstances and I would be very disappointed to have it said otherwise in our family's home.'

'A dancer you say? Is that what she told you?' Father O'Brien couldn't hold back a derisive chuckle. 'One of my parishioners saw her act and I can assure you it was hardly ballet.'

'I don't know what seedy clubs the men of your church frequent but Theresa was not the girl he saw. She was a professional dancer before the war – full stop.'

'Oh well, if that is the story you choose to believe...'

'I believe the woman I love, yes,' Peter's voice was steel-like now and Father O'Brien suddenly lost the desire to laugh. 'I recommend you believe her too, lest other stories, *true* stories about attempted theft and the manipulation of young women by certain men of the cloth come to light.' He was standing close and Father O'Brien felt suddenly very small next to the younger man's large, athletic frame.

'If you'll excuse me,' Peter finished, leaving abruptly.

Father O'Brien let out a long breath, cursing the legacy of Eve. What hope had mankind if they couldn't seem to resist the sins offered by women?

Theresa put on the dress and turned to look in the mirror, admitting to herself it really did suit her. The new cut had worked perfectly and it looked as fashionable as the latest styles in Pitt Street, despite the fact that the fabric was almost thirty years old. But such fabric! She stroked the gold satin reverently as it hugged her figure, the hues touching highlights in her hair, which she wore up on one side, fastened by an elegant gold and diamond clasp that had also belonged to her mother, the waves falling forward on the other. The overall effect was seductive and she knew Pete would find it hard to control himself, which sent her stomach into spirals.

She had to tell him the truth. She had resolved to, many times, but the moment never seemed right, especially when he wasn't up to physical exertion anyway. But now that they were here on holiday and he was strong again, the chemistry between them was charged. She knew she had to make her confession, particularly considering the wedding was now set for two weeks' time and soon after he would be sent back to fight. She wasn't willing to squander any more of the precious days they had left on waiting to be together. And she certainly didn't want to risk him finding out during the act, a possibility that could well eventuate if today was anything to go by.

There was something very sensual about this place, with its lush gardens and beauty. It was almost as if the jungle air had found them again and was cloaking them in its heat and seduction.

Last night at the family Christmas party she had found his eyes trailing her wherever she moved, watching her mouth as she talked and his hands glided against her as they danced in a slow, rhythmic way that caught her breath and made her wish they were alone.

She'd woken from a restless night to spend half her day distracted by his bare torso as they'd played with the children at the pool, finally managing a brief private moment together walking back from lunch.

'Come here,' he'd whispered, pulling her through the frangipani trees and into a hidden little copse. It was fast and frantic and he'd been desperate for her, kissing her throat and baring her to the waist in a sudden rush of wanting.

'Oh God, you're so beautiful.' He kissed her breasts and she felt the warmth of desire suffuse her entire body before he drew away, fighting for control. 'We have to stop,' he'd panted, leaning his forehead on hers. 'We can't.'

'I want to,' she protested, trailing kisses down his chest, the heat sweet in her veins.

'No love, we'll wait. The first time should be as man and wife.' He'd resisted, his fingers a little shaky as he'd pulled her costume back up and ran his hands over his face. 'But for pity's sake stop flashing all that skin my way. You're going to send me into a relapse.' He sent her a smile, his face lighting up in the incredibly handsome way that broke her heart, and she knew now was the time to tell him. But the words were left behind as he grabbed her hand and led her back to the pool, jumping in and laughing with the others. Cooling off in more ways than one. Theresa decided right there and then she would tell him before the day was over because it was becoming more than a secret, it was becoming a deception. Here he was, holding himself back for his 'virgin bride', and she was letting him believe that's what she was. He deserved better than that.

There was a knock at the door and she called out for him to enter. Pete stared at her entranced, letting out a long whistle.

'What are you trying to do? Kill me?' He walked over and kissed her softly, glancing down the front of her dress then up at the ceiling. 'Oh God, we're going to have to get married tonight. I can't take it.' He was smiling but it seemed a little forced.

Theresa tilted her head to one side. 'Is something the matter?'

'No, nothing, nothing.' Pete said, pausing. 'Well it's just...'

'Pete, there's something I need...'

They both laughed a little and he kissed her on the forehead. 'You go first.'

'Perhaps it may be better if you sit down.'

Pete looked at her uncertainly.

'Alright.' He sat on the bed and waited as she began to pace. The late sun streamed across the room, causing the gold dress to cast soft mirrors of light upon the walls as she moved.

'There's something I need to tell you. Something I should have said before and I'm afraid…of how you'll react. I don't even know how to say it but I have to be fair to you and…I've got to get this out.' She sat on the bed next to him as her legs gave out, the fear of his response threatening to overwhelm her.

'You're scaring me, love.' He held her hand, waiting.

'You know how you want to…to wait for our wedding night before we…'

He watched her carefully. 'Well no, of course I don't *want* to wait but I know you want the whole white wedding bit and all so...'

'Yes well, that's the thing.' She took a deep breath. 'Pete I…I shouldn't really wear a white dress. I'm not…I'm not a virgin.' She searched for courage as he stared at her in disbelief. 'I mean, I have slept with a man before. One man. He had proposed to me and I thought he meant it and he…lied. I am so sorry. I know I should have said something before now but I couldn't bring myself to tell you. I was afraid.' Her eyes pleaded with him as he sat as if frozen.

'When?'

'When I was a dancer. Actually, when I stopped being a dancer. He left for war the next day.'

He remained still for a moment, staring at her, then stood suddenly. 'You're damn right you should have said something before.'

She watched as he walked over to the window then turned to study her, frowning.

'Is that the whole truth?'

'Yes...of course.'

He nodded then seemed to battle against something, shaking his head as if in denial. 'Alright...alright. I'm going to ask you something and I want an honest answer because I'm starting to realise it can't be a coincidence, can it?'

'What can't?' she asked, confused.

'The fact that Father O'Brien is here telling stories and all of a sudden you want to make a confession.'

She started in horror. '*Father O'Brien?* From St Reuben's? But... what is he doing at Greenshades?'

'Well I didn't get to ask him that because I was too busy defending your bloody reputation!'

'I...I can't believe it,' she said, stunned.

'You mean to tell me you didn't know he was downstairs, sharing your sordid past with God knows who?'

'No! And I don't have a sordid past, I told you, it was just that one man...that one time.'

'Father O'Brien said one of his parishioners saw your act and that you were working the streets of Kings Cross, and now you tell me some story about not being a virgin but it only being one man...?'

'It's not a story...it's true!'

He pinned her with a look, his blue eyes blazing. 'Did you or did you not work in Kings Cross?'

'I...I did.'

'Holy hell, Theresa,' he said, rubbing at his eyes, 'and did you or did you not...perform in front of men when you were there?'

'I...it wasn't like that.'

A flash of memory crossed his face. 'Oh God, that night in Port Moresby. When you were dancing for all the boys. That's something you did all the time, isn't it? Were you…were you a *stripper* or something?'

She stood, shaking. 'No. Of course not. And I'd appreciate it if you kept your voice down.'

But he banged the wall instead and she could see his rage had taken over. 'Just what kind of a *slut* were you?'

'How dare you say that word to me?' she exploded, suddenly furious herself. 'Actually, just get out. We'll talk about it later when you've calmed down– '

'What do you mean get out? This is *my* family, *my* life. *You get out*,' he yelled back at her.

'What are you saying…that you want me to leave?'

'Just get out of my sight. I don't even want to look at you. And for God's sake put some decent clothes on.'

'Five minutes ago you loved it.'

'Five minutes ago I didn't know that you were a *whore*.'

Theresa flinched. 'You don't seriously believe that.'

'*I don't know what to believe anymore.* All I know is you worked in the Cross and you've slept around...and now half my family probably bloody knows it too!'

'One man.'

He glared at her. 'You know, even if I believed that, you still lied to me. You still let me believe you were this good Catholic girl waiting for her white wedding day. Instead...instead you're what? A reformed *street worker*?'

Theresa's face was stony now as she picked up her purse. 'Tell me something before I go, just so we are clear. How many women have you slept with?'

He scoffed, his hands on his hips. 'It's different for men, and you know it.'

'How many?'

'I don't know, a few.'

'Were you engaged to them? Did you think that you were going to marry them? Or did you just pay them?'

'It's different. They knew the score.'

'Oh yes, the *score.* Men get whatever they want; women get either marriage or whoredom. Very fair. Let me tell you something, Peter Murphy, I just told you the hardest thing I've ever had to admit: that I slept with a man who offered me security, a home, the day I lost my job because I wouldn't turn whore. Yet here you are, someone who's had sex God knows how many times for the fun of it and you call me a slut? *Hypocrite*!'

He said nothing, his face still grim with fury.

She gestured around them. 'What do you know about the real world, growing up in….in mansions, food pouring in from the kitchen from your legions of admirers and loving family? The perfect goddamn golden-boy life. Aside from Missy I had nothing and no one and then he…he came along and he promised me marriage. A *family…*' Her voice broke slightly and she waited for him to speak but he still said nothing. 'I was betrayed, Pete, and I didn't want to betray you, so I'm telling you the truth.' He raised his eyes, hard and angry, and she tried one more time to reach the man inside, the one she trusted. 'I…I thought you would understand…'

'Well, I don't,' he said shortly.

She shook her head in frustration. '*Why not*? What happened to the man who forgives so easily? I mean…for God's sake…you can forgive the bloody *Japanese* but you can't forgive me?'

'Soldiers don't have a choice in what they do.'

They glared at each other, both unyielding.

'Do you still want me to leave?'

He walked over to the door and spoke to the wall before walking out. 'No, allow me.'

Theresa felt like screaming as she stared at the closed door, her whole being fuming at the unfairness of it all before marching towards it and flinging it open to go search for him. She wasn't letting him go that easily.

'There you are dear! Don't you look lovely? I have some friends I want you to meet.' Veronica looked nervous as she ushered Theresa over to some guests who had just arrived and she found herself trapped in a circle of polite introductions as she scanned the room for Pete. She found him, standing in the corner and downing a large glass of whisky, glaring across at Father O'Brien who was holding court with familiar arrogance. The priest raised his eyes and met her glance, leaning forward purposefully to whisper his lies into one of the neighbour's ears. Theresa felt her cheeks burn in response but it wasn't from shame. This was plain, straight out fury.

'Drink, madam?' The waiter paused.

'Yes, thank you.' I'll give them something to talk about.

She didn't know how it had happened but she seemed to be surrounded by men in uniform, all eager to fetch her drinks or tell her jokes, which she laughed at with false appreciation. It pleased her to see how it infuriated Father O'Brien and even more so how it angered Pete, who was still glowering from the other side of the room.

'Care to dance?' asked one enterprising young corporal.

'Thank you,' she accepted, allowing herself to be sailed about the dance floor. She was really quite drunk she observed, somehow pleased at the notion.

'I hear you're engaged to Pete Murphy. Why isn't he dancing with you?'

'Because he's a royal buffoon,' she responded airily and he raised his eyebrows, obviously figuring he might have a chance with her after all.

By the time she had danced with several partners Pete looked to have had enough and a pathway cleared for him to stalk towards her.

'I told you it was déjà vu,' Pattie whispered to Mick as Veronica and Jack watched anxiously.

'May I have this dance?' he demanded through gritted teeth. Her partner acquiesced and he steered her away from the crowd and towards the door.

'Goodness, what will your family think? Dancing with a lowly whore like me.'

'Shut it, Theresa. You made your point.' He grabbed her arm and led her towards the parlour, where she flung herself onto the couch and poured another glass of champagne. 'Don't you think you've had enough?'

'Oh I don't know, I thought that was your verdict tonight. You've had enough!'

She pointed her hand in the air dramatically and sipped at her glass.

The door opened and Mildred walked in. 'A word alone with me granddaughter if ye don't mind, Peter.'

He threw his hands up and marched out. 'She's all yours!'

'That's what you…used to say. I got the hiccups.' She frowned at her glass.

Mildred stood, looking agitated, and Theresa patted the seat next to her on the lounge. 'Come sit down, Nana.'

'No, no, I think I'll stand for now. I know yer in the middle of an argument and all but I....I just needed ye t'know a few things for yer own good before y'go on. Things I suppose I should've said sooner, but there it 'tis. I guess I just didn't want to tell ye.' She paused, wringing at the material of her handkerchief and taking a large gulp of sherry.

'Come on,' said Pattie, dragging Veronica to the door to eavesdrop.

'But...'

'Shhh.' Pattie put her finger to her lips and they moved closer.

'We shouldn't,' Veronica whispered.

'Oh we already know what she's going to tell her anyway.'

And so, against Veronica's better judgement, they listened.

''Tis a very pretty dress,' Mildred began. 'I remember the night yer mother wore it.'

'Was that the night my father came and proposed here?'

'Aye, that was the night…only there was a complication. Theresa, yer mother did some things that people haven't forgotten and when ye wear her dresses and behave in a certain way, well, tongues will wag. Especially when certain people want to get them to wagging. That priest...'

'Charming man, isn't he?' Theresa observed dryly, sipping her champagne with a small hiccup.

'Dangerous,' Mildred warned. 'I wish you had told me about yer...dancing and so on...'

Theresa frowned, regretting her grandmother's embarrassment from all this. 'That's all it was, I promise...'

'Of course child, y'don't need to explain to me. I just want to be protecting ye now because some will think the worst. Reputations are fragile things and y'mother...rather damaged hers that Christmas.' She paused, looking pained. 'Ye'll be tarred with the same brush if yer not careful.'

'What do you mean?'

Mildred sat down and sighed, taking another sip of her drink. 'Yer mother was being courted by someone else for a few months and it seemed serious. In fact everyone expected them to announce their engagement, then yer father arrived out of blue...a stranger even to yer grandfather and I. It was quite the scandal when Gregory announced the betrothal here, especially in front of the man's family.'

Theresa put down her glass, starting to feel suddenly sober. 'Who did she do that to?'

Mildred paused before admitting it. 'Jack Murphy.'

Theresa felt sick, the photo taken right there at Greenshades all those years ago flashing through her mind. The crowd around the Sunbeam. Jack Murphy's arm around her mother's waist. Her mother had betrayed Pete's father? How could she do such a thing?

'I know, it seems hard t'understand how she could jilt a man so cruelly and at first I was most ashamed, I assure you. But t'was a reason you see. She didn't expect Gregory t'come back into her life and she was…in need of marriage.'

It took a moment for the truth to dawn. 'Christmas.'

'Aye.'

'And my birthday is in June.'

'Aye. I know, I know, but before ye go judgin' her harshly jus' think what t'would have been like t'have ye out of wedlock.'

'But…are you sure I'm Gregory's child?' she asked, aghast at the alternative.

'Of course. There's no mistaking that hair, child. Ye have no fear there.'

Theresa stood, somewhat unsteadily, and walked slowly over to the mantel. 'But no one can blame me for that. I mean, I was just an innocent baby...actually, I wasn't even born!'

'I know, I know,' Mildred said sadly, sipping at her sherry and holding her handkerchief across her heart. 'But you look so much like her in t'dress and all, and there y'were dancing with all those men...with the priest whispering his gossip and lies...people will tend t'think the worst.'

'Then more shame to them,' she said, raising her chin. 'I've done nothing wrong except dance, as a job for a while then tonight for a little fun. Since when is that a sin?'

'It's the sins of the mother ye have to consider...'

'But I'm not my mother...and anyway, maybe people would understand if they knew *why* she chose my father...'

'Perhaps...but not when they know the rest. And that they will, I'm afraid t'say. 'Tis only a matter of time.'

Veronica went to pull Pattie away, still trying to accept the fact that Rose had been pregnant when she courted Jack, but Pattie stood firm, wanting to know it all.

Theresa looked at her grandmother, confused. 'What is the rest?'

Mildred took another large gulp of sherry. 'I...I can't say... anyway ye'll find out soon enough...'

'Nana, what aren't you telling me?' Mildred sniffed against her tears and Theresa went over to hold her hands. 'What else do I have to live down?'

Her grandmother looked at their joined hands and spoke in a low voice.

'She did something else that will cause a great scandal when it is known. It's only that they are buried together...otherwise no one would ever find out.' She shrugged helplessly.

'Who is? My mother and father? Please, tell me.'

Mildred looked nervously around her, clutching at her glass and handkerchief, then took a deep breath. 'No, not your father. I wasn't entirely honest about him, dear. Truth was, he was a violent man. That's why she ran way with ye.' She paused, as Theresa tried to digest that terrible fact.

'I'm sure you know yerself that during war...things are different. Time seems so very precious...'

'She found someone else, didn't she?' Theresa knew in an instant it was true.

Mildred nodded. 'Aye, that she did. I only found out about him later, from her friend Beatrice, who she served with. She wrote me and told me…'

Theresa braced herself as the words continued to rock her, not wanting to know but needing to.

'This Beatrice, she said they were terrible in love. She found her happiness you see, but the man was someone close to home again and I'm afraid it will come back on ye when the truth comes out. It will only get worse when they know...' She wrung her hands anxiously and Theresa felt sick.

'When who knows?'

'His family,' she whispered.

Theresa felt the dread arrive just before the words landed.

''Twas the son of this house, Clarkson, Peter's uncle.'

Pattie let out a cry and they turned in shock to watch her storm into the room, closely trailed by a pale Veronica.

'*How could she? How?*' she sobbed.

Pete came in then, watching in confusion as his aunt accosted Mildred. 'Why him? Why not any other man? Isn't it bad enough she tried to trap my brother with Gregory's bastard?'

Theresa flinched. Now there was a new word to be hurled at her as well as orphan and slut.

'She had to steal my husband while I waited here, holding his baby?' She flung herself at Theresa, hurling the words in her face. '*It's all because of you.* If it hadn't been for you Rose never would have used Jack, she never would have married Gregory and run off to France and she never would have stolen my husband from me. *My husband.* Do you know how long we had together as man and wife? One week.' She paused, angry tears streaming as her face contorted with pain. '*Just one lousy week.* Long enough to get with child and that's about it. A child he never saw. And you, you're just the same. Father O'Brien is telling everyone about it. You're a slut, just like her,' she spat. 'Get out of this house! Hasn't your family done enough? Go! Tell her Pete, *tell her*!' Pattie screamed at him.

Theresa raised her gaze to Pete and she could see him torn, struggling to take it all in and find a way past his anger, past the sins of the parents. She waited, praying desperately it would be the way back to her, back to the place where it was just them.

Pete wouldn't let her down.

But the moment passed and somehow...he did.

'Come along, Nana.' Theresa stood, the euphoric effects of alcohol now dissolving into heaviness and nausea. From somewhere within she found the strength to pull back her shoulders, hold her tears and help her shaking grandmother to her feet. They made their way in silence to the door, silence broken only by Pattie's choking sobs.

'Theresa.' Veronica reached out to her, but she shook her head and kept walking. Without Pete's voice raised in loyalty there was nothing left to say.

Forty-seven

Numoikum, New Guinea, 15 August 1945

They sat, weary and hot, accustomed to both and past caring, just tired of it all. Squinting against the horizon, watching the warships as another plane took off in the waters below. The 16th Battalion were seasoned now, like many of their fathers before them, ambivalent about the politics of war, past the mutterings of surrender. They'd heard it for too long as they chased the Japanese north, further and further away from Australia, through creeks, rivers, beaches, jungles and villages. All they knew was that the enemy was still biting in retreat, proud and cunning and remaining invisible to any man who felt a Jap bullet as the last thing he ever knew. They feared them now, more than ever, as stories grew of torture and mindless cruelty in prisoner-of-war camps. Peter hated those sadistic monsters, that he couldn't deny. But the average Jap soldier was a pathetic sight these past months, skin and bone and many of them starved to death by the time the Aussies found them on the jungle floor. It made Pete sick to see the waste of life, even after all these years.

He sat against a palm tree near the village, half watching the planes, the paper and pen idle in his lap. The page was blank save the words at the top: *Dear Theresa.*

All the words that should follow had already been written a hundred times over and sent to Mildred or Missy or anyone else he could think of who might know where she was hiding in London. No one would give him an address but at least he knew she was receiving his letters: Mildred had assured him of that much. According to the same she was also refusing to read any of them.

Pete sighed, lifting the page and looking at the photo underneath of a woman in a shimmering dress, eyes like fire as she tilted her chin at a photographer who little knew this beauty was filled with outrage that Christmas night, two and a half years earlier. Simon had asked him once: why this photo? Why not ones that brought back memories of happier times? One that might give him hope? Pete hadn't offered an explanation at the time, but the truth was that the memories of happier times were easy to conjure. They lived like a beautiful gallery in his mind that he visited every night as he closed his eyes against hell and war. But this photo…this photo gave him something more important than hope: it gave him conviction. He knew this side of Theresa would never surrender to lesser emotions. She would always have passion in her blood and he would need that the most when the time came, because he was gambling, with whatever life he had left owing after the war, that she would face him again. And fight him. Having it out was the only way.

He would have to stoke her outrage and anger until it exploded, praying that it would wane into forgiveness and she would become soft once more. Loving. His. Any other ending was unimaginable. That outcome was the only thing keeping him sane in his nightmarish exile in the tropics. He felt he was paying for his sins now, forced to endure the brutality of man at his worst. Forced to examine his own shortcomings, his ability to lose himself in anger and hatred. The beast within. It was a battle they all waged but his father's words still sustained him. War wouldn't take his soul. And holding that photo helped him cling to that every day. He was more than a soldier, more than a body that took life. And he would spend the rest of his days being the rest of that man. With the woman he loved.

He sighed, folding the page and photo back up and putting them in his pocket, looking across at Simon as he smoked a cigarette, flicking the butt deep in thought. Wondering if his child has been born yet, Pete wagered. Only Simon shared any personal truths with him here; to the rest he was just 'Cap', the man charged with keeping the lot of them alive. Pete stood and stretched, walking over as Simon stubbed the butt out.

'It's quiet,' Simon said, looking up at him. The past few days had been strangely so, a lull in the carnage of the jungle hunt.

Pete was about to comment when the sound of guns thundered from the ships below, smoke billowing as they repeated in quick succession.

'What the hell…?' Pete stared. Simon jumped to his feet and the other soldiers came forward and they stood as one, watching the scene, searching for the cause of such sudden defence. The pounding continued until finally the sound of a runner crashed towards them, a young, thin teen, carrying a note.

'Cap…?'

Pete took it and opened it, reading it with hands that began to shake, then the words came at last, words he thought he might never get to say.

'The Japs have surrendered. It's…over.'

Men fell to their knees; others hugged and danced about, some just leant against a tree in shock while others wiped tears of joy and relief away.

One man sent a prayer of gratitude to heaven knowing he would now see his firstborn child.

Another placed his hand over the photo that lay against his heart, knowing every day from here would take him one step closer to her.

Across the sea and way down south a woman held her newborn son and was told peace had come at last.

And far, far away another woman slept, unaware that the ashes of letters in her grate were soon to come to life. The day was coming when she would hear their words from flesh and blood.

Forty-eight

London, December 1945

'Miss Mayfair, there's a gentleman here to see you. He says he's from Australia.' Missy put down her brush and told the doorman to let him in, wondering who had tracked her down all the way over here in London.

He held his hat as he walked in, a very good-looking man in a captain's uniform.

'Good morning, Miss Mayfair. I'm sorry to disturb you,' he began.

'Don't be silly. It's not every day I get to see a tall drink of water from home. What can I do for you, Captain?' She smiled sweetly, observing him with appreciation.

'I was hoping you might know the whereabouts of a friend of mine. I've been trying to find her for the past three years actually and I believe you are the mostly likely person to know where she is.'

She turned back to the mirror, the smile instantly fading. 'What makes you think I might know that?'

'Because she would never break ties with you, Missy.'

She picked up her lipstick, pausing as she applied it. 'You've been promoted, Peter.'

'They eventually do that if you keep surviving.'

Missy met his eye. 'You took your time getting here.'

'Would have helped if I hadn't been knee deep in mud trying not to get killed.'

'Why don't you tell me why you want to see her so badly and I'll tell you whether or not I know where she is.'

'I'm sure you already know why. I sent about a hundred letters to your address.'

'Speak.'

He ran his hands through his hair. 'Do you mind if I have a drink first? It's been a long journey.'

Missy reached for the decanter and some glasses, pouring two drinks and handing him one. 'And a long war,' she sighed. 'Here's to peace.'

She sat in the front box seat, like a bird in a gilded cage, her newly cut hair short about her face and tucked one stray curl behind her ear. The action mesmerised Pete and his hand gripped the opera glasses as she moved, every gesture a torture. The red dress hugged against her, reminding him of heated memories; the same memories that had plagued him in the endless cursed jungle that had prevented him from chasing her across the world.

Her grandmother sat next to her, arrived in London just that day with Iggy and beaming with pride as he took to the stage, Missy on his arm. It was opening night and the lure of the two stars playing together at last had made it a sell-out. Pete caught Missy's eye as she turned and winked at him from the stage. She had become his closest ally in London and he knew deep down she wished Theresa would relent. But the latter remained frustratingly immovable and Missy was steadfast in her loyalty, refusing to reveal Theresa's whereabouts no matter how much he pleaded. Missy had invited him to opening night, however, and he'd known Theresa wouldn't miss that.

Missy ran her hand along the piano, dazzling the crowd in her silver gown and capturing their hearts with her playful ease as she sang 'It Had to be You'.

Pete watched Theresa's face fill with pride and he felt the words leave his own heart and brush skin like a whisper.

He traced that skin with his eyes as she arched her neck to hear something her grandmother was saying and he snapped the glasses down. Bugger this bloody waiting. Pete stole behind, counting the bays until he found hers; he parted the heavy velvet, finding himself inches from her back.

Missy's words filled the remaining air between them. 'Wonderful you.'

She lowered her face, sensing someone's presence, and turned, her eyes widening in shock.

Rising, she brushed past him out into the foyer and he followed.

'You can't just run away,' he said, matching her steps.

'Watch me.'

'I've come halfway across the world, Theresa. I'm not giving up now.'

'You should,' she threw back at him, quickening her steps as she descended the stairs, the red dress trailing behind her.

He grabbed her hand, turning her around. 'Why haven't you answered any of my letters?'

'Let go of me.' She flung him away and walked on.

'I wrote hundreds, saying I'm sorry in every possible way known to man. What's it going to take, Theresa? Theresa? For God's sake stop running!'

She'd reached the street and the cabbie opened the door for her. 'Don't let him in, thank you,' she instructed and the beefy man obliged, holding up his hand.

'Please,' he said through the window as she stared straight ahead. 'Please give me a chance to explain. Theresa!' he called as the cab pulled away. Its tail-lights receded and he stared after them, his shoulders slumping.

'What did ye expect, lad?' Mildred asked from behind and he turned to her, meeting her understanding gaze.

'A chance.' He shrugged, feeling defeated and exhausted after years of imagining a different scenario, where she fell into his arms.

'So find another,' she suggested, 'and this time choose someplace where 'tis harder to escape.'

'I would have thought you'd hate me too.'

Mildred tucked her arm into his and steered him back to the theatre. 'If I hated every foolish man I'd met there'd only be women in me life and, bless them all, 'twould be terrible dull all the same.'

'He wants me to forgive him.'

'So forgive 'im.'

'I can't.'

'Why don't ya just tell 'im that then?'

Theresa looked over at former Private Ben Hill and sighed. 'Because that would involve facing him.'

They were sitting in a café near Hyde Park, where they had met regularly over the two and a half years she'd been in London. Initially, she had made enquiries of her father's family but the old widow Lady Chambers was long dead and the estate had gone bankrupt in the stock market crash. No other relatives were to be found but after what she'd heard of her father she deigned to pursue the title she should inherit.

She hadn't actually expected to find anyone who knew her mother but she'd put a notice in the papers anyway. To her shock Ben had responded the very next day, telling her he'd never forgotten 'Redsped'. She and her captain had been good friends to him during the war and he would be proud to know her daughter. Her planned search for her mother's friend Beatrice had never eventuated, cut short at that first lunch as Ben introduced the same Beatrice as his wife.

Since that day Beatrice rarely missed a meeting either but had stayed home tonight with their youngest daughter, who had fallen sick with the flu. Her name was Rosie.

Through them she had pieced together part of her mother's story: the way she worked, the courage she showed, her reckless driving and determined nature. Her love for a dashing Australian captain.

It seemed they had the last cursed fact in common.

'And why can't ya do that?' Ben's one eye was kind as he watched Theresa struggle with her emotions, her stubborn expression so like her mother's.

'Because he...he'll twist things around and make me feel confused.'

'Why don't ya just give 'im a chance?'

'Because he doesn't deserve it!' she blurted out.

'Y'want to punish 'im for hurting ya.'

She stubbed out her cigarette angrily. 'You don't understand, the things he said– '

'Were cruel.'

'And the way he just sat by while– '

'While his aunt tore ya to shreds, yes, y'told me many times.'

She was silent for a moment as she studied her glass.

'And now yer angry with me,' Ben said.

'Yes. Oh, I don't know. I'm just angry in general, I guess. Why couldn't he stay away?'

Ben leant forward and held her fingers gently. 'The same reason why ya can't stand to be near 'im is the same reason why he wants it so badly.'

'And what's that?'

'Ya won't be able to deny the truth when it's right in front of ya.'

She didn't say anything, just pulled her fingers back and lit another cigarette. They were all the same, Ben, Missy, Nana, even Uncle Iggy. They all thought she should forgive and forget but it wasn't that easy. Just as it hadn't been easy to force herself away from him, away from her newfound home and back to war, albeit in Europe this time. Far away, working in aerial transportation, bringing soldiers back to London, then studying medicine once the war was over. Fulfilling all the plans for her head and ignoring all the ones made by her heart.

She'd made a life for herself. She had Missy again. She had Ben and Beatrice, wonderful friends who had understood and loved her mother. She had family, regularly writing to them and seeing them on the happy occasions they came to England, such as now. She had her work. She had everything she needed. The fears that filled her dreams at night, dreams of Pete dying in battle, calling out her name in remorse, were just the foolish lamentations of her heart. Her head cleared them well away each morning.

Ben waited patiently while she processed her thoughts, knowing her well enough by now to almost read them as the shadows crossed her face.

'What are ya really afraid of, Theresa?' he said at last.

She shrugged, the words coming reluctantly. 'Maybe I…I am a fallen woman. I mean look at my mother…maybe it's in my blood.'

'Love?'

'*Lust.* Maybe I was always kidding myself…wanting a normal life with a respectable man. No one wanted me for anything like that until I met him. Just…sex. The boys in the country; the boys in the city. Maybe he will change his mind again, away from war. In real life. The priests and nuns always said that the sins of the flesh lead to damnation, so maybe I'm damned now. Maybe he… doesn't want that woman. Not really.'

'Seems pretty keen to me – three years of trying to win ya back. How much proof do ya want?'

'I tell you what I *don't* want: I don't want to go back to him only for him to…to resent me. To think that I'm just like her. Rose's daughter.'

Ben shook his head, his smile filled with affection. 'Can't think of no better compliment than that.'

Forty-nine

Calais, France

The day was clear but bitterly cold, the sky cornflower blue, as the woman bent down and placed the poppies on his grave. Theresa watched her curiously as she approached, the tall figure vaguely familiar.

She froze as Pattie turned and they met, face to face at last.

'Found a few out of season. They're strange little flowers, aren't they? More like paper than petals. Appropriate somehow, with the red.' Pattie shrugged, turning towards the sun. 'Why the chess piece?' she asked, nodding at the small queen standing guard, mounted between thc two headstones.

'He...gave it to her. I don't know why.' Theresa found her voice. 'She had it in her pocket when she died.'

Pattie frowned then shrugged against it. 'That sounds like something he would do.'

The wind whipped at their coats and Theresa bent to place the flowers she had brought with her as Pattie watched.

'I didn't expect you would ever want to come here,' Theresa said, arranging the blooms.

'No. Neither did I.' She shook her hair from her face, taking a deep breath. 'Veronica got it in her head I needed to come, kept going on about forgiveness and Pete needing me to talk to you. Wore me down in the end with her badgering. She's annoyingly good, you know.'

'Yes.' Theresa smiled a little. 'She is that.'

Pattie touched the headstone gently. 'She likes you. Believes you are meant to be in our lives. Destiny and all that nonsense.'

'A wartime dalliance is hardly fulfilling some grand vision of destiny.'

Pattie knelt down and traced the inscription on Clarkson's grave. 'So one would think.'

Theresa bit her lip, unsure what to say, but Pattie continued, pushing aside the tears that had gathered at the corners of her eyes. 'Did Pete ever mention he was born the day we buried Clarkson? Well, buried…we had a ceremony. There's no closure, you see. Not until you see a grave, then it feels…final.' She braced herself against the wind. 'I…I still hadn't quite let go and seeing you there, in his house…it was a painful way to find out and unfortunately you couldn't have been standing in a worse possible place at a worse possible time. I suppose I was seeing her, not you.'

Theresa stood still looking at the grave. 'And you hated me too.'

'No. No, I never hated you. I hated her, yes, I can't deny that.'

'So you've decided to come and stand here at my mother's graveside, all the way from Australia, just to tell me you hated her?'

'No.' Pattie shook her head. 'Hasn't it occurred to you that perhaps I have other reasons for standing here?'

Theresa looked at Clarkson's grave, feeling a little ashamed.

'I've come here to ask you to forgive.'

'You want me to forgive you?'

'No.' Pattie lifted her face and looked Theresa in the eye. 'Not me. I've come to ask you to forgive Pete. It's time.'

Theresa gaped at her. 'Of all the arrogant, self-important – '

'Please, hear me out.'

'Oh I hear you. Order the poor orphan to count herself lucky and take him back!'

'No, not order, I'm begging you. Please. Pete is…like my own son and the very best of men, Theresa, surely you know that. I can't live with the fact that I destroyed his chance at happiness because I was jealous and angry. I can't.' Pattie shook her head.

'He messed it up, not you. He destroyed it.'

'No, he just reacted badly. I destroyed it. I think I was ready to tear you down from the start and I succeeded, much to my regret. But he loves you, so much. I thought he might go mad when they sent him back to war and he couldn't find you and now, the first chance he gets, here he is and Mildred says you won't see him.' She held up her hand. 'I know, I know. You think he doesn't deserve forgiveness.' Pattie held her arms out, sweeping them at the white graves that spread out in a sea before them. 'But for God's sake, girl, look around you. Don't you think any one of them would give anything for this chance? To live? To feel happiness?'

Theresa fought the emotions that threatened to make her give a little and turned to leave.

Pattie sighed, making one final attempt to get through. 'I had a long time alone, Theresa, before my Mick came along and I found love again. Loneliness might protect you from getting hurt, but what about love? You can't tell me you're happy alone. I wouldn't believe you. I know a woman with a broken heart when I see one. I recognise that pain. Swallow your pride and choose love, Theresa.' She looked towards Clarkson's grave. 'Forgiveness is freeing.'

As she watched the young woman walk away, hunched against the cold and her own pride, Pattie shook her head. Stubborn as a mule that one.

A gust of wind made the flowers flutter against his name. *Reminds me of someone else I know.* She felt she could almost hear him say it.

Pattie stared at Clarkson's grave one last time, saying goodbye to the long-familiar place where he lived inside of her. Reaching into her handbag, she squished an old furry hat on her head and allowed him one last smile.

'Farewell, Mr C.'

Fifty

Theresa walked up the hill to the cliff, past the crumbling skeletons of buildings that marked the crush of war, inevitably to rise again but still for now, solemn in their wait. She breathed deeply of the ocean, finding solace in the monthly ritual she'd performed across the channel since she'd been in London. First Calais, to honour their deaths, then Boulogne to feel their lives.

It was cold and there were a few other people around as she watched a man approach, tall in his Australian uniform. Not uncommon here, they were usually tall, these Australians, so honoured for their courage around these parts where the graves of their fallen were meticulously tended by a grateful French people. He was headed this way and she felt her body tense.

She decided not to turn her back, not to run this time. She couldn't run forever, but as she faced every living, breathing detail of him before her she felt trapped, despite the space surrounding her.

'Hello Theresa,' he said simply. She didn't speak, finding herself without adequate words, eventually swinging her gaze towards the safety of the horizon.

'Missy sends her love. Told me to give you these.' He handed her a velvet box and she opened it, finding a string of pearls inside. 'Said to tell you some things are too precious to give away.'

She stared at them shaking her head. Typical of Missy to refuse to sell them all these years and even more typical to wait for the perfect dramatic moment to return them. She closed the box slowly.

'Theresa…'

'How's the law career going? You certainly have a way with getting people onside, don't you? Charming my friend and importing your aunt all the way from Sydney. Who else have you got tucked away? Is there a marching band around the corner?' She pretended to look for one over his shoulder.

'What do you mean, my aunt? When did you see Pattie?'

'About two hours ago at my mother's grave.'

'She…she went to the graveside? What did she say to you? Oh God help me…if she said anything to make things worse– '

'Well first of all that would be impossible and secondly she was actually there for…other reasons.'

'Such as?'

She began walking down the hill and he followed. 'None of your goddamn business.'

'Aren't you going to let me explain?'

'What's to explain? I didn't suit your world. *C'est la vie.*'

'No, no it wasn't that. Look, I behaved badly. For God's sake, Theresa, I've played it a million ways in my mind and it comes back to the same thing. I let you down and I'm sorrier than you could ever know.'

She turned and looked up at him. 'Behaved badly? Is that what you call it? I could come up with some stronger words than that for calling me a slut and a whore and…and letting me be cast out of your family's home.'

'I…I never really thought those things. I was just shocked,' he said, exasperated, beginning to recount the facts on his fingers. 'I mean for God's sake…one, I'd just found out you worked in the Cross and you'd slept with someone else, two, your mother jilted my father because she was pregnant with you and then, three, she had an affair with my uncle! That's a lot to take lying down!'

Theresa frowned. 'Still on trial, am I?'

'No, I'm just trying to explain– '

'How none of it is your fault.'

'No,' he said firmly. 'Mine is the greatest fault. I didn't just betray you…I betrayed *us*. Bloody hell, I was such a fool and, you were right, a hypocrite as well. I was jealous and stupid and…and upset, but Theresa don't harden your heart against me forever. Please,' his eyes begged her, 'I've longed for you every day, writing letters between battles, never giving up, not once, just waiting for this opportunity to tell you. Theresa, I'm *sorry*.' He reached and clasped her hand. 'I wouldn't care if you'd slept with a hundred men. I'd just count myself lucky to be the last.'

There they were. The words she really wanted. She shook herself, turning and walking down the hill once more, confused and fighting for every resolve she had now, her head and heart at war.

'You know something?' he called after her. 'You're a bloody pain in the arse.'

She stopped still as he stomped down after her. 'What did you say to me?'

'You're a bloody pain in the arse!'

'This is your apology.'

'No, you've run out of those. Now you're going to hear a few home truths. You're a bloody hypocrite too.'

'How the hell do you figure that?'

'Because at least I apologised for misjudging you. You can't even admit that you misjudged me!'

'In what possible way?'

'The Golden Digger, remember? The whole reason you're being a pain in the arse right now is because you're mad at yourself for not choosing a perfect man. Well I'm *not* perfect, Theresa. I never was.' He reached her side then and held her face with both palms. 'But I'm bloody well perfect for you.'

'I…I've worked so hard to get over you.'

'Then you've had more success than me.'

The truth was there at last, just as she'd feared it would be. He pulled her close and kissed her, every emotion and feeling transferring into her and she lost herself to the reality of him.

Pete.

The reasons she'd had to never take him back faded into that shared, incomparable place, the place where only they existed, a place inexplicable to anyone else.

Yes, he'd fallen down once when she needed him, but he wasn't just that one fall, he was hundreds of other moments. Moments that now flooded her senses: his face when they carried him out of the jungle, the moment he caught her as she threw herself off that table and into his arms, the tenderness in his eyes when he looked across at her in the plane coming home.

The longing. The letters. The regret.

Never a perfect man after all, but he was a good man. And she loved him.

It was time, Pattie was right. This was Pete, her Pete, and she wanted him back. She did want happiness. She did want to be free. And she did want to forgive. It was her turn.

Pete stroked her cheek, so very softly now. 'So will you marry me or do I have to call for the marching band?'

'I don't know. You're kind of a pain in the arse.'

His handsome face returned in full force as it lit up with that old, familiar grin. 'Told you we were meant to be.'

Theresa felt her own smile twitch, then she threw back her head and laughed, really laughed, and he joined her, catching her lips then eventually her hand, kissing it in promise.

He didn't let go as they walked down the hill to his car and drove away from Boulogne, leaving the high stone walls behind them.

The winter sun of France shone across her fields and nurtured the sleeping poppy plants, now fed by the blood of men who had become a part of her earth.

And, as the builders sorted through the rubble of her cities, two lovers found their way out of the debris at last, and into the hope of a new life.

Author's Note

Gallipoli Street is a work of fiction and although it is based on true events in history, artistic license has been employed at times to ensure cohesion is maintained.

Acknowledgements

Some of my fondest memories revert back to childhood when I would pore through my mother's marvellous book collection, pick a world to fall into and curl up on the couch with a nice red apple to do just that. I knew even then that I wanted to write, to fill a tome of my own one day, and wonderful heroines like Josephine March and Anne in her Green Gables taught me that in order to make that happen you need to write from the heart; to write what you truly know.

Now, due to my wonderful publishing family at Harlequin, I hold my own novel in my hands at last. I like to picture my readers curled up on their couches, falling into this world, and feel grateful for the people who made it possible, not only the publishing staff (Annabel and Sue – you are an author's dream come true), but family and friends who share my life.

So much of this novel comes from my heart, so without them there would have been little to say.

For example, the relationships between mothers and daughters. How could I have written a word about maternal love if not for the first-hand experience of my own mother's gentle care and patience? Dorn Best, you instilled in me a passion for literature and I would never have become a writer without it. Thank you also for the many, many hours of editing and discussion. This is our book.

Then there's Dad, a man who began his professional creative career at the same age as I am now, becoming a successful and much loved artist. Kevin Best, you taught me to 'follow your star' and showed me first hand how much happiness that can bring. A father's faith and love echo in these pages because of you, just as they echo in my heart forever. My inspiration, my hero.

To my beautiful sisters, sisters-in-law, nieces and girlfriends, how could I have written about the bond of sisterhood without you all? Thank you for the hours of reading, dissecting and discussing and for inspiring some of the main characters herein. (Perhaps our girly lunches could encompass more than one subject from now on!) In particular, Theresa Meury, my real life muse and confidant, and Benison O'Reilly, the voice of reason and my personal mentor, thank you for believing in me.

To my brothers, brothers-in-law, nephews and 'mates', thank you for teaching me what the latter truly means. I could not have imagined what our forefathers endured without understanding the ties that hold men to such depths of loyalty and bravery. Nor could I have imagined how vital a part humour played in keeping them going. Those words are born from you. (A special mention must be noted to my brother James for helping his poor sister understand some of the finer points of warfare. I now know that WWI tanks could not swing and aim at one particular man with accuracy, not even one as villainous as Gregory Chambers. A machine gun would have to suffice.)

To my large, wonderful, Irish-Catholic Australian families, how could I have written about such an upbringing without you? I am sure you have recognised some first-hand memories embedded in the story and thank you for sharing them with me. (And yes, Nana was 'witchy'. How she ever knew Uncle Jack was coming home from war that day is anyone's guess and yes, she did enjoy the term 'ugly man's dog', bestowing it on Uncle John Colgan on more than one occasion.)

To the community I live in, Hornsby Ku-ring-gai, how wonderful it felt to write about our home in days gone by and how grateful I am to have been born and raised, 'barefoot and unencumbered', in the Bushland Shire. I hope you all enjoy envisaging it as it was during this era as much as I did researching and writing about it.

To my husband Anthony, it is only because of you that I could find the words to express what enduring love truly means. Thank you for being the safe, warm centre of my world. Additionally, without your patient support while I tapped away for thousands of hours this novel could never have eventuated. (Sorry about the many requests for cups of tea and for hogging the computer. I'm sure I owe you a boy's golf weekend or two).

To my children, James (Jimmy) and Jack, you make every day brighter and give meaning to everything I do. I can only imagine what it must have been like to send a son to war and my deep love for you made such contemplation possible. I am so grateful to live in times of (relative) peace and pray that you never have to fight or give your life for Australia. You are being raised in a land where democracy reigns and freedom of speech is your right. You have your forefathers to thank for that and may you never take it for granted.

Thank you for being patient while Mummy locked herself away and for being not-so-patient sometimes and giving me cuddles and little boy chats. Love you my angels.

And so to my last acknowledgement: the Anzac generation, in particular my maternal grandparents, James Dennis Clancy (my Da) and Gladys Mary Veronica Clancy (my Nana).

Gallipoli Street is dedicated to these two amazing people and, although this is a work of fiction, some elements of their story have wound their way into my tale.

To begin with, James did serve in Gallipoli. He joined the army, not as a Lighthorseman, but as an infantryman when he was only seventeen, four years underage. James soon found himself at the Mena Camp in Egypt. Tales have been handed down of a young man climbing the pyramids at sunset and enjoying himself with his mates in the Wazza district during time off. Like the character Jack in the novel, he received a silk scarf from King George whilst in Cairo and wrote his rank, name and date on it that day. They remain there still, in one hundred year old ink, for our family to trace in wonder.

James was shipped across to Gallipoli and endured horrors he would never speak of to my mum or her sisters. 'Little girls don't need to know about things like that'. She believes it never left him and he carried some of those unspoken images for the rest of his days. Whilst there, he nearly lost his life to dysentery and was evacuated to Cairo where he received an honourable discharge. However as soon as he was able to he rejoined, because, as he said to my mother years later, 'you can't just leave your mates to face it alone'.

James served in the Somme, a bloody, muddy business, the only highlight of which was sharing Christmas Eve with the German soldiers, swapping cigarettes and playing soccer on that famous night in history. He never forgot it and spoke of it often to his children. Soon after he was injured, receiving nasty shrapnel wounds that needed immediate surgery, however they had run out of morphine. In the end James had to be knocked out by drinking large amounts of French champagne. He survived, again, was discharged, again, and rejoined, again.

James served out the war in the Middle East and returned home to marry the girl with the curls whom he had long admired in mass, Gladys. This spirited young woman had spent much of her formative years on a dairy farm in Beecroft and had been known to race a cart along a dirt track on occasion. Although five years his junior she matched him in every way and could find a hidden penny no matter how hard he tried to trick her, even the one hidden in the bedpost. They struggled through the Great Depression living in Braidwood on a small farm and using a dug-out anthill for their oven. They had eight children, one dying in infancy, and managed to get through those difficult years living on rabbit and panning for gold in the creek, with James travelling wide and far for any carpentry work he could find.

They returned to Sydney and after a time Gladys fell in love with a house on a hill with a rose garden and a wide verandah. It was situated on Gallipoli Street in Hurstville. It is family folklore that she used every bit of willpower and a fair dose of prayer, even burying a holy medal in the garden, to get that house. She succeeded, and it was by all accounts the happiest days of their lives living there, marred only by a new development shadowing over them: World War II. Their son Jack tried to join up underage but the army turned him down. Ironically James was offered the role of sergeant at a training camp for underage soldiers at Liverpool and Jack was sent there to be trained under his father's tutorage. Uncle Jack tells me there were merry times at that camp as he played guitar and his dad played the fiddle and many an impromptu party ensued.

The parties soon ended, however, and Jack was sent to New Guinea. One day a telegram arrived and Gladys had to sit and wait all day for James to come home from work as the postmaster wouldn't let her open it. Jack had been injured but would survive. Not so his brother-in-law. Iris, their eldest daughter, received a telegram on Valentine's Day. At the age of only eighteen she was informed that her husband Wally had been killed. She was seven months pregnant with the family's first grandchild, my beautiful cousin Daphne.

The war ended just as James and Gladys's other son Des finished his training as a pilot, and both boys lives were spared in the end.

My grandparents spent the rest of their married life together in Gallipoli Street. One day their second youngest daughter rang from the hospital to tell them they had a new grandchild, one of many by then. Her name was Linda Jayne and she was born on Anzac Day.

'What a beautiful name,' James said to Dorn. They were the last words he ever spoke to my mother. James passed away in his sleep a few days later.

Nana lived to a great age and saw great-grandchildren and even great-great-grandchildren come into the world. She was the kindest woman I ever knew and never, ever complained about anything, despite living through such turbulent times. She passed away surrounded by her loving family and I believe she and Da watch over us all.

Such were my grandparents. Such were these years in my family. Such were the Anzac generation to me.

Thankyou for giving so very, very much and for inspiring these words, firstly, in my heart.

Lest we forget.

talk about it

Let's talk about books.

Join the conversation:

on facebook.com/harlequinaustralia

on Twitter @harlequinaus

www.harlequinbooks.com.au

If you love reading and want to know about our authors and titles, then let's talk about it.